ELVISH JEWEL

TRACY RENEE ROSS
AND
JAMES DANIEL ROSS

TriMoon Eclipse — Winter Wolf PUBLICATIONS | Cincinnati, Ohio

This is a work of fiction. All names, characters, places, and events are either products of the author's imagination or are used fictitiously. Any resemblance to actual events or persons is entirely coincidental. All trademarks and registered and are the property of their respective owners.

All rights reserved. No part of this publication may be copied, reproduced, stored, archived or transmitted in any form or by any means without prior written permission from the publisher.

Copyright © 2017, Tracy Renée Ross & James Daniel Ross
Cover Design & Art © 2019, by Miriam Chowdhury
Edited by Tracy Renée Ross
Interior Design by Tract Renée Ross

Published by TriMoon Eclipse,
An imprint of Winter Wolf Publications, LLC

ISBN: 978-1-945039-18-8 (paperback)

Other Work by Tracy Renee Ross (aka T.R. Chowdhury)

Shadow Over Shandahar
Dark Storm Rising
Echoes of Time
Whispers of Prophecy
Breaking Destiny
Embers at Dawn
Dark Mists of Ansalar
Blood of Dragons
Shade of the Fallen
Forging the Bond
The Inn of the Hapless Cenloryan

Other Work by James Daniel Ross

Radiation Angels
The Chimerium Gambit
The Key to Damocles
The Legend of Fox Crow
I Know Not
The Opus Discordia
The Saga of Those Before
The Echoes of Those Before
The Secrets of Those Before
The Fate of Those Before
The Whispering of Dragons
The Last Dragoon

Dedication

*M*ore today than yesterday. *M*ore tomorrow than today.
*F*orever.

–James Daniel Ross

*F*or everyone who believes that love can transcend all things-
all ages, all races, all genders, all distances, all spaces, and all
time.

–Tracy Renée Ross

"I have love in me the likes of which you can scarcely imagine and rage the likes of which you would not believe. If I cannot satisfy the one, I will indulge the other."
— *Mary Shelley, Frankenstein*

"Hatred paralyzes life; love releases it. Hatred confuses life; love harmonizes it. Hatred darkens life; love illuminates it."
— *Martin Luther King Jr.*

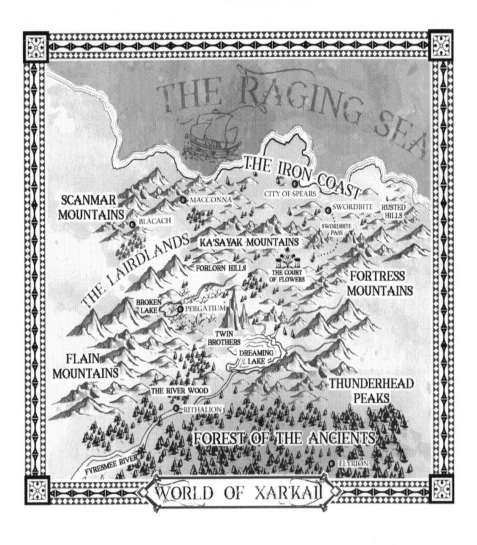

THE RAGING SEA

THE IRON COAST

SCANMAR MOUNTAINS

MACCONNA

CITY OF SPEARS

SWORDBITE

RUSTED HILLS

BLACACH

SWORDBITE PASS

THE LAIRDLANDS

KA'SAYAK MOUNTAINS

FORLORN HILLS

THE COURT OF FLOWERS

FORTRESS MOUNTAINS

BROKEN LAKE

PERGATIUM

TWIN BROTHERS

FLAIN MOUNTAINS

DREAMING LAKE

THE RIVER WOOD

THUNDERHEAD PEAKS

RITHALION

FOREST OF THE ANCIENTS

FYRESMEE RIVER

ELYRION

WORLD OF XAR'KAI

Prologue

It was a beautiful day. The sun shone bright, and the sweet scent of wildflowers was strong in the air. The unfamiliar sound of laughter echoed throughout the mountain cavern. Actually, not entirely unfamiliar, not since SHE had come to stay in his home. She was like no one he had ever met before, and he had met many people in his rather long life. She was young, maybe a couple of decades past one hundred, and her beauty shone like a beacon in the night. And her children...

...they were exceptional.

They were twins, a boy and a girl, aged at about three summers. The boy was certainly elvin, for he had begun to develop those features, the most obvious one being his ears, which were becoming long and pointed like those of the higher caste in Elvish society. He was remarkably bright for an elf his age, grasping concepts that most didn't comprehend until years later. But then again, he had to keep up with the girl.

Esgrynn walked to the opening of the cavern and looked out over the serene 'scape. On one side there was a crystal clear lake surrounded by rocks, and on their other was a hardwood forest. The children played hide and seek among the tall, thick trunks, their laughter pealing through the air as their mother tried to find them and catch them.

He closed his eyes, allowing himself to luxuriate in the scene, and when he opened them again, it was dark. The evening meal had been prepared and eaten, and everyone was settling down for the night. The children were curled along each side of their mother, and they looked up at her with adoring eyes as she spoke. Her voice had a sing-song quality to it, and he knew she was telling them a story. The words weren't important to him, rather, the look on her face as she told it. Her eyes shimmered with unshed tears, ready to fall for the man whom the story was about. It was obvious she was in love with him.

Suddenly sensing a presence before him, Esgrynn looked down to see that the girl had approached. Unlike her brother, she had not developed Elvish features. Rather, she looked to be quite human. However, her appearance was where her human-ness ended. She was a strange one, always looking at him, watching him with intense grey eyes. She was bright beyond her years and spoke like one who was much, much older.

"Who are you?" Her words were spoken with the utmost of solemnity.

He stopped himself from smiling, instead giving her the seriousness she gave him. "They call me The Warlock."

She narrowed her eyes and screwed up her face the way children do when trying to figure out a difficult puzzle. "Who are you really?"

Esgrynn opened his mouth to reply when another voice abruptly entered his mind, a woman's voice. "Esgrynn, listen to me. Please listen!"

The image of the girl wavered and he struggled to hold onto it. He didn't want to listen. He wanted to keep speaking with the child.

"There is danger! They have done the unthinkable and cleft the mountainside. The waters are coming, coming to flood the city. Please, please listen to me!"

Esgrynn snapped awake and inhaled deeply. He just lay there for a moment, untangling dreams from reality. It was dark, and the sultry air lay heavily against his skin. It was unusually quiet, the night devoid of the of the locust song that had been so characteristic of every waking and sleeping moment for the past month.

The voice was gone, but he knew it had been real. It had a clarity borne of magic instead of a construct of his mind in the form of a dream. It was a voice he'd heard many times before in many other dreams throughout his life, and he wished he heard it much more often in reality.

It was Chevonne, the woman he loved more than any other, the one he'd hoped time and time again would accede to be his partner in life. And if her voice was real, then so was her warning...

Esgrynn leapt out of bed, grabbing the trousers lying over a nearby chair. He struggled with them for a moment before his legs were in and he was pulling them over his hips. If the warning was true he didn't have much time.

It was then he heard it, an ominous, almost imperceptible CRACK! in the distance up in the mountains. *Oh gods...*

He ran. He ran through the dark halls of the house he shared with his sister and her husband. It was a large one, three stories high, and able to bed his niece and nephews, their spouses, and many others. He careened around the corner and rushed into their bedroom. He stopped at the entry, looked at them as they slept soundly in their bed. *By the gods, the entire city is asleep!*

His shout was a desperate cry. "Shaladrea! Xadrian! Wake up, we have to go!"

Xadrian was up in a heartbeat, is warrior's training kicking into full gear. Shaladrea was slower, but the fear in his voice roused her better than any siren. She reached for her nightgown, but his tone stopped her. "There's no time for modesty. Come on!"

Xadrian grabbed her hand and followed behind Esgrynn as he flew up the stairs to the third storey. The sound of distant crashing became louder by the moment, a counterpoint to the thundering of his heartbeat in his ears. They topped the stairs then rushed down the hall and out onto the balcony. Then they stopped.

The sound was horrifying.

He felt a hand place itself within his and he looked down at his sister. Illuminated by the light of the crescent moon, her face was pale and her eyes wide. "Esgrynn, what is it?"

He fought past the lump in his throat, the reality of what was about to happen to Pergatium descending upon his soul. "The dragon mages used their magic to cleft the mountain. The sound you hear is the waters of Shining Lake rushing down towards the city."

Her hand flinched within his, and her lips trembled.

"Now let me concentrate. I need to get us away from here."

Her hand tightened onto his with a death grip. "Just us? What about my children? We must warn them and save them too!"

Xadrian put a hand on Esgrynn's shoulder and pried Shaladrea's hand away. "Hush, dearheart. Let him work now."

Her voice rose over the approaching waters, waters that could only be heard, not seen, a sound that was terrifying. "But we need to get the children. We must hurry!"

Esgrynn concentrated on his spell as Xadrian responded in a soothing tone. "No Shaladrea. It is too late."

An agonized wail, followed by wracking sobs nearly distracted him from his work. Through the power of his spell, he made his summons. It wasn't as mighty as a dragon, but the wyvern would suffice to make good their escape.

Xadrian held Shaladrea tightly against him, their nude bodies outlined by the pale moonlight. "No, I don't want to leave. I want to stay here with my children. They need me!"

Xadrian's voice remained soothing. "No, no my dear. They don't need you anymore."

"I can't leave! I belong here with them!"

Xadrian's voice cracked. "No, they are being called to the gods now. It is their destiny, not yours."

The floodwaters crashed through the city. Esgrynn imagined he could hear the buildings and everything within them being demolished, but in truth, all he could hear was the thundering wave.

Shaladrea's voice barely made it over the flood. "I don't believe you!"

Xadrian's reply was almost lost. "Then I will believe enough for the both of us!"

Esgrynn felt a wave of weakness just as the wyvern appeared. It was a large male, plenty big enough to carry three adult passengers. The serpentine beast winged towards them, and just behind...

...was a massive wall of foaming water.

Shaladrea screamed as Esgrynn pulled her and Xadrian back from the railing. The wyvern alighted, muscular legs breaking the railing into splinters, massive wings creating a wind that blew the hair back from his face. Without hesitation he wrapped an arm around the sinuous neck and pulled himself up. Once astride, he wrapped his legs firmly around him, sliding back just enough until the back of his legs hit the thick muscle that controlled his wings. He then leaned down, his hand outstretched.

"Sister, give me your hand!"

Fear contorted her features and she adamantly shook her head. She took one step back, then another, then...

As it turned out she didn't have a choice. She hit the wall of Xadrian's chest just as he gripped her about the waist and lifted her up. With all his strength, Esgrynn took her from his brother in law and pulled her astride ahead of him while Xadrian swung himself up behind.

And then their time was up.

The wave hit the balcony just as the wyvern lifted off. The cold spray washed over them, entering their mouths and noses. The wyvern's wings stretched and reached, reached, reached for the sky as they gasped and choked. Cold and exhausted, they clutched at the each other and the beast beneath them, watched as the waters washed through their beloved home.

They continued to watch as long as they could see, until the darkness of the night hid the story of Pergatium from their questing eyes. Esgrynn's heart ached, reeling at the agony that sang through every fiber of his being, for, like every other elf, he could sense the passing of his brethren. It was strange, unlike battle, there were no screams to mark the passing of so many people. There was only the terrible feeling of their lives being snuffed out all at once...

Chapter One
The Ambush

They came out of the shadows, dark blotches against the green and brown landscape. They had successfully hidden from the scouts, wrapped in the bloody hides of animals to cover their stench. Now they roared like beasts and descended upon the reindeer drawn carriage in a wave. Humans.

Perhaps a pure elf would have seen them and they never would have gotten so far, but the guards were all low-elves, with the gift so thin they carried only an iota of the Blessings of Creation. All but the lady inside the carriage, and the half-blood witch that stood atop it.

Vivien had spent decades of her life in the school of magic in Rithalion. She had neither dedicated her time to the peaceful pursuit of knowledge, nor the contemplative plumbing of nature. She had learned to conjure the fae of energy and direction, of force and focus. She was a conduit to the wind and the wild, chaos and rapture. Vivien was a war mage, and the first group of humans to break from the brush discovered this as they rushed to their doom.

She motioned and screamed words of power, names scribed on the bones of the universe. Gouts of black fire leapt from her hands, streaming into tiny faery stones that burst into obsidian knives upon the first, second, and third man rushing the party. Human flesh shredded and they died terribly with screams on their lips.

But there were many, many more.

The defenders drew upon their Elvish blood and steeled themselves. Their giant cat mounts, the tir-reath shrieked and spat. What came for them was like every tale spun by older siblings in the dark of night, and every one of them felt their hearts shudder and quail. Dirty, tattooed humans cased in filthy rags and beaten metal came pouring out of the dark like maggots from a rotten skull. Covered in tanned leathers and plates of shining steel, low-elvin footmen lowered spears or loosed arrows, both with deadly aim. Tir-reath disemboweled enemy at will. Humans fell screaming.

Then, from out of the trees, the elvin bowmen were peppered by thick, black bolts. Tir-reath screamed and threw their riders; elves choked and died as the foul metal corroded their flesh. The survivors hefted shields, but more came. The humans met Elvish steel with poisonous iron. The elves moved with unmatched grace and perfection, and each low-born elf could summon enough of the Blessing to become a terrible wind of steel that cut like broken glass. But, though they were killing in droves, they were losing by numbers...

Vivien balled up her fear and shoved it aside as the humans whooped and screamed. She turned her ears to other places, hidden behind the veil of the material world. She heard a warning inside her screech of possibilities in the fabric of fate, and she threw herself to the side. An iron tipped arrow flew above and she pulled again at the nature of time and space with her will.

She threw out her hand and a dozen blindingly white fae coalesced from the coldest shards of sunlight. They sucked in all heat, creating voids in the world that wept snow from jagged wings. They flew out in a fan, hurling into the trees toward the hidden human bowmen. A single head appeared, then ducked behind the bole of the tree, but the fae did not slow. They passed near branches that instantly encased in ice and froze leaves solid. The fae bolted forward and passed through trees, sounding like the crunch of boots in packed snow. The hidden bowmen fell from their perches. Petrified pale and blue in the midst of aiming or loading, half a dozen ambushers teetered from hidden places and fell to the ground below, shedding icicles and shattering to pieces.

Yet, there were so many more.

Bolts found elves, black iron slipping its fingers into flesh and erupting in blood that would not be staunched. The wounds instantly became angry pink and yet pale, infected by the ancient bane of all elvin people. More black stinger wasps flew from the forest. Tir-reath screamed as they fell, dear friends lost forever. More elves fell, lives that could not be replaced within mere human life spans.

Just before her one carriage elf fell to a duet of bolts. The second grabbed at the fallen reins, leaping back to the seat with unnatural grace. He smiled cockily back at Vivien for a moment and started to flick the leather straps, hauling the reindeer to the side and urging them onward. A screaming human bounded onto the side of the cart. Vivien flung an open hand that lashed out with a cloud of thousand burning embers. The human screamed as the burning fae entered his face, making sizzling black spots, and exited the other side as gouts of bloody steam. But the ambusher's axe still fell, still severed the carriage driver's arm, and the precious reins fell away. Bolts came and felled the two lead reindeer moments later. Their screaming deaths locked the carriage where it was, and ensured no escape was possible. They must fight or die.

The speed, the brutality of loss swept over the witch. Tears began to press from between her eyes, a morbid string of diamonds for every one of the fallen elf folk. Heat pulsed along her skin as the battle washed over her and the soldiers, drowning them.

It whispered of her defeat.

She trembled and reached deeper, feeling the seed of Elvishness inside of her and letting her soul drink from that power, becoming faster, fiercer, feeding from a bloodline that went back a thousand, thousand years. She reached to the sky and spoke a wyrd.

Even the humans paused, for the weight of the wyrd could be felt even by those with half dead souls. The sky grew dark as clouds coalesced and came together like an angry fist smacked into a palm. A dark fae flashed in the sky, from horizon to horizon, and then it shrieked. Lightning, primal and wild, smashed into the nearest tree, splintering it. Blue tentacles lashed out and burned the life from attacker after attacker, blinding eyes and deafening ears with the sound of bullwhips.

Then came the counterstroke.

Such a simple thing, hurled from the dirty fist of a savage. It was an innovation, a thought brought into malignant being by a spark of genius. A simple, burlap sack was hurled, the fragile strings that held the contents straining against the weight. It struck Vivien in the chest, the canvas and string shredding with the impact, and the force barely that of a well placed punch. But the innards were then free, and they splashed in the air like a cloud of angry, black bees. Iron flakes shaved as fine as dust erupted around her, covering her in a heavy cloud that cut off all magic, all feeling, and all comfort. She screamed, and then the cloud was inside her and she retched as it began to burn.

Cold iron, the bane of magic, covered her and consumed her as she fell from atop the carriage. Weightlessness gripped her as she tumbled forever, burning and choking, the forest not a comforting thing, but a nightmare landscape she could barely see through eyes tearing with blood. She landed. It was like being kicked by a reindeer, and she struggled to rise, only to shift feebly. She could not fight, nor contact the aether, but she could hear.

What she heard was her kinsmen dying, one by bloody one.

The harsh language of humans filled the air as elvin screams finally ended. Hope kindled as the doors to the carriage flew open. The Lady had emerged. Far beyond the ken of mortals, her radiant beauty surely struck the attackers dumb. The Lady uttered the fluid words of magic, and fae erupted from trees, raging dryads that snatched thorns of steel hard wood from the trunks and hurled them with deadly accuracy. Many humans fled. Those that stood were surely to be massacred. But then there was an imperceptible sound of a ball in flight, then many.

She moved like the wind, but the missiles struck the ground, the carriage, and even a branch above the road. Iron shards rained down upon the Lady, a pure elf, and she only barely managed to choke back a scream. Vivien heard her fall like a titan to the ancient paving stones of the Elvish road. Without her will, the dryads decayed into splinters.

Footsteps approached as Vivien wiped at her eyes, tears desperately trying to wash the sharp iron from under her lids. Rough hands grabbed her and she heard laughter and ripping cloth from the direction of the Lady. She cursed bitterly as one eye opened, a red swollen mess, to see a sharpened tip hovering inches from her face. She desperately clawed a dagger free from her belt and moved it across her body, barely catching the iron sword and shifting the tip just enough so that it plunged into the turf by her head.

Retaining hold of the sword, the human cursed and lurched back. Her heart thundered against her ribs. She could see it in her mind's eye– within moments he would thrust and her little blade would prove useless parrying the direct power of the blow. Still, she held it aloft, defiant. There was a scream from behind her– the Lady. The pureblood's fate would be far slower, far worse...

Then she saw it.

Like a wolf, a dark form bounded towards her through the woods. The first shape that resolved was a massive axe held in one hand, a short blade with an absurdly long handle glittering in the other. Wild hair flew in all directions, an untamed beard fluttering like a flag. It was savage, primal, but human. *Oh Gods, we are truly lost.*

The sword swung back. Just as it began its descent, the shadowy figure fell to a crouch and leapt. Her executioner faltered, heeded instinct and turned just as the barbarian landed behind him. The Wolf bellowed so loud it made Vivien's heart stutter to a brief halt.

But she would live to see another day.

The Wolf charged and slammed into the man standing over her. The sound was made of meeting flesh and crunching bone, and the swordsman flew back as if struck by a charging horse. His blade fell amongst a rain of blood and viscera that trailed him as inhuman noises came from the Wolf. Another rose up against him, and the Wolf peeled to the far side of the carriage. His first foe fell bleating like a lamb, crumpled to the ground in a pathetic heap. There were still plenty more.

Vivien rolled over, her hand randomly landing on a spent steel arrow in the soil. On this side of the grand carriage, a human straddled the Lady's hips, agog at the wild man who had felled his comrades. Men began to shout, but only after several blows that sounded like squealing metal giving way to chopping meat. Vivien raised the Elvish arrow and choked out a single word of power. Her brain suddenly felt bathed in needles as she pushed past the iron but the missile flung from her hand and buried itself in the neck of the one savaging the Lady. With a strangled cry he fell back. Wrenching herself past the pain of the iron dust stabbing her mind and burning her skin, she crawled to her liege's side.

The sounds of carnage continued as the Wolf growled and roared, axe and blade cleaving a continuous path through the ambushers. Some threw iron satchels at him, but he easily batted them aside, flying through the clouds of iron dust to cut down archer and swordsman, armored and half naked alike. He was human and the dust was like nothing to him. Arrows flew and found his flesh, but he barely broke stride as he cleft men in twain with his mighty axe. Faced with such fury, most of the few remaining attackers broke and fled.

Vivien dragged the choking Lady to the shadow of the carriage as the sounds of battle slowly ended. The woman's dress was torn and blood streamed from her eyes, nose, and mouth. Vivien desperately tried to brush the dust from the Lady's porcelain flesh, but it seemed useless. With a desperate moan, she glanced around and grabbed an Elvish sword from the unfeeling hand that held it. Despite the fatigue enveloping her like a sodden cloak, she reached for magic.

Her head pounded to her spine, heart warbling with missed beats, and the flow was feeble, but there. She leant the power of the sky fae to the metal, little sparking winged dots flowed up and down the metal, charging the steel. More and more, she gathered to her cause and let the fae dance onto the blade until the iron filings quivered, stood at attention, and then flew to the metal in a frenzy. She felt them dance from inside her clothes and strain to escape the folds of her skin. They crawled like bugs from inside her mouth and screeched against her eyelids to fly like raining tears black to the weapon. The blade got heavier and heavier, the silver sheen and carvings of hawks obliterated by a growing coat of iron fur.

Finally, the filings were mostly gone, and the weapon had grown far too heavy. She cast it aside into the sudden silence of the forest.

Something shifted to avoid being hit by the lump of metal and Vivien looked up. It was him– the Wolf.

He smelled of coppery blood and unwashed animal. He wore nothing but primitive boots and a kilt of the mountain barbarians held in place by a thick, rough leather belt. Crossbow bolts stuck out from one leg, his arm, and a shoulder. Other wounds bled where he had snapped the heads free and pulled out the shafts. He was covered in shallow cuts, and at least two thrusts bled freely. Each would become an ugly scar in a map-work of them on his body, but none of the myriad of wounds would ever overshadow the old, massive, twisted scar that bisected his muscular chest.

His axe was gone, but the left fist held an ornate broken sword barely the length of a long dagger, like the death warrant signed by a god. Harsh breathing filled the air, his body curled around the pains that plagued him, but his eyes were clear and bright. As red as blood and glowing as though burning from some internal inferno, they stared directly into her with the wonder of a child. His breath came in heavy gasps like the workings of a bellows, and his breath steamed in the air... or perhaps smoked.

A last attacker appeared behind the Wolf, hammer raised and shield held ready. Vivien made the barest start of a cry as the barbarian spun on his heel. The hammer landed a vicious blow on his right shoulder, and she saw the bones shift as they shattered. The Wolf let out a terrible howl, but still brought the broken sword up in a short arc. The blade flashed, cleaving shield and arm, armor and bones, and a spray of warm blood flew skyward. The dagger reversed, and flashed back downward into the last ambusher's face, instantly sending him to oblivion. The body fell, the forest again as silent as any graveyard and strewn with more corpses.

Ignoring his shoulder and other wounds, the barbarian slowly turned back to Vivien. It was a motion devoid of menace, without hate or violence. Though fresh blood dried and steamed in the cool air, he looked for all the world like a small animal approaching the doors of some ancient temple. For heartbeat after heartbeat, there was nothing in the universe but they two. He tossed matted locks of brown hair from his face, but never broke eye contact. As sand trickled through the glass, her fear of him faded, but new trepidation began to course thorough her. She felt a stirring of his emotions beneath his skin and knew in her bones his passion was not for blood. He spared a glance for the Lady and sheathed the broken sword. Gathering his kilt, he took it from around his hips and offered it to cover her modesty even as he exposed himself. The Lady nodded slowly and took the stinking rag, but the Wolf's eyes never left Vivien's. Inside them was a massive power, something larger than life and hotter than a coal fire. It bathed her and warmed her, but also made her heart tremble.

The Lady covered herself and nodded. "Thank you."

Vivien fought past the sudden fog of her reason. She lowered her hood in the universal Elvish gesture of peace and camaraderie. "Yes, thank you."

The barbarian said something. His accent was thick, the words familiar to her, yet foreign. There was no doubt that he meant them like a pledge taken upon the lives of innocents. When he finished, he bowed his head, not to the Lady, but to Vivien.

ELVISh Jewel

The hum of bowstrings gave only the barest of warnings. Three arrows erupted from the chest of the mountain man, two in one lung, one in the other. His eyes flashed wide. He gurgled in rage as he bent away from the impacts to his back. He staggered as three more arrows hit him, spraying hot blood across Vivien and the Lady. Tasting it on her lips, Vivien noticed it was like eating from a fierce pepper. He went to his knees. His eyes flickered, empty of hope and full of sadness. For a moment he was small, so very small in Vivien's eyes. Then the light went out.

The barbarian slumped forward and collapsed upon the forested turf. The advanced guard, drawn back to their location by the sounds of battle, came to tend to her and the Lady. Two took up the pure elf, glowing jewel of beauty marred by attempted rape and wicked iron. The third reached for the witch, but she pushed him away, diving over the iron-furred sword to roll the barbarian onto his side.

He was just a human, a wild thing, but her heart crashed about in her chest with each beat, wanting, needing him to survive. She saw the bleeding wounds, saw the many arrows and she clenched her teeth as she brushed matted chestnut locks from his face. Tears escaped her eyes and she cursed them and their uselessness even as questions forced their way from between her lips.

"Who are you? Who are you?"

She never expected to hear an answer, but the man opened his eyes, rubies so dark they were almost black. He weakly brought his left hand up to trail a tender touch across her cheek, then said something in the guttural tongue of the mountains, a language she had once learned as a child, but since forgotten. His hand then dropped and his head slumped to the side, passing into what seemed to be a deathlike sleep. Without caring how it looked, Vivien lowered her head between the forest of arrow shafts sticking out of his chest and pressed an ear to his skin.

His spicy, pungent scent was overwhelming, but aside from her aversion, she heard his heart. In fact, when she sat back up, she heard it too. In the silence of the woods, if she listened closely, she could hear it thumping like the war drums of the immortals. It was powerful, indignant, alive. Vivien shook her head and looked back to where the guards stood with the Lady.

Unbent, unbroken, the Lady nodded solemnly, holding the ragged kilt over her modesty. "He lives. We will bring him with us."

Vivien looked at the sword hilt protruding from the dagger sheath where it hung from the belt around his waist. It was a work of gold and silver, of scaly drake hide and amethyst settings. She had no doubt there was Elvish script on the blade and she wondered how he'd come upon it.

A guard began cutting the arrow and pulling the heads clear of the barbarian's body. "Who is he?"

"Whoever he is, he has survived Pergatium." The guards shivered at hearing the name from the Lady's lips. "But he has saved us, and for that we shall see him live so we may thank him."

Vivien turned back to stare at the powerful, naked creature. The footman attempted to bandage the wounds, but they refused to gush the required blood. Instead they wept in impotent rage, blood steaming despite the warm air. Meanwhile, the rest of the vanguard quickly made way to go, collecting arrows and preparing for a fast escape from this bloody place. Most of the guards were dead, but a few clung to life and were placed in or on the carriage. The reindeer were all lame or dead, and so the few tir-reath the vanguard had were repurposed. Most of these yowled and fidgeted as they were tied to the carriage, while the few remaining were made ready to ride.

Vivien kept watch over the barbarian the entire time, but as the soldiers moved him to the carriage roof, she made her way to where the Lady of Moonlight and Love sat atop the gentlest tir-reath, a fresh dress and cloak covering most of the outward signs of attack. Vivien coughed, her lungs aching from the iron dust she'd inhaled, dust that her magic was unable to remove. She certainly needed a healer once she returned home, and the Lady did as well. Her insides churned as she watched the vanguard grudgingly load their savior into place, his body limp and unmoving. *Dear gods, would he survive?*

Vivien frowned. "What did he say to us?"

The Lady's voice was soft and fragile, "What he said to *you*."

Cold fingers gripped Vivien's heart. "To me?"

Feeling a gentle hand on her shoulder, she turned to see fear in the eyes of the Lady, fear, and a sadness deep and wide as any ocean. She blinked languidly and whispered, "He said that he has known you all his life, and now he has finally found you again."

Vivien backed away from her touch, shaking her head, "H...he knows me?"

The Lady nodded. "And even more... he loves you."

Chapter Two
The Engagement

Horns blew, bagpipes blared, and drum-rolls rattled off of the stone walls of the wooden buildings on all sides of Castle Blacach. Ravn looked to his parents, resplendent in fine, bright clothes. In particular, his father wore a massive green patterned kilt that fell in sharp plaits from his waist, draped over one shoulder. On his hip he wore an ancient blood blade. Ornate beyond description, the short iron blade was the badge of the Laird of Blacach. No need for swords or axes today, for it was a time for joy.

That thought had him lean out of line to look at the far end where the guards stood with kilts and spears flying the family tartan. The man at arms of the castle did not move, but Ravn thought he detected a hint of a smile under the openings in the helm. He waved to Moray, who stood a little straighter.

Ravn's father glanced down at him, beaming through his tightly trimmed brown beard, his golden crown of small branches and stag horns glinting in the sun. Ravn turned to his mother, Aileen, who was far less sure, but putting forth a brave smile as she fiddled with blonde hair that kept getting blown into her face by the incessant wind. He understood the pressure. The visitor was a huge figure in every one of the stories his father used to tell, stories of war and glory from his youth. Though only eleven, he knew that this was an important meeting, setting the course of his domain for the lifetime to come. He adjusted his own tartan sash and stood tall as the party came through the cheering mob of people, riders carrying spears topped with red tartan, the gigantic feathered feet of the horses stepping high and brisk.

Laird MacConna rode at the front of the procession. He was an enormous man, rippling with powerful muscle run to middle aged gut. His head was a blossom of blonde like a thistle and his beard wild and free. It was the grand smile that turned his impressive visage from frightful to friendly. The massive horse had yet to fully stop when he leapt down from its back and ran to the arms of Laird Blacach. The embrace between them was like bears wrestling, and they slapped each other on the back as they roared in laughter.

Lady Blacach smiled more timidly at the display as her opposing number came to the door of the carriage when it stopped. The Lady MacConna was also gigantic, but from a whole other perspective. Red haired, clothed in thick furs trimmed in red tartan, she levered herself from the carriage, rolled her eyes skyward, and silently thanked the Gods the long trip was over. Still, when she approached, her bright smile and round cheeks almost overtook her overwhelming laugh and loud voice. She was clearly a woman for whom size was not a choice, but a dedication of both mind, body and soul. Ravn instantly liked and feared her.

Aileen smiled in greeting and the women began their nattering, their first meeting as far as Ravn knew. He did not bother to listen, instead glancing around MacConna's wide hips and even wider furs in an attempt to catch a glance of the only visitor that truly interested him.

Ravn was the only child born to the family Blacach, and as such, their heir. On the other hand, the MacConna's had no such trouble. The children emerged in a wave, letting servants take the horses, but standing back until introduced like proper nobles. There were four sons from early adulthood to younger than Ravn, and four daughters from a babe in the arms of a wetnurse to a plump beauty just at marriageable age. All were dressed like mother or father, with varying shades of red or blonde hair. Ravn, however, only saw three of the daughters, and he fidgeted to see more clearly, standing on tiptoes and searching intently.

"Is this him? Oh, just look at this young man!" Lady MacConna turned her considerable attention to Ravn. "So handsome and polite! What lovely gray eyes. They look like the sky over the mountains. And quiet like his mother! Ooooh that will be a blessing to his future wife, to be sure. Ernan is forever bellowing in his halls, driving one to drink!"

Ravn shrunk under the scrutiny, but Laird Ernan MacConna saved him by breaking in, "What's this, woman? You love my fiery disposition!"

She smiled wryly, "I love it more in the silence of you drinking and eating than the sound of you ordering another mug or plate, you brute!"

Ravn giggled, for the words were sharp, but the intent was not, and the Laird swept his wife into his arms, "Liam Blacach, my sword brother and dearest friend, this is Mòrag, my blessed bride and mother of my children."

Liam nodded as he took her hand, smiling warmly, "Any woman who could take the wild out of Ernan is a mighty wife, indeed."

Ernan recoiled, "Take the wild out of me? How do you figure?"

"You live in a castle." Liam replied wryly.

"And?"

"It is still standing. You are going soft."

Anything more, Ravn missed. The MacConna children were becoming restless and had moved one, tiny figure from the back of the group to the front. She was willowy and thin as a reed, with none of the telltale traits to distinguish her from a boy as of yet. She looked like she had seen about ten summers, with lank brown hair and mournful blue eyes. They glistened wetly as she looked at Ravn.

Ernan noticed her presence and jumped formality to seize the moment, "Ah! My little sparrow. Ròs, may I present Laird and Lady Blacach and their son, Ravn."

Ravn blinked, smiling weakly. He was unsure of really what was expected, but the girl seemed so thin, and tiny, though near his own height and only a couple summers younger. This moment was supposed to be important, but now that it had arrived, silence reigned but for the milling of the guards and commoners in the street. He felt the pressure build, all the parents looking on expectantly.

Ravn cleared his throat and tried to bow like a civilized adult, "Hello Ròs MacConna. Welcome to my home."

Parents beamed and turned to the little girl.

Ravn felt it coming before the blow landed. It was like a storm rolling in over the mountains and it started at the trembling of her lips and the misting of her eyes. Her hands balled into fists and her face contorted, "I HATE HIM! I HATE HIM AND I WILL NEVER MARRY HIM!"

Then she ran off through the crowd of her siblings toward the carriage. The door slammed with finality against a backdrop of utter and complete silence.

Ravn's father was not smiling. Ernan was looking embarrassed and his wife was, almost impossibly, shocked wordless. His mother looked like she wanted to bundle him off as if he had been cut on a practice blade in the yard. He carefully cleared his throat again even as his young heart trembled and broke inside.

"It has been a long journey. She is understandably tired." The whole group relaxed. Early betrothal was a long tradition in the Lairdlands, and this one would be gossiped about for generations for the breech in protocol. "And she is clearly frightened. I am frightened, too. But she speaks her mind and an honest wife is more precious than one who follows meekly."

Ernan guffawed and slapped Ravn across the back, nearly bowling him over. His mother squeezed his shoulder sadly. The traditional presentations ruined, the party started to disperse. Mòrag ran to look after her distraught daughter. Aileen took charge of the guest Laird and his pack of children, showing them to their rooms. Moray walked away from the soldiers falling out of a line, nodded proudly to Ravn, then followed his charges.

Liam, a huge and powerful figure even at his age, took Ravn aside and knelt to speak with him eye to eye, "You showed great wisdom today, and you have made me proud."

Ravn blushed and shrugged, "She is pretty."

Liam smiled and nodded, "Pretty fades. Strength flees. All things wander and corrode like iron in the rain. Even passion may falter given enough disdain or disuse." He set a hand on Ravn's shoulder, "But love... to whomever or whatever she decides to be, that can sustain anything against even the wrath of a giant."

Ravn listened closely and nodded. "Yes, Father."

"You have behaved as befitting a man, son. Tomorrow you will have your kilting."

As Liam walked off to see to his guests, the young Blacach stood, stunned, until a rotund young woman glided before him. Hair of red gold, blending her father and mother perfectly, she smiled at Ravn sadly. Ròs was just the pretty side of plain, but this girl was truly beautiful and blessed by her mother's plumpness. She had a kind face and she touched his cheek as he would imagine an aunt would.

"You were very kind to spare my sister public rebuke."

Ravn blushed again, "A husband, even a future husband, should be kind."

"Kindness is often in the shortest of supply in this world, young man. From here we travel to my marriage to Lairdson Erik McCarr in the Lowlands. I hope he is half the man you will be, Lairdson Ravn Blacach."

She smiled and then was gone, leaving Ravn amongst the business and bustle of the streets outside the castle that were trying to return to normal. He looked over and saw a small, pale face with red-rimmed eyes glaring at him from the MacConna carriage. Tentatively he gave a wave, and it disappeared.

Chapter Three
The Wolf

Vivien clutched the worn book to her chest and blinked at the healer with uncomprehending eyes. "Awake?"

"Awake, yes," he said serenely, "and in chains."

She almost dropped the book as her voice rose. "In chains?"

Like herself, the healer was a half blood, and had she been anything less, he would have had the right to scold her. Even so, he visibly restrained himself, "Of course! He is a human, after all, and a wild one at that. If he were an animal, I would say rabid. He tried to escape when barely able to walk and he broke two arms and a jaw before he could be stopped. We put him in chains for his own safety as much as anyone else's."

Vivien shook her head, wondering at this capacity for violence and strength from a man ridden with a dozen arrow wounds, let alone sword lacerations and crushing hammer blows, to wreak so much havoc. Then she remembered his shoulder, the one shattered near the end of the battle. "Did you save his arm? The one struck by the hammer?"

The healer's eyebrows flew up, "I did nothing of the sort!"

Vivien recoiled at the acerbic reply, for so much effort had gone into saving the man's life. She and the one of the guards had wrapped the Wolf's wounds as best they could in the field because the only one skilled in healing had been killed in the fray. It had taken three days to reach Rithalion, traveling day and night, swapping tir-reath on the carriage to make certain they did not expire from the strain. During that time, the Wolf had never awakened.

She frowned, hazel eyes sparking, "But the Lady—"

The man before her set his jaw and licked his lips in annoyance. Both of them were hooded, as befitted their station in Elvish society, but now the healer lowered his red cowl to step away from his duty and speak to her more informally.

"Listen to me carefully. We did nothing for the human."

"But—"

The healer's eyes flashed as he cut the air with his palm. "I said listen! We tried. We summoned the fae to heal his wounds. They would not heal him."

Vivien felt gooseflesh prickle over her body. Elvin magic tapped into the fae of the seleighe, the very building blocks of the world. The very idea that the fae would not, or could not, touch the human... Vivien's mind spun, unable to conceive of the meaning, "The Lady–"

"The Lady, who you are not, left clear instructions. If you have other questions, please address them to the Grand Magister." He turned, raised his hood, and left her standing in the causeway, walking away with an air of purpose, red healer's robes flapping behind.

Vivien clenched her teeth as he left. The great arch, one of many, spanned from one side of the gorge to the other, flying high above the forest below. It was a bright place, covered from rain or direct sunlight, where birds rested and sung. Yet its beauty was lost upon her and she stared out the open sides upon the Elvish city.

Fall had come to Rithalion. The western stronghold was a riot of blazing colors that were at odds with the cool air. The city spread across the gorge, carved out of the broken gray rocks that lined each side. A rushing river leapt from the crest in the west and flowed like sparkling ivory and sapphire through the center, reflecting the tracery of bridges, bulwarks, and buildings carved into the native stone. The whole of the city was serene, safe, but somehow she could not find any tranquility within.

She slammed the book down on the carved stone rail and cursed. Her hands traced the strange markings, stubby and ugly, that marked the human script beneath the far more beautiful Elvish. She had known this language of the Lairdlands in her youth, but it had been forgotten beneath decades of magic lessons and memories...

She closed her eyes and concentrated, purging the chaos from her as she had been taught by her masters through time. She finally found her center, snatched up the book, and walked down the causeway to the south face of the gorge. From there she passed the sculptured rock, the many carvings, the beautifully appointed doors and sparkling crystal windows of the healer's passages of the Western Hospice, past the more spartan barracks, to the dark jails in the roots of the rock face. Once she was close, she could hear him. Without realizing it, she had started to run.

The jail was a massive chamber carved on a ramp that went far into the rock. Here, there were no beautiful carvings, no signs that there ever had been a sun, or wind, or stars. It was a place for those doomed. The cells were carved into the walls, with iron bars to gate a prisoner from all comforting things. With only one way in or out of the prison, and no place to hide, it inspired a chill in all elves.

Green and brown clad guards laughed and joked outside of one such hole. It was there she ran. From inside there came a rhythmic crashing of metal that rang through the empty chambers like a fierce, fast, metallic heartbeat.

Elvish Jewel

The soldiers were low elves; children of children of elves and humans. They came to attention as she ran up to them, everyone suddenly about their duty. The Captain stepped forward, steel armor clacking as he planted the butt of his spear on the ground and snapped a salute.

In command of the mostly-empty prison and thus of her presence, his tone was brusque. "Business?"

Vivien narrowed her eyes and made sure her hood was up, clutching the book in her arms. The clanging rhythm continued and necessitated a shout to be heard over the clamor, "I am in service to the Lady and was there when this human was apprehended. I am here to check on him."

The Captain recoiled slightly. "Check on *him*? I would think it more likely you should check on *us*. I don't know how you captured this monster but–"

Her words came out in an explosion, "He is not a monster!"

In the silence that followed, the clanging continued, once every few seconds. Meanwhile, the other guards stood in mute shock at the depth of her passion. Finally the Captain bowed slightly in submission and stood aside, allowing her to move forward and look into the cell.

It was the Wolf. His kilt, boots and belt were gone, but he'd been given rough spun pants held in place by braided twine. Bandages covered his body and were so saturated that rivulets of blood crept from beneath. They had cleansed him of the filth that had covered him in the wilds, and trimmed the beard peppered with strands of silver. The naked parts of him portrayed a violent life through multitudes of blemishes long healed, and through the light smattering of reddish hair over his chest was a massive, ropy scar that crisscrossed over his heart like a dread curse. His hair had been shorn at the ends and braided during his care, but wild curling tendrils had come out of the plaits to create a mass that made him appear almost just as untamed as before. She marveled at the silver that frosted his mane, made more obvious due to cleaning and collection into ropes. It told that he was old for a human, at least in his forties, but his face was unlined with age. Every sinew was taut, and his body glistened with sweat as he blocked out the world and bent to his task.

He was held not on a bed of straw or sitting on the floor, but in a kneeling position, with arms cast wide to the sides. Each scarred limb was chained at the wrist to the opposing wall, one of the few uses of dreaded iron inside the Elvish kingdom. But he was human, and it did not burn him, did not weaken him. All it could do was keep his arms from hanging side, keep him from sleeping comfortably if at all, and keep him from bringing his hands together.

Then he flexed.

It was like watching a predator leap. Muscles bunched in perfect sequence, building in a wave that culminated in a dual fist punch, taking up all slack in the chains and slamming the links taut in a metallic crash. She jumped and dust emerged from the mounting brackets set into the walls. Slowly, the arms lowered, then rested, tensed, and leapt again. Another crash and she jumped once more. The power there was frightening.

The Captain flourished an arm, "Here is your not-a-monster." She felt the men smirking behind her and anger simmered deep within. A few plates of food sat, untouched, in front of him, along with pots of drink that had been set on the floor though the bars. Vivien clenched her jaws. Uncouth barbarian he might be, but the cause for his rage was evident.

She turned back to the Captain, "Are you responsible for providing his meals?"

The man nodded, "I am."

Her reply hissed between clenched teeth, "There is no way for him to reach the food!"

He shrugged nonchalantly. "I am also responsible for the safety of my men."

Her temper burned brightly and the words leapt from her lips, "Open the door!"

The guards, as one, recoiled. "You can't be–"

"Never mind!" The words were like a slap, and shifting the tome to rest in one arm, Vivien caressed the steel lock and murmured strange, cryptic words. Tiny, dark fae flittered about her fingers, leaping into the mechanism and spinning latches until the lock fell open.

The door moved effortlessly ajar.

The guardsmen scrambled for spears and shields as she stepped defiantly through the gate and into the room. The Wolf, head hanging low, caught sight of the hem of her blue robes. His head snapped up. His face was at first the epitome of bestial rage, but when he recognized her, it abruptly transformed to a peaceful gaze of embarrassed wonder. Thoughtlessly, he went to stand. She startled as the harsh sound of the unforgiving chains yanked him back down to one knee. *Oh gods, what have they done to you?*

A rumble began to sound from deep within his chest. His body crouched into a coiled bunch and the chains slackened. It was like the calm before a great battle is fought, or the peace before a child is born. Then he lunged. The Wolf put every muscle into pulling the chains with such force, Vivien heard his joints pop in agony.

"Wait!" She rushed forward without thought, dropping the precious book on the floor. "Please, wait!"

Instantly he stopped. He knelt there before her, massive chest heaving, breath stirring frayed, chestnut braids hanging in front of his face. For a moment longer the air rang with his attempt to destroy the irons. The guards shouted something from where they remained behind her, but she ignored them and crouched before the man they called "monster".

The chamber was suddenly silent, the atmosphere filled with tense anticipation. Her heart beat a staccato rhythm as she looked into his eyes, eyes that were like none she'd ever seen before, colored red as freshly spilled blood. The Wolf's large hand slowly rose towards her face and a chill raced down her spine. Her breaths stilled as his fingertips touched her cheek ever so gently. The caress was reminiscent of the one from that day on the battlefield, like she was the most precious thing in the world.

However, the sensation that she was in the presence of something wild persevered. Beyond any shadow of doubt, she was at the mercy of a being with great power.

And she was afraid.

Vivien instinctively jerked back. The hand followed and the iron clinked, the man's arm at the end of its range. He knelt there, hand extended, like a man falling from a cliff to his doom, reaching for the last hope that would save him from gravity's cruel embrace. She remained just out of reach; the light in his eyes dimmed and the hand finally fell, chains clanging against the stone floor. All life seemed to leave him as his back bowed and his shoulders slumped. At that moment, she was certain of her judgment prior to entering the chamber.

This is no monster. She sat there for a moment, regarding the broken man before her. *Who is he? Where is he from? Why did he save us?*

Tentatively, she reached out, little by little. It wasn't just fear that made her so hesitant; she'd learned to overcome many fears during her apprenticeship. It was something more, something she couldn't define. It made her belly clench and her heartbeat increase in tempo. It made her breathe a little faster and made her palms sweat.

Finally her hand touched the top of his head. Despite the runaway strands, his hair was smooth, soft even. He slowly looked up and her fingertips slid over the thick, wavy strands. His eyes were mesmerizing, darker than they had been a few moments ago. The red was still there, but less intense, like the color of her favorite dress, the one she liked to wear in court. Trembling, her fingers continued down his temple to his cheek, where she felt the stubbled, silver flecked beard. She placed her hand beneath his chin, and with the other, picked up the large mug lying nearby. She brought it over and carefully placed it to his dried, cracked lips.

He drank deeply of the watered wine, his throat rising and falling with each swallow. Unlike many men, he didn't grab the mug away from her to drink faster, but seemed to bask in the care she offered and took only what she gave. She saw the deep abrasions on his wrists and the trails of blood that crept down his arms to his elbows. A surge of anger swept through her like a wild river and she pitched her voice back to the guardsmen, "Give me the keys to his manacles."

The guards began to argue the seriousness of her request. Her temper flared again and the torches flickered. "Give them now!"

A heavy bronze ring with a single key bounced over the uneven floor to her side just as the door clanged shut. She lowered the empty mug and picked it up. Without further thought, she gently unlocked his left arm, making sure not to touch his wounds or the dire metal of his bond. Then, at the guard's protest, she tossed the ring back towards the closed door. She grabbed one of the trays of uneaten food, the one that looked freshest, and brought it to her side. Turning back, she found the Wolf's face a mere two inches from hers.

She blinked. The skin around his eyes was crinkled, and he had silvering hairs scattered about in his eyebrows to match those in his hair and beard. Her eyes traced the lines around his mouth… *would they disappear when he smiled?* His posture displayed vulnerability without losing power powerful, very dangerous indeed. Her heart pounded against her ribs as he reached out his freed hand and placed it at the back of her head, scandalously pushing off her hood. He then gently pulled her forward and placed his forehead against hers.

She let out the breath she'd been holding at the same time he released a gusty sigh. He whispered something, muttered in words she couldn't understand. His hand was warm and she allowed herself to relax. His scent tickled her olfactory nerve; he'd been washed but still smelled like an animal, his musk spicy and woody. Tendrils of his long hair hung alongside their faces, thick and smooth like the fur of his namesake. The guards shrieked in the distance behind her, but she easily ignored them. The passion of the moment was couched with power, pillowed by gentleness that touched her soul. For that brief time, she allowed herself to live in the moment, something she rarely did anymore.

When they finally parted, Vivien fetched a pitcher of water from near the door. Only with great reluctance did he let her go. When she sat back down on the floor before him, he gestured for her instead to sit at his side. He pressed gently against her, touching her without making her feel oppressed. She filled the mug with the water and handed him the best pieces of slightly staled bread, slices of dried meat, and raw vegetables from the platters that had taunted him not long before. She knew he must be starving, but he ate slowly and took only what she offered. When she'd sifted through the most edible bits, she shouted for the guards to bring a fresh platter.

As though doused by an avalanche, the thrumming rage that burned inside the Wolf flickered out. He ate the fresh food that was brought, his wrists a mass of torn skin from surging against his bonds. Vivien picked up her book and searched for the appropriate pages. She finally found what she was looking for, a translation from Elvish to the rough speech of the Lairdlands, the most likely language of a man moving through life wearing a kilt. She found the familiar phrase, "Who are you?" and spoke it aloud. She hoped it didn't sound too terrible to his ears.

The Wolf sat up straight like a predator that has a man mimic noises back at it. He reached for the book with only a moment's hesitation, flipping pages until he replied in horribly accented Elvish, "I am your servant."

Vivien's brows beetled, and she struggled with the shock of him reading the Laird's script as much as his reply. He was educated, definitely not a commoner. She shifted pages again, "No...no. What is your name? Who are you?"

He smiled sadly, shrugging. He looked to the guards with spears outside the gate, a freshly summoned junior healer staring in shock through the bars, and the tall, almost glowing presence of the newly arrived Grand Magister hovering like an elder spirit behind them. It took several seconds for her to translate the reply.

"I am no one."

The voice of the pureblood elder was like a physical thing in the echoing halls of the prison. "Vivien, I would have some words with you."

The reaction from the Wolf was immediate. She watched his whole posture shift simply by tensing muscles. Instantly he went from chained in a squatting position to being crouched for a pounce. His eyes flashed bright red for only an instant, as if a trick of the light. She caressed his arm and they returned to a dull red, so dark they might as well be black.

Vivien rose slowly, raised her hood, and crossed meekly to the side of the simmering, elder, full-blood elf.

Made by the Deep Green and the Mother of Light at the beginning of time, the elves were the purest expression of their love. The raw power of these two beings was infused into their first children– all things growing and living, withering and dying. All of this was embodied in the Grand Magister.

Timeless, ageless, he stood outside the squalor of the prison like a pillar of light, platinum hair glowing around his shoulders. His robes were a heavy cobalt of endless night, but he shone from beneath the hood nonetheless. Even as he frowned slightly, Vivien felt the mote of joy behind his eyes that he always saved for her. She walked out of the cage and the guards slammed the bars shut behind her. Vivien jumped, and opened her mouth to protest when the Grand Magister demanded her attention with soft, yet sonorous words.

"You are safe, young one. I rejoice in your wholeness through the storm of battle. I have spoken to the Lady of Moonlight and Love. She says you were unshakable."

His words flooded her with warmth and she smiled, a blush flushing her face. Yet a seed of doubt, the remembered hail of burning iron, the blade poised before her face, the screams of the dying, shook her as if she had returned to that exact moment. She trembled. Then she looked back, past the dead iron bars to the Wolf.

The human was there, but no longer a dangerous thing snapping at his chains. He sat against a wall, slowly eating from the plates on floor and watching her with forlorn eyes. "Magister... Lord," She corrected, speaking to him not as the teacher and leader of the Elvish Kingdom's mages, but as a noble full blood elf, "We would have failed had it not been for this human. He..."

The Magister only nodded, but it stopped her as she spoke. She could feel the fear and confusion her words inspired in the low elves guarding the Wolf behind her. How much more aware was the pure blood that stood before her? Her teacher smiled slightly, "Walk with me."

It was not a request, and Vivien could not fathom refusal. He walked and she fell respectfully a step behind and to the side, following him in his calm, serene gait up the spiraling stairs, out of the cold, lightless place of iron and torches and into the light of day. It was cool, but bright. They came back to the halls that lined the gorge and the common elves of lesser bloodlines moved about their business. Children playing a game of Capture the Rod, swarmed around the Magister with joyful giggles. Bareheaded and free, they scampered dexterously among doting adults who smiled at their antics. For a moment she envied them their exuberance, laughter, and innocence, feeling a measure of loss when they left.

The question came from nowhere and knocked the wind from her, "Have you yet thought of childbearing, Vivien?"

She gave a deep breath, struggled to get control of emotions that suddenly surged through her mind. In truth she had not, but the lie came easily to her lips, mayhap too easily. "Of course, but my duties, and the time..."

Her voice trailed off but the Magister waited. Elves were masters of waiting, knowing every day from that moment on was theirs by right of blood that did not weaken and die like that of humans, not for centuries upon centuries. They turned and walked onto one of the grand arches that linked the west and east side of the gorge. It was near the apex the Magister turned and walked onto one of the balconies. The pressure of the silence was oppressive and she finished clumsily, "There have been conversations, Grand Magister."

He did not reply, but looked over the swath of the forest that stood below, as beautiful and wild as any in creation. The blue ribbon of the rocky Fyresmee River far below reflected the sky and sunlight as a glittering seam of silver. She could feel the Grand Magister's serenity, and she wished to find it for herself. Thoughts and worries whirling within gave her no peace.

"Magister, the human... he saved the Lady of Moonlight and Love. Is this what we owe him? A cage?"

He affixed her with eyes so blue they were like the sky on a cloudless summer day. Yet, they reflected the weight of thoughts she could only conjecture about. When he was ready, the Magister spoke again. "The thing in the cage downstairs, he is not human."

Vivien recoiled. "But, Magister…"

He shook his head. "During the battle he was dealt mortal wounds, Vivien. You know this to be true. He was brought here to be healed of these, except our greatest soothers of pain and suffering found nothing but ugly scars and the shallowest of hurts."

Forgetting herself, Vivien interrupted. "But when we were on the road he was near death for days!" Shocked, she covered her mouth to stop it from further betrayal.

The Magister's eyes glittered but he chose to ignore her temerity. "Even his shoulder has somehow mended, with only bits of broken bone protruding from the skin where his body has expelling them like splinters. The healing fae would not touch him, Vivien, and even I am still searching for an explanation to that. No, he is not human. If he ever was."

Vivien blinked furiously, realizing how her act of entering the Wolf's cage was pigheaded and foolhardy. "Might he be possessed by one of the elder fae?"

The Magister's brows came together ever so slightly, not in anger, but in concerned consideration. All accepted Elvish magic revolved around the harnessing and taming of the most basic motes of creation, the faeries. Sometimes they were corrupted, but could still be controlled by a sufficiently powerful and skilled wizard. Finally he shook his head, "No. The fae recoil from him, Vivien. Whatever made him is a darker magic, and I daresay, an older kind than even we have seen."

Those words threw a chill down her spine again. In the chaos of creation, the void dispossessed by light and life held things so dark they could blast even an elf's sanity to pieces. She shook her head fiercely, childishly, "He is not evil! I would have sensed it, Magister."

Then the Magister changed. He lowered the hood on his robes and, for a brief instant, he seemed as old as he was, over a five hundred years behind him and hundreds more before him. She hurried to bring down her hood as he raised a kindly hand and laid it on her shoulder. "Young one, the Wolf is not evil, but he has sharp teeth. It seems we owe this one a debt, but so far you are the only one to get through to him. It is because we owe him we must let him loose, but in your care. It is for that reason I must ask– if needed, can you kill him?"

The question drove an ice cold spike into her heart. It fluttered in beating, and shriveled with a painful need to run and hide. Yet there, looking into the eyes of the Magister, there could be only one answer. "Yes." Though the truth of it she had no idea.

"Take some time. Learn his language. You knew it when you were young. Then let us discuss bringing him forth from imprisonment. The Lady wishes to thank him, but then we must find a safe place to release him back into the wild, my dear." He smiled warmly. "You are a good daughter. I am proud to call you my own."

He gathered her in a caring embrace that brought little comfort. All she could see in her mind was the lost and needful eyes of the Wolf who named himself Nobody.

Chapter Four
The Noble

L ydia looked through the bars of the cell, preparing herself to enter. She crinkled her nose from the stench and wondered, not for the first time, why she'd been asked to perform this duty. But every time she really thought about it, she knew the reason. Vivien believed in her, believed she would see past this man's outward appearance to see what lay deep inside.

She hardly remembered her life in the Lairdlands. As the daughter of a merchant, her marriage prospects had been limited. But she was young, and pretty, so when some elves passed through one day, one of the men took notice. He swept her off her feet and promised to make her a lady befitting his station. Her life with him had been a very rewarding one, filled with all of the things he'd promised, and more. She never missed her old life, so she let it creep back into the recesses of her mind.

Except the language. The language stayed with her.

Lydia took a deep breath. She'd heard of the violent tirade that had damaged dozens of men. She considered her old bones and figured this man could kill her with a casual sweep of his bare arm. The Wolf crouched at the far end of the cell, a mountain of a human with curled, untamed hair on his head and even more on the rest of him. She tried not to focus on trails of scars across his chest, ribs and back, massive muscles won over a lifetime of survival and conflict. She tried to understand what Vivien saw in the hulking brute, as tall as any elf and twice as wide.

Vivien had left one of his arms free so he could eat and sleep; the guards had been too afraid to chain him again. He poured over a large book lying in the palm of his free hand and she wondered where he'd acquired it. She shook her head slowly as she imagined he was actually reading the thing.

Lydia nodded to the guards and they opened the cell door. One of them unceremoniously thrust a tray of food into her arms as she entered. Time had sucked much of the muscle from her limbs, but she toddled into the cell without a walking stick. She hated walking sticks; they made her feel old. A useless vanity, but in a land of those who do not age, it was her one act of defiance to time and her human heritage. She kept her gaze riveted on the Wolf, who stared at her intently from eyes so dark, one could become lost in them. A wave of fear suddenly enveloped her and she stopped in the middle of the cell. The tray shook in her unsteady hands and broth spilled over the sides of the bowl. She set the tray down and proceeded to do the first thing that came to mind.

The Wolf sat there and calmly watched as she cleaned up the mess that had accumulated over the last few days. She swept up the old food and took away the stale water. She poured a bucket of it down the stinking latrine, swiftly followed by a second. She picked up all the discarded trays, bowls, and mugs. She tried to keep one eye on him and the other on her tasks. The moment she forgot to do so, he crept towards the newest tray and picked it up. Realizing how close he was, she startled and stepped on the thick chain that bound his right arm. She toppled over. Trays, bowls, and mugs flew in every direction as she curved into herself, desperately hoping nothing broke when she hit the cold, stone floor.

Though her landing was hard, it was nothing like she expected. It was much too giving, and warm. Lydia opened her eyes and found herself looking into the ruby black eyes of the man the guards called "monster". Where she lay in the cradle of his arm, he looked at her curiously, calmly, without malice or violence. He smelled of spice and animal musk. Across his chest, as if he had been horribly maimed at some time by an awful claw, there was a scar that stood red and angry from neck to navel, and nipple to nipple. She knew he wasn't truly human, but this old wound provided evidence of his mortality. And perhaps he wasn't as fearsome as the men liked to make him out to be...

The door swung open and the guards thrust their spears into the cell, shouting as though she was in the direst of danger. The Wolf looked up and, as if caught by the light of the setting sun, his eyes flashed blood red. His whole body tensed beneath her and she threw up a hand, "Stop! That is enough!"

In shock, the men ceased their juvenile hollering. Trembling more at her audacity than her current situation, she carefully picked herself up out of the barbarian's arms. In spite of her increased status as a great teacher, she was still only human, and beneath almost every inhabitant of Rithalion. The only exception was the lowest of the elves, her age giving her status above those having so little of the ancient blood they were almost entirely of human descent.

The guards calmed as she arranged her robes to lay befitting a proper lady and she nodded to the Wolf. "Thank you."

The man's eyes had shifted back to dark, but somehow they brightened and he gave a nod. She waited a moment, then spoke again. "My name is Lydia." The Wolf nodded again. With no more forthcoming, she tried to be more direct. "What is your name?"

She expected him to be confused, or to at least have to think a great deal about picking his humanity out of the mass of wildness that coated him. When he replied, however, his voice was clean and clipped, certain, not guttural in the least. His face clouded, as if with some sad memory, and he said in a deep voice, "I am nobody."

Lydia blinked and her reply was indignant. "You most certainly are someone!"

The Wolf's face fell and he retreated to the back corner, left arm strung out before him. There he sat, his face dark and his brows beetled low to cast his eyes in shadow.

Lydia watched as he retreated into his mind. She pulled herself up and addressed him more officially, "I am here to teach you to speak!"

The Wolf flicked his eyes at her, his voice monotone. "I can speak."

She set her jaw, caught between beast and burden, "I am to teach you Elvish."

The Wolf suddenly became intent. "Is Vivien returning?"

Lydia frowned and shook her head, "Why would she?"

The change was instantaneous. The Wolf seemed to collapse in upon himself without even moving. He just slumped, all of his endless fire quenched. Lydia gasped in understanding, then walked forward. Before she realized what she was doing, she had her arms around someone who was really just a man, albeit a large hairy one. He wrapped one arm around her with gentle awkwardness.

She held him a long time, and when they parted, his eyes radiated gratitude. He nodded, picked up the book he had been reading from the floor, and passed it to her.

"Could you return this to her?"

Lydia flipped through the book, a book that translated her native language to that of the elves. Finally she looked up at him, staring incredulously. "You can read this?"

He simply nodded.

"Who are you?"

He stared into her eyes– deep, dark pools swirling with emotion like a far off storm. "I am nobody."

"She calls you 'Wolf.'"

He didn't ask who. He didn't even flinch. "As she wishes."

Lydia opened her mouth, thought better of it, then pursed her lips and sighed. "All right, Wolf. Where are you from?"

He gave her an appraising glare, backed by obvious pain, "The deepest places in the forests claimed by no nation or race."

She tried again. "Your language is of the mountain folk. In fact, you speak the tongue like a noble."

He gestured to the cell and his stained, ragged pants, "You could tell from my grand accommodations and my fine garments?"

She sat back on her haunches, ignoring the protests of muscle and bone. "Fine. But I am still assigned the task to teach you Elvish."

The Wolf thought on this, then nodded towards the guards. "Then you had better get a chair from the brave ones in armor cowering outside. Your old body will not want to stand or sit on the stones with me."

Her face clouded and she thought of doing no such thing just to spite him. But finally she turned and spoke to the guards, requiring quite a bit of convincing, until a small, unpadded stool was passed through an open door guarded by two spears. The Wolf shook his head and continued to page through the language book. Lydia brought the chair next to the Wolf's pallet and sat primly.

"Can you really read that book or are you foxing?"

He furiously turned pages, then spoke in Elvish, "*I can reading, sir.*"

Lydia sniffed as if detecting some off odor. "I don't think a wolf would be capable of speaking Elvish any more than reading a book." He just looked at her. She had taught hundreds of children in her day, and this one was proving as truculent as any she had ever met. "It seems you are far more than the wild beast they think you are."

The Wolf smiled for a moment, then caressed the book like it was a love charm. He looked to the door as though hoping the mage would appear, and when she did not, his smile died. He shrugged and said in Elvish, "No."

Lydia breathed deeply, "Perhaps. Perhaps not. But we will start." Again, the Wolf looked to the door, then slumped onto his bedding. For long seconds, she watched the mighty human become progressively smaller. She left her chair, slowly, as if approaching a wild animal. She held out a hand, trembled for just a moment, then drew close and whispered, "Keep the book. Read it. If you learn, she just might return after all."

His head snapped up. Nostrils flared as his breathing seemed to act as a bellows that turned his banked fire into a raging forge. He nodded.

She smiled and began the lesson for the day. He consumed it like it was his last meal, tearing off whole sections and swallowing them whole. He guarded his knowledge jealously, and constantly pressed forward for more.

Wolf, indeed.

Chapter Five
Attack of the Liath

Castle Blacach was a wooden and stone fort near the top of a mountain, built on an unassailable spring, and surrounded by hearty, thick wooden buildings. It was a place of laughter and labor, of honest feelings and simple beauty.

But not this day. This day it was a place of smoke. And fear. And blood.

Ravn Blacach huddled in the Kirk of the Chorus, crying. The old priest, Angus, held him tightly, harsh woolen robe scratchy against Ravn's face. Screams pierced the air and Angus winced, covering the boy's head with his long sleeves. But neither the robe, nor the walls, did anything to mute the shouts and cries that fluttered through the broken doors, nor disperse the smoke of the burning village.

Bright flames licked the buildings while black iron axes fell upon the townspeople, shining with blood that flew from each swing in sparkling droplets. The terrified screams grew louder with every passing moment as the horrors increased. Inside Ravn just cowered.

"LORDLING!" A gruff voice rattled the rafters, and cut through the background misery. "LORDLING! Come and face me, you little cunt!"

Ravn glanced at the door, shivering, but the priest held him even more tightly. "No! Those creatures of darkness dare not come in here. They dare not touch the kirk. Stay with me, and we will be safe."

Ravn huddled back into the wool like a child, tears soaking the cloth. There was another scream, higher pitched than what any man, woman, or boy could manage. It was made of sheer panic.

"Come now, boy! Come now and watch what happens next to this dull little bit of a mouse!"

Angus shunted aside Ravn and was instantly on his feet. He then hurried to the shattered doors that lay askew like broken teeth barring entry to the kirk. He poked his head out an opening, face flushing with rage at the scene beyond.

"How dare you! Let the young lady go at once! She is no threat to you, barbarian! She is the daughter of Laird MacC–"

The arrow struck with a gruesome crunch. In horror, Ravn watched as the man who had taught him numbers and letters, history and songs, fell back from the opening with an arrow sticking out of one eye. He collapsed to the holy marble floor, blood swiftly pooling outward as depraved laughter emanated from the outside.

The girl's scream came again.

"Come now, boy! Buy her life! I have two Blacach nobles out here. I only need one more to end this."

The Liath lied, Ravn knew he lied. Ravn's mother was behind several feet of timber and stone and his father was a mighty warrior. But he feared the Liath did not really lie at all, and that he just might be telling the truth.

The Far Liath had stuck in the middle of the night. They had summoned thick fogs to dull the senses and came down upon the village surrounding Blacach castle without mercy. They had made no move on the castle's unassailable walls, only letting the tortured screams of their victims crush the souls of those inside. The gates had been locked. The gates had been barred. Then the Liath began hurling parts of men over the walls. Then parts of women. Then whole, living children. Ravn's father mustered the guards and marched out into the blinding fog to meet them. They never made it past the gate.

Hundreds of them had flooded in, screaming like demons and holding leather wrapped iron blades. They crashed into the defenders like molten metal poured over wax. He saw his father press into the yard beyond. Moray retreated under a clot of the creatures. Ravn and the priest had made it to the kirk.

Ravn heard the laughter outside, the cruel sharp sounds slamming into him. He turned over on numb limbs, looking onto the faces of the Chorus, the pantheon of gods that looked upon him with sad eyes. He recoiled from them, afraid they would see his weakness and find him wanting.

He staggered to his feet, reflexively glancing back to the door. Priest Angus was still dead, his off white robe turning dark red. The metallic smell of blood soaked into him and he feared it would never leave.

Ravn smoothed out his kilt. He looked down at his hands. It was two years now since he had been declared a man. He lived in a castle, he had the best clothes, and the best food. All he had to do was defend his people, people that were now being chopped up out on the streets.

There was another scream.

Winter had brought another trip from the MacConnas. They had left Ròs at Castle Blacach to get to know Ravn, hoping to convince her of their future plans. She had been quiet, and distant. Now she was out in the streets, screaming, while those men did gods only knew.

Another scream abruptly cut off by horrid laughter.

Fear ran wild across his skin like a broken nest of spiders, but his thoughts remained. *Ròs is a guest in my home. She is my future wife. I am a man.*

His hands clenched into fists.

Outside Blacach had become a twisted nightmare. Fog flowed through the streets as blood trickled between the cobblestones. Bodies lay in pieces strewn everywhere and the Liath tore through houses looking for silver and gold. Their weapon of choice were thin bladed axes of beaten iron, handles wrapped in leather cord. They used them on doors, and walls, and animals, and people.

The crooked planks of the kirk door shuddered and the laughing stopped. Multiple eyes the color of blood, rust, and pus shifted to the opening as it yawned wide, exposing a plump boy in a pleated skirt. The Liath slithered from the shadows on all sides, sometimes leaving entertainment behind that wailed, whimpered, and cried.

The sun was weak and far away through the thick mucus in the air, but it spared no detail of the carnage. In the street, splayed like a broken bird, lay a man on his back, his front a mass of hacked meat and crimson stains. Everywhere Ravn's eyes landed, horror built upon horror, but each echoed hollowly inside his heart. His steps came weakly, but one followed after another until he stood over the body of his father.

The Liath had not lied.

An eternal titan lay there, destroyed by insurmountable darkness. There in the middle of the street, broken and battered, hair matted with blood, he looked different. He looked empty. Nothing but a shell left behind. Liam's mighty sword was shattered and his shield still strapped to his broken arm.

Next to him was sprawled the body of his mother. Bright blue dress stained black by blood, she was a death to all the music he had ever loved. She was an end to all the comfort, all the safety, he would ever feel. She had died reaching for her husband, drawn out by his death, struck down in her grief.

Words caressed Ravn's ears like rusty knives, leaving runnels in his brain, "Ah, the little lord of Blacach. Welcome, Laird. Please, join the festivities."

Numbly, Ravn's brought his gaze to meet the yellow eyes of the leader of the Liath. The creature stood as a man, but was serpentine and sharp. He sat on a pile of corpses laid out like a throne facing the kirk. The damnable attackers were twisted, dark, and malevolent in appearance and action. Ròs whimpered at the foot of the throne, covered in blood. The leader growled and backhanded her so viciously her head rocked back on her neck and made her cry out.

Again, the voice of gravel and night, "What do you think of my music?"

Without answering, Ravn bent down and unstrapped the targe from his father's arm, slipping it onto his own. He sadly glanced at Liam's shattered sword and instead he drew the long, iron knife from its bloody sheath. The honor blade was heavy, ancient, passed from laird to laird down through time. Words were etched in the blade from tongues no longer spoken by any man. They promised darkness. He tried to remember everything the master-at-arms had ever taught him, but his mind was clear as a windblown sea. The only detail that came to him was an old tradition. He scraped the iron blade against the steel center of the targe and the sound rang through the street. It was a single peal of challenge.

The inhuman creature before him smiled, its mouth a mass of jagged yellow fangs. "Well, if you don't know the words to my song, at least you know the dance." He reached to the side and yanked a sword from the corpse of the boy that cleaned the stables. It was sharp, the edge bright beneath a coat of thick, dark clots. Ravn took up a fighting stance and leaned far back, pushing the shield before him as he was taught, blade hidden behind his only defense.

The Liath laughed. He swung the sword in a tight circle as he swiftly grabbed a fistful of mouse brown locks, slicing them away from Ròs' head. She whimpered again as he smelled them obscenely and flicked the fine strands into the air.

Ravn suddenly felt something build from inside, a pressure from somewhere deep within, a place he didn't know existed. His body shook with the power of it and he opened his mouth to proclaim, to order, to command. But the explosion fizzled into empty words that warbled weakly and barely penetrated the fog, "Leave my home. Leave my wife."

The Liath slunk off his throne, stepping slowly. He struck the ground with the sword and the metal rang discordantly, drawing the last few Liath from the darkest corners to watch. "So, now you are giving the orders, are you?"

Ravn's mouth was suddenly dry, full of raw wool. But his voice was a bit stronger. "Leave my home. Leave my wife."

Then the Liath was fast and seemingly struck from three directions at once. Ravn stumbled back but there was nowhere to go. The sword came again, biting through the cloth of his tunic to slice into his skin, causing slick streams of blood to cover his protruding belly.

"What did you say, boy?"

Ravn tripped over an outstretched arm. He fell hard and realized it belonged to his father. The foul creature cut at Ravn's legs and he pulled them up and rolled to the side.

"What did you say, you little shit?"

Ravn gathered himself on his knees and raised the targe as another storm of blows ensued. He pulled the shield higher, higher, higher to stop the next attack from taking his head.

Ravn sometimes sparred with his father on the training ground. Liam never held anything back, and his favorite move was to strike high.

"What did you say?!"

Liam would strike high again.

He held the targe high and the sword rang off it.

Then his father would go low, taking one of his calves.

Ravn extended his arm, absorbing the next blow that fell far more mightily.

And there he was, exposed from waist down for the perfect strike to make him into many different pieces.

Without thought, without even fully knowing why, Ravn brought the targe all the way down, slamming the shield into the cobblestones just as the Liath came with a casual backhand. Instead of sweeping his legs from the boy's torso the sword struck against the targe's center boss, ringing it like a bell. The lord of Blacach looked up to see the Liath smiling with a mouth full of misshapen teeth like razors and needles. But the eyes, the yellow eyes shifted in that instant.

Ravn leapt. He exploded from the ground, shield held to the side as the sword scraped along the metal center. The Liath shifted back, but far too late. The boy leapt at it like an animal, iron blade of his forefathers shooting forward. The Liath's eyes widened as the honor blade plunged into his chest to the hilt, sizzling on demon blood as it crashed off a rib and slipping into the hollows between. The black, twisted, greasy mass it found could only vaguely be called a heart. Piercing it in two had the same effect.

Ravn landed awkwardly, but he landed. The Liath fell back with a finality now familiar to the streets of Blacach. And for a second, there was no sound, no cries. Only the gentle wheeze of escaping breath and the hiss of the iron eating at the flesh of the evil thing.

Ravn tried to shout, tried to roar, but his voice was a mere shriek, "Leave my home! Leave my wife!"

And, to his amazement, the razor fanged faces and iron axes slipped back into the shadows. The mists receded and the sun's rays pierced the gloom.

Ravn dropped the shield from nerveless fingers. Moray, man-at-arms, and a handful of people ran from the keep into the street to see him there as the final bit of dark faded from the sky. They saw their lord victorious. Moray knelt. The others followed suit.

Ravn heard the words come from someone who sounded much older and wiser, someone speaking with his voice but his father's words, "Find the survivors, help anyone who lives. Get runners to warn the local lairds. The Liath are raiding."

He did not see if his commands had been followed. Instead, he walked away from the dead body of the evil thing he'd felled and over to a blood soaked Ròs. She trembled like a newborn animal, weeping for so long now she was out of tears, out of sounds. He pulled her thin body into his arms and held her tight, closing his eyes against the gore-spattered landscape all around.

His voice was filled with the conviction of all the years he would spend as Laird. "I will never abandon you. I will never dishonor you. I will ever stand in your defense."

She wrapped her arms around his neck and hugged him back with a fierceness borne of the greatest fear. However, in spite of her relief and gratitude, her heart was never in it.

Chapter Six
Vivien and Torialvah

Vivien walked slowly through the garden. She whispered the words to the incantation, putting it to memory along with all the others, hoping to use it when the need arose. Her mind refused to let go of the horrors of that fateful day. Though a week passed, she could not shake the feelings of helplessness that had swept over her like an untamed sea as the ambushers killed her people without mercy. It didn't matter how strong the elves were, they were no match against the sheer number of the humans.

And therein lay so much of the problem. Numbers. The humans bred like rodents, a child every year, maybe two. There was little to hold their populations in check except disease. Other than that, there was only other humans, for they were very good at fighting with one another.

Vivien stopped in the middle of the path and stared into the space before her. Yes, the elves had lost so much that day, and there was a way she could aid her people in regaining what had been taken.

She had only to produce a child.

Vivien took a deep shuddering breath and felt her belly churn uncomfortably. She and her husband had been at odds much too often as of recent. It was worse after the ambush. He had been openly concerned as she recovered from her wounds, but afterward, there had been a strained tension in the air she couldn't identify.

She blinked away the tears that suddenly gathered at the corners of her eyes. Torialvah was possibly the handsomest man she had ever known, and at one time, she had been pleased to be his wife. That was at the beginning. It didn't take her long to realize he did not necessarily feel the same way about being her husband. Not even close.

Vivien felt her soul approach a deep, dark pit in her mind. She looked over the edge into the dark churning waters below, and deliberately turned away from that path. Over their twenty years of marriage, she had thrown herself into her studies and was applauded as the highest ranking mage in her class. She had hoped her husband would be proud of this achievement.

She was met only with disappointment.

The tears fell down her face and onto her silk dress. Before they were married she had thought of him with fondness. He had been kinder then, more caring. Through the years, that had dwindled away and all that was left was a coldness that chilled her every time he was near.

New thoughts arose, rogues who ought to fight the rising tide of despair. Whatever Torialvah lacked as a husband, he more than made up for in other things! He was a strong warrior, a great provider, an excellent smith, and an accomplished leader. Well before she had even met him, Torialvah's service to the elvin community had allowed him to rise in rank to someone who bore significant status. He could ask for anything, and before long, he would have it.

She supposed that was how he had acquired her.

Vivien had once hoped the Lord of Ice and Steel would come to love her. Over the years that dream had turned to dust along with any others she had once fancied as they pertained to Torialvah and any happiness they might share. As her thoughts shifted to love, an image of the Wolf formed in her mind. She recoiled instantly, remembering the stinking, harsh, dull lines of the beastly human. Yet, she could not get the Lady's words out of her mind, the words he had spoken as he fell unconscious from his wounds the day of the ambush. That he loved her.

"No one has ever loved me before."

She was startled to realize she whispered the words aloud and looked around even though she knew she was alone. Her heart beat fast, like a rabbit under the shadow of a hawk flying overhead. She twisted her fingers together trying to regain calm, and the excess of emotion leaked into the aether. Teeny-tiny fae the size of gnats glittered in a waterfall from her fingers as if being ground from limestone. *Really, how can that be? How can a man love someone he had never met, and then having seen only across a battlefield?*

After that one visit, she had not returned to the prison, her duties keeping her away. A part of her did not want to go back. Everyone was agreed that the human was not a human at all, and whatever strange power he possessed had been inflicted upon her the day she had made her visit. She called upon her elvin blood and cast thick cords of will across the chaos tumbling about within her. In truth, she didn't know what to think about that and had no faith it was a fact. The confusion had to be dealt with privately, far away from the Wolf and all he had begun to mean.

However, it didn't stop her from asking Lydia to go in her stead.

Vivien shook herself free of the thoughts, and was about to start walking again, when she heard someone call her name. Her heart skipped a beat and the blood in her veins turned to ice. The voice was angry, and it belonged to Torialvah.

"Vivien! I know you are out here somewhere. I would like to have some words with you!"

The fae went out like candle flames extinguished by a sudden wind. She shuddered and thought about going off the path and hiding behind the nearest rosebush. She hated fighting with him, and by the tone of his voice, she could tell that was the course of her near future. She wrung her hands and looked down the path behind her, whispering to herself. "Vivien! You silly thing. Hiding behind rosebushes? Really?"

She just stood there and waited. She didn't have the courage to answer back. Some days were better, and she felt stronger. This was not one of those days. Her heart thundered against her ribs and she hoped the altercation would be minimal. Besides, what reason did he have to be angry with her for?

Torialvah came around the curve and stopped when he found her standing there. "Did you not hear me calling for you?"

Her husband was a pure elf, a full blood noble of her people and, as always, she was struck by his beauty. He was tall, standing at least a foot higher than she. His hair was so dark it was black, and long enough to weave a plait that lay over his shoulder to dangle near his elbow. His blue eyes were so pale, they were like ice– fists of frozen water powerful enough to face the burning rods of iron he had beaten into brave Elvish steel during his youth, sheets of glacier that showed brutal constancy and control, winter diamonds that formed intricate sculptures, truly beautiful things, so rare like his displays of affection for her.

She just stood there, not dignifying him with an answer. She wondered what he saw when he looked at her. Of course he saw her hair, colored a reddish blond. People liked to say it looked like the sun was trapped in it. He must see her eyes, colored an indistinct gray that liked to shift into varying shades of green every now and then. But what else did he see? She was loath to imagine it for he had not paid her a compliment since the early days of their marriage.

He frowned and narrowed his eyes. "Come back to the house. I would like to speak with you behind the privacy of walls."

She nodded and walked behind him, heart sinking in her chest. Even though the garden was considered their private property, they could still be heard if their voices rose too much. He meant to argue with her, but she had time now to fortify herself for the battle.

The moment they entered the house, Torialvah's demeanor changed. Even though his back was turned, she saw his shoulders relax and when he spoke, his voice had not the edge to it she heard in the garden. "We haven't spoken much in the past few days. My work has, by necessity, kept me away and your studies have monopolized much of your time."

Vivien stiffened at his choice of words. He never addressed her work as important as his, even though it had gained her the honored position as Mage Escort for The Lady of Moonlight and Love. But she let his diminution go, like she always did now, because it simply wasn't worth the argument. She'd come to realize that he was so self absorbed, he didn't even realize he did it.

"Yes, I have been busy."

He turned around to face her. "So how fares the human?"

She regarded him intently, wondering why he bothered asking her about the Wolf. He didn't seem to care when they first arrived back in Rithalion, and appeared disturbed that they had even deigned to save him.

"I believe he is doing well."

His dark brows furrowed. "You do not know?"

She heard something in his tone, something that warned her to tread carefully, but she didn't know what it was she had to be wary about.

"I would like to believe he is doing well, but I have not seen him..."

Torialvah's lips pursed and his eyes flashed. He didn't bother to let her finish. "Then what is this tale I have heard told of you going to the prison?" His voice rose. "A tale that goes so far as to tell how you entered the captive's cell, demanded the key to his manacles, and fed him food from your hand?"

Vivien took a deep breath and just stood there. In his anger, her husband was larger than life, his aura so big it filled the entire room.

"Yes, but that was days ago. I do not know how he fares..."

"It doesn't matter when it happened!" he interrupted again. "You had no business entering that cell." His eyes narrowed and his upper lip curled. "What were you thinking? Did you have any care for how that looked?" He took a deep breath, huffed, and when she did not defend herself pressed on further, "Or have any care for your safety?"

She took note of which of those statements came first. Of course he cared more for appearances than anything else. She never imagined her action would be a cause of embarrassment, not to mention, the source of anyone's storytelling. Thinking on it now, she understood how it could be an entertaining conversation piece, especially if it came from the mouth of one of the guards on duty that day.

She kept her voice low and calm. "I didn't think I would have to take such action. But when I saw the conditions in which he was being kept, I felt I had to intervene."

"The conditions? Vivien, he is being kept in prison! What do you expect?"

Her temper flared. "Yes, the conditions! He wasn't able to reach the food trays! He would die of starvation and no one would care. So I made decisions, the ones I felt were the right ones to make at the time!"

His eyes flashed again. By the look on his face, he didn't care about anyone starving. He pointed at her and his voice was scathing. "Your decisions affect more than just you and your precious human. They affect everyone around you, and like a stone cast into a still pond, they ripple outward to encompass a city." He didn't have to move to make her feel like he was getting closer, looming over her. "I never want this to happen again. If you do something asinine, please tell me about it yourself."

Torialvah swept out of the house without a backward glance. Vivien watched, glad to see him leave. Tears gathered in her eyes and thoughts of the conversation she had shared with the Grand Magister came to mind.

She hated thinking about having children with her husband, and that realization alone was enough to make her cry.

At least now she could do it alone without anyone to hear.

Chapter Seven
Freedom

The Wolf was restless. He had taken to pacing as far as his chain would permit. Lydia would come in the mornings to find him docile, but the wrist that bore the manacle was red and weeping blood. The guards told her that he liked to work himself into a sweat, sometimes using his body as a weight to train his muscles and at others straining against his bond as long as his endurance would allow. The display of power was awesome, but the guards had lost their fear. She could see it in their eyes as they strode into the cell and kicked the food trays in every morning and evening. They wouldn't admit it, but it was their unease of Vivien that moved them to be certain he could reach the trays.

And yet they were determined to not let their captive pass the bars into the light.

Days passed into weeks. There was only so much learning that could be done by book and wrote. Perhaps it was cruelty passing as caution that lead to her mad plan. Maybe plan was too much a word for it. At one point she went to a clothier and picked up something civilized for the Wolf to wear. Many mornings came and went and she went to his cell without the bundle. Every night she returned to her small home and saw the bundle waiting for its recipient. Then came a morning that dawned crisp and clean. It was a day that would make any soul smile, and she thought of the dour man, filled with pain, far from the sky with no sun to succor him. She dressed in a beautiful, simple white robe trimmed in bright red embroidered flowers, pulled up the hood, filled a small pack with the clothes, and slung it over her shoulders.

The morning was busy in the kitchens of many of the high born elves. There was one in particular in which she'd been a familiar figure for many years, and it was there where she started her day. The flurry made it easy to slip into places she was not supposed to be, to gather things she had no right to, helping the unwitting staff as the vague idea solidified in her mind. Perhaps the Wolf's growth of beard reminded Lydia of her life before Rithalion, or mayhap of a past lover, or her father. It mattered not once she touched the bottle of dream wine.

She brought two platters, one sparse and one piled, and two pitchers, one with wine and the other water. She walked the familiar path, across the gorge and down the steps, out of the morning and into the torch lit darkness. As always, her ancient bones protested, and she had to rest her joints every so often. Today she did not give them long to recover.

Once there, she passed the night guards and met the morning sentries in their normal place, glowering at the Wolf. She suspected they teased him when she was not there. They did not even notice her until she was upon them, and they each jumped when she entered the ring of light from the two torches by this, the only occupied cell.

"What goes?" said the eldest guard, the one in charge. Lydia had not bothered to learn their names.

She frowned, careful to tighten her shoulders and clench her jaw. "I had expected to find the night crew still here. I owed..." she trailed off.

He smiled, looking at the plate laden with stuffed vegetables and fresh baked bread. "Well, I am surprised you missed them. Still, carrying that all the way back to–"

Lydia frowned, "No, no, I am not carrying this back up to the kitchens."

She briskly set the platter down on the table. The guards had already broken their fast, but there was no sense in missing out on extra food, especially rich food such as this. They lustily converged on the extra fare as Lydia turned and set the Wolf's tray and pitcher on a nearby outcropping. The leader fumbled with the ring of keys. Lydia took them and placed the pitcher of wine in his hands. Rather than protest, he smelled the rose liquor and smiled like a child getting away with a good prank.

Lydia opened the door and saw the Wolf sitting in the corner. The rattling keys opening the door brought his gaze in their direction, but the guards paid him the slightest of heed as they focused on the sumptuous meal. Lydia adjusted her pack, picked up the tray and pitcher, and entered the cell.

The Wolf held a book in his lap. It looked old and tattered from wear and beyond any shadow of doubt, she knew he studied it even when she was not there, early in the day until far at night. She spoke in Elvish, a small smile playing on her face. "More lessons today."

The Wolf glanced at the door, which stood slightly ajar, but when it did not grant him the reward he wished, he turned away dejectedly. He just nodded and shrugged. It was as if she could feel the constant confinement, the eternal night, the time away from Vivien, was all slowly eroding his will. The lack of bleeding from his shackled hand may be mistaken as a good sign by some, but Lydia saw it as a surrender of sorts. Vivien was an accomplished warmage, and she doubtlessly had much on her plate if even half the whispers flying across the city were true. Yet, she hoped for the Wolf's sake she would take some time to visit. Today should help, but...

The guards laughed raucously and she smiled wider instead of letting her darker thoughts show. They had tasted the sweet dream wine and were quaffing it as if it were water. Lydia opened her satchel and brought out a fresh towel, an Elvish hood, a pair of light brown breeches, a wide black belt, and a simple white shirt. The Wolf picked up the shirt, and said the word in Elvish easily. Before he could reach for the breeches, Lydia jerked her chin at him, "Put it on."

He looked wryly at her and lifted the wrist still bound to the wall. Lydia responded by dangling the large ring of ornate keys.

His reaction was immediate. The Wolf glanced at the guards, who had become sluggish and quiet. His whole body tensed, thrummed even, with an energy not unlike the strings of a harp tightened until they were about to snap. His eyes darted back and forth from the keys to the door, back and forth, back and forth. They flashed red like glowing blood.

Lydia put the keys behind her long skirt and regarded him intently. "Wolf, you must swear to remain with me at all times. You must never leave my side."

The man gaped at her, then ran his free hand over the full growth across his chin and cheeks. It was frosted with silver beneath the dark chestnut, but added a scheming look to his squinting eyes as he appraised her. For a brief moment, Lydia felt the desire to leave, return the keys to the guards, and return tomorrow as if nothing had happened. But then the Wolf nodded. She stepped close and looked deeply into his eyes. She saw the sincerity there and allowed herself to believe in him.

Lydia unlocked the iron cuff. The guards barely stirred as it clattered to the stone floor. She was aghast at the thick ring around his wrist, an old bloody collection of scars and oozing wounds. The Wolf stood tall, but Lydia matched him as a matronly force that held out the towel and the pitcher of water. She said in Elvish, "Wash first."

He had spent weeks in a cell, voiding himself into a hole in the floor without access to soap or water for cleaning. He scrubbed himself without a modicum of shame. The water cleaned the worst of the foulness away, and she hoped it was enough. The wrist she washed herself, ripping off a bit of clean towel to bind it. He donned the shirt, pants, and belt, pulled the points of the pants through the holes in the shirt made for the purpose and tied them to the belt to hold up the breeches. She watched him and felt again that he had not always been the animal everyone thought him to be. If she could get away with taking the time to loosen and re-braid his hair, she would do it, but his energy was too wild.

The Wolf started for the door. Lydia stopped him with a firm hand and held up a mantled hood. "You must cover your head. Keep the hood up and do not take it off."

He looked at her quizzically for a moment before donning the hood and starting towards the open cell door again.

"Wolf!" the teacher barked. Her towering student, free of his bonds, turned. "Your promise!" He looked to the door, to her, then back and forth.

Finally he stood still.

Lydia made sure she had the keys in her satchel, then walked with him out of the cell. She closed the door with an ominous clang. The two looked at the guards, slumped in their seats around a table half full of food, sleeping as the dream wine let them frolic through imaginary gardens like children.

She felt his excitement, a physical need, to leave his prison behind, yet he kept his word and walked beside her. Barefoot, but upright, they exited the dungeon and into the fullness of daylight. He squinted at the sun, for he had not seen it in so long, but as his eyes became accustomed to the light, she led him onto a balcony that opened up the view of entire gorge.

His eyes widened with wonder. The walls on either side were clad in several levels of shops and homes. Delicate bridges spanned from wall to wall and beautiful stone stairs flew from one level to the next in graceful arcs. Above were patches of forest canopy and far below was a modest river that rushed through the center of the gorge.

The Wolf shook his head and gestured, "There are deer in that garden."

Lydia smiled but scolded him gently, "In Elvish."

He said it again, and managed a passable job, so she answered, "It is no garden. Elves live in harmony with nature. It is so here. All the animals of the forest live on the valley floor as we live in the walls."

His face clouded, "What of the dangerous animals?"

Lydia smiled again and touched his arm, "They learn we are not prey."

A group of children ran behind them, laughing and cavorting as they played a game of tag where they shot sheared cattail at one another using a makeshift bow constructed of woven green sticks and a bark twine string. The Wolf shook his head, "We? You and I are the only ones here without pointed ears."

Lydia nodded, "It may seem that way, but there are many humans that have the honor and privilege of living here among the eternal folk. Come."

She led him over the bridge to the other side of the gorge to the House of Laws. Elves of every caste gazed curiously at him as they walked, and more than one passed and wrinkled their nose. But no one stopped them.

The Wolf watched them back boldly, but quietly, flexing his hands as if to remind himself the manacles were truly gone, "The elves live forever, then?"

Lydia smiled wryly, "Well, no. Even the lowest blood elf will outlive men by many generations. Pure elves can even live to eight hundred years, but seven is more likely. Eternal in comparison to us."

If she didn't know better she would say that the Wolf looked slightly embarrassed. He said nothing, however, as they came to the front doors. Lydia pointed, speaking slowly as she showed the bas relief that framed the door in figures carved only one hand tall.

"Is it a story?" he asked, his limited Elvish making him even more childlike.

"A thousand years ago, not very long as elves understand it, there were many elves." The Wolf looked on. She tried to see it new through his eyes, being amazed all over again at the detail of every tiny figure, noticing some figures were repeated from scene to scene, recognizable even as they changed clothes, while others died and were never used again in the storyline. "But seven hundred years ago a creeping darkness came from across the mountains. A young wizard named Kalshamar brought forbidden knowledge into the kingdom, a knowledge that brought war between elves and their brothers. After a hundred years of war, the elves' numbers had depleted and a great fear took over many of them. The traitor elves took the side of the darkness and betrayed their kin rather than be destroyed. They took the city of Pergatium, and the forces of the fae elves laid siege." That panel, just short of the middle over the doors, was a horrific scene with the portrayal of violent death. She shuddered a bit, remembering the deadly stories of that day, "After a fierce battle four hundred years ago, Pergatium was retaken by the fae elves. The whole city was turned into a graveyard. None survived." It ended at the top of the right door. Lydia took the Wolf's arm and lead him away without telling the rest. "The elves have survived, but only just. Elves procreate very slowly. Their numbers would never be able to defend the kingdom again. Not for a thousand, thousand years."

The Wolf looked to the city around them. "And this?"

Lydia looked down and noticed she was walking arm and arm with this strapping man, like a noble and a lady strolling a garden. And while he was far from young, he was at least two generations younger than she. Lydia suppressed a giggle and found it disturbingly difficult to do so.

Another group of children ran by. "Those children have elvin blood, but are not full blooded elves. When higher blood elves come of age, they go into the world and find human lovers. The women return carrying half-blood children, the men return with wives with whom they have their children. It is these lower blooded elves that you see. They man the cities while the elves renew the numbers of the pure."

The Wolf smirked, "What, these elves can have just anyone?"

Lydia chuckled. "Well you must understand, elves are some of the most beautiful beings ever created. They can beset and bedazzle most mortals. And it isn't a bad life, especially for the wives. We are brought to paradise to live in a safe land of plenty. Our children are young for a long time, and they love us long into our golden years..." Lydia smiled wistfully, thinking of her many beautiful sons. "These children fight for their elders, run the kingdom, and always try to breed together to make more elvin children. They are the most precious part of our whole world. The word for an infant is... Wolf?"

The barbarian stood still, bereft, "Is that what she did to me?"

Lydia laughed, carefree. "The Lady of Moonlight and Love? I would expect so."

Again the Wolf blanched. "Is that her title?"

"That is her name of sorts. True names were used to horrible effect during the war, so now they hide..." She stopped speaking and stared at him. The Lady had been there that day he was taken, but... "Exactly who do you mean, Wolf?"

"Vivien. Did she bring me here to use me as a mating stud?"

Lydia smiled. "Vivien is beautiful, but I speak of the Lady. She must have smitten you when you saw her in Vivien's presence that day in the woods."

The Wolf looked confused, reverting a bit to animal as he growled, "There was a beautiful woman there, but..."

Lydia's eyes widened and she covered her mouth. *He does not remember her. The fairest face of any mortal and he does not remember her next to...* She pursed her lips. "It is not polite to speak of others without their presence. Time grows short, let's continue your lesson."

The same group of children ran by again as they started across the bridge back to the side of the gorge that contained the prison. There was much here to learn: the words for the types of trees, the flowers, the birds, everything. But they had to be back before the guards awoke from their sleep, before–

The laughter ahead became excited and loud, then suddenly turned to shrill screams. At the first sign, the Wolf dropped all pretense of civilization. He did nothing but tense, but in that split second he was no longer a man, but an animal. He pulled forward and Lydia pushed her aching joints and old bones to try to keep up. He got to the apex of the bridge twenty long strides ahead of her, where a crowd had gathered around two guards and the group of children.

"Its Tanjen!"one cried. "He climbed over the rail to move the branches so we could keep watching the bear. He fell!"

Lydia heard the boy wail from far below at the gorge floor.

She joined the crowd pressing to the edge, but could see nothing. The fir tree that grew a little higher to the bridge must have blocked the boy's sight and broken his fall. Then they heard it, the roar of an angry beast. All those with elf-blood shuddered, for they could hear the anger in the noise. It was a mother bear defending her young.

The crowd looked to one another, and all expected doom.

An answering roar staggered them, one that came from their ranks. The crowd parted as the Wolf came through, whipping off his hood and bounding forward like a wild thing. Lydia caught her breath and the guards didn't have even a second to react. He grabbed a spear in each hand and leapt over the rail, holding the shafts across and above his head as he plunged into the green embrace of the fir tree.

Chapter Eight
The Bears

She saw, half the city saw. The calls of a child in danger brought anxious crowds to the rails. Vivien was unsure if they all held their breath as she did. From the side of the gorge she saw through a break in the trees as the Wolf leapt from the apex of the bridge. Concern swallowed her shock to see him out and free, but there was no mistaking his primal roar, his bulky frame and wild hair. The tree rippled as the spears, held doubled up and across the lay of the branches, caught the young weak spars at the top and slowed his descent, breaking with the sound of crackling thunder. Heart in her throat, she watched as he came to the lower branches, which were thick enough to slow him further, and then bounce him off of his path and tumble him through the remaining layers. He lost the spears as the bear roared again, but she could see the Wolf's progress as he tumbled from branch to branch like a marble through a sea of pegs.

Vivien ran a dozen yards to find another vantage, one where she could see the child, too terrified to even wail as the bear scented the dirty, frightened thing before her. She snuffled the air mere yards from the elf-boy, unsure of the meaning of his blood and frightened by the chance meeting with a small predator. She stood on two hind feet, upper body bobbing in irritation. Then she stood full upright, as tall as a man but far more dense.

The bear had come to a decision.

Paws ending in wickedly sharp talons flexed as she roared again. All the elves became silent. Not a single breath was drawn as the terrifying sound punished every ear, rattled the ground, and shook loose leaves from the trees. A trill of fear washed over Vivien, followed by memories of another time, another place. She heard something in that voice, a menace—that it was best to end this puny, squalling thing than risk...

Suddenly there came an answer, a challenge. It came like an army of raised fists, struck like angry hail, and thundered like the storm of a volcanic eruption. It was fire, and faith, and fury. Pebbles shuddered and jumped on the soil. Leaves securely fastened blew from their perches and fell like shimmering green tears. The bear retreated back from the boy, shaking her head. From the mantle of the fir that had swallowed him whole, the Wolf emerged like the wrath of all things mankind; terrifying and brutal.

He had stripped off his tunic and hood, wrapping them like a shield around his left arm. In his right he held the two spears, one point up and the other point down. He was battered, bleeding from a thousand scratches, and a bleak purple and green spot was forming over one shoulder where he had hit loam. Yet his body thrummed with primordial energy. His muscles rippled unnaturally, as if growing larger and more powerful every moment. The weather was warm, but his breath exhaled puffs of thin steam as if it were winter. His untamed hair flooded over his shoulders in random frazzled ringlets that wafted about in the breeze.

And then there was his eyes.

They glowed blood red in the dim shelter of the forest below, comets that cast his face into demonic light. The Wolf looked at the boy, stuck a spear into the ground to mark the place to where he dare not retreat, flexed his mighty hand around the remaining weapon, and bared his teeth in challenge.

"So angry..." someone nearby whispered in Elvish.

Vivien did not spare a look, for the bear was up, and lumbering at the Wolf on all fours. Rage answered rage, the Wolf's bare feet chewing into soft soil like spades to launch him forward. At the last second, the human veered to the side and leapt. The bear lunged, catching nothing but air as the Wolf sailed by, swatting back and below to leave a shallow slice at the animal's side. Vivien gasped as the Wolf rolled out of sight.

She bolted, pushing through a crowd that gasped at her as she shouldered them aside to breathe air clear of their pressure. She left the last of them behind and sprinted for another section of the gorge overlook. She skidded to a halt when she saw the Wolf and the bear dancing along a path away from the child. The bear swept forward, claws extended, lunging for the big man with the intent to disembowel. The Wolf struck back, deadly spear turned aside by thick hide and dense bone, leaving bloody marks but doing little to truly hurt the beast.

Vivien's heart stuttered in her chest as more memories flooded through her mind, memories of pain and powerlessness. *Dear gods...*

The Wolf thrust and missed. The bear reared back and lurched forward. It gathered the huge man into an embrace and Vivien heard a scream. Blood sluiced down the man's back and he disappeared down into the wall of matted brown fur.

The screaming continued.

The Wolf re-emerged, tumbling out of the side of the bear's grip, leaving behind the long torn shreds of his arm wrap. The bear turned, but the barbarian was already spinning, putting his whole weight behind a strike that landed squarely on the animal's snout. The bear stumbled and the Wolf scrambled for the remains of his spear, coming up without a piercing head.

The screaming stopped. Vivien abruptly realized there were dozens of hands touching her on her shoulders, her back, her hands. She glanced left and right into eyes of blue, green, amber and brown that regarded her sadly. She saw their hurt for her as she felt the rawness in her throat. She struggled for control, confining those memories to the dark recesses of her mind. Shame flooded her senses at the outburst. The strain of the moment, the...

Vivien stilled. She glanced down at the Wolf who wielded the thick spear haft like a sword, beating the bear with precision strikes, yet giving ground before claws that already had him lagging, leaking blood in streams. On either side of the gorge there were guarded entrances to the wilderness within. Help was already on its way, but the it would never reach him or the boy in time.

Suddenly it all fell away. The sounds of the crowd died away as her walls rose. She pushed her way clear of the people and ran to the bridge over the battlefield. The robes of her esteemed station as a battle mage bought her passage through the line of soldiers claiming the spot where the boy had fallen. A rope had already been lowered when she arrived, and without hesitation, she took it in hand.

Accompanied by murmuring from the guards, Vivien swung over the edge of the bridge and climbed down. Halfway to the ground she began to slip, the rough hemp burning her hands. She breathed through the pain and called to the wind and the clouds, to the fae imprinted on every breath of the world. Tiny figures carved of mirrors forged in magic flitted to her aid and caught her as she let go. Her robes fluttered madly about before the fae slowed her fall. She still landed hard, but safely, into the tall green grass.

Vivien didn't bother raising her hood as she ran towards the sounds of battle. The bear shrieked in pain and anger, but this time there was no reply from the Wolf. Fear battered at her walls but they stood firm, and when she saw the combatants, she stopped. The Wolf was quiet, but seemed to have gotten the upper hand. The blade had been sheared from the spear shaft, but he struck with thick wood with unending focus. The bear's fur was matted with blood, and she staggered back from his latest attack. He couldn't kill it, but he could bring it pain. He hit the eyes, the nose, and gave vicious jabs to the belly.

Finally, finally, the beast wailed and retreated, backing away from the devilish attack and wheeling to rumble off into the brush.

And there he was. The cloths wrapped around his left arm were naught but bloody tatters. A swipe to his chest had caught the barest amount of skin, but left nasty runnels that bled freely. A bite to his thigh had savaged the flesh to expose the meat of his muscle. He staggered to one knee breathing hard, eyes fading from glowing coals to burgundy pools. He raised his head, lungs still running like a bellows, but the moment he saw her face, his whole being changed. The animal fell away from him, leaving something powerful– more powerful than the being he'd been.

And he smiled.

Vivien's breath hitched as she felt gentle fingers caress her insides, recognizing the yearning of his heart and feeling it echo distantly inside of her. The moment was torn away by a momentary bleating from behind her. She turned, heard strong footsteps race up to her. But she threw up a hand that had the Wolf skid to a stop.

The boy lay in a crumpled heap. Many of his bones had been shattered from the long fall, and his limbs were twisted in awful directions. The Wolf stood, trapped between scooping up the child and staring in horror. Vivien shook her head, "You cannot help here."

Obediently, he watched as Vivien called forth a surge of Elvish will that suffused her whole being. This formidable will brought all the strings of reality into alignment, and she contacted the fae with a song written by her soul. Again the trees shivered, the wind whipped, and the mirror sheen fae answered her call. Their presence matted the tall grass around the boy as they gently, effortlessly, slowly, cradled the child and lifted him into the air. The air spun more and more, driving their scents deeper into the woods, but hoisting the injured child on a cushion of air, higher and higher to the bridge far above.

Beside her, the Wolf watched, gaping like a child. He chuckled despite his wounds, entranced at the tiny luminescent people who flitted about on gossamer wings.

Suddenly, a roar punctured the air, one deeper, and much more fearsome than the one they'd been hearing before. Vivien's concentration fluttered and a dozen fae winked out, the body of the boy jerking in midair before she could make him rise again. Her heart shuddered against her ribs and she cursed, *This was not just a bear with cubs. It was a mated pair. Oh gods, no...*

From out of the nearby trees, a dark form barreled towards them. It was huge, larger than his mate by at least two feet. He stood on his hind legs and roared again, spittle flying from an open mouth full of sharp teeth.

"Save the child!" the Wolf said in Elvish. He yanked the second spear out of the ground next to her and then bolted from her sight.

Her eyes were locked on the boy, will pouring into the commands to the fae to take him higher, faster. She could not see the battle, and the horrible sounds reached her ears as a masterful nightmare played out writ in blood and fear.

Her ears picked out the whoosh of a massive paw aimed at the Wolf. The gristly sound of tearing flesh told her that, this time, the human wasn't fast enough to dodge out of the way. Grass tearing, soil sliding underfoot, she imagined the Wolf spun around by the force of the hit, bloody sweat flying in all directions. She heard him land heavily on the ground, his broken body sprawled before the angry male bear.

The boy was going higher, higher, almost there. Arms were reaching for him.

The bear roared. The Wolf answered with a power beyond human. Flesh met flesh as mighty blows were exchanged. Then there was the tearing of flesh under claws. Above, the boy was gently gathered onto the bridge as she heard a very mortal scream behind her. It was a sound that mined into her soul and left it all but hollow.

She spun as the bear, up on two legs, bleeding and caught through the belly with a spear, shook the Wolf like a dog with a rat. The huge jaws were around the shoulder at the neck, and the mighty man's body flopped lifelessly. The bear had opened his back to the bone and now tossed the body like a discarded toy almost twenty feet to tumble where she stood. It was coming again, not necessarily for her, but for the one that had dared stand up to him: the Wolf.

Despite her thick walls, something inside Vivien snapped.

The incantation came to her lips without thought. She spoke the words as though in a dream– succinctly, perfectly, with deadly accuracy. She drew runes in the air, the symbols glowing in the recesses of her mind where only she could see them. Her voice rose and the power that gathered at her beck caused the air to stir. The leaves rustled in the trees and her unbound hair blew around her head like a halo that darkened with shadow.

The bear sniffed at the sudden winds and roared again, this time with a tinge of confusion, of fear. Her hands moved to shape her magic, sculpting the design she desired in her innermost mind. The call went out, but not a voice of harmony, but one of discordant radiance. The first fae darted from beneath a rotted log. It was simple, and it was small. It dripped with vileness and bore the stigma of fetid danger. It flew at the bear, who swatted at it, but it was far too late already.

Another unseleighe appeared, and another. Some looked like wasps, others like ants, bees or roaches, flies and spiders. These tiny predators came in a massive, hungry cloud as the beast took one more lunge at the two figures, only covering half the distance before doom was upon him. It roared and was choked by a living cloud forcing its way into the mouth, cutting into the sinuses through the nostrils, burrowing into the ears, and exploding into the eyeballs with single minded intent.

The beast wailed, a frightening, frail sound. It wheezed and coughed, screaming and crying forlornly. As the moments passed, she watched as the bear shrunk, insides devoured in an orgy of destruction. Rents appeared in the flesh and the creature deflated before her, half digested muscle and tissue oozing out in streams.

The incantation ended and there was a pregnant pause, as though every living thing in the area stopped to watch.

Everyone looked on as the unseleighe, untamable and dark, devoured the bear from the inside out. They would not stop, would never stop, not until they had consumed nearly everything. It was darkly beautiful and horrifically fast. The bear made only two steps, blind and in unspeakable agony, before it collapsed. As she watched, the last things to be devoured were the brain, the heart, and the very essence of the proud creature. She let go of the tide of destruction and the unseleighe went back to the dark places from which they had come, leaving a bear skin covered in hideous tears and tented on brittle bones that cracked and strained under the weight.

The enormity of the transgression beat upon Vivien's mind but she dared not answer. Instead, she took two shaky steps forward to the broken and bleeding body of the Wolf. She turned him over onto his back, hands and robe instantly soaked in his hot blood.

Please, please be alive!

Against all odds, his eyes flicked open, gaze flickering like the dying light of a fire in a rainstorm.

"Wolf? Wolf?" She trembled and could not stop. Tears made it hard to see and she couldn't breathe.

He saw her, focused on her eyes as if she were the only thing in the world. He said "I am learning Elvish..."

She shook her head, a barking laugh coming out fueled by pain coming close to sheer panic, "What? What?"

When he spoke again, she was sure it was just him continuing a sentence, not a new one. His voice was a whisper, "...so I can tell you I love you."

What fear and grief had not taken from her, the summoning of the unseleighe had ripped from her heart. Her vision swam and she lay her head on his chest.

She heard his heart beating, somehow still beating.

Inside her mind, she became convinced that, as long as she listened, it would not stop.

She listened very, very hard.

Chapter Nine
The Ceremony

avn reached for the navy silk cloak and pulled. It slid silently from the metal frame, exposing his gift for his bride. The long expanse of beaten and polished silver had cost a small fortune. However, the massive goose-down bed with warm sheets of soft, twenty-times washed wool had been easy to afford.

He turned and regarded himself in the large, silver mirror. He was smartly dressed in black suede and green tartan with a white linen shirt. "Well my lad, you're the very image of him, that is for certain." From his place at the table, Laird MacConna smiled like a golden sun eclipsed by the massive beer mug.

Ravn continued to stare at himself. His hair was curly chestnut like his father's had been, and his eyes stormcloud-gray like his mother's. Yet, he did not think he looked like either of them. He looked like…

…nobody, really.

The chair screeched against the wooden floor as Ernan stood and came over to stand beside him. When the man's heavy hand fell on Ravn's shoulder, he dutifully turned. The older Laird had spent many months at Blacach to supervise business. The severe strife and shortages of the first year after the Liath attack had given way to bounty. The coal mines had given way to more coal, and when more surveyors had been sent out, seams of iron were discovered. Within the last three years, Blacach had transformed from an empty keep to the start of dozens of caravans heading into the lowlands. Caravans that meant trade, trade that meant wealth.

As Ravn looked into the large man's blue eyes, he saw true love reflected there. Ernan doubtlessly missed his wife back at Castle MacConna, but he often stayed to help Ravn at Blacach, fighting the creeping frost in his yellow hair with ales of increasing strength. The once mighty man had become soft, and his size no longer had much to do with prowess in the sparring yards.

For miles in every direction, Ravn was known as the boy who had killed the Liath chieftain. To Ernan he would always be the boy who had saved his Ròs.

"I have seen you grow from an early-kilted, round little boy into the fine warrior I see now. Oh, don't look like that. You and I practice the blade in the yards for an hour a day. The hour after sunrise, old Moray trains you as well."

Ravn felt pressure behind his eyes and he blinked away the wetness that threatened. Ernan stepped back to give the young noble some space and refilled his mug from the pitcher on the table. "Late at night, you practice again alone, with bow and axe, sword and shield." Ravn started and met the older man's gaze. "I know I have never said this before, but I believe there is no better man in a thousand miles to protect my Ròs, and for that, I feel the utmost of pride."

Ernan's words touched upon the memory Ravn tried to keep at bay, and it blossomed behind his eyes like a spontaneous summer storm. It poured fire from the sky of his soul, starting a pyre that looked like a carnage filled square of Old Blacach. The hellish light showed the broken body of his fallen father. Alongside was his mother, who had been eviscerated and dragged down the street after him, discarded like a piece of trash. It was an endless fire, a molten, living thing. Ravn stared at his feet until Ernan came back and put a hand under his chin.

"Never gaze at the ground, boy. You are a Laird of a strong name in a sturdy castle. Keep your eyes on the slopes and the sky, for you are joining your blood to mine and you should be proud." Ravn tried to look past the turmoil inside, tried to nod bravely. He must have managed it, for the older Laird smiled and nodded back. "'Tis almost time… son."

He left, the door shutting as silently as snow falling across the limbs of a dead tree. Ravn turned back to his reflection in the mirror. He tried hard to see what others seemed to see. He spoke, and servants responded. He judged, and judged with mercy. He laughed, and laughed from his heart. But in her many visits, Ròs never once seemed to take joy from his presence. She smiled from time to time, and found peace in her crafts, or with her handmaidens. But never with him.

And now…

A knock came at the door. It opened without time for him to give any leave. Red gold hair, bright blue eyes, and a belly distended from several months of pregnancy walked into the room. Ravn felt the corners of his mouth twitch to see Nora, sister to his betrothed, the young woman who had been so impressed with his mercy the first day they met.

"Oop!" She grinned. "You nearly smiled. Your face may break, Laird."

Ravn felt himself blush and he stared at her shoes until it passed. She tutted, "Come now, hasn't my father given you the 'skies and slopes' speech?"

He nodded, chuckling despite himself.

Elvish Jewel

Her eyes softened and she gathered him in as close a hug as her swollen belly allowed. "Dear, you have grown so much, but you are still but a boy in there, aren't you?" Ravn opened his mouth, then shut it. "Has anyone told you exactly what you have to do tonight?"

Apprehension rippled down his back and rebounded up from his heels. He gaped as Nora laughed softly. "You poor, poor boy." She took a vial from her sash. "This is Turnipseed oil. It will… ease things." She handed it to him and he nearly dropped it, so she set it on the table beside the bed. She turned back and cupped his face in her hands, "You are so sweet. Tonight, however, you must be strong enough for you both. You will hurt her at first, but only to give her great joy later. I pray you give me a nephew or a niece."

After she, too, left, Ravn sunk onto the bed, looking at the little vial of golden oil. He understood the gross mechanics, and knew that his whole world was about to change again, but he knew so little about… why.

Horns blazed brassily and he shot to his feet. The door opened and he started to see the guard outside his door was none other than Moray, master-at-arms, captain of the guard, and the man with whom he had sparred every day since he could remember. If success had been a trial for Laird MacConna, it had been a plague for Duncan Moray. The last three years had seen his fair hair fade to white. His toned body had sloughed toward his feet, and wine and whiskey had stolen his muscle. His face had been ravaged and rounded, his nose a map of red vessels.

Ravn moved woodenly to the doorway and paused as Moray tried to snap to a salute in a cloud of alcohol fumes. Ravn studied him, as MacConna had studied Ravn, and the older man shrunk as Ravn had. The young Laird had watched the aging servant of his family from afar with the men. He had seen him at dawn every single day to practice how to kill. At those times, he seemed normal, cunning, the man of old. But other than that, he was a recluse, quiet, ashamed.

During the Liath attack, Moray had been forced back, pushed out of the courtyard and into the kitchens. He had fought there, killing half a dozen of the deadly enemy before Ravn struck down their leader. The servants who survived the attack had survived because of Moray's skill with a hammer, shield, and sword. Those he was not there to defend did not live. Just as Ravn had not been there when…

…the storm of fire and thunder rumbled in the recesses of his mind.

Ravn blinked and gazed into the eyes of the older man. He was grief stricken at the pale, lifeless thing that looked back. Moray spoke in a subdued tone, "A happy day, eh Milord?"

Ravn nodded. A moment or two passed. "It was not your fault."

Moray twitched, then met his lord's gaze with certain, serious understanding. A tear flushed from Moray's eye. Before it struck the ground, Ravn was engulfed by arms that had once been burly, and crushed into the chest of the last living man he truly thought of as family.

The trumpets blared again, impatiently. The two separated. Moray summoned three breaths before he choked huskily, "Thank you, Milord."

Ravn nodded and received one in return. He gave one survivor something only another could give; forgiveness for having lived.

Everything else was a blur. Walking downstairs, to the renovated and fortified kirk. Nodding to MacConna smiling beside a tiny, cloaked figure. Past the musicians and the beautiful, ghostly tune. Past the hundreds gathered in the pews. Down the aisle of sun yellow carpet of cat's ear flowers. To the altar.

Then his bride. More music as her father brought her cloaked in his own, red tartan. The moment where she was unveiled came, and he held his breath.

She was so slight, and simple. The crown of gold-wrought roses looked dull in the colored light that managed to pass through the stained glass. Her dishwater brown hair fell sorrowfully down her back, her blue eyes red and puffy from crying. Even her white dress edged in gold hung limply. Her hands wrung one another with white knuckles nearly translucent on pale fingers.

There were words said. Ravn did his part. A long swatch of green tartan was used to bind their hands. More words. She nodded at the end, choked by tears. Ravn took the tartan and clumsily tied it into a loop. He draped it over his lady, taking her into his house. It hung loosely for she could not fill it.

Then the crowd erupted into cheering.

The mass of people swept them from the altar, out of the kirk, through the hall set for banquet, then up the stairs and into their bedroom. The door shut.

The wed couple was alone.

Ròs wept silently, openly, as she shed her dress. With trembling hands Ravn unbuckled his belt and let his kilt fall. Ròs turned away and let her underdress slip down while Ravn shed his shirt and vest. He saw nothing but the smoothness of her skin, the delicate curves of her thin body. His heart thundered like a herd of wild horses and he realized what the ribald minstrels sang about.

Slowly, as if a marionette pulled by clumsy strings, she crawled into bed and lay on her back, eyes squeezed shut. With leaden legs Ravn approached the bed and lay beside her. Ròs shuddered as he touched her with his most gentle of caresses. He moved her. She resisted at first, then slowly eased against him. He found himself holding her in his arms across his body, like a father with his child. Suddenly she was clinging to him, naked and crying. Her body shuddered all throughout the night, so much he could feel her ribs as she breathed great gulps of air.

Ravn took a strange comfort in her grip, in her warmth, in her alien softness. But he was not sure if she was ever really holding him.

Sometime in the middle of the night, by the light of the dimming torches, he looked to the little golden vial of turnipseed oil. It went unused.

Chapter Ten
Memories and Mercy

Vivien rode through the city, Sherika's long strides eating up the distance between her home and the sanatorium, shiny black mane rippling in the wind. The guards had borne the Wolf away with uncharacteristic gentleness, but the hospice where he had been taken was so far from the scene of battle that she had run instead for her home. Once there, she had shucked the blood-covered robe and donned another, rushing back out as fast as she could. At the base of the trees, amongst the carefully carved pillars that held up the graceful platform above, lay a wooden structure open to the world with just enough enclosed to keep in heat and shield from the weather.

She had paused and given a breathless whistle.

The answering purr could be felt inside the chest of the listener. A pair of large, green eyes blinked from the recesses of the den. Vivien smiled in instant relief and rushed forward. She wrapped herself around the neck of the big, black tir-reath feeling the heat from the neck and the silky softness of the long mane. The beast got to her feet, and nearly lifted Vivien from her own.

She loosened her grip and took hold of the feline cheeks to make the creature look at her directly. "Sherika. He needs me."

The tir-reath blinked, and then stood still and ready. It took only a few seconds for Vivien to throw the light, supple saddle onto her furry mount.

The forests used to teem with the tir-reath in ages long past. Elves rode them into battle in numbers uncounted when they were tasked with husbandry over all the lands, and the lesser peoples rebelled. That was thousands of years ago, and now there were bare handfuls of the long legged cats left. As a high noble, Torialvah had been given one. Seconds after being introduced to Sherika, the cat and Vivien truly belonged to each other.

Tir-reath stood slightly taller than a horse or reindeer, with thicker legs and wider paws by far. Their teeth were fearsome, their claws deadly, and while they ran nothing like a bobcat or mountain lion, they could still leap dozens of feet into the air, making a horde of riders seem like an eruption of angry elves from a treeline in the days of old.

Sherika whuffed as Vivien tightened the soft leather straps and swung into the saddle. As soon as she felt Vivien grab the long black fur of her mane, she was off, steered in the correct direction with gentle motions. Along the forest floor of the gorge, Vivien pointed Sherika and let the tir-reath run, dodging undergrowth and over barriers. The shadowy mount shot beneath the bridges far above, flying like an arrow to the nearest stair up to where she imagined the Wolf was being kept.

She lay low over the lithe body, felt the muscles bunching and relaxing as her friend ran. She patted the soft fur along Sherika's neck and breathed in her musky scent. The big, long legged cat connected with the Elvishness inside her, barely needing coached as she felt where she needed her to go. Sometimes Vivien would ride her just for the company, and Sherika never seemed to mind, always happy to oblige. Today the rider needed the mount more than ever before, and Sherika seemed to know it and refused all distraction. *You are the best things Tor has ever done. I will never forget the day he brought you home to me.*

Vivien sat up and back as they approached the stairs. At the cue, the big cat slowed to a jog and then to a walk. The guards saw her blue mage's robe and pulled the massive ornate gates open as if they weighted nothing at all, and she lay back down over the back of the tir-reath. Sherika took the cue, leaping from one landing, then thirty feet to the next. There she skidded around the pillar and then skipped the next step with a following leap. People nearby sensed the tremors from the cat and whistled warnings up and down the levels, clearing the way as Sherika took floor after floor to very near the top.

Once at the door to the expansive building, Vivien slipped down from the tall back and patted Sherika's shoulder with one hand while flipping up her hood with the other. She then took the cat's face in her hands and looked into viridian eyes. "Stay here and wait for me."

Sherika obediently sat on her haunches and wrapped her long tail around her front legs. Vivien lovingly stroked the soft black face and scratched behind the rounded ears before she turned to walk into the building carved into the face of the native rock. Other elves walking in the area stopped to admire the tir-reath, who stood like the statues carved into the tombs of their ancestors, preening and cleaning long legs fastidiously.

Though carved into the sides of the canyon, it was not dark inside. Like most similar buildings, tunnels were carved to the surface and used polished quartz discs and mirrors to reflect the rays of the sun down into the complex warren. Unlike other times she'd been there, guards stood in the entry. The low-elves looked at her as she walked in and moved to stand in her path. Her temper rose, but Vivien quashed it down. Anger was not the first recourse in dealing with these men. *A show of strength, yes. Anger, no.*

"Please step out of my way. I am here to see the human."

One of the guards shook his head. "I am sorry Lady Vivien. We have orders to keep everyone out."

She frowned. "Orders from who?"

The guard shifted uncomfortably. "The Captain, Lady."

"I am certain I outrank your Captain. I insist you allow me passage."

The guard shook his head. "I am sorry Lady, but I cannot do that."

A new voice came from behind the guards, "It is alright Lamar. Let her through. She will be my responsibility."

Vivien looked in the direction of the familiar voice and saw the red-robed Mikarvan standing there. She felt her walls tremble, tired and knowing there was support nearby. *Oh gods, I haven't seen him in so long...*

The guard grudgingly stood aside to let her pass and she swept by him in a flourish of robes. She walked towards her old friend and they rounded the corner together. The instant they were out of public view, the healer lowered his hood and she followed suit, his solemn demeanor shifting into one of happiness. His blond hair was trimmed short on the sides, but the top was a bit longer and hung over his forehead. He brushed it back to reveal sparkling, light brown eyes, and his expressive lips curved into a smile. "Vivien, it is good to see you!"

She smiled and touched the rich red of the robes of the master healer. "It seems you have become very good at your profession, though I miss your long hair. When were you transferred here? I would have come to see you."

Mikarvan's expression shifted to one of sadness. "Would you?"

Vivien stopped when she stood before him, saw the hurt he tried to keep concealed beneath his aura of strength and professionalism. She looked away from his marked gaze, settling on the wall above his left ear.

"That's what I thought. The Lord of Ice and Steel keeps you well beneath him in your marriage bed," he said.

Her temper flared and she felt the customary power gather in response. Small wisps of control slipped through her mental fist and summoned tiny red fae that flickered uselessly around her head before winking out. She hardened her gaze and swung her eyes back over to meet his. "So you came out here to debase me?"

Mikarvan was instantly contrite, "I did not mean–"

"You did. You decided to mock me. Well you have succeeded." Inside her, the temple where she held Mikarvan, all her heroes, of friends and family, shook a bit. The walls wept with tears, but she kept them from her eyes. "Can I see the human now?"

The healer took a deep breath, realizing his own hurt had become a weapon in his mouth and he lowered his eyes in real shame. "Vivien, I'm sorry. I didn't mean to hurt you."

She narrowed her eyes. "Yes you did. You wanted me to know how much my actions, or lack thereof, have made you feel. You have been clear."

He raised his hands in supplication. "Vivien, please..."

"Are you going to take me to my man or not?"

Mikarvan regarded her intently. "He is down this hallway, first entry to the right." He regarded her intently for a moment. "So he is yours, this barbarian?"

Her tone was icy. "He is not your concern."

"What is going on? You used to tell me everything."

It was her turn to feel a surge of lost closeness. "We are no longer children. And quite truthfully, I am afraid you don't know me anymore."

She moved to step past him, but he put a hand on her arm. "I do know you. I know your heart."

"My heart? That has been withered and locked away for a long time now. Thank you for your reminder of this." She cursed her voice for shaking a bit, cursing the human-ness of it. She looked down at her arm. "Please let me go."

He hesitated. "The human, he has been aggressive, but has allowed us to tend him."

"He is awake?"

Mikarvan's eyes glittered seriously behind his blonde locks, "Awake, and deadly."

Vivien gave him a smirk. "I have been near him; he is not deadly."

Again, Mikarvan raised his hands in surrender, "A wounded animal may be even more dangerous than a caged one." She shook her head, but he continued, "You know the fae will not heal him?" He read her eyes, "You do!"

"That doesn't mean anything sinister."

Though alone, Mikarvan looked up and down the corridor and got close to Vivien, nearly whispering, "He is healing himself. Wounds to the bone already have new skin. Torn meat has become whole muscle. He has scars, wet and red, but the wounds *are healing*."

Vivien took this in, flipping through decades of teachings to find the reason, how it was even possible, for the Wolf to reject the fae and yet heal. "Has he attacked anyone?"

Mikarvan hesitated, then shook his head. "But there was a bear claw imbedded in a rib of his back. He growled at Iovana when she removed it, but did not attack." Vivien breathed in relief, but then saw there was more to come. "She cut herself on the claw, and her finger was covered in the human's blood. The cut burned as if drenched in lemon juice. Yet, by the time she cleaned it, the wound had closed."

Vivien grabbed Mikarvan and pulled him close, but no matter how deeply she searched his eyes, she detected no lie or exaggeration. She took a deep breath, "How much love does Iovana bear for you?"

"Vivien–"

"You can tell no one of this. No one!" Mikarvan looked almost sick, shifting from foot to foot and trying to back away from her. She pulled him closer. "Promise me!"

He said nothing, but nodded. And that, if it did not repair the damage done to her image of him, at least set some repairs in order. She nodded and started to turn away. Mikarvan caught her arm and his demeanor shifted. She saw a man who would protect her with his life. "He is not really human, you know that?"

She nodded. "I do."

"Yet, you have no fear of him?"

She contemplated this question and slowly shook her head. "No, no I do not."

He stepped close, well within the boundaries of customary personal space. His voice was again a whisper, "You know we have been given orders to keep you out of here?"

She looked up at him, took in his handsome face. "Then why are you doing this? Why are you risking yourself for me?"

His eyes darkened and he brushed his fingertips gently over her cheek. "Because, no matter what they say, I believe you have the best interests of your people at heart."

She stared at him for a moment, looked deep into his eyes and quashed asking of who 'they' might be. She saw the truth lingering there and nodded.

She turned to go when he spoke again, "The boy..." Vivien turned back to him, "The boy you saved. He will live."

She flashed him an honest grin. "Good, I'm glad."

He gave her a sad smile, dropped his hand, and stood aside.

Vivien took a deep breath and walked towards the room Mikarvan had said contained "her man". She wondered when he had become her possession and she recoiled at that thought. *No, not my possession, my responsibility.* She reached the entry and hesitated. *Why am I so nervous? I know he won't hurt me.* She shook her head. *No, that's not what makes me so giddy.* She knew the reason but she was afraid to articulate it, even in the deep recesses of her mind.

Vivien entered the chamber. Asleep, the Wolf lay, bound, on a bed in the middle of the room. He wore nothing but short-chained manacles around his wrists, not even a cloth to cover his genitals. She glanced around and was not surprised to see a blanket lying on the floor on the other side of the bed.

With another deep breath and her lightest step, she walked around the bed to retrieve it. It seemed wrong that the powerful man capable of staggering a bear with bare fists was so exposed, so vulnerable to anyone who may harm him. Vivien picked up the blanket. The quality of the cloth was higher than she expected, and she smiled. *This man deserves so much more. He is human, but he cares about people regardless of their race, as if he were raised among us.*

She raised the blanket and snapped it gently in the air, billowing it above him to settle gently over his legs and groin. She tucked it close to his side and startled when a large hand swiftly grabbed her wrist. She gasped as the Wolf sat up, squeezing so tight the bones popped.

She cried out and he focused on her, the light in his blood-red eyes winking out within the space of a heartbeat. His brow furrowed. "Vivien?" He instantly relaxed his grip, closed his eyes, and murmured in his foreign tongue. It sounded like a prayer, and when he looked at her, his eyes were dark, fathomless. His words were thickly accented, but she understood him. "I've been waiting for you."

Her breath hitched in her throat. "Why?"

He looked into her eyes, searching. "Because I love you."

He released her wrist she stepped back from the bed until her back reached the wall. Suddenly she wondered if she had been blind or a fool to ignore the danger he represented. "How can that be? You don't even know me."

His expression saddened, his hand still extended as far as the short chain on the manacle would allow. "I don't need to. I can see what lies in your heart."

She shook her head. "You cannot possibly know that."

"Believe me when I say I do. I have seen you before. I have seen you in a place far, far away from here."

"What? You have never seen me, human. And anyway, why would I believe you?"

His gaze intensified. "Why would I lie?" Silence reigned. "Why did you save me from the bear?"

She swallowed past the painful lump lodged in her throat and blinked her eyes free of the tears that threatened.

His gaze softened. "Come here." When she didn't move, his tone became supplicating. "Please."

Elvish Jewel

Of their own accord, Vivien's feet carried her back to the bedside. Her heartbeat thundered in her ears and the world bled away until all she could see was the Wolf. The long, tightly curled hair lying over his chest, the scars, the freshly sealed sequence of wounds where bear teeth had tried to savage his arm from his torso at the shoulder. He shifted his body to the side, just a touch gingerly. She hesitated before accepting the unspoken request, carefully sitting down. Her eyes widened when he reached out to touch her face with an unbound hand, the manacle still intact, but the chain broken. He replied to her question before she uttered it. "Elves seem..." he searched for the word, "fickle in their gratitude. I freed my hand this morning. I am so glad I did."

He slowly rose into a sitting position, his eyes fastened to hers. She could see a flicker of pain deep within their depths, but he didn't flinch a single muscle. He slid his hand to her arm and gave a gentle tug. "Come closer."

She breathed harder, faster.

He blinked. "I promise I will not hurt you."

"I...I know that."

She scooted closer, her breaths now rapid and shallow. The Wolf then placed his hand at her back and pulled her towards him into an embrace.

Just like she did that day in the prison, she relaxed into him.

It was an endless moment, beautiful and simple. He held her without demand or promise, without formality or form. It contained only warmth. It reached into the deepest parts of her and found cracks that had built over a lifetime. She melted into him and reached around to the tender, new skin covering the horrific wounds she had seen him receive.

She drew back, her face a barest whisper from his. She could feel his raw desire, his almost physical need, to kiss her. His lips trembled and his breath smelled of smoke and fire, yet he did not come forward, dared not presume. But she could feel his heart beneath the horrible scar on his chest against her breasts thumping like the stampede of a thousand horses. It echoed inside of her, and found an answering call as clear as any lupine calling to mother moon. She wanted to move forward, ached for their lips to meet. She steeled herself...

Then she moved away.

He did not grab her, did not chase her. He stayed utterly immobile, and let her go wherever she will. It was different, a feeling of utter freedom she had never known. All men who claimed to love sought to possess, to constrain. He simply waited, and was content for whatever she chose to give him.

Or not.

"Let me see your back."

Obediently, the Wolf turned over and she saw the truth of Mikarvan's words. The skin had closed, angry and red, over mortal wounds to leave him far more whole already than any elf could ever hope to be without the aid of summoned fae.

"You are amazing." she breathed.

He shrugged, somehow capturing a lifetime of doubt, regret, and loss into three words, "I am nobody."

Vivien drew back as if slapped. She gazed at him like a lunatic who declares that fish walk at night and drink blood. She marshaled her arguments: the boy, the Lady of Moonlight and Love, she herself... but the sound of hard boots on stone interrupted them.

It was the Captain, sheepish guards in tow. He did not take off his helmet. "You have been summoned to the council," he said to Vivien, and then to the Wolf, "and you are to be placed into your cell."

Vivien had known this was coming, could feel the creeping doom approaching since this morning. "I need to get my tir-reath..."

He cut the air horizontally with his hand, "Your mount has been sent home. The Council does not wait for you patiently, nor does your cell for you, human."

The Wolf bared his teeth and growled, an incredible mimicry of his namesake. Vivien touched him lightly and he stopped, "Go peacefully to your cell, Wolf. Promise me."

He frowned, but nodded. Then he said as if a curse, "Fickle."

Chapter Eleven
Race Out of the Dark

As he promised, the Wolf was docile, but noting the broken manacle, the elves still bound him tightly. They placed him into a reindeer drawn carriage, and he was quiet, not moving a muscle. His mind, while alert, was focused on other things, things that were nowhere near his moving penitentiary. Vivien was everywhere: the smell of her on his skin, the feel of her breath against his jaw, the color of her eyes as she looked at him with such solemnity, her warmth against his side as he held her. He was worried, wondered where they were taking her and what they were going to say to her.

Once at the prison, they descended into the darkness. They had new, if simple, clothes for him, though for who's benefit it was hard to say. They walked around the circular shaft until they reached the familiar cell. The Captain motioned the Wolf in, and was followed by him two of the guards who had accompanied them. One of the elves fumbled with the cuff to his left hand. The iron burned him and he dropped it twice before stopping to put his gloves on so he could handle the damned thing.

Footsteps covered by his motions suddenly caught everyone's ears.

Lydia tottled into view, near collapsing into the stunned arms of the other guard as she struggled for breath to enter her old, rickety frame. The Wolf shot to his feet, and the chain would no longer reach his wrist.

"Teacher?"

Lydia looked all about, trying to take in the scene, "Wolf! Oh, Wolf! You cannot go! She must face all of this herself. It is her burden to bear."

"What?" He tried to question, but when his Elvish would not come fast enough, he switched to his native tongue, "Speak plainly!"

"Vivien, she was called to the council!"

"Yes, I heard. I was there." He meant to walk forward, but the guard behind him had hold of his wrist. He glared at the elf, clenched his fists, but allowed himself to be pulled back as he'd promised.

Lydia pulled herself up, trying in vain to hide her fear behind the veneer of her teaching face. "She killed that bear, young man!"

"She saved a boy!" he retorted angrily.

One of guards laughed. "Listen to him, he sounds even more like an animal than ever, speaking in that human gibberish! The old woman too!"

The Wolf struggled to ignore the outburst, focusing instead on Lydia. "She did it with the unseleighe... dark magic... forbidden magic. There is no one to speak for her and they will punish her harshly."

The Wolf barely quelled the urge to surge forward, legs trembling. "But she saved me!"

Lydia shook her head, her eyes reflecting the hopelessness she felt. "The ends do not justify the means, Wolf. There is no one there to stand for her, no one to speak in her defense. Saving you will not save her from their judgment."

The Wolf listened hard and heard her true words, the ones she left unspoken between them– *Please go to her. Somehow, save her!*

The Wolf forced himself to remain relaxed. The guards were alert, but not ready for violence. He didn't want to do anything that might tip them off. His nostrils flared as he deeply inhaled, taking in the woody scent of them inside their armor. His stomach roiled as he felt the tight snap of the manacle around his wrist, watched as the Captain gave a nod. The guards outside were reinforced, confident, relaxed. Lydia's old woman scent, like dried paper, was overcome with the sour smell of her fear.

From lowered lids the Wolf considered the manacle on his wrist as the lackey went for the other, now far too short to reach him. He felt the fires burning within him as he lifted his gaze and fixed it upon the senior man. "Captain?"

The half elf frowned, then crossed his arms, took a step forward to show his lack of fear, and frowned at the Wolf. "What?"

He felt the firestorm rise, one fed by the otherworldly thing deep within him. Out of the corner of his eye he saw Lydia step back from the cell door, so attuned to him she could feel it coming. He found his focus and the Elvish sprang to his lips like he'd known it for years, "Are we agreed I have come peacefully to my cell, Captain?"

The other man chuckled nastily, "Yes. I would say you are quite captive in your cell, animal."

The soldier with manacle duty grabbed at his free arm, pulling him back so that he could shackle him with the other one, the one that had never been replaced after Vivien had freed him from it.

They meant to punish him, to make him suffer. Not this day.

The Wolf nodded. "So be it."

And he spun.

Weakened from weeks of being yanked hour after hour, day after day...the manacle held, the thick chain links held, but the bolts that mounted to the wall, battered and abused, shrieked as they were wrenched free. The spin ended with the Wolf's fist in the gut of the guard who held him, sending him flying back to the toilet hole, retching.

The Captain started to react... far too late. The Wolf whirled his left arm in a tight arc, bringing the chain in a ever shrinking spiral that covered his forearm in a lattice of iron. The Captain reached for him, but the Wolf lunged forward and drove a vicious elbow into his chest. The weighted stroke dented the steel armor and robbed the soldier of all breath. He began to collapse as the Wolf hurled him back into the lap of the first victim. The last elf in the cell had a chance to get his sword, but not draw it fully. Instead, the Wolf's foot connected with the hand, still clenching the hilt, as it came across the belly. The force sheathed the sword with a snap and threw the guard back into the bars, which rung as if struck with a massive hammer, and he slumped to the floor.

Of the three outside, one appeared at the door, spear ready. The Wolf grabbed just past the spearhead with his right hand and simply walked out, his superior mass pushing the off balance guard back, back, back until his heels hung out over the void of the central shaft. Another spear came from the right, and the Wolf decapitated it with a slight shift and a vicious slash of the chain used as a whip. He turned to face the last two guards, spear held like a wall before him. He jiggled the shaft and the poor sod holding onto it yelped as he almost fell to certain doom.

The other two paused.

The Wolf smiled grimly. "Get in the cell, or he falls."

The decision took only a moment. To be precise, it took a moment... and another shake of the spear.

The other two sullenly filed in, dropping weapons and trudging glumly. The Wolf pulled the last from the edge of the circular ramp and shoved him roughly in, then he slammed the iron bars shut and picked up the keys from the guards' table.

It had taken only seconds, yet the violence had been immediate, complete, and vengeful. The Wolf took no weapon, not sword or spear, but unlocked the hated manacle and let it fall to the floor. He winced and worked his back muscles. Tender skin had split and he felt the dampness of blood where it soaked the unbleached cotton shirt he had been given.

He turned to Lydia and spoke in Lairdstongue, "Grandmother, where is she?"

She stared up at him. "Wolf you can't..." Her voice was weak under his rage, which simmered just below the surface. "You can't!"

"Where?" The tone of his words descended into the range of a faithful hound, a good hound, that was reminding the master it was only one generation from being a wild thing and his equal.

"Go west along the wall eight bridges. You will see the tallest spire in the center of the gorge. That is the Great Council Hall."

"The place with the stories around the doors?"

Lydia blinked, seemingly surprised that he remembered. "Yes. Yes that's it." He locked the door, and the three men awake and aware inside slumped a little further. Lydia sighed. "Wolf, when you are gone, I'll have to let them out."

She looked at the keys in his hand as he continued to work the wounded muscles along his back and shoulder. He grunted, "I suppose you will." He then tossed the keys off the edge. It took several seconds for them to hit the ground below.

Lydia came close, holding up a small rolled parchment. "Take this. Give it to the council. The doors will be sealed by magic. I don't know if anyone can get in, but I hope you can. Promise me!"

The Wolf accepted the scroll and slipped it into his belt, nodding respectfully. Lydia pursed her lips, once again becoming the teacher as he turned and began to jog away. "Remember, you cannot stop the council. You must bend to them!"

His jog shifted into a run, then a sprint, up the circular ramp to the surface. "She will not be punished for my sake, Grandmother! She will not!"

Vivien's nostrils twitched. They had allowed her to wash, but she still stank of blood. She wondered balefully if she would ever be free of it. When she closed her eyes it surrounded her like a thick blanket, but that was not the worst. Hiding from the world brought back the vertigo feeling of discarded control, the cloud of unseleighe, and the slowly disintegrating corpse of the bear. She went cold as she thought of the swarm of hunger that had consumed the animal, turning it into a sieve of muscle and sinew... Vivien shook her head to clear the thoughts from her mind, but when she opened her eyes, the nightmare continued.

The council chambers vaulted high overhead, emerging from the walls on every side with balcony after balcony, cunningly carved from stone to provide seats for the full-blood elves of the city who would sit in judgment. There was easily room for five hundred or more, once limited to the oldest and wisest of the True Folk, but now all two hundred and thirteen full-blooded elves left in Rithalion could sit in judgment and leave space to spare. The gallery above was open to all who wished to see the city's laws in action. Considering the public nature of her offense, it was packed with every half-blood and less in the city that could spare the day. She had already been placed in the center of the room, surrounded by eyes, wrists in bronze chains as she stood on the round, raised podium in the center. She shrank under the weight of the stares until a voice brought her to her feet.

"How do you fare, my daughter?"

Vivien barely suppressed a wail of dismay. There, in chains, before all men and women of the city, her father had come to witness her dishonor. And of course he should, he was the Grand Magister, after all. She felt a momentary flash of fear at his wrath and she winced, her eyes closing in shame, for there was never anything to fear from this man. Ever.

She smelled blood, saw the bear, felt the hopelessness and the pain all over again. Her heart thundered in her chest and a child's voice screamed...

The Grand Magister touched her hair with a gentle hand. She startled, but when she opened her eyes, he met her gaze with eyes just like her own, and inside their hazel depths reflected his profound love. She fell into his waiting arms, the heavy chains clinking around her. The Grand Magister held her tightly for as long as she clung to him, and when she was ready, allowed her to pull away.

Her voice nearly broke as she asked, "Father, do you know what I have done?"

He nodded and looked at her through sad eyes.

She came close and whispered, "I am afraid."

"I know, but you will get through this." He gripped her shoulders. "You are strong."

Another rogue thought caught up to her and filled her with dread. "What will my husband say? What will he do?"

The Grand Magister frowned with concern. "My dear, is this something you fear?"

Vivien hesitated. She hadn't meant to say that aloud. Her father knew very little about her life with Torialvah, and she needed to keep it that way.

She shook her head. "No, of course not. I just hate for him to have to answer a lot of questions from people when he is trying to work."

The Grand Magister gave a small smile. "He will manage, I'm sure. Your Lord has many years of wisdom."

Vivien only nodded, wishing it was that easy. The Magister gripped her arm strongly and leaned in, eyes serious, "You have done wrong, Vivien. You summoned unseleighe, and here of all places." He lowered his voice further, "I know I have ever been indulgent, especially after your mother died. But I warn you, be humble. Be humble, and mercy may come. Be defiant and it shall certainly go badly."

A wind that did not exist suddenly roared in her ears. Her father lingered but only a moment longer before a far away bell tolled mournfully. Pure elves began filtering into the balconies. Magical light from nowhere sprung from runes on the circular podium, lighting her up for all to see, so that none could mistake her shame.

The world shifted and wavered and as ears rang. She raised her head and her vision swam, walls tilting this way and that. She reached for the curved railing surrounding her and the surface beneath her palms rose and slumped. *Oh gods...*

She looked up toward the chambers in the walls and saw the pure bloods of the city, the wisdom of centuries behind each pair of eyes, stern and uncompromising. More waves of weakness impaled her heart even as she tried to stand straight, *Oh gods, what have I done?*

Runes on the railing flared more brightly, forcing her face upwards. The gallery was far above, but beneath these the elves watched on, bodies in shadow of the balconies, appearing to be disembodied, glowing heads in the caves along the walls. But these were all advisors to the four at the imposing oak podium that loomed above her.

Vivien stood silently before the High Council. They were the eldest and wisest in the city. They were so old, their hair was a transparent silver, and they wore elegantly embroidered robes colored deep hues of purple and burgundy. They sat before a large oak table polished to a high sheen, and before each was a vial of ink and a stylus. The four elders stared at her from faces that were the epitome of solemnity. They had filed in under the cover of her despair, and were now ready to sit in judgment of her.

There was no preamble, no introductions. Everyone knew why they were here, and they went to their grim business.

Master Orinoco, Lord of Flame and Forge, was the first to express his displeasure. "Warmage, you didn't just kill that bear, you obliterated it! You disobeyed the laws of Rithalion and violated an ages-old truce with the creatures who share this place with us. Just as important, you misused your power to do it. There are always dark patches in the light, and so it is with the unseleighe. Their use is inexcusable. What have you to say in your defense?"

A thousand arguments crowded to the back of her throat, but none was strong enough to lift her tongue. Vivien lowered her head in shame. "Nothing, my Lord. It is just as you said. I was wrong to use my power to summon the unseleighe to this place."

Silence reigned for several moments. She looked up at the Council again, wondering what kept them from their verdict. Mistress Swansee, The Lady of Principle and Grace, narrowed her eyes and gestured dismissively, "Yes, yes. But the crime is only half of the matter. There is motivation, the reason why, child. Speak now in your defense."

Vivien's mouth opened. Thousands of reasons and excuses pounded for release from her throat again, but under the judging eyes of the council she remained silent. Then she looked to the balconies where the pure blood elves watched on. She wondered if her husband was in attendance, and went cold and numb. She lowered her head and shook it meekly.

Oilariann, Lord of Honor and Victory, frowned deeply. "Child, speak. There is none other here to defend you, for none were there during your transgression. We may mitigate your sentence for the life of the child you saved..."

The Lady of Principle and Grace snapped, "Your impartiality, Lord!"

Oilariann tossed his head slowly and waved her to silence. "Recognizing the facts does not make me partial. A boy is alive because of her. Just as we were not there, but we know her summoning to be a fact, a child is breathing because of her efforts. A half-elf besides!"

Kilcahnn, The Lord of Discipline and Morality, shifted ever so slightly. "And the law states it is for she and her defenders to argue her virtue against her vice." He leaned forward, and it could be imagined that his creaking bones echoed in the hall as his long hair fell to frame his face, "Do you have any that would defend you?"

Vivien felt herself sinking faster, faster into the dark well within her soul. She shook her head. "No, Lord. I do not."

"I see."

The council members looked to one another, unspeaking. Finally, The Lady of Principle and Grace stood and faced Vivien with a face both stern and distant, "Lady Vivien Valdera, we the High Council feel it is in the best interest of justice for you to undergo the following punishment: for one year you will be prohibited from using your magic. You shall not practice it, and you also shall not participate in any studying of it. If you are discovered breaking this decree, you shall suffer dire consequences."

Vivien's heart bottomed out all the way down to her knees. For elves, a year was not really a long time, barely a blink of an eye. But to not practice one's vocation for any length of time could be very taxing. Spellcasters were more the rule for this, and never an exception. Their suffering was great, for there were physical and mental consequences. Her heart, her very soul, would starve, and a year would feel like an eternity.

However, it could have been worse, much worse.

Vivien bowed before the Council. "I offer many thanks for your leniency."

"Then The Book of Shame shall be gaveled and the punishment entered." The Lord of Discipline and Morality grabbed the heavy book in front of him, lifting it inches from the heavy oak surface. "It shall be written. It shall be judged–"

BOOM!

The sound came from the entry doors, inexplicably, and for the first time anyone could remember, the Book was not gaveled. It hung there as the gallery erupted into chatter. After a moment, the Lady of Principle and Grace raised her voice in scandalous disappointment, "Silence!"

The gallery fell silent. The Lord of Discipline and Morality began again. "It shall be written. It shall–"

BOOM!

Guards appeared from shadowed nooks along the floor level of the chamber.

BOOM!

BOOM! BOOM! BOOM!

There was a pregnant pause before the door careened open with flying splinters.

Chapter Twelve
Judgment and War

The Wolf ran past the elves of the city, but none sought to stop him. He raced like the wind, the ornate face of the carved gorge on one side, the twisted flowery railing guarding against the drop to the river gorge below on the other. Between the two was an avenue wide enough to run two carriages abreast without danger of touching. Even during the busiest hours of the day he could have rushed through. With so many of the population at the trial his will lent him speed without cause to pause or crash into obstacle. He sprinted like a madman, lungs pumping like a bellows, heart nearly audible as he rushed by on legs punishing the ground with inhuman strength. Finally, he turned on the correct bridge, heading out into the middle of the gorge to the lone spire of rock upon which the Council Chambers were built.

He knew there would be guards, and he was not disappointed. Two half-elves stood before the door. They wore heavy, orate armor of layered steel strips and they came to attention as he approached. The Wolf lowered his head and pushed harder, faster, waiting for the moment where they would lower their spears and challenge him, a moment that did not come. He barreled past them and into the door, shoulder leading, arm curled into a shield against his ribs, At the last moment he gathered his legs to work with his momentum and crash through the massive double doors that–

The world was ringing, burning. There was a whiplash of pain as his right shoulder popped back into place, cartilage cracking and snapping. Laying there on the ground, the Wolf shook himself as voices came into focus over the sound of his beating heart.

"It's hard to think we share some of the same bloodline."

"Be thankful for your lineage, Jeahann. I certainly am."

The Wolf looked past the men to the ornate door, which glowed blue. He thought he could see brighter veins among the glow, long women shaped like gossamer winged salamanders. The Wolf shook his head, yet the door refused to fully focus. He stood raggedly to his feet.

A crowd was gathering at the disturbance, keeping their distance and whispering. The one called Jeahann was leaning on his spear, Elvish features twisted into a mocking smirk. The other was moving forward, but kindly and slow, as if approaching a wounded animal.

"You're the Wolf, right? You helped save that boy–"

He shook his head, his eyes seeing nothing but the door to the council. "Vivien is in there?"

Jeahann shifted from one bored foot to another. "The accused is in there being judged–"

The Wolf threw himself forward, again slamming into the door with a resounding BOOM. There was a bright flash. The fae that held the door shut hissed, and he was thrown to the ground, sliding twelve feet from the adamant portal. The Wolf nearly missed the crowd, gasping.

The kindly guard dropped his spear and came over to help him off the ground. "The accused is being judged, Master Wolf. They have sealed the court and it cannot be opened until the verdict is rendered." He gasped, "Your wounds! On your back! You have torn them open!"

The Wolf felt warm wetness over his back where bear claws had bitten deeply. His blood quickly soaked the shirt and slid down his back like drops of rain from a wounded and uncaring sky. However, he ignored it as he turned to the guard, "She cannot be judged without me. It is my life she saved!"

Jeahann was the one who answered, "It is done. The court is sealed, and can only be opened by the aged and wise elder purebloods who closed them. The elf-blood conjurer will survive without you–"

There was something more the snide elf was about to say, and it felt like a pejorative, but the Wolf did not wait. He leapt forward, hammering the blue glowing door with a bloody shoulder.

It was tiny, infinitesimal, but it was there, an ounce of give. The Wolf looked up for only a second, but there he saw his blood on the door. It smoldered and steamed. The glow began to fade as if spun sugar struck by rain. He backed up just a step and hit it again, again, pain stabbing at his back as trickles of blood became angry smears on the door.

"Don't! You'll hurt yourself!" said one guard.

"Let him!" Jeahann sneered. "Then he will be easier to return to prison for his disrespect of the law!"

The Wolf saw the door, felt the ancient wards and powerful fae shudder away from his blood. He leapt away from it and then gathered for a spring. The crowd behind was shouting for him to stop and blood streamed from his shoulder. The sun and the wind shone and blew respectively without care for the drama or the stakes. But inside the Wolf, there was nothing but the heartbeat of his mind, and it spoke a single word...

Vivien.

He roared and leapt, hitting the door like a force of nature. Bronze plates cracked and split, wood splintered. Locks gave way as a blue flash painfully blotted out the world. But it fell before him, and he tumbled into

the darkened hall, with the council of the city looking on in shocked silence.

Vivien recoiled from the flying splinters and thundering crash. In the wreckage, he stood tall and indomitable, long hair flying in chestnut spirals. His muscles rippled as blood turned his white shirt red. In the darkened hall, his eyes glowed like red lamps.

He roared in Elvish, unable to see as he went from daylight to the chamber's twilight. The name inside of him made its escape, "Vivien! Are you in here?"

High above, one of the purebloods shouted ancient names forgotten by most living. Disembodied, fae hands appeared out of the shadows and clamped upon the Wolf's arms, becoming chains that yanked him to the floor. The weight and the shock pulled him to his knees as effectively as a blow to the head. His reaction was immediate and instinctive. He growled deep in his chest, the sound rumbling off the tall walls like a prowling pack. The fae created chains that sparked and blazed around his bloodied wrists. The Wolf wrenched at them as if they were physical things, and the hall gasped as one as the chains, strong as the finest steel, shattered around his efforts and dissolved as if they had never been. Vivien just watched, stunned.

Immediately, three more elves stood and called upon ancient pacts with the fae. Ropes of trickling sunlight, chains of solid air, and a net of swirling leaves descended upon him. The moment they touched his bloody body, the fae creations began to smoke and burn. He thrashed free, sending little half-seen, winged bodies flying back into the aether.

"Stop this! I would speak and be spoken to!" He bellowed in indignation, eyes flashing with the beating of his heart. The raw power on display caused every soul to pause. All but one.

Discarding the rules of her people and the shame of her position, Vivien answered, "I am here, Wolf! I am here."

He swung around to look in her direction, and when he saw her in the circle of her prison, his eyes narrowed dangerously.

Vivian vaulted over the railing, chains jingling, and ran to within a few steps of the barbarian, hands raised to halt him. "Please stay calm; they will kill you!"

He considered her, then the soldiers, the council seated in balconies as high as the light went, and shook his head, "My life belongs to you. If it takes its loss to speak in your defense, so be it." His voice rose. "But I have a letter in your support!"

The court erupted, and though the elders silenced it merely by raising their hands, they were clearly scandalized by the need. Silence reigned for several moments.

Swansee's voice rang with deliberation, "Fetch this letter!"

The nearest guardsman snapped to attention, handed off his spear, and came forward. His first steps were disciplined and crisp, but as he came close to the Wolf, he faltered. The Wolf glowered at the lower elf, and even though he took the rolled parchment from his belt and handed it over with a bloody hand, there was the implication of a growl, if not an actual one.

The soldier retreated quickly and brought the scroll to the Council. When Swansee was finished reading it, she passed it to Orinoco on her right. He then passed it to his right, and onward until all had read it.

Swansee regarded Vivien from eyes full of compassion and conviction. She was the one to whom all the elves depended for unadulterated justice based on the edicts of their society. "It seems you have a loyal friend in Rithalion. Lydia Skylander has spoken on your behalf."

Vivien's breath lodged in her chest. *Oh gods, Lydia, no. You were supposed to stay out of this!*

"The first thing she states in her letter is that you would not want her to speak up in your defense. Why is that?"

Vivien blinked away her tears and answered with all of the truth within her. "Because I do not wish for her to share in any punishment I deserve, Lady."

Swansee nodded. "She also says that you had no knowledge that she would be allowing the human out of his cell. Is this the truth?"

"Yes, Lady. I did not know about that."

"So, do you not feel that the old woman should be punished for this transgression?"

"No, Lady. She does not deserve punishment."

Swansee furrowed her brows. "And why not?"

"Because the only reason Lydia was there to see the Wolf at all is because I asked her to do so. She was making visits to his cell as a favor to me."

"Wolf. This is your name for the human?"

Vivien nodded. "He will give himself none other."

Swansee regarded her intently, gaze inscrutable. "So you wish to accept punishment on behalf of Lydia Skylander?"

"Yes, Lady. I do."

"You are aware that the severity of your punishment will possibly be doubled?"

Vivien closed her eyes, fear causing her belly to clench spasmodically. "Yes Lady."

"NO!" roared the Wolf, "If she can take Grandmother's punishment, then I shall take hers!"

The whole of the room gaped at his impudence. He stood there, unbowed and unbent. Defiant. She made to speak, but he looked at her with such conviction she fell silent.

Vivien felt something grow inside her, filling her chest and making her heart beat loud. It was hard to breathe. His ruby eyes held no guile or subterfuge. He was honestly pledging his life in her defense. He had defied sharpened steel, somehow defeated the fae seals on the door, embarrassed himself and risked further imprisonment for her. He was so intense, like a bonfire at the height of summer, beautiful and destructive. She could not fathom him.

She regarded him, finally realizing that at some point he'd come to join her in her prison. He turned his head to look back at her and Vivien gasped to see that his eyes were a cerulean blue. She'd never seen them that color before. Then he blinked, and they were again blood red. She opened her mouth but never got to speak.

"Warmage!"

Vivien turned, and beyond the ring of brandished spear heads, the pureblood elves of the Council and gallery stretched out and up the walls. She could feel the weight of the long, cold silence that had descended. She saw anger... anger, outrage, and fear.

She bowed her head, "Yes, Elder?"

Orinoco was frowning, "Instruct your animal that he should go back to the jail and—"

The Wolf's voice rang through the chamber. "For what crime?"

In every balcony seat, elves looked to one another. Orinoco sneered, "For your own safety."

"How many bears do you think there are—"

Vivien put a solid hand on the Wolf's chest. "He has asked his crime, and has proved difficult to kill. Does our protection not seem unneeded, wise one?"

Mistress Swansee shifted in her seat. "Perhaps it is not for his protection, but that of our people?"

The Wolf growled, "Do you have many more children who need protection from being saved from bears?"

Vivien clutched the Wolf's shirt in her fist as she turned and gave him an icy glare. When she turned back, she caught stares of embarrassed disapproval, but also a ghost of a wry smile on the face of Oilariann, Lord of Honor and Victory.

The Lord of Discipline and Morality huffed, "Speak though he may wish, judgment has been rendered. The time is passed."

Oilariann raised a hand and patted the desk in front of him, which had the effect of banging a gavel to the assembled whispering throng. "Kilcahnn," he said "the judgment was not entered into the Book of Shame by official proclamation. There is still, thus, time to speak."

Kilcahnn, offended by the use of his name rather than title, glared at his opposing number, "Thank you, Oilariann, for bringing that into light." He set his jaw and glared down at Vivien.

Orinoco pursed his lips at the others sitting in judgment. "Fine then. Does the animal have anything to say to mitigate the manner in which you killed that unfortunate bear?"

The Wolf's face clouded as he tried to parse the language, so Vivien translated it into Lairdstongue as best she could. He frowned and spoke in Elvish, though his pronunciation was deplorable, "She saved me. I am the prize she won."

Shocked, Vivien spun around, but his next words were already spoken. "If you must take anything from her, take me." She looked up into his dark, ruby eyes, but he wasn't looking at the elders. He was looking at her. She shook her head slightly, but in his eyes she saw no regret. He was not a being of regrets, only action.

Her heart sank. "Oh gods, they will jail you for your whole life!" she whispered.

He did not whisper, or yell. He rumbled, "As long as you are not."

His proclamation had set the room tittering, and even the judges looked from one to the other, uncertain. They all made to speak at once, but Oilariann made it first, "This shall be allowed, but you understand that there will be no mercy for you?"

The Wolf nodded, not taking his eyes off of Vivien. "Yes, I understand."

Anger swelled within her. *This is my responsibility! How dare he take it from me?* In spite of the small distance between them, she could feel the heat radiating from him. *He means it. He would actually die for me.*

She hardened inside and turned to renew her protest, but a massive hollow boom rang through the chamber. It was the Book of Shame landing on the judge's bench, silencing all. The voice of the Lord of Discipline and Morality rang loud enough for all to hear. "The Book of Shame has been gaveled and the crime and intents entered."

"No!" The protest ripped from Vivien's chest without thought.

"Sorceress, be silent!" Orinoco snapped. "Human known as the Wolf, you have been found guilty of gross violations of Rithalion law!"

Kilcahnn nodded, "We sentence you to the service of the people of Rithalion. You will serve in all things, and not be free to leave without let, to travel without order, to kill without permission. This shall be for a period of fifty yea–"

"Seasons!" Swansee blurted, shocking all. Kilcahnn glared and she pressed her lips into a thin line. Lithe, ancient hands smoothed out her silvery robes and she peered down at Vivien and the Wolf, sadness and understanding in her eyes. "We recognize the risks taken for the life of the elf-blood child. And so you shall be in service to our people for the next fifty seasons."

Vivien felt her breath escape as a gasp. Twelve and a half years was a long time for a human, but it was better than fifty. She turned to the Wolf, her whispered voice pained. "Please don't do this! You will be their slave; you will not be able to leave!"

The Book of Shame fell again, then was opened to allow Orinoco to enter the sentence.

The Wolf spoke in a low, deep voice. "They may think what they wish, but I am slave to no man or elf." He curved his lips into a smile, "And I do not wish to be anywhere else, Vivien."

Her breath stilled for a moment. His smile was honest and deep, unfamiliar, like he wasn't used to doing it. It changed his entire face, giving him an attractiveness she hadn't seen before. She looked into his eyes, astounded to see that they were blue again. She blinked and they were their customary deep red.

But the judgment was not done. "Lady Vivien Valdera, for the period of two years you shall be prohibited from using your magic. You shall not practice it, and you shall not participate in any studying of it. If you are discovered breaking this decree, you shall suffer dire consequences."

The Wolf opened his mouth to speak but then closed it at Swansee's upraised hand. "However, this sentence has been reduced back to the original one year. It is just. Half of her doubled punishment to you, Wolf, and half to her. Be at peace."

The barbarian stood shocked, trembling, however Vivien knew it could have been worse, much worse. Just like before, she bowed before the Council. "Again, I offer many thanks for your leniency."

"The Book of Shame shall now be gaveled and the punishment entered." Kilcahnn lifted the heavy book and it fell on the bench, the sound of it reverberating with finality. "It shall be written. It shall be judged. It shall be done."

Silence reigned for a moment before Oilariann spoke, "And now we must assign you a keeper, Wolf."

Orinoco paused in his writing to look up, "I suggest–"

From the entry came a voice. It was perfect, powerful, and strong. It vaulted off the walls to every ear, "I will be responsible for him."

All eyes turned to the destroyed doorway into the chamber. With all the majesty of a queen, Shaladrea, the Lady of Moonlight and Love stood silhouetted in fading light, shining like a sun, hands folded meekly, her posture anything but. The crowd of onlookers pressed forward to see the exchange.

Lord Kilcahnn huffed, "This is highly irregular."

Lord Orilarann nodded, "Who better to make sure his term is served to both the benefit of our people and himself?"

Lady Swansee nodded, "She is fit to serve in this capacity, and it shall be allowed."

Lord Orinoco pursed his lips and gestured to the Wolf. "And why would you ever want to saddle yourself with... with this?" he growled. Throughout the room of watchers there was a smattering of chuckles. The Wolf frowned deeply and crimson flashes danced dangerously in his eyes.

"Because," The Lady practically floated into the room past the ring of guards still brandishing weapons at the Wolf, her gown of palest blue flowing behind her like wings, "a war is coming. This man may be many baser things, but he is brave." She stopped within arm's reach of the Wolf. He glanced at her, but only a glance before turning his gaze back to Vivien. "And we shall need all the courage we can get."

The elves, from those in the tall bench that acted as a seat for the elders, to the vaulted balconies of the assembled witnesses, one looked to another and held their collective breath.

Orinoco frowned, "Is this the proper place to discuss the coming War?"

"The people should know. The humans of the Iron Coast are out of timber." The Lady of Moonlight and Love moved gracefully towards the center of the chamber. The soldiers took to their knees, bowing their heads before her illuminating beauty. She glided to stand beside the sorceress, who took her hand and placed a gentle kiss on top. Shaladrea spared the Wolf a glance before turning to the elders. "They have been arming kingdoms with the accoutrements of war for fifty years. They have forged swords and shields. They have built ships.

"The trip north proved true many of my fears. The size of the force that attacked us was easily fifty men strong. It was no mere scouting force or simple band of wanderers. It was an exploratory force. I believe they are coming. They are coming for our trees."

The silence was almost deafening.

Orinoco's frown deepened. "You must find out how this animal broke the wards into this hallowed chamber. Why his body rejects the fae. He could be a great danger to all elvinkind."

Shaladrea shook her head, smiled sadly, and moved to face the Wolf. Her beauty was legendary, indescribable by immortal poets and songwriters. Even in a dark room she was lambent. No one who looked into her eyes could ever remember the color. But for one, shining moment, she looked at the Wolf and simply was. He looked upon her without fear, without modesty, and without movement. He glanced at Vivien kneeling at his side, slowly followed her cue and took to his knee.

The Lady touched his head gently and spoke to the assembled multitude, "He is no danger to us, but he is in great pain. We shall ease it and thereby find its source. He is a great ally, a powerful warrior. We shall bring him under our aegis and give him the chance to champion us."

Chapter Thirteen
Consummation

It was with a light step that Ravn walked to his wife's chamber suite. The balcony was finally complete, and he looked forward to showing it to her. Situated near the top of the cliff beside the castle, it looked out upon all the Blacach lands: the verdant fields, the small woods, and the surrounding town. For their convenience, there was a connecting chamber, complete with furnishings, and an upward leading tunnel staircase led from the main castle to this highest point. Ròs had once said that she enjoyed looking down on everything, and so he'd had the balcony made as a gift to her. It also happened to now be his favorite place in the castle.

Ravn smiled as he got closer to her chamber suite. She had insisted they have separate ones right after they married. He acquiesced, but only under the condition that they be close to his. So he had the bed he'd had made for her taken down and moved to the suites down the hall from his, and he took back the bed he'd slept in prior to their nuptials.

Ravn slowed when he heard voices coming from behind the door to Ròs's chamber. It was slightly ajar. He got closer and identified the loudest one as Nora, his wife's elder sister. She seemed upset, very upset, and Ravn couldn't help but eavesdrop to find out why.

"Ròs, do you understand the import of this? Ravn is your husband! You swore your body to him when you married!"

"I never wanted to marry him!" Ròs spat.

"It doesn't matter that you didn't want marriage, but it is what you got! And you have a duty to your husband and your family!"

"Duty," she huffed. "I've had enough of duty."

"What do you mean? You've yet to fulfill any of it. By the gods, you haven't even consummated your marriage! I can barely believe he has let you get by so long, over an entire year!"

"He's a sniveling weakling! Just the thought of his hands on me makes me feel sick."

Ravn closed his eyes and swallowed heavily. His heart ached a hundred times over to hear those words even though he'd always known she felt that way.

"Do you really hear yourself Ròs? You can't be serious! Are we talking about the same man? The man who killed the leader of those twisted elves all those year ago? The man who saved your life in doing so? The man who goes to the sparring fields every day and wins every mock battle? The man who presides over this place and issues judgment with such thoughtful sincerity that his people adore him?"

Silence reigned.

"You have been blessed Ròs! Blessed! Many women would cut off an arm to have a husband like your Laird!"

"Well, they can have him, because I want nothing to do with him."

Ravn felt Ròs' words cut him like a knife and he blinked back tears. His heart beat hard in his chest, as if seeking warm blood now that all of his had turned to ice.

"Well that's no longer your decision to make. You gave yourself to him on the day you married him, and it is your duty as his wife to have him in your bed. 'Tis what wives do! It is your duty to give him children, at least one heir to carry on his family name!"

"I don't care!"

Nora's voice lowered and for the first time since Ravn had known her, she sounded dangerous. "Well you had better care, sister, because you are breaking your oath to your Laird and his castle. That is a crime!"

Ròs's tone lost some of its arrogance and was tinged with uncertainty. "It is not."

"It damn well is! Punishable by imprisonment!"

Her voice became so low, Ravn strained to hear it. "No, I won't do it. I won't have his cock thrusting away inside me like a bull in rut."

Ravn closed his eyes again, squeezed until hot tears finally spilled from the sides. Shame suffused him, for that was all he'd wanted to do for the past several weeks, take her just the way she said it to Nora. His mind simply could not forget the image of her standing before him, nude, on their wedding day. He climaxed in his dreams every so many nights– and he hated himself.

He had to strain again to hear Nora's response. "You will do it. You want to know why? Because I am going to tell everyone what you have done."

Ròs's voice was a whimper, "You wouldn't."

"Try me."

There was silence, and then, like a banshee from the hells, there emerged such a hideous wail from the chamber that Ravn almost fell back. "I hate you! I hate you! I hate you!"

Ravn hastily retreated back from the chamber, and when he was far enough away, turned and ran. He ran as though for his very life, past his own chamber suite and down the stairs. He ran though the castle until he was outside in the bailey.

"Giles! Bring me Dancer!"

The man bowed and was about to make towards the stables, when Ravn swept past him. "Never mind. I will get him myself."

"Yes Laird!"

Once in the stable he went right to The Dancer's stall. The stallion was the finest horse he'd bred thus far, young and fiery. The animal snorted when Ravn opened the stall door, but stood still as he slipped the bit into his mouth and the bridle over his head.

Ravn led the beast out of the stable, and as his usual, The Dancer was doing what he did best. He pranced around Ravn, tail held high, snorted, and whinnied, fighting to keep the saddle from placed onto his shiny chestnut back.

Ravn pursed his lips. "Fine, have it your way then." He vaulted onto the stallion's bare back, took control of the reins, and got the fractious animal under control. They clattered out of the bailey and through the streets of Blacach Towne. He kept the horse under control until they reached the outskirts, then gave The Dancer his head.

And then they ran. They ran as far from the castle as he could, and only when he felt the wild stallion finally begin to tire, he turned around. On the way back, he thought of the next day, his favorite day of the week, where he would settle conflicts between the people who lived in town. He loved to help them resolve their disputes, and more often than not, restore friendships.

Once back at the castle, he handed The Dancer off to Giles, then bounded up the castle steps, two at a time. The scent of freshly prepared food assailed his nostrils when he opened the door, and it was only then he remembered he hadn't eaten all day.

He glanced over at the head cook, who had entered when she heard his arrival, "Hannah, I will take supper in my chambers this evening!"

"Yes, Laird!"

He rushed up the stairs to his chamber suite the same way he did the outside steps to the castle. He felt so much better after his run, and his head was cleared of the conversation he'd overheard earlier that day. He wouldn't let on he'd heard it. Perhaps he could continue to give her the freedom she desired. It would break his heart, and mayhap anger the gods, but there had to be a way for her to remain happy. In the meantime, he would just eat and rest, show Ròs the balcony in the morning.

Ravn opened the door to his chamber, stepped in, and abruptly stopped. There, standing in the center of the room, was Ròs. She wore a sheer nightgown splattered with embroidered flowers, and her brown hair lay tumbled around her shoulders. In spite of the cruel words he'd heard uttered from her earlier that day, his body stirred at the sight of her.

Ravn was proud how swiftly he regained his composure. "Ròs, is everything alright? Can I get you something?"

She was quiet for a moment, just staring at him through watery blue eyes. He waited patiently for her reply, not moving from his spot. "I...I've come to realize that it may be wrong of me to keep you so far from me all the time. I'm ready to make our union legitimate in every way."

For a moment he couldn't believe what he was hearing, no matter what threats Nora had proposed earlier that day. Ròs flinched as he began to slowly move towards her, and when he stopped before her, she looked at the wall of his chest. He was nervous to ask, but did so anyways. "Are you saying that you wish to share my bed?"

Again there was a moment of quiet before she responded. "I...only if you wish it."

Her words spoken to Nora rang through his mind, but he reached out a tentative hand and brushed it gently over her shoulder. She shook at the light touch, but didn't back away. Perhaps this was it, the way to the closeness they lacked in their relationship. Encouraged, he brought the hand up to her face and caressed her cheek, but she turned away and he let his hand drop to his side.

Ravn moved away from her, his heart thundering against his ribs. Even now, after all this time, he'd held true to his vow and he'd never taken another woman to his bed. He had a castle full of them; it would have been easy. But every day he endeavored to be a man his father would be proud of, and above all things, his father had loved his mother and treated her with the utmost respect. Always.

He took off his boots, followed by his shirt. Even though a robust fire burned in the fireplace, he kept his socks on to keep his feet from the cold stone floor. He climbed onto the bed and then beneath the covers. He looked at Ròs, noticed that she hadn't stirred from her place, not even to watch him.

This was it, this was the moment where he let her go or took her as his. "Is this what you want, Ròs? Are you certain this is what you want?"

Her voice was small, and frightened, but certain, "Yes."

"Come into the bed with me."

Stiffly, she did as he bid, walking to the other side of the bed and laying down on it. She didn't look at him, just stared up at the ceiling. He considered not pursuing this, her every action telling him she didn't want it, but he couldn't bring himself to stop. This was something he'd wanted for almost a year and a half, more than that if he counted the times he yearned for her before their nuptials. He had heard that most women were afraid of the first time, but after that, the fear would pass. He would be gentle and treat her like the lady she was. She would certainly love him after they had become one. *She had to.*

Ravn scooted over to her side of the bed, and once he was beside her, he once more reached out to touch her arm. She didn't look at him as he caressed it through the fabric of her nightgown. He slowly trailed his hand down to hers where it rested against her flat belly, then left it to move to her torso and rest beneath her breasts. He felt her breaths quicken. He looked up to her face and saw that her eyes were closed. She lay unmoving beside him, and remained that way even when he cupped his hand around one small breast.

His body roared to life. He raised himself on his elbow, looked down at her as he ran his hand over her breasts, his erection pressing painfully against his trousers. For the first time ever, he placed his lips on hers and gently kissed her with all the love he had in his heart, hoping, praying she would return it.

Nothing happened.

Ravn stopped to catch his breath, his mind battling with his body. Meanwhile, he unbuckled his belt and pushed off his trousers, freeing his sex and allowing him a sigh of relief. *Maybe, just maybe I can make her want me.* He put his hand on her again, felt her tremor at his touch. He worked at the laces of her nightgown, pulled the garment apart to finally expose her.

Her milky white breasts lay before him, perfect in their small roundness. All he could think to do was kiss her. So he did just that, placed his lips over the tiny rosebud nipple of one breast. Her body shuddered, and he continued, kissing it with his lips and licking it with his tongue. Then he did it with the other one. He ran his hand down her torso, under her hands, and down to the juncture of her thighs. Then he just rubbed her there, not knowing what else to do since her gown was in the way.

Ròs continued to lay there, unmoving and unresponsive.

Ravn rose from her chest, his erection throbbing for release. He finally took the initiative and pulled up her gown to expose the white skin of her legs beneath. Her smallclothes were there, and suppressing a growl of frustration, he pulled them down over her narrow hips. He looked at the thatch of curls over her womanhood and paused. *Finally I will be truly married; finally she will be my wife.* The thought invigorated him and gave him a happiness he hadn't felt in a long time.

Ravn looked up at her face again, looking for any response. All her saw was her lips pressed into a thin line, and her eyes closed tightly shut. He swallowed heavily, his body reacting to her lack of interest. But it wasn't enough to quench his thirst for her. He rose over her, gently spread her legs and situated himself there. *This is going to be good for us. It will bring us closer.* He leaned forward to kiss her again, hoping for a response... He pressed himself against her, then again, and again, harder and more insistent.

And then he was inside. Ròs gave a sharp inhale and her breath shook as she let it out. He moved inside, slowly at first, and then a bit faster, and then...

His body stiffened with the power of his climax and it was over. He lingered over her for a moment, noticed the tears creeping down her cheeks and withdrew. He looked down and saw the blood covering his receding shaft, between her legs, on the bed linens. *This is more than I thought it would be. They didn't warn me it would be this much...*

Ròs shifted beneath him, drew her legs together, hastily pulled down her nightgown and crawled out from beneath him. Without a single word, she slid out of the bed, pattered across the stone floor as she opened the door to his chamber, and left.

Ravn just kneeled there on the bed, his shoulders slumped, while the fire crackled in the fireplace. He wondered if he would ever be able to make his wife happy.

Chapter Fourteen
Bound

Vivien caressed the soft fur, letting it slide beneath her fingertips. The large head in her lap moved and luminous green eyes looked up at her with utmost love and devotion. "I'm sorry I couldn't ride home with you yesterday," she whispered. "I felt terrible."

Sherika reached out and put a soft paw on her face. Vivien held it there for a moment, and the first tears began to stream down her cheeks. They were hot and fast, dripping onto the gown she still wore from the council meeting.

"You...you are my best friend. I love you so much."

The big feline closed her eyes into slits and purred.

"It's the truth. No matter what I say, you will love me. No matter what I DO, you will love me."

The purr deepened.

The tears continued, and Vivien's shoulders shook with the force of her sobs. Sherika curved her lithe feline form around her, enveloped her in warmth and security. The purring was strong; she could feel it in her bones, and it was comforting. Then something caught Sherika's attention and she began to sniff, her long whiskers trembling with each inhale. She whuffed and sniffed, finally coming to Vivien's hand.

Vivien took a deep breath, curtailed the tears, gave a gusty exhale. "Yes, that is my punishment." Strangely, somehow, Vivien sensed the questioning confusion in Sherika's mind. The tir-reath were wonderful that way when deeply bonded with their companions. They could feel one another's deepest emotions. Vivien turned her hand, letting the light play across her pale skin. Delicate runes shone in the sun's rays, glistening briefly metallic gold before disappearing once more.

Sherika sneezed.

Through her tears, Vivien grinned. "Yes, I know. The spell is a bit caustic and tickles the nose."

Her friend proceeded to lick one hand, and then the other, her warm raspy tongue seeking to take the beautiful runes away. It had pained her father to place the spell upon her; he'd held her close the entire time, the way he used to do when she was a child. In the end he just grasped her hands and spoke the complex incantations that bound her, magic that would keep her from using her own.

He cried when he did it. She'd never see never father cry before. Ever.

Vivien's chest tightened with the memory, and the tears began anew. Sherika stopped the licking and pressed her body closer against Vivien, settled around her the way a mother does a litter of cubs. Vivien fell back and lay against the soft, dark belly, crying in earnest. She didn't just cry for herself, but for her mother, who was long deceased, for her father, for Lydia, and for... the Wolf.

What had he been thinking? What craziness had entered his mind for him to do what he had done? He was insane to want to stay, to live in Rithalion as a servant when he could be wild and free.

"Wild and free." Vivien rolled the words about on her tongue. They sang a song to her, one she wished to embrace. *He has given away the one thing I dream about the most. And now, bound like an animal, I am nothing.*

The magnitude of the thought struck her and she jolted. She recalled the Wolf once saying something terribly similar when he first arrived in Rithalion. *"I am nobody."*

Sherika's body suddenly stiffened, and Vivien knew she sensed someone approaching. A trill of dread washed over her. *Torialvah.*

Sherika felt the shift in her demeanor and the purring abruptly ceased. The tir-reath had made it clear how she felt about the Lord of Ice and Steel many years ago and avoided his company whenever possible. However, instead of stalking back to her den like usual, she stood at Vivien's side when she rose.

Torialvah sauntered into view and stopped when he saw Vivien standing there. His dark brows furrowed, and his sour expression shifted to one of annoyance. "There you are. I wondered where you had gone after the council meeting adjourned."

"I went to see my father," she said quietly.

He pursed his lips. "Oh yes, that's right." His upper lip curled into a spiteful sneer. "How was that? I'm certain the old man was gratified to punish his only daughter in the worst way possible."

Her lower lip trembled. *No, I can't cry. He hates it when I cry.* Sherika bumped up against her side, a loving presence to soothe her. Vivien curved her fingers into the thick fur and clenched her fist as tightly as she could.

"The Grand Magister is just fine. Thank you for inquiring."

Tor scoffed. "Impudence doesn't flatter you, Vivien."

She struggled to keep her voice from wavering. "Neither does cruelty suit you, Torialvah."

He gave a mirthless chuckle. "Ahhh, you think I'm being mean to you? Is that it?" He stepped towards her. "No, my dear, just being truthful."

Sherika gave a brief trilling moan, a sound that indicated displeasure. Tor's eyes darted to the tir-reath and his voice was low and scathing. "Tell your pet to leave us or come inside the house."

Vivien inhaled deeply, then slowly released Sherika's fur. She patted her companion for a moment before stepping away to follow Tor into the house. She could already imagine what he was going to say. She had lay a hand on the Wolf in the council chamber, right in the middle of his chest. It was an infraction she hadn't considered at the time, but now she would suffer the consequences. Even in a society like theirs, where people take many lovers throughout their long lives, there were societal norms that were adhered to. She had blatantly disregarded them in this case, and it would be frowned upon.

Tor didn't stop when he entered the house, but silently continued through the hall towards the bedchamber. Vivien just continued to follow, rubbing her forearms of the strange sensation that enveloped them, looking around the place and, even after twenty years of marriage, feeling like it still wasn't hers. It was Tor's home. He had lived there for decades before her, and he would possibly live there decades more after her.

Once in the bedchamber he turned to face her again, his pale gaze clouded with the storm in his mind. His voice was low, but built into a dull roar, "I thought I told you that if you were to do something imbecilic, that you would come tell me about it yourself."

Vivien frowned. "It's not like I had a chance to tell you anything at all, imbecilic or not!"

"Yes, I heard. You were found at the hospice with that animal you dragged in from the wilds several weeks ago."

She lifted her chin in defiance. "I wished to know if he was still alive."

"Really Vivien? All you had to do was ask Mikarvan when you arrived there."

She looked away, remembering what the young healer had said about her husband just the day before. At this moment she supposed he was right. Indeed, she lived beneath Tor's boot-heel, she supposed maybe a bit more than other women of her station in Rithalion did their husbands. She'd thought about it before, but only in passing. Now it was a glaring element of her life that just served to perpetuate her unhappiness.

"I wanted to see him with my own eyes."

"Ahhh, so you couldn't trust Mikarvan?"

She shook her head. *No, it wasn't that, it was...*

It was like he spoke to the unspoken words in her mind, but really just a response to her headshake. "Then what was it Vivien?" His voice was raised again. What is it about that stinking human that makes you do the most damnable things? You are lucky he was there to save your silly hide in council today after you took the fall for that foolish old woman!" His tone dripped with sarcasm, "Very commendable of you, by the way. I suppose you owe it to Lydia, after all, by making her go to see your animal every day!"

Torialvah began disrobing, his movements jerky as he went about a task he usually did with gorgeous fluidity. When her eyes rested upon his nude body, she felt nothing, no stirring deep inside like she used to feel when they were naked in each other's presence. She supposed he'd stolen that away from her, desire to be with a man and have him be a part of her the way men and women were made to be.

Instead, anger coiled within her belly. Tor was right, the Wolf had 'saved' her. She didn't need his help, didn't need his saving. Lydia was her responsibility, and Vivien deserved to wear the binders her father had placed on her for twice the length of her allotted time– binders that now burned as she unconsciously fed the fires that called the fae with her anger.

Vivien turned and left the bedchamber. There was no point in speaking with him, he was so full of anger and rancor. She walked down the corridor and into the common room. She was tempted to refute him, that she hadn't made Lydia do anything, that it had been a request. But she knew better. The old woman would never have gone to see the Wolf without her prompting, never bothered to teach him anything.

Vivien settled herself on the plush sofa that dominated the room. With Sherika there, it would be perfect, but she didn't want the potential fight if Tor happened to walk in and decide he didn't like the tir-reath being there. It seemed he'd had enough of animals as of late, and anything or anyone that came to offer her solace was going to be one, whether they really were animals or not.

Chapter Fifteen
The Fortress

The carriage ran along the road of carved stone along the walls of the gorge. The elaborate housing structures built along the boughs of the ancient and proud trees, the flying bridges, and dense forest faded behind giving way to rolling hills as the walls of the pass grew further and further apart.

Lydia appeared to doze, but the Wolf watched out the open windows as the sun painted the sky a cerulean blue. He had been washed free of blood and was mending again. He was given a handsome blue hooded shirt, thick brown vest, boots, and rugged pants, but he constantly rubbed at the seamless bronze bands on his wrists. The thick manacles were devoid of chains or bars, but they would tell the Council where he was at all times, and could compel him back into Elvish lands if he were to wander.

Not that he was likely to wander. He spent all the day of the judgment and the next being as docile as a lamb. He did not struggle when they fitted the magical cuffs to his arms, or when they examined his closing wounds. He did not complain when scholars and magicians came from the college to poke and prod and collect vials of blood, hair, and even spit. Yet, every time someone came in, he looked up with hope, and every time retreated into his walled mind of silence.

For each time it was not Vivien.

Lydia sighed. They had been left alone in the parade of carriages, for none really wanted to be near the dangerous giant and his explosive temper. The city that had once begun to accept and love him now tempered their gratitude with fear. The wards on the council chambers had been ancient, unbreakable things, and he had pushed through them with all the grace of a boar in rut. The road left behind all but a few scattered homes built into the side of the rock face and began to angle down to the level of the ground below. At the first bump of leaving the carved rock for the thick hexagonal paving stones of the road, Lydia's eyes snapped open and she yawned largely.

"Are we leaving the city?" The Wolf asked in Lairdstongue.

"*Elthari!*" Lydia snapped. *In Elvish.*

The Wolf frowned, then had to think through the words before he could ask again.

"No, Wolf." She answered, "Elvish cities are far less..." she searched for the right word, "...defined than human ones. But we are headed for the palace of the Lady of Moonlight and Love, and that is what is considered the border of Rithalion."

The Wolf huffed. "Palace?"

Lydia shrugged. "If you look, you can see it now."

And he could. As the carriage train crested a hill down to a more gentle valley leading into plains beyond, they saw gorgeous towers and delicate threads connecting tall spires. The sun arced into its descent, and the light streamed past. He examined the far off palace as he did everything, with the greatest of intensity. Lydia moved to the other side of the carriage to sit next to him and looked at his strong features. He was thinning, but still thick from his bull neck down to his legs that looked like logs. The elves were delicate, lithe, but this was a man who had punched a bear and had it recoil. He was scarred, wild, and frightfully powerful. As the carriage *thunked* over the seams between the huge hexagonal plates of the road, she imagined she could hear the mighty beating of his heart.

Lydia shook away the thought and smiled at the intently brooding barbarian, then off to the palace as it grew larger. "So, what do you think?"

The Wolf did not know the word, so he spoke his native tongue, "It is a fortress."

Lydia started, "What? Don't be silly!"

The Wolf shrugged and turned away from the window, a brief flash of red in his eyes that betrayed his annoyance.

"Oh, poor boy." Lydia chided, "The world of elves is often confusing to the likes of us at first."

She felt she had no need to explain 'us' to any non-elf. This was an Elvish kingdom and Lydia had lived with the elves since she had been barely a woman. She ruminated on the past just for a moment, and then looked back at the Wolf.

"So where are you from? I have guessed the Lairdlands, but who are you? What is your name?"

He gave her a dangerous look, "I am the Wolf. Vivien named me."

Lydia shook her head, "Certainly, but you have to be at least forty years old. What was your name before now?"

The anger slowly dissolved, and Lydia watched his eyes go out of focus. He was no longer looking at her, but through her. She started to reach out, but he snapped from his reverie and recoiled like a cornered dog, ready to either snap or shy away.

"I was nobody."

His reaction was startling, confusing, and a little bit frightening. She was compelled to bite her tongue, but somehow she found her voice again, albeit a much smaller one. "Wolf? What *was* your name?"

He gnashed his teeth, baring them to her the way a frightened animal might. "I had many."

Lydia sat forward, her adamant will filling the space between them, ignoring the raw emotion thrumming off of him in waves. Her voice was soft and entreated him to speak to her. "What were they?"

She watched his face flash with sadness, anger, sadness again, pure rage, hurt, and then frustration before becoming serene. He pierced her with eyes that glowed like banked coals. When he answered it was in his native tongue, "My names were given in love and respect, as gifts into the mouths of people who then chewed and swallowed them."

Abruptly he flipped the handle to the carriage and bolted from the seat. Lydia came to that side, saw him racing ahead of the convoy of royalty and their guards. Soldiers watched him pass on swift legs and shrugged, but Lydia watched intently as he ran and ran...

Away from her.

She sighed, latched the door and sat back in the seat as the carriage rolled on, rocking her gently. Elves did not give their names except to those they knew and trusted. She did not know more than two dozen herself. Otherwise they used title, honorifics, nicknames that could not be seared into magic and used to attack them. That was a lesson from the civil war they would never likely forget. But the Wolf was a human. He should share his name, or at least trust enough to. She was as close to a friend as anything he had in the kingdom, and she needed to help him if he was ever to find a place here now that he was bound to their service. And maybe she needed him a little bit too. He had given her something to do to fill the days of her golden years, a purpose.

Lydia pursed her lips at this thought, but meanwhile the palace grew larger on the 'scape. Out of new eyes she regarded it and she began to reconsider the Wolf's words. She saw the palace in a new light, one that made her uncomfortable. Vivien had brought her here before, and it had seemed wondrous if not slightly nonsensical. Now she noted the tall, orate walls riddled with places for archers, the towers set to bolster against attack. The motte upon which it sat was marked by the road of the elves, but below the entrance it serpentined back and forth up the hill, allowing extra time for defenders to winnow attackers. As they got closer she became more certain that the Wolf was right, and she could not shake the feeling it foretold of some dire need.

The proud reindeer pulled the carriage up the winding slope and she saw the tiny shrubs she remembered from years ago now grown to mighty trees. Planted by hand in regular lines, they stood watch over the slopes as vigilantly as any soldier. As the carriages rumbled to a stop, Lydia saw the Wolf in those trees, resting against one of the trunks.

"Silly," she muttered as she slowly and painfully disembarked, pulling her hood up modestly. But her eyes traveled from the august assemblage up at the gates to the palace and she saw not the fanciful things she once imagined, but thick and imposing blockades to siege. She shook her head and motioned to the Wolf, who obliged and came over.

The doors opened languidly, possessing not so much grace as she might have imagined, but great weight. The Lady of Moonlight and Love came to greet them, exquisitely beautiful elvin dancers cavorting on all sides and enveloping the crowd by casting wildflowers, playing musical instruments, and singing songs of harmony and welcome. The carriages were moved in through a large, and equally imposing, side door with the servants. Lydia made to take the Wolf that way, but a call stopped them.

The Lady of Moonlight and Love swept up to them. Lydia snatched the Wolf's hood to pull it up as was proper, but he moved to shy away. The Lady herself lowered hers, meeting them without covering and making Lydia cease her fretting over the Wolf's cover to focus on removing her own.

"Please, please, friends. Come inside and be at ease. You are not here as servants, but honored guests." Lydia barely heard her. She had seen the Lady from a distance before, but now that she was in her presence, she was certain all the legends were true. She was beautiful, so beautiful her heart ached. Her radiance smote all that looked upon her, a glamour that reached into the soul and healed all ills. All bodily aches forgotten, Lydia went to one knee in her presence, and the Wolf followed suit falteringly.

The Lady smiled. "Please rise and come in with the group so you might be given your shelter and sustenance."

The Wolf nodded silently as the Lady turned away. Lydia, released from the Lady's presence, snatched at the Wolf's hood and put it up. He glanced at her with an annoyed frown as he pushed it back down. "Why do you do that?"

Lydia pursed her lips, guiding the much larger man to the back of the line by taking his elbow as if her were a small child. "Civilized folk cover their heads in public unless speaking to a close friends. The Lady," she paused as the memory of such beauty washed over her, "was very kind to take down her head covering for you and I."

The Wolf pointed with the jerk of his chin as elves entered the huge archway into the palace, lowering hoods and removing hats. Only armored helms stayed on, "And now?"

Elvish Jewel

"They are inside, guests," she replied primly as they passed the lintel posts and lowered her own hood, "As are we. To be covered inside is to mark oneself a stranger, an interloper, or an enemy."

The Wolf looked meaningfully at the bronze manacles that encircled his wrists. As light played across the surface, hidden shadows of runes fluttered across the surface. Lydia nodded sadly and made sure to speak in Elvish, "Dwell not upon that. Come." And she took his elbow and walked in as if on the arm of a great lord.

Servants took lords and ladies, servants and guards, from the procession, leading them to suites where they could rest and allowed the main body to move on. The halls were brilliantly decorated, with metal shutters far above reflecting the light of the setting sun down into the halls with a golden glow. More of the Lady's servants flitted through the halls, picking up globes of clear oil in which beautiful flowers floated, and touching tapers to the pestles to create soft, easy light. Dry ivy climbed pillars throughout the wide open lanes of the halls, and each door was carved of thick oak and festooned with images of poetry and nature even as they clunked securely to shut out the world from those within. Lydia watched the final group cast she and the Wolf a curious glance as they were lead into their suite of rooms. Lydia had to shake off the word 'fortress' again as they passed by the last one.

This left only the two and one lonely low-elf servant that smiled and motioned them to follow her. She spoke with a voice full of summer meadows and cavorting deer, happy and simple and bright, "Please come with me."

Lydia smiled back, infected by the young woman's bright green eyes and golden hair. Her beautiful yellow dress was edged in a complicated knotwork of roses and sunflowers, and moved like a second skin. "I hope it is not far, these old bones are in need of rest."

She smiled again, all contentment and serenity, "No, not far."

They climbed stairs into higher levels of the palace, the Wolf dour and searching every shadow, Lydia marveling at the wonderfully spun tapestries, lights, and vaulted ceilings while further dismayed by stair after stair after stair. She had begun to huff when she finally asked, "Have you been in service to the Lady for long?"

The low-elf laughed, a carefree and musical thing, "I have been with the Lady for three decades, but I can consider it service only in that she is in the same service to me." They took a sharp turn and there was a beautifully carved door, made in the scene of a lady and her lord, holding one another in the warmest embrace. When the tall double doors opened, the two lovers were parted, and the shadows cast made them appear to weep. The woman motioned them inside. "She is, after all, my wife."

113

Lydia accepted the news with aplomb, and smiled honest congratulations. The Wolf shook his head as if to dislodge a fly, "Wife?"

The woman closed the doors behind them and laughed again, "The Lady of Moonlight and Love has four wives, and we are blessed to share her life."

"No husbands?"

The woman stood before him, unabashed. "The Lady had two husbands. One died in the war, the other no longer shares her life anymore."

The Wolf considered these words as he continued into the room, passed Lydia who was gaping at the décor. The rest of the palace was white marble, hints of wood and swaths of green. This was rose petals and wood. It was inviting, close, and intimate like an embrace from a paramour. Sparse gold inlays sparkled in the candlelight, and the thick red carpets absorbed all sound. With characteristic bluntness but uncharacteristic impropriety, Lydia blurted, "These chambers are far above our station."

The woman laughed, and it was joined by a musical sound that made her sweetness seem a bell being rung against the might of an orchestra. Still wearing her glowing white, the Lady of Moonlight and Love swept into the room. She first moved to embrace her wife warmly, then addressed the two newcomers. "These are my chambers. You are staying as my guests and you will share them with my wives and I for the duration of your stay."

Lydia stood shocked. The Wolf tossed his mane of hair in irritation. The Lady glided before him and lay a tender hand over his heart, "You are my man, Wolf. I am responsible for you, and share in your crimes and successes. In return I will share my home and my food. Do you understand?"

Lydia watched the Wolf stare into the eyes of the Lady, a vision that glowed with life and light, like staring into a sun without blinking. He bowed his head, and when he raised it, the Lady cupped his bearded cheek in one perfect hand, "You do not love me. You will never know how attractive that is to me."

The Wolf rumbled, "I love—"

The Lady put her dainty fingers over his mouth to shush him, smiling sadly. "I know."

Lydia took in the whole scene with baited breath. The Lady's wife stood, just as shocked. Everyone, everyone who looked upon the Lady loved her in ways large and small. But before her was the one man in history to not. Then the moment passed, and the Lady took her wife by the arm and lead them deeper into the chambers and down a wide staircase to a set of suites. "Here are your chambers."

While less lushly appointed than those upstairs, they were still beautifully done in stained wood and soft whites. There were rooms made up as bedrooms, an eating area, a small library, and even a wide balcony that overlooked the land around from the safety of the inner bailey. Heavy chairs were spread here, with a fireplace set into the stone wall and a large railing of carved marble that guarded from the hundred foot drop below. A dozen or more could cavort comfortably here, and the domed ceiling allowed for even a juggler to perform. Lydia bowed low. "Lady you are too generous."

She smiled back. "Nonsense. A man of the wild will need space to move, and you have been sent by Vivien to teach him and you will need space for instruction. Servants will bring you food and provide your needs. We will have clothes made for the Wolf." She turned to address him directly and stepped closely. "The borders of Rithalion are not far. And you are forbidden to pass over them without my leave."

The Wolf frowned. "How will I know?"

Her smile became sad and she tapped one of the bronze manacles with an impeccably manicured nail. "You will know."

The Wolf's face clouded. "Whose rooms were these?"

The wife's eyes went wide behind the Lady, and the Lady's face became sad, like broken clouds striped with light to turn the rain into a glittering hail of diamonds. "They were my youngest son's."

The Wolf nodded. "Will he return soon?"

The wife turned her back, and even the Wolf lowered his head as the Lady wiped away a lonely tear, "My son is not with us anymore. He died in a skirmish with the Liath many years ago."

"I am sorry."

The Lady composed herself, pulling the sadness that had suddenly flooded the room back into herself. She moved to her wife and took her arm, "You should instruct him, Lydia. So much of his life will be shaped by history he does not know."

Lydia curtseyed, knees aching, "Yes, Lady."

The Wolf nodded silently and the Lady turned away. She and her beautiful wife left for the main chambers, and the room became darker for it. The towering barbarian walked to the center of the room, through the unshuttered doorway onto the balcony, and breathed easier, his hunched shoulders loosening.

Lydia shook her head and went to the small library, returning with a glass decanter and two goblets. The Wolf had moved to the railing, and was sitting on the floor looking wistfully past the walls to the forests beyond.

The teacher scoffed and motioned to a chair, "If you are a wolf, you should have been put in the kennels. If you want to be treated as a man, then sit like a man."

The Wolf frowned at her, but then stood to move toward one large padded chair. He startled and pointed. "Vermin?"

Lydia chuckled as she glanced over and poured herself a drink, "That's a tirinian. They eat pests here in Rithalion. They are prized for keeping a house clean of bugs, and gravitate toward love and goodness." She held out another, full glass. "They are good luck and warn of guests with evil intentions."

The Wolf took the glass absently, staring at the little creature with the body and face of a cat, the legs and tail of a squirrel, and enormous tufted ears. He reached down to pick it up and it scampered onto his hand. Though the bushy tail hung off, the body was only the length of his fingertips to his wrist, and the thing stared at him with knowing black eyes rimmed with thick auburn fur. He regarded the tirinian for a moment, then held his hand over a table next to his chosen seat and waited. When the animal didn't move, he turned his hand over to dump the creature onto it. With a flip of its tail it scampered to the other side of his hand and continued to stare. The barbarian sighed wearily and shook his hand, but the little animal scurried up his arm with sharp claws on fabric to sit on his shoulder.

Lydia took a long sip, "Oh, unseleighe dancing! Sit down, Wolf. Having one sit on you is good luck!"

She concentrated on the beautifully aged berry liquor, relishing the slight, smooth burn and tart sweetness.

"Grandmother, in which war did her husband die?"

Lydia frowned, then sighed, but smiled when she looked at him, tirinian curled in his lap. The little thing was purring contentedly, a tiny *tik-tik-tik-tik* at the edge of hearing. "She likes you. You are now, officially, welcome in the home."

But he didn't look welcome. He looked slightly uncomfortable like a new father with someone else's newborn asleep on his lap.

Lydia laughed, and gave only the slightest attempt to curb the sound at the man's frown. He drained his glass in one pull, not tasting the stuff, the lights from inside the apartment winking off of his bronze cuff. She sighed, "Wolf, you live at a moment in the Elvish nation that is the tip of a mountain whose body is covered in fog." She looked back to him, and he stared at her as intently as any predator on the prowl. Seeing he was not to be dissuaded, she filled her glass again and settled in.

Lydia sat and sifted through the stories, the memories, the shared pains and tears he had watched elves shed while they thought that she wasn't looking. "A long time ago the elves had two kinds of magic. There was the magic of creation, the fae, and the magic of destruction, the dragons. The fae, and those that could contact and summon them were celebrated. Those that did the same for the dragons were feared. The two factions were never at rest, for the spirits of nature, the fae, will always be at odds with the elemental expressions, the dragons." She glanced over, "You have another visitor! That's very good luck."

And, indeed, the Wolf had two tirinian sitting on his lap. He looked twice as uncomfortable. She wanted to smile, but the weight of the subject drew her back to her memories and her drink.

"Hundreds of years ago there was a civil war. Nobody knows how it started, but everyone agrees it started in Pergatium, at the old wizard's college there. It spilled out into the streets, and had elves taking sides." Lydia trailed off, thinking of the horrors that followed. The silence went on and on, until the old woman looked to the Wolf and saw him watching as intently as ever. "It caused a rift in society. Brothers marched against brothers in that doomed place. Unbelievable magicks were unleashed. Terrible things happened." She looked into the bluish black liquid, then drank it and whispered, "Terrible things."

Again silence stretched, this time until the Wolf rumbled, "Wars are where terrible things happen."

Lydia looked at him, her face stricken, "Elves live for hundreds of years, and mate slowly. They lost lovers, friends, and relatives that had been in their lives longer than human kingdoms have existed. The loss was felt so deeply it altered them, and bred an anger inside of them that burned." She filled her glass and sipped again, eyes focusing on something far away. "They once loved each other as a whole race. They gave their names freely, in love of one another. And then..." Her voice broke, "...and then the hate began. The Great Hatred seeped into all of their hearts and the battles became massacres where no mercy was asked or given.

"They murdered one another's wives and children, killed one another in their beds. And then, then their names..." She took a shaky breath and sipped again, "...they began to use name magic. They wrought the names of those they once loved into horrible spells that reached out and twisted those that summoned the elemental dragons. The dragon elves were driven from the city of Pergatium and into the wilderness beyond. The massed armies of those who summoned the fae marched into the city to fortify it and give chase, knowing that both groups could never coexist.

Broken, battered, exiled, the elves of the dragons knew their doom would come swiftly after them... and so...

"And so..." Lydia took a deep, shuddering breath, passionate tears full of sorrow pouring down her face, "A mighty river flowed past the high mouth to the valley, leaving only the barest stream to descend and feed the golden city of Pergatium. Using dragons of earth and water, they redirected the river into the valley." She screwed her eyes shut, "The dragon elves flooded the valley and drowned them all."

Seconds ticked by. Lydia set down her drink on the side table and held her belly tightly. "Elves are the most sensitive of creatures. The mothers especially. They often realize they are pregnant before they miss their menses, and they can feel their children all of their lives. Elves died by the thousands, tens of thousands. Mothers felt their children die. They had felt and hurt the entire ten years of the war, and it had bred white hot anger on both sides. But the day Pergatium fell, that sealed the fate on the hatred forever."

The frail old woman leaned forward, slumped, "Human women who take elvin seed share the blood of the child, not enough to be considered even a low-elf, but enough to feel them faintly. When my boys grew into men and went off to the Northern Marshes to sell steel, I felt them get ambushed. I was working in the garden when I felt their light, a warmth my whole life, be snuffed out. My sons, my husband, gone. I cannot imagine what the elvin mothers felt. And after that..."

Lydia breathed deeply, letting the memories of loss wash over her. They were very old wounds, and had never fully healed. She had learned to pull the covers over them, live with them, but they would never go away. *They were supposed to outlive me...*

She breathed in cool night air and breathed out until her bunched muscles relaxed, and the tightness in her heart subsided. She found the place of peace inside her that had carried her through the darkest of years. She opened her eyes and looked at the Wolf.

It was not the cackle of an old woman, but the shadow of a girl's musical giggle that escaped her then. A joyous sound that had captured the heart of a high-blood elvin man over half a century ago. The barbarian was covered from one end to the other, with both thighs, shoulders, arms and one foot buried in little purring balls of fur that slept contentedly as he sat rigid and immobile. Lydia gasped and giggled again, feeling the berry liquor burning through her and helping cast away the shadows of loss. The Wolf frowned mightily and she stood slowly, wobbly and moved to him,

"Oh, it is so difficult to be loved and respected, isn't it young man? Shoo! Shoo!"

The tirinian leapt from him regretfully, languidly, and watched him intently as he stood and took the older woman's unsteady arm. "I have a feeling, Wolf, that the elvin people will be grateful to have you fight for them in the coming battles, even if they do not know what to make of you right now." She put a hand on the center of his chest and patted him absently, "Grateful, very grateful. Now come to bed."

She half pulled, and was far more than half supported by the big man as they reentered the apartments. He guided her into the first room with a bed and let her sit down on the soft goose down mattress. She protested for a moment, but sleep was overtaking her before she was straight on the bed. The Wolf tenderly laid her head on the feather pillows and pulled the thick knit covers over her sparse frame to her pointed chin. Then he turned in the near complete darkness and left as quietly as a tear rolling down the cheek.

Old aches roused Lydia well before dawn. She could see naught but the slightest outlines of the objects around her, but she slowly built herself into a standing position and walked painfully into the hall. The candles had been doused and she had not learned where the lamp was stored yet. She found the other bedroom, but it was empty, blankets missing. The kitchen was empty. The library, empty. Finally she braved the shutter doors to the balcony where the chill night wind was whipping mercilessly. There, in the corner near the fireplace where coals lay like dull red eyes, the Wolf lay curled against the elements on his blankets. The wind stirred his hair, and fluttered his new clothes, and mussed the fur of at least two dozen tirinian that slept on him as a living blanket.

She shook her head in wonder and whispered, "Very grateful."

Chapter Sixteen
The Proving Grounds

imrudian sauntered into the apartments, assured and relaxed. His clothes were rugged, tunic and trousers of brown and dark green hues that had seen their fair share of miles. On his back was slung a human made cloak canted at a jaunty angle even as it trailed behind him. He scratched at the many days growth of black beard and flashed a charming smile at the handsome, brown eyed man who looked back at him in the mirrors he passed.

He had a job to do, and he was certain he could accomplish his mission. Barbarians could be tiresome, but were unlikely to be cultured or imbued with the needed subtlety to match his wits. He heard the elderly teacher giving her lessons in Elthari, smelled the remains of a delicious chicken they must have enjoyed for lunch. He had made a visit with the kitchen staff earlier that morning to be sure that the wine they had consumed was not as watered down as customary, so as to dull them ever so slightly. *At times like this, it paid to use all the advantages one could acquire.* His soft-soled boots made little noise on the polished wooden floor, and as such, as he appeared in the doorway, he expected an undisturbed moment to observe, not a pair of piercing ruby eyes flashing and narrowing at him.

Sim was stopped in his stride by those eyes, suddenly as big as the room. He blinked and the illusion faded. They had the barbarian dressed simply, with a thick hooded brown shirt and leather vest. However, there were no trousers. The man had obtained a length of harsh woolen cloth and tied it in pleats around his waist secured by a cinched belt. It looked like a short dress, and his hairy legs stuck like tree trunks into the boots he had been provided. He stood like an animal, ready for anything that might happen, muscles bunched. But then he walked across the floor and extended his fingers. Sim blinked for a moment and extended his own so the fingertips touched, the Elvish way of greeting.

Sim was very elvin, but never looked it. More than that, unlike most, he could *feel* so very acutely. At the touch, he got flashes of blood, death, long cold nights. Above all, he saw the face of Lady Vivien Valdera, very young, atop a crude castle wall. He jerked away from the contact, trying to shake the powerful images away.

The old woman, withered and spare, smiled at the Wolf, "Ga'thallaa enus-ataba, La'ath." *Very good, I am proud of you, Wolf.*

Sim forced a smile that had fooled crafty tradesmen and suspicious guards across the human lands, replying in Elthari, "I am called Sim. The Lord of Swords and Truth has asked to meet you at the training yards and I am to be your guide."

It was a simple message, delivered with expertly designed sincerity and innocence. Yet, the Wolf's eyes narrowed. His nostrils flared.

This one is suspicious. Sim did not let his smile flicker. The dark red eyes became darker, brows puckering with some hidden instinct. *Get him moving and not thinking.* Sim bowed, "If you will follow me."

Sim turned to go, but after three steps, he noticed he was alone. He took one light step back and strained his ears to hear the low conversation from the library.

"Wolf, one does not simply ignore the invitation of a Lord."

The reply was deep and rumbling. "Come with me."

"Seleighe in the walls! You don't need the protection of an old woman like you are a child! You must stand alone among them sometime. These will be your people for a good portion of your life going forward. You must become one of them, as I have."

There was a pause. "As you wish, Grandmother."

Sim took a long, light step away from the door, clasping his hands modestly before him and waiting like the picture of innocence. The Wolf appeared a moment later, tall and brooding. Sim bowed and turned. They made a direct line out of the palace, but it had transformed into a hive of activity. Since the Wolf's arrival at the Lady's palace the War Council had met a dozen times in the month that had passed. The Lady had thrown open many chambers in the fortress that had been long sealed, revealing apartments to be used by visiting mages from the college. These men and women would gather in the ballrooms, which were being used as serviceable training areas. The college was a place of learning and understanding. This fortress was being used to hone skills gained there into weapons.

The Wolf watched the students pass with calm disinterest, and kept following. Sim smiled to himself as the big man let down his guard. "Wolf? You called your tutor Grandmother? Is that possible or did she just remind you of your grandmother?"

When a few paces garnered no answer, he looked back at the following human. The look he was cast was one of mild dislike. Sim feigned innocence until the Wolf huffed. "It is a form of respectful address by my people."

They took a few more steps together, Sim perfecting polite interest, "What people are those?"

The two had to stop while a cloud of students went by, each mage trying desperately to hold three fiery fae in glowing globes before them while struggling to concentrate on wading through a room full of people, a magister murmuring encouragement from behind.

The barbarian loomed over Sim, causing him to turn. The large man's beard was long and shaggy, and he showed no intention of trimming it close as was customary for humans in Rithalion. It was split by a feral smile that hadn't an iota of happiness. "Humans."

And then he was past Sim and moving briskly through the crowded corridor toward the rear gates. Sim was an expert at moving quietly, gently. The Wolf simply moved like an ox through waves of grain, his presence creating a prow that got others out of his way. Sim was tossed a bit in the wake.

Very soon, the businesslike steps exited the open rear gates and they stood at the top of the serpentine road that headed down the motte. Thick, fat flakes of snow were falling silently in the light breeze, frosting the tips of the trees, grass, and rocks a far as the eyes could see. The Wolf, even in his light clothing was untroubled by the chill, or the way his breath frosted in the air. Sim stopped next to him, slightly disheveled from his trouble. He tried to hide his irritation and tried to pry once more, "So you say you are from the Lairdlands, then?"

The Wolf gave him another meat eating grin, "In fact, I didn't. Now where is this Lord of Swords and Truth?"

Here, the arc away from the front of the palace became obvious as it formed a massive crescent that held a small valley full of trees in the center in loving arms. "He is at the training yard down in the valley."

And the barbarian was off. Not down the stairs, or along the more gentle switchback path, but straight down the slope with hair and kilt flying. He had not even bothered to put his hood up. Sim growled in frustration and jogged to the staircase, taking two at a time as he tried in vain to catch up to the racing man who was threading the space between marching trees.

He reached the bottom out of breath just after the Wolf did. The tall trees suddenly parted, and before them was a wide arena laid out as an amphitheater. Raked seating on all sides was carved out of the soil and then faced with beautiful stones. Seats were made of tenderly trained saplings tied into shapes to hold the sitter in comfort. Now that the light snows fell upon the green seats, they looks like they were covered in delicate white silks, all facing where the warriors of Rithalion sparred and marshaled. Some were moving through obstacles, others practiced sword-play. The clatter of wooden water weapons was a constant sound that littered the air.

The Wolf watched, body tensed, as Sim paused to raise his hood after the mad dash. He took several deep breaths and took his place calmly beside the giant man. The Wolf spared him not a glance, but Sim had the feeling if he had been an animal, his ear would have cocked to capture his soft footfalls of approach.

"They call this place the Arena. Magnificent, is it not?"

The Wolf did not reply.

Sim waited politely, and the barbarian went to his haunches to watch intently. His muscles were bunched, his fingers twitching slightly just above the ground. It became clear he meant to say nothing. The low-elf shrugged and motioned down the final steps and out onto the field. The Wolf huffed, stood, and walked ahead.

They passed clusters of men running in groups, fighting with weapons, and fighting with their hands. Some staggered, some paused, others gawped openly at the Wolf. He moved amongst them without the slightest misstep. His confidence radiated from him in an aura that all the elves could feel, along with barely suppressed suspicion. All avoided him and his path, like dogs in a kennel making way for his namesake. Both had sharp teeth, but their proficiency was earned. He was born to it and they all knew.

At the center of the Arena there were a series of tents. Their festive colors were at odds with the elves who wore off whites and greens spattered with brown from the day's labors in the mud. Outside, speaking with lords, captains, and generals, there sat one elf. He wore a simple, white fur cloak with the hood down, serviceable leather plates over nondescript padding, and heavy leather gauntlets reinforced with steel plates as if he were likely to engage in sparring like the rest. Like the High Council members, he was ancient beyond the reckoning of mortal men. He, however, possessed a vitality about him they did not. His head was shaved, eschewing all prettiness for practicality. This was not an elf of quiet contemplation, but a being of ready action. He saw them coming from hundreds of yards off, yet did not pause his conversations, pouring over documents, creating dispatches, or scrying at maps until the last seconds. Yet when he did stop, all business was concluded. He stood, moved around the table, and received them at the precise instant discipline required.

Sim began to bow even as the Wolf did not. The Lord waved a dismissal. "Do not bother."

Sim would have stumbled if he had been truly human, but instead recovered fluidly. "Lord Of Swords and Truth, may I present–"

The old man frowned, "I am Xadrian, War Commander of the armies of Rithalion."

Sim caught his breath at the sound of the Lord's true name. He looked back to the barbarian, waiting for a some kind of crude bravado. Instead the commander's silver eyes dissected the Wolf without mercy, and the deep red gaze of the big man took him in with guarded caution. Finally the human replied, "I am nobody."

Sim's mouth went dry at the breech in etiquette. *A true name given to be rebuffed–*

The Commander nodded. "I do not believe that is true, but I also believe that you have that as the truth in your heart, and accept it. The warmage, Vivien, has called you Wolf. Will that be acceptable to you?" The human nodded. "Good. Calling you 'Nobody' might be poetic, but it will cause useless confusion. You are here to be of service to the elvin people, do you understand?"

By way of reply, the Wolf held up the twin manacles of bronze that encompassed his wrists and rang them together.

Xadrian nodded again. "Bad business that. Yet I have been put in command of you, and I need you. Do you understand?"

The Wolf only nodded.

Xadrian nodded back. "But, honor first." He stepped back and very slowly gripped the hilt of the sword that hung at his side. He drew it slowly, eyes never leaving the Wolf's suddenly tensed frame. The sword began to come forth, but after a little more than a foot and a half of blade it ended abruptly in a ragged edge. Xadrian balanced the truncated blade, ornate and deadly, on flat palms before the Wolf. "This is Arisil, better known as Doomslayer. It has been in my family for five thousand years. It was lost in the flooding of Pergatium. I had given it to my second during the last battle. She never returned, and I and I was never able to go retrieve it. Its loss, and hers, has been a stain on my honor for four hundred years." He offered it to the Wolf. "You recovered it and it was taken from you when you were imprisoned by my people."

The Wolf took the broken blade. He considered the ornate carvings, the flawless amethysts, the fine scrollwork, the supernatural keenness of the edges. Then he sat it back upon Xadrian's palms.

The Lord of Swords and Truth narrowed his eyes. "You return it?"

The Wolf nodded. Sim realized he was not breathing and took a brief quaff of air.

Xadrian sheathed Arisil. "May I ask why?"

The Wolf chewed on his answer. "I have lost. If I can make right another man's loss, then perhaps my own will be so lessened one day."

Xadrian smiled broadly with an expression Sim had never seen him make in all the years he'd known him. "I knew I had the measure of you. I believe you are the brother of my soul, and I welcome you to my table if you are ever hungry, to my home if you are ever cold, and to my family if you are ever heartbroken."

Sim blinked at the turn of events, the Lord all but adopting the uncouth barbarian as a son. Yet, the tall muscled man only hung his head, hair falling to cover his face. "You are kind, but I am not deserving of a home or a family."

Xadrian put a hand on the Wolf's shoulder and Sim squelched a warning. Yet, the human tamely let it sit there as the Lord spoke gently, "Maybe now, but you are my blood. The people of this realm will learn that and accept it. They do not understand you, but they will. They will see and love you, for you have as much to teach us as we have to teach you."

The Wolf's headshake was nearly imperceptible, "What can I possibly teach you?"

Without warning, Xadrian struck. The master of Elthari sath'hara, Elvish hand-and-foot combat, made a simple lunge to the midsection. Fast and hard, it was born of hundreds of years of training, powerful honed muscles, and rock hard bones. Sim recoiled at the sound of a side of beef being struck by a hammer. But the strike, masterfully made, had been caught by one massive hand. The Wolf's counterstrike, a foot to the Lord's chest, sent the old elf sprawling end over end for a half dozen paces backward. The ground had been churned by hundreds of feet moving to mash the light snow into the soil and it gave under the commander, his passage leaving a furrow behind that coated him and his cloak.

All activity stopped on the field. Soldiers came running from all directions, but the Lord had come to rest only for a moment on all fours like an animal. Then with a shrug, he divested himself of sword, sheath, cloak, and belt, and tossed them all at Sim who barely caught them. Before he had them arranged in his arms, the Commander was moving.

The Lord struck like lightning, but the Wolf met his skill with unimaginable power. Blows rained upon the human's hunched shoulders, curled arms and meaty midsection. Elves cheered until the Wolf grappled the old soldier and slammed him into the muddy ground. There was no victory in it, for the Commander had spun his hand into the human's beard and the Wolf's head jerked mercilessly as the elf hit the turf. Xadrian rolled away, but painfully, slowly as the Wolf backed away and held his face growling. They were both spattered in dirt now, but ignored it as they circled and considered one another.

The men leapt and met again like two titans. The Lord of Swords flipped the Wolf's hair into his face, then landed two skilled shots to the jaw. The third stroke, however, the Wolf lurched back, grasped the Lord's wrist, and kicked him in the midsection hard enough that the breath *whooshed* from his lungs.

The crowd no longer cheered, no longer called, they only watched these two fighters stagger for a moment and shake themselves back into combat.

Xadrian took a poetic stance, arms spread and waiting. The Wolf hunched his shoulder like a bull, legs ready to spring. Both roared like beasts and they ran at each other, closing the gap, building speed. Feet churned the soil and their footsteps sounded like the heartbeat of racing gods.

Then Xadrian went to his knees, sliding under the Wolf's mighty fists, and came to a stop several steps behind.

The Wolf recovered and spun, only to see the back of his opponent's head as he knelt. Sim watched in awe as the Wolf paused in confusion, then stalked back. Yet Xadrian did not move, breathed only deeply and calmly.

The Wolf's lungs were going like bellows, veins standing out everywhere flesh was seen from face to legs. He paused, sure of a trap, then like his namesake circled the commander at a safe distance. His hands shook with repressed violence, his sweat steamed in the air. His visage, however, took on a confused wonder as he came face to face with Xadrian. The commander exuded serenity, devoid of sharpness or aggression. Still the crowd watched with bated breath.

Then the Wolf came close and kneeled before the commander, who smiled. Then he spoke, "I have no home. I have no kin."

"You do now. And you will teach us utter aggression. In return we will teach you peace. Do you understand?"

The Wolf nodded.

"Good. Now shave your beard and tame your hair. I would never have matched you otherwise." He slowly stood and looked on all sides where generals and footmen alike watched in confused silence, "Did someone call an end to the war? You all seem eager to abandon your training. Could any of you face the Wolf next?"

The crowds scrambled back to their duties, and the Wolf watched them on his knees, stunned, as Xadrian went to Sim and regained his belt and weapon.

The Lord's voice was low. "He will say no more for now. He is mine, and has my trust and I his. Report to your master and tell them. If there is evil to find, I will find it, but mark my words, he is my man."

"But Lord, your wife has claimed him al–" Sim swallowed his protest as Xadrian stabbed him with a vicious look.

"The Lady of Moonlight is no longer my wife." He growled, then swallowed his bitterness. His eyes had a flinty edge. "He is her man, but she knows only half his heart. I know the other, and that is mine. You will deliver the message I send. You will do it *now*."

Sim bowed in acquiescence, then watched as Xadrian, covered in dirt, went back to the human. With an offered hand he brought the big man to his feet. "Come, Wolf. You have faced many of these men from the Iron Coast and lived where our soldiers died. I would know why."

The two mud-spattered warriors walked back to the table, albeit a little stiffly. The training would begin in earnest on the morrow.

Chapter Seventeen
The Request

Vivien stared numbly at the missive held loosely in one hand, her breath misting in the air before her. It was a beautiful invitation, written in the Lady's own hand, upon the finest parchment. Above any other emotion, confusion reigned, and she wondered why the Lady requested her presence.

For the thousandth time, she looked at the intricate runic design that crawled up the length of her forearm. Over the past four weeks she'd come to despise it more than she thought she ever would. Magic that used to come naturally to her without beckoning now caused a visceral pain that originated deep within her belly and spread outward to touch every part of her. It was soul-wrenching, and many days all she wanted was to hide behind the walls of Torialvah's home, stay curled in her bed, and sleep the days away until it was over.

But now she had this invitation from the Lady of Moonlight and Love to come to her home. Vivien didn't want to go, but propriety dictated she should. *The Wolf is there...*

She frowned and released the tension, letting the missive curl back into a roll. *What will Tor say? Do I care what he says?* She went into the bedroom and packed a small bag. She felt a couple changes of clothes and toiletries was good enough, then donned her fur-lined winter cloak. She left a brief message as to her whereabouts on the mantle, then went back outside.

Sherika had sensed something in her thoughts and slunk out of her den just as she approached. The lithe, tir-reath stretched languorously and then sat back on her haunches, waiting patiently as Vivien got the travel harness. She was still as Vivien snapped it into position, and even shifted to make it easy for her to tighten it in the appropriate places.

The bag was tied down first, and then Vivien settled onto her back. At the proper cue, Sherika rose and padded out of the courtyard. Vivien glanced around for a moment, indecisively wondering if she should accept the invitation, but then nudged the tir-reath into motion. Sherika bounded ahead and Vivien instinctively pressed low, moving rhythmically with the big cat as she ate mile after mile with her long legs.

And then she was there. Shaladrea's fortress sat atop a motte, situated among the sprawling foothills of the Flain Mountains north and west of the city of Rithlion. She slowed Sherika to a jog and they took the long, serpentine road up to a mighty gate made entirely of stone. Carved within it was an image of the moon and the beautiful Goddess Arshemi. Vivien reached into her bag and took out a small horn, the one the Lady had given her when she first went into her service. She blew on it four times in succession, then waited.

A deep grinding sound filled the air and the gate slowly moved. It opened until there was just enough space for passage, then Vivien entered. The sound of the gate closing filled her ears as she found herself in the middle of an immense hallway. On either side it continued and broke off into smaller passages that led to the various rooms making up the Lady's home. A servant girl danced up to her and gave a winning smile. "You must be Lady Valdera. The Lady of the house has been expecting you."

Vivien suppressed a frown of dismay at being so predictable, nodded amicably, and slid down from Sherika's back. She followed the girl up a series of stairs, high and wide enough for three tir-reath of Sherika's build to walk abreast. At the end, they reached a set of double doors made of solid oak. Together they formed the image of a man and woman in a sensual embrace, the Deep Green and The Moon Goddess.

The girl opened the rightmost door and Vivien bade Sherika stay outside as she entered the chamber suite. It was just as she remembered it, with ornate tapestries, plush rugs, velvet sofas, and massive floor braziers made of gold. Straight ahead was a large pair of shutters that Vivien recalled led out to the balcony. To the right were two doorways, one leading to Shaladrea's rooms, and the other down some stairs into a set of rooms below it.

The girl gestured, "Come, the Lady is awaiting you through here." Vivien followed, and just as she was about to enter, an old, tottering woman emerged up the stairs.

"My dear Vivien! What a sight you are for these old eyes!" Lydia exclaimed.

Vivien embraced her friend, took in Lydia's old-lady smell, and reveled in her presence. They hadn't seen one another since before the trial. The servant girl stood unobtrusively to the side as Vivien and Lydia seated themselves on the nearest sofa. "How have you fared here these past weeks?" Vivien asked.

"The Lady treats us well, like we are her family!"

Vivien smiled, unsurprised by this act of generosity, but then became solemn. "The Wolf, he is happy here?"

Lydia nodded. "He is adjusting. It's taking him some time, but he's getting there. He talks a little more now."

"He speaks his mind."

Lydia smiled, "To you. And a little to me. Less to anyone else."

Vivien nodded and forced another smile. "This is such a wondrous place, filled with such beauty. It still boggles me that underneath it all, it's naught but a massive stronghold."

Lydia's brows pulled together in consternation. "Stronghold?"

"Why yes, this fortress is huge, bigger than any I've ever seen before. It's hard to believe that a gentle soul such as the Lady would ever think of building anything like it."

Lydia simply nodded. "Yes, yes of course."

Vivien rose. "She is expecting me. Let's talk more later."

Lydia followed suit. "Yes, hopefully I will see you for the evening meal and..."

A deep voice interrupted, "Vivien?"

Both women looked over to find the Wolf standing there. His clothes were an arrangement born of both elvin and human worlds, and his wild, curling hair uncharacteristically tied back from his shoulders. His face was most startling, for his beard was closely shaven. For the first time she saw a square jaw-line, the shape of his mouth, and his nose didn't appear quite so narrow.

Vivien blinked and stared before looking away, a wave of familiarity washing over her. *Where in the world could I have possibly seen him before the ambush all those weeks ago?* Sudden ire bubbled beneath the surface, for she still had not come to terms with what he had done in the council chamber to reduce her sentence. *He thinks of me as a weakling woman, and thus feels he has power over me. Let's see where that gets him...*

Without answering, Vivien looked away from the Wolf and to the young woman standing discreetly to the side. "I am ready to see the Lady now." She turned back to Lydia before walking away. "I shall see you tonight for dinner."

The girl opened the door to the Lady's private chamber. Vivien barely glanced at the Wolf as she walked past him to enter. She could feel his hurt, but she slammed up her barriers and didn't look back. If she ever had the inclination, she would deal with him then.

Her thoughts left him as she heard the Lady's voice, and Shaladrea glided into view. "Vivien! I'm so glad to see you! Thank you for accepting my invitation."

Vivien gave a brief bow. "But Lady, I know I am welcome here anytime, without invitation. You have told me so many times before."

Shaladrea took her hands, eyes colored a warm honey brown. "True, you are my dear. But I wanted to see you today in particular."

Vivien cocked her head and waited patiently for an elaboration. As a child she'd learned the virtue of patience early on, often a difficult concept for low- or half-elvin children to grasp. Something about their human ancestry made it so, for humans tended to rush about life like there was no tomorrow. But Vivien was exceedingly patient, and she settled down to wait as long as necessary to hear out her friend.

Shaladrea stepped across the room and moments later came back with a goblet of dark red wine. Vivien graciously accepted the goblet and took a long sip. Of course it was good; the Lady's wines were always good. They sat in companionable silence until Shaladrea spoke again.

"In preparation for the upcoming war, I have opened my home to many of those who will be playing a role in it. As we speak, our men are practicing and sparring with one another across the Arena, hoping to make themselves better than any of their human adversaries. However, I didn't just issue an invitation to Rithalion's warriors, but to her spellcasters as well.

Vivien was about to take another drink but stopped before the goblet reached her lips. She regarded the Lady intently, a myriad emotions coursing through her all at once. She was suddenly very aware of her forearms, and they felt like they were being squeezed ever so slightly, a reminder of her failure.

She brought the goblet down and held it in her lap, the trembling of her hands making the burgundy liquid almost slosh over the sides. "I...I'm glad you have done so, Lady. To have both mage and warrior study and practice together will be a great thing, and mayhap make them a more cohesive unit in battle. I hope you will keep me abreast on the progress being made here."

Shaladrea smiled, a loving smile that Vivien imagined her mother may have bestowed upon her before she passed so long ago. "I don't believe I will need to pass along progress, for I would like you to be here as it happens."

A lump came to Vivien's throat, a burning one that tried to keep her from speaking the way she wanted, with patience and decorum. "Lady, you know I would love to see the progress, but the temptation is strong, and the pain, even for the most rudimentary of things, is extraordinary. Please, I beg that you understand..."

The Lady raised a finger to Vivien's lips. "Shhh. Hush my dear. I am aware of your pain." Her smile changed into one of sadness. "I would like to help you, if you will let me. I am not asking you to stay here to tempt you. Rather, I would like to have you here as a teacher. I believe there is none better than you to bring our warriors and spellcasters together. I remember all of the talks we shared about this very subject, and your ideas are sound."

Vivien shook her head. "Thank you for the extraordinary compliment, but how can I teach anyone anything if I cannot use my magic as demonstration?"

Shaladrea placed a small hand on her shoulder. "You will use your words, and over time, you will find the perfect ones. Your words will be like magic and they will fit inside every man and woman's mind to create the perfect image of what you want them to do. And when they succeed, you will know you have accomplished your task."

Vivien gave a deep sigh and contemplated what the Lady had said. She supposed it was possible, albeit not the perfect means of communication. Showing was always so much easier, and often better, than mere words alone.

"But Lady, why not find another who can simply show them? Someone who is also good at what they do, someone who can use their magic?"

Shaladrea's gaze became intense. "Because there is none other as good as you."

Vivien shook her head. "I don't believe that."

Shaladrea gave a shrug and let her hand slip away. "Believe what you wish, but you know how I feel, and I want you. Will you do this for me in my service? Or not?"

Vivien breathed deeply. Already she was in Shaladrea's service; the Lady could ask for anything and Vivien would be bound to provide it. However, she was asking for Vivien to do this for her, a request instead of a demand. Vivien wanted to give Shaladrea anything she wanted, but feelings of inadequacy were difficult to dispel.

"I can try to do as you ask, but I am still not..."

Shaladrea's eyes brightened and her smile lit up the room. "I knew you would do this for me. I also know you are the best one to teach our warriors and mages how to come together, no matter what you might think." Her voice was emphatic. "I believe in you Vivien."

Chapter Eighteen
The Letter

She stepped out of the practice room, leaving the sounds of the young apprentices practicing their spellcasting behind. Vivien smiled to herself, pleased with the progress they had made in the three short weeks she'd had them under her tutelage. They were smart, every last one of them, and would make great warmages. As it turned out, they had arrived a couple weeks before Vivien had been called in, time given to each one of them to decide to opt out if they so chose. The vocation they had chosen was a difficult one and, especially in these times, fraught with peril. They deserved nothing less.

There were twelve of them: nine men and three women. Each was young, and had been taken from the college at a very defining moment in their arcane studies, the one that told the magisters what type of spellcaster they would be dealing with in future tutelage. Some of them went on to be mere dabblers, others were healers, and a few aided in the architectural marvels that surrounded her every day. Not many people had the ability to cast magic, and when youths were discovered to have this ability, they were instantly taken to the college, where they would have the best influences and training as possible, right from the start. The men and women in the chamber behind her... they had shown a propensity for the magic one would see cast in battle. And thus, they were the newest minds that would define the term 'warmage' for the next several years. what a privilege it was, and an honor, to have the opportunity to mold them!

"Lady! Lady Valdera!" Vivien turned to see a boy running up to her, a scroll in his hand. "This message came for you this morning!"

She smiled and accepted the message. "Thank you, Aaron! I appreciate the extra time you took to find me."

His cheeks flushed red before he gave a brief bow and scampered off.

She chuckled and popped open the seal, the sound swiftly dying away when she began reading. She read the message again, just to be sure she read it right, and then read it a third time. The letter was signed in her husband's own hand, and when she looked at the seal, saw that it was stamped with the crest of his house, making it difficult to disbelieve the unbelievable.

Tor was asking her to come home. Not demanding she come home. Asking.

Because he missed her.

Vivien looked up and down the hall, then pinched herself to be sure she really was rooted in reality and not one of the dreams her mind often concocted to make life seem better than it was. She twisted the skin and left gouges with her fingernails. Tiny droplets of blood welled and she hissed at the burning sensation.

"Mistress Vivien!"

She quickly lowered her sleeve and turned toward the voice. It was Tyrell, one of the spellcasters she'd been training for the past three weeks. He was the most promising out of the entire class, showing exemplary technique, determination, and a steel will that exceeded all the others. He shared her vision for a unified fighting force, and she could see him being the one she could trust to be at her side during battle.

She smiled as he approached. As always, his dark brown hair was neatly braided, a stark contrast to the light blue tunic that accented the blue in his gray eyes. He was a half-elf, and like herself, his mother had passed a long time ago. They had many similarities in their upbringing, and she felt a kinship with him she rarely felt with others. He didn't seem to mind that she was his superior, and he was a quick learner, embracing all she had to teach with aplomb.

"Mistress, Larissa needs a bit of help with her spells. You have told me many times I execute them rather well, and I was wondering if it was all right with you if I gave her some aid."

Vivien's smile widened, and she momentarily forgot the message from Torialvah. "Tyrell, thank you for asking me. I appreciate your thoughtfulness. Yes, of course it is all right for you to help. Maybe you can offer her some insight that I cannot..."

Her voice trailed off as waves of embarrassment and ineptitude washed over her. In spite of the success she'd experienced as a teacher for the mages chosen to be a part of Lady Shaladrea's program, Vivien continued to struggle within herself. It was students like Larissa who needed that little bit of 'more' that she could not provide, and it made her feel a failure.

Sensing the shift in her demeanor, and understanding the reason, Tyrell reached out a hand and placed it gently on her shoulder. He stepped closer and bent down a bit to look into her downturned face. "Mistress, I want you to know how much you have done for all of us in the program. Without using your own magic, you have taught all of us to begin casting spells with our sword-bearing counterparts in mind, and to use our magic to enhance their abilities. I can't wait for the next phase of our training to begin. We couldn't have made it this far without you."

Silence reigned as Vivien fought to keep her tears at bay.

"Mistress," Tyrell's voice lowered and became deep, "we all know why you can't use your magic, but still we stand by you. You are a good teacher and a brilliant warmage. We are honored to have you instruct us." His voice deepened even further, "And I would be even more honored to have you by my side in any battle."

Hesitantly, Tyrell reached out and brushed a thumb down her cheek before turning to leave. She listened as his footsteps died away before lifting her face and allowing a few errant tears to finally flow. His words were nice to hear, wonderful actually, and made her feel worthwhile. He didn't know the pain she endured daily, and how, late at night, in her sleep, it often became so agonizing, she would just sit up until the sun rose in the morning.

Hopefully he would never know.

Vivien moved down the hallway and contemplated the message clutched in one hand, more tears threatening at any moment. *Why is Tor writing me now when I am busy with important work? How can he miss me when he's never done so before? I suppose I've never been away from home for so long, but really, what do I have there? Sherika is here with me, and Shaladrea has given me more clothing than I can possibly wear.*

Raw emotion rushed through her and sent her mind skidding on doubtful ice. *Tor has made it very clear he does not want me on more than one occasion. He considers me a nuisance and a burden. Truthfully, I'm not certain why we are still married.* A trickle of anger infiltrated. *Yes, why am I married to a man who hates me so much?*

Vivien abruptly took the next turn and began to walk up the stairway into Shaladrea's tower suite. *Regardless, I should go and see what he wants; he is my husband after all. I need to tell the Lady I am leaving for a while in case she needs me.*

She continued up the winding staircases, and had almost made it to the apartment, when she heard a heavy pair of boots start downward. *Oh gods, no.* She thought about scurrying back down to avoid a confrontation, but it was much too late.

The Wolf emerged from around the bend and stopped in his tracks.

His energy was so massive, it filled the stairway and made her want to press up against the cold stone wall that she suddenly felt at her back. Like a predator he closed the distance between them, slowly...slowly, and his dark eyes drank her in like a much coveted wine he'd gone too long without.

His deep voice was monotone. "Vivien."

She made hers the same. "Wolf."

He stopped when he stood before her. "I have barely seen you in weeks. When I have, you are gone in an instant."

She felt a flash sweep through her, anger she was certain reflected in her eyes. She simply shrugged, not trusting herself to speak.

"Lydia says you are teaching here, yet we have not spoken."

It was then she noticed how good his Elvish had become, and in spite of the anger, she felt a bit of pride. She shrugged again. "I have no need to talk to you."

His brows furrowed and his eyes reflected the hurt he felt. She watched some realization sweep over him, and his shoulders slumped. "I am that unimportant to you?"

The anger rose and she lashed out before she could stop. "No! You should know that's not it!"

"Then what is it Vivien?"

"It's what you did, in the council chamber. You had no right to do what you did!"

His gaze reflected surprise and shock. "I came in and I helped you. We stood together like we did when we fought the bears."

"No, you came in thinking you could save me. I don't need you, or anyone, trying to save me! Lydia was my responsibility. I deserved her sentence AND mine. You took that away from me."

He digested her words, then tried to find the suitable ones to utter back to her in Elvish, his mouth opening and closing like a giant fish. He raised his arms and the cuffs he was forced to wear winked in the light, stabbing her with guilt.

She continued, "This happened for all to see, for all to scrutinize. You have no idea what you did to me that day!"

When he couldn't find the words, he didn't bother reverting to Lairdstongue. Instead he closed himself away like a genie in a bottle.

"I don't need you Wolf! I can protect myself, and I have responsibilities. I don't need you running around here trying to divest me of them in the name of help. Just...just leave me alone!"

With that, she proceeded past him up the stairs and into the Lady's apartment suite.

The Wolf just stood there, alone and broken.

Chapter Nineteen
Seduction

The Lord of Ice and Steel knew when his wife was home. He could hear her speaking to that infernal feline he'd brought for her when they were newly married. What Vivien didn't know was that the cub was the last of a large litter, small compared to its heartier siblings, and unwanted by anyone who came to see it. Tor had taken the poor, ugly, cub out of pity, and thought to offer it to his wife, who seemed to have a propensity for pathetic things.

Vivien named the cub a variant of the Elvish word for 'moonlight', *Sherika*. Who knew that drab gray cub would grow into the gorgeous, lithe form he would see a year later. The pitch black color was the absence of light, but if anyone asked Vivien, the tir-reath was all the light in her world.

Torialvah squelched his feelings of annoyance and instead focused on his wife's voice. It was like none other he'd heard before, not too high like many women, but definitely not low enough to be a man. It had a sultry tone to it that stirred him if he allowed it, and when he first brought her home fifty years ago, he did.

Tor moved away from the entryway and into the hall leading to the bedchamber before she opened the door. Let her be forced to find him as opposed to him just standing there, waiting for her like a fool. He'd already sounded enough an idiot by the message he'd sent, imploring her to come home.

Tor entered the bedchamber and walked over to the window. He stood there, looking out, and frowned. Once, they had been on good terms, but Shaladrea would get no favors from him in the future. The Lady of Moonlight and Love had another thing coming if she thought she could monopolize Vivien, especially during wartime for a cause he did not want her being a part of. He didn't care that she was the best in her class, or that she ranked higher than the other mages of her status. First and foremost, she was his wife, and that mattered more than anything right now, especially when she could bear him a child, a child that that would rank above most others in Rithalion, not just because it would be a high-born elf, but one that had arcane ancestry.

Vivien had never mentioned wanting a child, and he'd never really thought much of it himself, until recently. The impending war had everyone in a tizzy, and more than once he'd gotten the question, "Lord, have you and your beautiful wife yet considered the future? Should she really be out there on the front lines, when she could be here at home heavy with your son or daughter?"

He'd grown to hate that question, but he had come to see the truth in it.

Indeed, why was Vivien defending Lords and Ladies from ambushers when she could be in his bed giving him the sons and daughters needed to make Rithalion strong again? And even if she wasn't in his bed at all, why did she need to be the one on the front lines? Find another warmage to be there. Certainly there was another that would work just as well?

Tor turned away from the window when he heard her enter the bedchamber. She was a vision of beauty, wearing a gown he'd never seen before, wavy gold hair tinged with red falling over one shoulder, gray-green eyes wide with uncertainty, lips curved downward in the pout that he always liked.

"Thank you for responding to my message and coming home."

Her brow furrowed and bewilderment crossed her face. She walked across the chamber until she stood in front of him. "I don't understand; why do you need me here?"

He reached out and stroked her hair. She blinked in surprise and just stood there, seemingly not knowing what to do, or what to say.

"I know you are busy, as am I, but knowing you are here at the end of every day is comforting. Since you have been staying away, I have come to realize what your presence here means to me." He stepped close, deliberately entering her personal space. He watched her grapple with her desire to step away, but ultimately accepted him there.

He stepped closer and plunged his fingers into the thick waves of her hair. "I miss you in my bed," he whispered.

Her breathing stopped and she just stood there, her eyes wide.

"I have missed you there for a long time."

A flash of sadness crossed her face. "Why have you never told me this before?"

Tor studied her for a moment, wondering what she was feeling. He always had such a hard time reading her, when he never seemed to have a problem with anyone else. He struggled to answer her question and finally arrived with a vague reply. "I didn't know how."

She gave a heavy swallow and simply nodded.

"I'm tired of arguing, Vivien. I want us to do what we both do best and then come home and share our lives together. I want us to have children to share that life."

Her expression shifted to mild consternation. "Wait...what?"

"Yes, I want to have children together. With the war coming, it's been on my mind. Rithalion needs the new blood. WE need it for our family."

She shook her head. "No, it's a terrible time...much too dangerous for a child!"

He caressed the side of her face, bringing his hand down the curve of her neck to the swell of her breast. His breath hitched in his throat. He hadn't allowed himself to get this close to her in a long while. The scent of her was intoxicating, and the soft feel of her stole away his senses. "Now is the perfect time."

Her voice wavered. "I have a job to do, and people are relying on me. I...I can't have a baby now."

"Vivien," he breathed her name into her ear and gently steered her backward towards the large bed that dominated the room, "stay with me." He kissed her cheek, then trailed his lips down to her neck. He heard her soft intake of breath and he felt a tightening in his groin. He always enjoyed hearing the small sounds she made during lovemaking, and this was just the beginning.

She put her hands on his chest. "Tor, wait..."

He pushed her back and followed her down onto the soft pillows. He poised his lips above hers. "I want you here with me. Need you."

"Torialvah, why now? Can't we talk more about this?"

She sounded breathless and he smiled as his lips gently brushed hers. He'd had taken many women in his three hundred years, and he knew he was a good lover. He'd always had a strong affect on Vivien, and he loved bringing her to her knees. "Talking can wait."

He crushed his lips to hers with fierce abandon, pressing her into the pillows. He wrapped one arm around her waist while sweeping the other over her breasts, down her belly, to slide over her that place between her thighs. She moaned against his lips and pressed her hands to his chest again.

She barely managed to turn her face away, her voice a raspy whisper, "Tor, please stop."

He slid his hand to her back and his fingers easily worked the clasps to her gown. She made to speak again, but his lips locked back onto hers, kissing away any thoughts of resistance. He slid the gown down over her shoulders to expose full, milky white breasts. The nipples already stood at attention, just waiting for him to suckle them.

His arousal pressed painfully against his pants. His lips tore away from hers as he reached down to release himself, his voice deep with the lust built up for months of keeping her from him. He didn't even remember why he'd done it, but for the fact that she constantly infuriated him one way or another. "Why would I stop? You are my wife, and I want you, Vivien." His voice shifted so low it was almost a growl. "And I know you want me."

Again, the pressure of her hands against his chest, and his sex throbbed in response. Gods, she'd never been so insistent before, and he found he was enjoying it. He drew one nipple into his mouth, suckled it the way their children would once they were born. He heard her hiss, realized he must be pulling too hard, and brought his lips back up to hers. Despite her staying hands against his chest, Vivien returned the kiss.

The gesture sent a wave of heat washing over him, urging him on. Torialvah grabbed the skirt of the gown and began pulling it up. When he was done, it bunched around her hips to reveal the length of her shapely legs, the curve of her hips, and the lacy smallclothes hiding her womanhood. He put his hand there and shifted the fabric aside, feeling the wet heat of her envelop his fingers.

Yes, she wanted him. She always wanted him.

She moaned as he shifted over her, her hands once again putting pressure on his chest. She arched her back, her hips pressing upward against him, and he bit back his own groan of response. He released her mouth and took her hips in both hands, positioning her beneath him. Her tone was a breathy whisper in his ear, a plea, "Tor...Tor, wait..."

He pushed hard and Vivien cried out with pleasure. She took his breath away and he knew he would never keep her from him again.

Chapter Twenty
The Run

Once, he had a home. Once, he had a name. No more. He had lived for longer than he could really remember as a being of passion, of action. He had traded at dozens of villages, met hundreds of people. Yet, he had never been at home. Instead he always retreated to the safety of the woods and the wild, the only thing he understood. It was a place of bounty, of beauty, but it would try to kill if it was taken for granted. He knew its fickle care and accepted it as it accepted him. Winter had settled in without disturbance by the elvin people in these pristine lands. The silence of the sleeping winter world allowed his internal chaos to burn freely. It was here that he ran.

Unknowable rage fueled him like a blacksmith's forge. It was the only warmth he had, the only power to keep the dark thoughts of his past at bay. Whenever it lagged, he felt weightless, spinning in midair as the earth came to kiss him with rocky, fatal teeth. Shirt discarded miles ago, skin steaming as flakes melted on his shoulders and in his hair, his legs churned drifts of snow in a ragged line. His kilt flapped in a sudden burst of wind and he dodged giant oaks older than most kingdoms in his need to escape.

His legs hammered the ground and ice like he hated them. Silent sentinels of green, brown, and white flashed by as he tore the strip of cloth from his hair and let it fly free. He tossed it to the wind and bounded forward, seeking to put mile after mile between himself and Vivien's barbed words. He leapt a fallen log poking from the blankets of white, and then tumbled face forward as if dragged there by chains.

The Wolf heaved himself to his knees, arms pinioned to the ground by unimaginable force. He felt the bronze manacles of the elves grow hotter, and he pulled them, sizzling, from the snow only with great effort. They sought the ground as if carved into the side of the mountain, and though he growled and screamed, he barely managed to gain his feet. His arms trembled and burned with exertion, his joints popped as muscles thrummed with fury. He pulled at them, bit at them, and slammed the manacles together. The seamless bronze rings were unperturbed, unmarked, and unaffected by his anger. He roared at nothingness, wishing for a release, a target for his wrath, but none appeared. Instead his feet spoke his defiance, one before the other as the manacles moved further from their home and became heavier and heavier. He moved onward, faster and faster despite the unearthly burden, breaking into a run as the snow began to fall in earnest and covering where he was going, and where he had been.

He entered the next treeline, manacles sizzling and popping as flakes fell upon them, arms straight at his sides from the tension of their pull. He dove into a dark shadow between trees. He suddenly felt as if the world was shifting and his feet had trouble finding the ground. Moments later he burst from the treeline and into a long, wide clearing. He stumbled again, but the weight, the heat, were both gone. He skidded to a stop, chest heaving and expelling thick clouds of steamy breath. He spun, but saw nothing but forest surrounding him. He looked for his tracks in the snow, but they were not there.

What?

His eyes caught movement.

His shoulders hunched, and muscles bulged, fingers curled like claws forged of loss and anger. He roared and it blazed through the swirling flakes.

Ten steps away stood a wolf. Brown and black, with a muzzle gone gray, the creature dripped blood from a dozen wounds. It had been savaged and torn. One ear was missing, one eye swelled shut and bleeding from a fresh cut. He was an old soul, once in charge of his pack through many winters, and now defeated and exiled by a younger warrior. The animal raised his head and growled weakly.

The Wolf could feel the animal's loss of home, safety, and family. He could sense the emptiness inside of him, the realization that everything that made life worth living had been taken, and yet the body continued onward. His mental walls crumbled and he felt himself in freefall. Tears blinded the barbarian and streamed down his face in continuous lines. Two warriors faced one another without reason to live or reason to fight. The human fell to his knees and sobbed.

The wolf, unable to cry, unable to speak, came forward on shaking legs. He came up to the barbarian and looked into his eyes. Then he lay against him for warmth. The huge man gathered the animal into his arms and wept. He wept for murdered dreams and lost lives, for a wide swath of pain that had torn his heart so long he didn't know how to live without it, for the open scars that now wept in his soul. After so long alone in the wild, he did not think in words with this pain. Countless images flashed through his head. He relived them all, knowing without a doubt that he would always be worthless, unwanted, alone, abandoned. Even Vivien had cast him aside, and there was no light left in his soul without her.

The sun finally set, the moon rose, and the wolf died.

No matter what the elves whispered about him he was only human, without tools, he had no way to carve out the frozen ground. It wasn't how wolves died anyway. There was a sad thought there for him, a foreboding he accepted for its utter truth and naked doom. With the body of the dead wolf in his arms, he walked into the far line of trees. After a few moments more, he lay the body down.

"You..." He spun at the voice, reaching for a weapon that was not there. Beside a tree stood the fur-cloaked Lord of Swords and Truth. "...have been given a powerful sign, Wolf."

The Lord had always been rough, but kind This was one of two... now the only elf that seemed to actually enjoy his presence, given him respect. And he had been trying to flee his lawful sentence. The Wolf, staring at the ground, said nothing.

Xadrian watched him closely, then shook his bald head. "You have lost your shirt. Come, we are close to my manor."

The Wolf's brows beetled, but after they had gone a few dozen paces, they exited the copse of trees and saw the sprawling, wooden structure that Xadrian and his servants called home. It was rough hewn, and made of tightly carved and interlocked logs. It was built as if the Lord had spent too much time in the wilds, and never felt comfortable in the fanciful artistry of his people. Confusion whirled in his head, and the Wolf turned in place, looking to through the thin canopy to find direction. Xadrian smiled and took him by the arm. "You left the city boundaries, and we were told. *She* brought you here."

The Wolf frowned. "She? Who brought...?"

Xadrian opened the simple door and ushered the Wolf in. "Let us not speak her name, lest we summon her."

The answering voice was like sunlight filtered through honey, devoid of anger but tinged with sadness. "Summon who, my love?"

Xadrian breathed a deep sigh as he came in after the Wolf, unbuckling his sword belt and putting the broken Arisil in the mostly empty sheath on the stag head stand by the entryway. The Wolf saw a heavy weight sink deeply onto his shoulders and into his soul. "No one. Please do not call me that."

The Wolf, shirtless and dripping with melted snow, nodded to The Lady of Moonlight and Love, but kept his distance. The barbarian had noticed how everyone was in awe of her, had noticed that she was always haloed in some kind of light that reached out and sought to entrance any who saw her. It wasn't that he was unmoved, but that it never reached the deepest parts of him the way it did others. She was fantastically beautiful, but she could not replace Vivien's name in his soul. Her presence enveloped him in a warm embrace and she stepped forward to put a hand on his chest. "You went past the boarders of Rithalion. Why?"

The Wolf could not stop his face from showing his guilt. He averted his eyes. Xadrian was the one who spoke, his tone gruff. "Don't answer that. She never asks a question unless she knows the answer."

The bald man hung up his cloak and walked into the main room devoid of decorative halls or fancy carvings. The inside was as much as the outside as it could be. Posts were carved as trees that spread to support the roof. Rooms were partitioned in upper boughs by screens of wooden leaves. The main floor held fallen logs carved into well worn chairs and couches. Books sat in readiness along shelves carved from standing stones. A bar in the corner held bottles in niches of a crystal waterfall, twinkling with lights that shone through from the other side. A fire pit in the center of the room was burning low. Xadrian moved stiffly to the stack of logs and tossed two onto it, smoke and sparks flying upward into a chimney hood above and out into the world.

Shaladrea watched him sadly, her light feeling melancholy. "Why say such things, love?"

Xadrian turned from her and went to the crystal waterfall. "It is true, is it not?" The Wolf said nothing, but saw a deep longing in them both, and guessed it was for one another. They were so close, so familiar, but separated by vast oceans of grief and loss. He watched them both and felt a kinship for Xadrian grow, for he could understand that pain. In the silence that followed, the master of the house selected one bottle and poured two drinks.

Shaladrea bowed her head and closed her eyes, then turned back to the Wolf. "He is very hurt—"

Xadrian pushed past her and shoved a glass of something into the Wolf's unresisting hands. "Do not speak of our business, Shaladrea."

Now, as she stood only inches away, he could feel the true measure of the deep well of sadness within the Lady, feel her ache and sorrow. She had borne it a long time, and it had become a part of her. That too he could understand, as had he ever since…

"It is of the Wolf whom I speak." She affixed The Lord of Swords and Truth with those eyes, those beautiful golden eyes, and the Wolf felt the Lord's mental walls buckle, his heart quiver and quail though his face remained impassive, stoic. "He is in love, and it hurts him. I am sorry for it, but I cannot heal him. He will have to mend on his own."

Her words lit a fire inside Xadrian, and he frowned. "And if he can not?"

The Lord didn't flinch, didn't move, as the Lady placed a hand on his cheek. "I have hope."

Then she left, as gracefully as ever, out the front door. Her presence, a deafening music, left a shamed silence. Xadrian drained his glass and moved to the fire. He stared into it as the low flames ate at the fresh logs, becoming a dancing oracle of chaos.

The Wolf watched emotions war upon the commander's face, and felt his resignation as he sat heavily on a carved, wooden seat. The Lord's pain was so similar to his own, and yet the Lord could find peace, even let the warmth of the fire comfort him. Gathering courage, he finally spoke. "You love her."

Xadrian gave a brief chuckle. "Everyone loves her."

Quietly, the Wolf came over and sat down next to the Lord of Swords and Truth. He sipped the blackberry brandy and it burned a path down to his belly. He made a face as he set down the glass. Xadrian watched him, realization dawning. "But you don't."

Their eyes met. The Lord saw the truth, but the Wolf saw back. He spoke slowly "You love her like no one else, Lord of Swords."

Xadrian looked away into the fire, seeming to take solace in the formless dance. "We were married once." The silence pressed in, heavy. "I was her second husband. Her first had died in the war." And again, heavier. "We had many children." He could feel the silence, barely scratched by the crackle of the logs being consumed. "They all died in the flood…at Pergatium."

The Wolf nodded, staring at the floor. Silence reigned. He felt a pressure, a need, long forgotten, to share his pain. "I had a son. I lost him."

Xadrian started, running a hand over his bald head in search of hair he had long since shorn to the scalp. He blinked at the Wolf, an expression akin to bewilderment on his face, almost like he couldn't imagine him as a nurturing parent. The Wolf's mind felt at the ragged edges of the hole left by his son, a boy he would never hold, and felt it still raw and bloody. He appreciated the Lord and Lady even more.

"What happened?"

The Wolf's thoughts turned inward and darkened. Memories wreaked havoc in his mind, images that hadn't visited in decades coming to the fore. He remembered falling. Screaming. And then after...after... But he was still aware of Xadrian, very aware. The elvin warrior shifted uncomfortably as the Wolf's fingers curved inwards to massage his palms. He felt naked with no weapon, his spine tingling as if he were caught in an ambush and he wished more for battle and rage to shut off the memories that screamed and cried inside. He met Xadrian's eyes and knew the Lord guessed right, the human itched to have a weapon in his hands.

Hatred surged through the Wolf, hatred of what he had become and who had helped make him this way. He snatched up the brandy, downing in one gulp. His throat burned as he spoke. "He was murdered."

Xadrian sat and waited. And waited some more. He picked up the glasses, filled them nearly full from a bottle of clear liquid, handed one to the Wolf, and sat down again. They drank in silence, the harsh liquor stinging all the way down and writhing in his belly like a snake.

"Wolf, why did you take on Lady Valdera's punishment?"

The Wolf raised a brow, the answer without a possibility of any other, "Because I love her."

Xadrian shook his head. "She's married, and a warmage. Because of her arcane lineage, her destiny was to always be with a pure blood elf. Her husband is unlikely to allow her to take any other partners."

The human's heart beat hard in his chest, like a war gong. He affixed the Lord with an intense stare. "I know."

The Lord shifted in his seat, uncomfortable, but forging on. "That explains Vivien. But what about the child? The child who fell?" At the word 'fell' the Wolf felt a shock travel through his mind to his heart and he blanched. "The one at the bridge?"

Taken off guard, desperately trying to battle his memories back into caves set in his head, the Wolf's reply was shaky. "It was a child."

"You would do it again, wouldn't you?"

The Wolf paused only for a heartbeat. "Yes."

Xadrian set down his glass. "Even if Vivien cannot love you back, will you help me defend my nation? All the children within it?"

The Wolf lifted a bronze manacle.

"No! Not because you are told to and not because of her!" Xadrian was adamant. "Will you do it? Will you remember to never run away from that responsibility?"

The Wolf looked deep within himself. He remembered being useful, needed. At one time he had served and been served. He remembered community, acceptance, and purpose. He craved them, wished for them with almost as much power as he desired Vivien's forgiveness. He nodded.

Xadrian nodded back, picked up his glass again, and drank.

The fire popped and crackled as they sat in silence. The longer it went on, the more the Wolf could secret his memories into deep recesses, and the more Xadrian seemed to relax. Finally, there was a measure of peace, and the Wolf remembered Vivien, from before, when she trusted and wanted to see him. The Lord of Swords and Truth spoke. "You know, few living souls know how to appreciate a good silence. So much importance can be said in silence."

The Wolf, torn from his thoughts, regarded Xadrian thoughtfully. The older man, somehow divining his unspoken pain, did not press or pry. He simply nodded. They continued to sit there, and more silence reigned. The Wolf finally glanced at his companion again and knew that, as his mind had taken him to Vivien, the Lord's had taken him to his Lady of Moonlight and Love...

Chapter Twenty-One
Understanding

Vivien sat, alone, in her chamber suite. It was the same one she always had when she stayed with Shaladrea, a small tower located on the east side of the fortress. It had a bedroom, a study, a bathing room, and even a large arena for the practice of weaponry, or spells, or whatever she chose. This time she lay, slumped, over the plush sofa in the sitting room. Sherika sat on her feet, keeping them warm as she liked to do. Sadness and guilt enveloped her like a shroud, stripping away all other thought and leaving her cold and barren.

What was that? What had her husband done to her? She loved the thought that he'd magically found his affection for her, and that he truly wanted her. His seduction had shown her that, indeed, maybe he had. But it had also shown her other things, things that made her belly roil with confusion, and more frighteningly, fear.

He would be angry when he saw that she had left. After their lovemaking the day before, they had fallen asleep in one another's arms. He had spoken words of kindness and love and devotion, words he'd never bothered to speak before. He would feel a fool for having said them, and she could only imagine what his words would be when he saw her message telling him she'd gone back to the Lady's fortress.

No talking. No discussion. No anything. She'd simply left while he was out because she was too much of a coward to do it while he was there.

Vivien rose from her place, smiling when Sherika gave a squeak from her place on the floor. The tir-reath didn't mind staying with her indoors, much preferring her company than the open world of the outside as long as she had an adequate place to relieve herself. So Vivien had created that place, made of the fine shifting sands that dominated the banks of the lake Shaladrea had at the center of the wood behind her fortress.

Vivien went to the door and grabbed the hooded cloak hanging nearby. She had a long day ahead, but first, she had someone she needed to see before she proceeded with any of those things.

She walked town the tower stairs and into the vast hallways of Shaladrea's fortress. In her mind she picked it apart, saw all the defensible places and who might be arming them, saw the reinforced walls, the battlements high above, the massive gate made of three layers of Elvish steel. She wasn't precisely sure where she was going, but eventually made it out one of the rear doors. She found herself exactly where she wanted to be...the practice fields.

She walked among the fields, arena after arena of mud-spattered elvin men straining against one another with sword, hammer, and mace. She'd never seen anything like it before, accustomed to the traditional sword, spear, and bow. Before long she found the man she was looking for, just as filthy as all the rest.

Vivien stood beside the arena in which the Wolf was working. Within were two men with swords, each trying to get the upper hand over the other. Neither was above using brute strength to nail his opponent into the ground, which consisted of at least a half foot of mud. She watched in fascination, never having watched such a bestial display before, and it was then he noticed her standing there.

Shock was the first expression to cross his face, followed by sadness. Then all feeling seemed to leave him entirely as he slowly walked around the periphery of the arena. She watched him approach and felt much of the same sadness he must have been feeling. Finally he stood before her, his dark eyes taking her in the way they always did. They seemed to see every part of her, not just the parts everyone liked to see most.

"Vivien."

"Wolf."

"Can I do something for you?"

She nodded. "Yes, actually you can. I can see you are busy, but I was hoping you could give me some moments of your time."

He shrugged.

Vivien hesitated, not knowing if that was a yes or a no, but when he didn't turn to walk away, she took it as a yes. "When we spoke yesterday, I was very harsh."

The Wolf was impassive and remained silent.

Suddenly nervous, she swallowed convulsively. "I understand why you did what you did, even though I didn't want you to do it. I understand it wasn't all about just protecting me and that you thought of us as a partnership. You wanted to take the fall WITH me, not FOR me." She caught his gaze and looked into his eyes. "I don't want you to just 'leave me alone'. You are important to me and I want your friendship."

He nodded, sadly, then reached out one large finger and ran it down her arm, touching the places where her geas lay, and then held up the hand as a fist, showing off his manacle. "You have it. Always."

She smiled then, a smile that enveloped her being and touched her heart. "Thank you. I will always remember this moment, and hope you will do the same."

Close behind her, Vivien heard the sound of a man's throat clearing, and she turned to find the Lord of Swords and Truth standing there. She gave a slight inclination of her head. "Lord, it is good to see you; it has been a long time."

"Mistress Vivien, as always, it is good to see you too. I am here because I would like to ask how your students are getting along in their studies."

"They are doing very well, some better than others. I believe that all of them will be ready within a week or two."

Xadrian nodded. "The men have been working hard and I believe they will be ready by then as well." He turned to the Wolf. "There are many units we have been training, but we have a new plan for dealing with the men and their iron dust." His steely eyes shifted to the Wolf, "It's your men that will be working with the spellcasters. The soldiers will defend, the wizards will cast."

The barbarian's eyes widened, considered this, then nodded grimly. "Master Xadrian, that...that is an honor. I know how much this means. Are you certain you wish to place your hopes on me?"

Xadrian looked back and forth from him to Vivien. "We are placing our hopes not just on you, but Mistress Vivien as well."

Vivien stammered, "Lord...this is a fledgling idea. It sounds like you are placing a lot of faith in this. It may not work."

Xadrian gave a toothy smile. "It will work. Shaladrea and I believe you will make it work. Together." His voice rose. "We need to win this war!" He raised a fist for emphasis.

Vivien turned to look at the Wolf, only to find him staring at her. His dark eyes bore a look of concern, but more than that, fierce determination.

Glancing within herself, she realized there was no one else with whom she'd like to take on such a monumental task. "We will try our best for you and our people, Lord."

She hesitantly smiled at the Wolf. While his expression had not changed, there was an intensity there. She knew who would be standing beside her in the midst of battle. It gave her a strange feeling, one she could not identify.

The Wolf was first at the practice fields every morning. He was also the last one to leave. He instructed with a rough, silent manner, the lesser elvin troops respecting his skill and fearing his utter abandon in battle. The mages were unsettled at first, but over time, they also garnered a guarded respect for him. They called him An'drath, 'dark one', but the barbarian never seemed to notice. The mages groused about how hard he marched them, how he forgave no mistake, how he loomed with ferocious disappointment, until they saw how harshly he treated the soldiers.

Vivien and the Wolf stayed up late at night, talking hour after hour about their plans. The Wolf absorbed everything she had to say, crafting the two units, spellcasters and soldiers, into one hardened fist. When they entered battle, they would be a synchronized unit. They had practiced for weeks, and were becoming a single entity that fought with utter ferocity tempered with wisdom and discipline.

All lives were precious, but the casters were able to bring the fae to the battle. With the humans covered in iron, the soldiers were the literal shields that would bleed and die to keep them safe. At the same time, Vivien had made extensive efforts to research battlefield enchantments. Normally reserved for warmages to use on their own weapons and armor, they would now be used to make each warrior into a wielder of light, ice, thorns, and fire.

Vivien walked the periphery of the field. Her fingers twitched as she watched the two groups come together with wooden hammers, the ones playing the elves attacking with learned aggressiveness, seeking to demolish the heavily armored faux humans. She instinctively called the fae, and she felt hot needles along her spine. She shook off the call and the feeling faded. She wanted so much to be there when the battle was joined, to fight for her people. The pain was only a vague annoyance now, but for some reason, she couldn't quite shut the aether away. It nettled her and she would have to meditate on it later.

The Wolf, in the middle of the chaos, roared, "ARROWS!"

As one, the mages ducked and the soldiers stood tall, shields becoming a roof under which the spellcasters then sent waves of fae to assault the lines of elves playing at humans, keeping them from whittling at the soldiers providing their protection. A dozen heartbeats and then the Wolf roared again, "ARROWS LANDED!"

The mages summoned fae of the earth, causing lines of 'humans' to fall. The soldiers lowered their shields and went at them with hammers and maces, 'dispatching' whole rows of them before engaging again with the far smaller force. The weapons were brutal, the tactics ferocious, but they would crack open the iron armor in a way an elegant sword could not.

The Lord of Swords and Truth left his planning table in the far center of the practice fields and approached to walk beside Vivien. She nodded in greeting. They watched the Wolf set the men with what seemed an instinctual knowledge, smiling savagely as the maneuver went flawlessly. She shook her head. "It is like he was born to it."

Xadrian looked at her in surprise. "You think so?"

Vivien smiled, an expression that faded at the edges at his honest skepticism. "Is he not?"

Xadrian seemed to consider this, then nodded. He raised his arm at the practice battle. "Wolf! A word!"

The Wolf called a hold, extricated himself from the elves in their tattered, muddy, padded regalia and jogged through ankle deep slush to the two of them. Vivien watched him come, seeing the economy of movement, appreciating the powerful stride. He nodded to Xadrian, and then focused just a second upon her. His eyes were a bonfire that doused her with heat.

Xadrian ignored the look. "I need your opinion." The Wolf nodded and they traversed the slushy field to the central table next to a single tent. A map of Elvish lands and those beyond had been set there, edges pinned by an ornate bronze compass, an overturned glass, a dagger, and a rock. "Here is the Iron Coast. Here is Rithalion. Their forces have to come through this pass in the mountains here." He pointed to the map. "We must decide where to meet them. Many advise stopping them at the pass mouth. Others want to wait at the Lady's fortress at the edge of the gorge. Which do you prefer?"

The Lord stood back, waiting. Vivien watched, and had her own opinion, but she was trained to think about the moment to moment of a battle. This was a larger thought that had many factors she had not considered. It seemed unfair to ask the Wolf—

The barbarian stabbed a finger over one section, inside the forest, but far from the gorge. "Here. Meet them here."

Xadrian frowned. "But that is neither of the places I have suggested."

The human shrugged, "Both answers are wrong. If you wait here, they will spend months, maybe years, collecting trees to run their war machine, buy more mercenaries, and collect strength and build forts. They will be hard to dig out. If you meet them at the mountain pass, you will be too far from your supply lines." He pointed at the spot again. "Here."

Xadrian considered it. "Why?"

"To the east is Dreaming Lake. To the west is a steep slope into Pergatium, a swamp and a wall created by the mountains, The Two Brothers. It will box them in and funnel their forces so you know just where they will be. The ground closer to the pass will not sustain a fortress of any size." He folded his arms, "And our wagon trains of food and supplies are protected from attack if they have more forces coming behind."

Xadrian nodded. "Anything else?"

The Wolf considered it for a moment. His brow furrowed deeply and he frowned. "Yes. A flanking force should circle around the peaks through Pergatium."

Vivien gasped, her insides quivering slightly at the name. "Elves don't go near the Doomed City."

The Wolf shook his head. "They should."

Xadrian smiled dismissively. "The place is treacherous. A force of any size will get lost there, lose men. No one knows the lay of the land."

The Wolf closed his eyes, steeling himself. "I do." Vivien went cold. She could feel the shock coming off Xadrian in waves. "And a force, powerful but small, could make the trip. They could circle the enemy and hit their lines from behind, destroy their archers and generals if they are lucky. Certainly burn the baggage train and the food they need to move forward. Catch them between hammer and anvil." He glanced meaningfully where the unit Vivien and he were training had reset for another run. "And we have such a force right here."

Xadrian had gone pale. He nodded at the Wolf and gave a curt dismissal. Vivien watched the big man run back to his unit. They howled a greeting at him. He returned it in kind.

Vivien almost smiled at how the men had accepted him, almost adopted him as one of their own. His final words, however, still stung. "We can't go into Pergatium."

Xadrian shook his head, banishing ghosts that danced behind his eyes. "No, he is right. We must."

Vivien felt herself go cold again. A tingle went up and down her arms, across her spine. "It is madness!"

The Lord nodded, his steel gray eyes boring into her. "Then maybe the way out of the madness of this war lies through insanity itself."

Vivien shook her head and glanced back at the Wolf, who was calling for the men to reform and start again. Her vision wavered briefly, and she caught herself against the table before she stumbled. "So what did that prove, general? Asking his opinion?"

The Lord kept his feet through willpower alone, searching the map over and over, looking over the options, seeing the possibilities. "Fighting bears in the wood will make a man fierce. It will make a man strong. This, this is something different. No one is born to look at a map like that."

Vivien's brow furrowed, and she shook her head as the dizzy spell lasted a bit longer than she expected. "What do you mean?"

"I saw the map and knew just how to read the line, knew that the place he pointed to is where we should hold our line, the exact spot I chose myself. I spoke with my generals and they all agree. None thought to flank through the Doomed City, but he is right, this is the best place to meet an enemy." Xadrian frowned at the Wolf as he voiced his thoughts long unsaid. "Someone taught that man to lead men into combat, to wage war. That takes time and it takes power." He sighed. "The Wolf fought for someone in his past, and he was a leader of men. That much is certain." Xadrian's expression suddenly shifted to concern. "Lady Valdera, are you all right?"

Vivien blinked a few times, put a hand to her forehead, and leaned against the table. "Lord, I feel...I feel unwell."

Xadrian grunted. "Go rest. Tell no one of my suspicions or of the plan to go through Pergatium. I will assemble the other generals in the next few days."

Vivien nodded distractedly and left the field. She climbed the many steps to the fortress of Moonlight and Love, and then many more into the tower the Lady kept for her. She stripped from the customary attire for a warmage, the bottom of the pants muddy from the fields and the long tunic spattered with the same. Naked, she settled onto the ermine fur rug in front of the fireplace, legs folded under her, and centered herself.

Her muscles began to relax. The warmth of the fire helped as she imagined great roots growing from her legs into the stone of the castle, and billowing clouds escaping her mind as she let go of all her stray thoughts. She lost her focus when another dizzy spell swept over her, accompanied by mild nausea. She lay back on the rug, rubbed her backside on the thick softness. She'd been feeling strange since she'd awakened that morning, and thinking back on it, she'd been feeling a bit lackluster the entire past two days.

What is wrong with me? Why do I feel so out of sorts? I just want to go back to the practice field and be with the unit.

Vivien rose and walked over to her discarded clothing. She bent to pick up the muddy pants when a thought flitted through her mind and struck her dumb. The realization almost toppled her to the floor and she stumbled over and barely caught herself against the bedpost.

No, it can't be. But it was. She was certain of it.

Vivien spent the next two days in a haze. It was a secret she kept to herself, for there was no one she wanted to tell. She'd never had many friends growing up under the shadow of the Grand Magister. Girls always seemed to be too intimidated by her uncanny arcane skill, and friendships with young men fled with her marriage to Torialvah. Her only confidante for a long time had been Lydia, but these days her age was catching up to her, and the old woman spent more days just resting, eating and slowly ambling about the fortress grounds. Vivien had a good friend in the Wolf. They had become close the last two weeks as they trained the unit for combat. But somehow, she didn't think he would take news like this very well, and she hated to compromise a friendship that had barely lifted off the ground.

A small part of her wanted to tell Tor. He would be happy about it. It was what he wanted, after all. She remembered the night they shared with mixed feelings, and now saw the seduction for what it was. He'd been angry when she left early the following morning after he'd gone to the forges for the day. He'd sent her a hateful message two days later telling her how bad of a wife she was, and how he deserved so much better. She'd ripped it up and thrown it into the fireplace, watched as the flames burned it into ash. She'd then refocused herself and went out to the practice fields to participate in her first session alongside the Wolf.

Certainly Torialvah would be happy he'd gotten from her what he wanted, but he would also try and make her come back home, uncaring of her work here. He would get his way of course, and use her delicate condition to do it. And she would sit there in his house all day, all night, with nothing.

By the third day, Vivien accepted her lot in life. The haze lifted and she knew what she had to do. She had important work, work that might mean the difference between victory and defeat, between life and death. She would take extra care of herself as she set upon her task, and she would keep the secret to herself until she could no longer do so. She was happy, happier than she had been in a long time. Even though Tor got what he wanted, she realized it was something she wanted as well.

For the child resting inside her wasn't just Tor's, it was hers too. And she had fallen in love with it.

Chapter Twenty-Two
Simrudian the Spy

In Rithalion, everyone of worth was elvin. Others denied it, but Simrudian knew it to be true. He stood and walked back to the road, drawing a branch over his tracks to cover them in the snow. The air was cold, but as he hitched up the human-made, iron long knife at his hip and the mandolin on his shoulder, he felt the familiar flutter in his chest and smiled. He looked to the spot where two pine trees leaned together into an arch near the road and marked it well. If anything went wrong, this would be his first stash of emergency supplies. He had many more leading like a trail of breadcrumbs back to Rithalion. He would not need them. He never did.

He was a low-elf... not half, not even a quarterling. His parents had fought bitterly in the years after he was born, when his ears never lengthened and became pointed, when his eyes never developed their almond shape. His father, a half-elf, was aware that society leaned towards multiple partners, but his wife had dedicated herself to him in honor of First Rights Tradition in order to be sure to give him a child. But then there was a boy who was clearly no elf at all. His father had left in a rage, and by the time the truth of his Elvish heritage was discovered, neither Sim nor his mother had any need of him.

Sim had grown up in a world where everyone saw him as a human. And in that, was his strength. Sim knew he was elvin. He had grown up talking easily, playing music effortlessly, teasing out secrets from others masterfully. When Lord Kilcahann had approached him in his youth, it almost had seemed inevitable. He had been given purpose, and he was eternally grateful. He may have passed his years back home without ever doing anything meaningful, set aside for more Elvish-looking suitors. Out here, in the world, his Elvishness helped him in every way. The hidden nature of his blood made it so any human enemy would never notice. So it would be with the Iron Coast.

So he hummed a happy tune as he came down out of Swordbite Pass. He rounded a bend and caught sight of the massed, stinking beast far below, the city of Swordbite. Again his heart fluttered, for he knew what awaited. He picked up his pace.

Sim had been there seven years ago, and remembered the dirty streets, the flat stone buildings. He had entertained at the homes of the rich the last time. Now he would stay on the street of inns, and almost certainly not meet anyone he had contact with before. Within hours, the hunkered, blunt, uninspired architecture became easy to pick out from the black and gray background. Chimneys belched stinking smoke into the sky, some from cooking fires, but most from the endless forges that went day and night. The forest, thin and young to begin with, ended abruptly, with stumps marching all the way to the city gates. The whole country was like this, stripped to naked ground and then some, leaving gaping holes looking for coal, tar, and metals to feed the war machine sold to any country with a bidder. They truly had little left.

To the north of the city, opposite from where he stood, there were masses of men composing a mighty army. For a moment his soul fluttered to see the veritable ocean of tents that marked their camp. It was truly a gigantic force. He estimated the tents and gave up somewhere around fifteen thousand men. He saw large pens for exercising horses, massive iron cages made for some gargantuan creature he feared to imagine, and siege engines in varying states of being built, or being disassembled. The sheer number of the enemy here was staggering, but Sim shoved his fear into a tight ball and placed it in the back of his mind. He had to get an accurate count, then get home.

Sim came to the gates and smiled at the gatemen, who waved him through without comment. The smell of the place was already fierce in his nose. Animals, food, sweat, and excrement told him more fully than his eyes could that he was in a foreign place again, and he felt like a cat on the hunt. The clandestine elf chuckled as he passed under the hunched gates that humans must think were intimidating. Everything was so small and blocky. So...human. He wandered along half remembered streets, everyday humans yelling or arguing, talking or laughing. The language was harsh, but he had mastered it before his first excursion there. The sheer chaos of the place infected him like always, and the dangers of approaching war made the subterfuge that much more delicious.

The elves all imagined human cities were lockboxes full of secrets and dangers. In the end, Sim's task was almost always laughably easy. Criers were everywhere, offering gold as a bonus for any able bodied man that wanted to join the expedition to crush the elves. It was all anyone was talking about. He stood on street corners and in taverns for most of the afternoon, playing softly and gathering a few copper coins while he listened to every conversation. He had trained himself to separate out the noise so he never had to draw attention to himself, and he never had to ask questions.

The army had giants. They had catapults. They were fielding cavalry. A force of this size was impossible to hide, and everyone loved to talk about it and the giant of a man, a drunkard, that led it, named Ignagamus the Tactician.

Fear slowly leaked from that locked chamber in the back of his mind and heightened his every sense. The human food and drink was a blaring cacophony of tastes without subtlety. Sim had always loved it. The voices and noises, so unguarded and brash, made him feel drunk with his own Elvishness. And always, always, he knew he was the most handsome man in any room. Tightly trimmed beard, delicate fingers, slim physique, he packed away the fear again and began casting around for something soft to warm the chill night.

Sim always looked upon it as a favor when he bedded a human woman. Often saggy and slightly slow, smelly and primal, they rutted like animals and were ever so grateful for his seed. He loved prowling amongst them as the night closed in, picking just the right mix of beauty and pedestrian that made his loins quiver.

It didn't take long to find her. It never did. A raven haired, wild eyed girl who marveled at his interest in her. They always did. Princess or whore, married or maiden, he always found them willing. He never stayed. He never had to pay. By the time he had spilled himself inside her she had finished three times, bucking against him with the heat of an open furnace. Afterwards, he dressed silently and crept from the room as he always did.

It had been fun, but the morning was a complication he didn't need. Elvin births to human women were often difficult, and without the help of Elvish care, almost never successful.

He walked down the stairs, his mind ticking off another victory. Now he had to sleep. He ambled down the road before the row of inns and picked one at random. He entered the establishment, sniffed at the fire burning low and the crowd winding down in the darkness. A group of soldiers sat staring into their ales, probably the victim of some expert player in a game of chance. Even the whores were lounging lazily in the corner, disinterested and fighting the chill.

Sim made his way to the innkeep and popped a few meager coins from his pouch. Fear was still everywhere, but it was a drug mixed with the heady scent of sex that surrounded him. He smiled winningly, "A room for the night, if you please."

The innkeep nodded and opened his mouth, but it was a voice behind him that shrieked, "YOU!"

Sim spun to look at the soldiers, but it was from the whores that the call had come. A young woman, thin and wasted, weathered beyond her years, stood and stared at him from across the room. Her fingers were like claws as she charged. He grabbed her wrists and smelled the rotgut over blackened teeth as she spat at him, "Bastard! Father to bastards! Evil thing! You left me! You left me!"

The room barely took notice, except for the soldiers, who laughed. Sim struggled against her maniac strength and she bit at his face. "Woman!" he cried, "Woman, get off of me!"

The innkeeper frowned, "Stella, stop this or you can sleep in the street!"

But she did not stop, she thrashed more, kicking at the taller, healthier Sim. "You left me!"

Sim pushed her back, almost knocking her over a table, his mind racing, "I have only just arrived woman! I do not know you!"

Stella righted herself and hunched her shoulders like a prowling animal. "Don't know me, eh? I bet you would never forget my white dress, my braided hair, or my untouched silky purse."

One of the soldiers chuckled. "She's on about being rich again."

Stella whirled on him and spat again. "To hell with you Acacius! I was rich." Sim looked to sweep up his coin and leave, but the innkeep already had them. The whore swung on him and closed to just out of arms reach and snarled, "This was the minstrel that played for my father, the one who took my maidenhead. He got me with child and my family cast me out!"

The room stood shocked, that embarrassed silence that provoked uncomfortable laughter as the wild haired woman licked her teeth for the coming revenge. Sim suddenly remembered her– the fair, young daughter of one of the merchants in town. He had spent a week in clandestine meetings, teaching her the pleasures of her own body. Then he had left, and reported back to Lord Kilcahann. Sim shook his head and made to pass by. "I don't know you."

Stella swung wildly, and clipped his face with her hardened nails, scraping four furrows into his cheek. Sim recoiled and the soldiers stood in a shot. Sim batted her attacking arms away as the soldiers surrounded them. He felt his insides grow cold as the soldiers approached. She was drawing attention to him, and he could feel imminent danger as the rush of the hunt was snuffed out.

One grabbed Stella from behind and kept her from her rampage. She screamed. "Marius, let me go!"

Marius held her kindly, gently, but firmly. "Stella, calm down. You don't even have a child."

Sim felt his spinning world settle beneath him. He stood up taller and adjusted his clothing. Then she said, "My father cast me out! I had to live on the streets. I birthed in an alley because old Iduma didn't want me to bleed all over his inn. I had to whore for three years to feed the damn thing. But then I saw it wasn't natural. I left it out in the hot night to die!" she finished triumphantly.

Everyone there had heard her stories of the charming man who had taken her virtue. Some had even heard of the child. None had asked what happened to it. They all looked to Sim, who knew his face was a mask of shock, pale and starting to sweat. He tried to regain control. "Ma'am, I just arrived here. I'm sorry."

Marius nodded at him while casting pitying eyes at Stella, "You had better go, friend."

Sim nodded over and over, pressing through the soldiers that surrounded the whore as she thrashed. "No! NO! I know his secret!"

Sim left the group and made straight for the door. The soldiers started to break up their group, returning to their drinks. Marius let her go as she stamped her feet and fumed.

"I saw the baby change!" she shrieked.

Sim placed his hand on the door and stopped.

"Oi," the innkeep snarled, "settle down, now!"

"The baby was an elfling!"

The room froze.

Sim's instincts screamed. *Run. Run*! But he paused at the door and turned.

"That man is an ELF!" From her pouch she had drawn two papery lumps. Strung like a necklace on a leather thong dangled two delicate, dried ears, definitively pointed. "I killed the little demon! HIS demon! He looks like a man but he's an elf!"

The soldiers slowly turned back to Sim.

RUN!

He broke out of the door and into the night. He did not make it far. The soldiers had him in minutes. Burning iron chains came soon after.

Chapter Twenty-Three
The Geas

Vivien awoke to agonizing pain. The chamber was dark, and she was alone. She cried out as it gripped her entire body, spidering through her guts and making her arms and legs spasm with painful intensity. She recognized it as the pain from the spell her father had cast upon her, but it was so much greater than it had ever been.

She screamed. It was a lonely, forlorn sound that made her ache all the more. It echoed into the empty chamber, seeking caring ears and finding none. *Where is my partner in this life? Where is he? Oh yes, he is busy with his anger.* Tears streamed down her face and she screamed again, the pain wracking her body in waves that felt like they would never end. She tried to let go of the threads to the fae, tried to ground herself to this place and this time, but it no longer had even the slightest affect on the sharp teeth of the geas. She tried again, shutting off her connection to the magic with titanic mental effort, but the pain grew worse and drew another scream.

Then it came to her. As if answering her plea, the pain briefly subsided, allowing her a moment of perfect clarity. She understood why the geas tormented her so, just as another wave of punishment swooped in and began to savage her with invisible claws. In spite of the terrible pain, it made her pause and reality swooped over her like a hawk over unwitting prey.

It was her unborn child. One day he would be a spellcaster.

Oh gods no. Please NO!

She cried pathetic tears into the bed-sheets, lamenting the loss of something she'd never had, something she'd never have. The love of a mate was powerful, more powerful than anything. It would have seen her through this cruel and all-encompassing torture. The pain shook her again and she cried some more, until the sheets were wet with tears and sweat, and she heaved great wrenching sobs that broke her heart into millions of pieces.

But then, something was there. It was large and soft. It scraped the skin on her forearms with a great, raspy tongue, and when it lay down beside her, purring rattled her bones in a counter to the pain. In her loneliness and loss, her calls had found succor. Vivien grabbed onto her friend, big handfuls of black fur that made Sherika squeak in protest. Yet, the beast didn't move, just continued to lick away at the thing causing Vivien so much agony.

Then, for just a moment, it was over. The pain calmed and Vivien took the beautiful feline face in both her hands. She felt the connection between them tremble, and then become as strong as steel. "Sherika, I need you to get the Lady. Bring her here." Vivien rested her forehead against Sherika's. "Bring the Lady back here to me."

As the pain overtook her again, Vivien forgot that the door to her chamber was closed.

Vivien became enveloped by agony: her body, her mind, her soul. All that existed was pain, and the frustrated growls and snarls of a large feline trying to get out.

But then it was over again, and the chamber was quiet. Her breath came in ragged gasps and her body grew chilled. "Sherika?" Vivien called out fearfully. "Sherika, are you here with me?"

She heard the chamber door fly open to bang against the wall behind it, and within moments, the Lady of Moonlight and Love was there at her side, followed closely by one of her wives.

"Vivien! My dear, sweet Vivien, your Sherika is right here!" The Lady's hand enveloped hers and placed it on top of the familiar furry head.

Vivien smiled and Sherika purred in contentment, the feline knowing she had done good work.

The Lady's voice grew alarmed. "Vivien, why are you so wet? What's happened?"

Her voice was a whisper. "Shaladrea, I need to tell you something." The Lady's eyes widened with Vivien's use of her name, for she'd hardly ever used it before. "I..."

But the pain was there again, taking her breath and her words away, making her body convulse and the sweat to trickle from every pore.

The Lady just held her tightly, held her, held her. And Vivien imagined perhaps it was how her mother would have held her if she was there.

When the pain ceased once more, "I...I'm sorry I kept it a secret," Vivien breathed.

Tears crept down the Lady's face. "What is it dear. Please let me help you."

"I didn't want to believe it at first," her voice broke, "but I am with child."

The Lady's tender gaze turned to one of horror and she abruptly stood from the bedside. "Betina! You must go to the Grand Magister now, this very instant!" She gestured to Sherika. "The tir-reath will take you!"

Vivien 'thought' the location to her companion just as the pain overtook her again. She uttered another mournful cry, and then there was only darkness.

"Vivien? Vivien?" She slowly opened her eyes to see the face of her father above her.

She frowned. "Wh...what happened?"

The Grand Magister's eyes were filled with fear. "Vivien, I am so glad you have awakened. I was afraid you would not."

She tried to move, tried to sit up, but her body ached with such ferocity, it refused. Every muscle, every tendon felt strained and bruised from some monumental effort. A sickness swept over her, and her stomach churned. Before she could issue a warning, she heaved. She vomited a nasty green fluid that her father caught in a bowl, and when she was done, he took it away.

It was at that moment, feeling so weak and unable to move, that she knew she was not just miserable, but also very sick. She was in great danger, and the Grand Magister, Master Jor'aidan, Lord of Magic, was afraid he could not help her.

Tears sprang to her eyes and she gripped the wide sleeve of his robes. "Father, you know?"

He cupped her face in one hand. "Yes, daughter, I know."

"Please, you need to save me. Save HIM!"

He shook his head, tears gathering at the corners of his eyes. "I...I have tried. But, somehow, I have not yet been able to remove the spell. I have managed to take away much of the pain you feel, but the spell is still taking its toll on you."

Vivien allowed this reality sink in to her consciousness. "I don't understand. You were the one to place it on me. Why can't you remove it?"

"I believe it has to do with the baby growing within. The spell has taken hold of him, and because he is not here for me to touch as I remove the spell, it remains attached to you both."

She breathed deeply, knowing what the Magister was saying. Her time was limited.

Jor'aidan took her hand and squeezed it. "I am not giving up, Vivien. I am going to keep trying." He swept his hand over her forehead, and an expression she couldn't identify passed over his face, "Your husband has been called, and he should be here any moment."

She nodded and chose that moment to glance around the chamber. The Lady was there with her first wife, Naomi. Master Xadrian, his customary stoic visage showing worry, was also there. Sherika lay at her feet, keeping them warm with her lithe body, and Lydia stood there too, one wrinkled hand smoothing over the shiny black fur. Vivien did a second pass, but he wasn't there, the face she'd hoped to see. Sadness swept over her and she wondered why *his* presence mattered so much.

Shaladrea swiftly approached the bed, gently bumped the Magister out of the way, and leaned close to Vivien's ear. Her voice was the barest of whispers, her breath sweet against her cheek, "He is here, against the wall on the other side of your bed. If you but ask, he will come."

Vivien squeezed her hand with gratitude, and when Shaladrea stepped back, she turned her head.

He was there, just as the Lady said he was. His crazy, curly hair lay, unbound, around his broad shoulders like a frosted chestnut mantle, his large hands at his hips, his back resting against the stone wall. He appeared to be relaxed, nonchalant, but she could see the wolf within, ready to leap forth and fight any battle that came his way. His dark eyes regarded her intently, but today, unlike any other day, she could see through them and into his soul. There, she saw fear and concern, both forged from love. It gave her a warm feeling, and for just a moment, she wanted to bask in it forever. Her mouth moved a little, but she didn't really know what to say. Her fingers twitched toward him...

His eyes locked to hers, he pulled away from the wall. He knelt at her bedside, gently took her hand, and enveloped it within his larger ones. His voice was deep, deeper than she'd ever heard it before. "Your father, he will not give up. I will not give up either. I know you told me you don't need saving, but if I have to, I will do it."

A tear trickled down her temple and she nodded. "All right, Wolf. I suppose I can let you save me, just this one time."

In spite of the seriousness of the moment, he smiled sadly.

The Grand Magister stood outside the door to his daughter's chamber suite, anguish simmering just beneath the surface of his being. He hated himself, hated what he'd done, hated that other people had dictated he do it. What kind of world did he live in where fathers were told to place spells on their children? Spells that could give them so much pain? Spells that could mean the difference between life and death?

It wasn't a world he wanted to be a part of.

Vivien was his last child, his love child. For her he would do anything. For her, he would give his life. For her, he would give other lives.

The last thought made him cringe inside, but at least he was being honest with himself. Perhaps he was no longer fit to be Grand Magister. He had held the title for a very long time. Perhaps, after this war, he needed to pass the title along to someone younger, someone more attuned to the people.

Perhaps.

Jor'aiden heard boot-heels coming up the stairs and knew who it was before he looked up to see Torialvah turning the bend. The other man stopped when he saw him standing there. The Lord of Ice and Steel inclined his head in respect. "Grand Magister, how is she?"

The words that sprang from his mouth weren't what he intended, but he supposed they got the response he wanted. "She is dying."

Torialvah's complexion paled and Jor'aidan watched a myriad emotions pass over the younger elf's face. He kept going, his anger needing some release, no matter if the recipient deserved it or not. In the case of his son-in-law, he believed he did, even though he had no concrete evidence of that.

"Why did I need to call you? You know your wife has important and rigorous business in this place. Why aren't you here to be with her?"

Much to his credit, Tor stammered a response. "Grand Magister, I also have many responsibilities. People rely on me to make sure my work gets done."

Jor'aidan nodded. "Fair enough; your work is important, but hers is *critical* to the people of Rithalion and to herself. You should have known that. In light of Vivien's condition, I assumed you would have delegated that work to others and come to be here with her."

Torialvah looked confused.

The Magister's anger was re-ignited. His daughter had been too afraid even to tell her husband about her pregnancy. It told him much about their relationship, and at that moment, he regretted giving her to this man in marriage.

"Yes, Father, I came as soon as I knew she was ill. I would like to see her now if you would allow me to pass."

Jor'aidan frowned. "So you don't know why she is so sick?"

"No, Magister. This is the first I've heard anything about Vivien in over four weeks."

His anger surged, and he fought to keep himself from saying all the hostile things that came to his mind. "So you are unaware that your wife is carrying a child?"

Tor's eyes widened and he took a step back as though he'd been delivered a physical blow. Finally he spoke, his voice shaking. "No, I had no idea."

The Magister was on him in an instant, his hand gripping the neckline of Tor's tunic. "And why not? Why don't you know? What is wrong with you, man, that your wife can't even tell you the things that most partners share with one another as soon as they realize it?" He barely paused before he continued. "Your wife is dying, and you had no inkling of the reasons why before being called here today." His last words were a sneer, sharpened by everything he knew of Torialvah into a stylus, "You are pathetic."

Jor'aidan released his tunic and pushed him away. Torialvah stumbled back down a couple steps before regaining his footing. The Magister's voice was a monotone. "You best get inside. My daughter is expecting her husband."

He proceeded past Tor down the stairs before the other man could recover himself. He then made his way through the fortress to the appropriate meeting chamber, the one where, barely several weeks from now, they would be strategizing over a war they never asked for, never wanted. When he arrived, he was taken aback to see that the Council was already there. He supposed he shouldn't be too surprised, for they always had a tendency of being early.

Lady Swansee was the first to rise. "Grand Magister, I came the moment I got your missive about Vivien. I am immensely sorry for her illness. You have called us all here. Pray, tell us what you feel we can do for her."

Jor'aidan looked around the circular table. Soon it would be filled with maps, figurines, and tiny structures that would embody every resource the elves had. Master Oilariann bore an expression of utmost sadness and regret, while Kilcahann tried to remain stoic under the extenuating circumstances. Master Orinoco tried to keep his facade of arrogance in spite of the might of the powerful magic user standing before him, the most powerful in all of Rithalion, and maybe even all of Xar'Kaii.

"She is dying, and has maybe a week at best. There is nothing you can do."

Swansee gave a small moan of dismay, and Oilariann lowered his head in deference. Out of the Council, he always liked them the most, for their demeanors were those of tolerance and exoneration as opposed to unmitigated castigation. Where Swansee and Oilariann seemed to understand that life was often filled with mistakes that should be dealt with tolerance and understanding, Kilcahann and Orinoco were quick to preach justice to the letter of the law, often with an air of insularity.

However, all four Council members had agreed on Vivien's punishment that day, and the Magister blamed them all for what was happening to her now.

"Magister, what is it that is ailing her? There must be something to be done for her!" Swansee exclaimed.

He gave a mirthless smile. "My dear Council, you haven't figured it out yet? Why would I bother calling you here to witness the death of my daughter if you didn't have something to do with it?"

Everyone's eyes were suddenly fixed on him. No one looked down, or across the room. They looked at the Grand Magister of Rithalion, who had drawn himself up in all his robed glory.

"Vivien is in the middle of her prime, and as such, in the beginning, and most opportune, of her childbearing years. She is pregnant."

"But that is wonderful news, Magister! Our healers will take extra care of her as they offer whatever remedies they can to make her well again," said Kilcahann.

The other two men nodded their agreement. Swansee was the only one to grasp the awfulness of what had happened. She put a trembling hand over her mouth, stared at the Magister until he gave a slight nod, affirming her worst thoughts.

"The spell the law ordered I place on her has attached itself to her unborn child, for he was destined to become a spellcaster one day. As of yet, I have been unable to remove it from either him or the mother."

Silence filled the chamber as understanding filled every mind of the Council. Never in the history of Rithalion had a punishment caused the death of the recipient, and it showed they had become too harsh in their punishments. Horror filled every face, including Orinoco, and he could see the sour taste their ruling left in their mouths.

Swansee was the first to rise, tears in her eyes. "We will leave you here in peace with your daughter while the rest of us convene to be certain something like this never happens again."

The Grand Magister raised a hand and Swansee immediately took her seat once more. Everyone knew who was in power at this meeting, and they were subject to obey.

"I will fight for my daughter until she takes her last breath. After that, I believe it will be best that I renounce my Magister's robes. I have no wish to remain in a city whose laws allow things like this to happen to its most beautiful and promising youth, even more, that those laws make fathers hand down punishments to their own children." He lowered his head in shame. "A new Magister, you will need to find."

Again the Council was silent. Every member wanted to object, but not one dared.

"But before that, none of you will be leaving anywhere before you *SEE* what you have wrought." He gestured towards the entry. "Come, come and see what your decision has done to your celebrated warmage, the one who had *ONE* lapse of judgment but was punished as harshly as she could be for all of twelve months."

The Council rose from their seats and moved to follow the Magister, when suddenly the great magic user rounded on them and stopped to stand before Master Orinoco, a finger pointed in his face. "Just so you know, both Vivien's tir-reath and the Wolf are in her bedchamber. I will reiterate now that there are NO ANIMALS in that room. Do you understand me sir?" The Magister's voice shook with the strength of his emotion.

Orinoco stumbled back a step and blinked rapidly. He barely hesitated before inclining his head in deference. "Yes, Magister, I understand fully."

Jor'aidan led the Council through the fortress and to Vivien's tower. Halfway up the stairwell, he began to hear agonized screaming. Forgetting his mission, the Grand Magister leapt up the remaining stairs. He found Naomi crying outside the door to the chamber and he swept passed her to enter.

Vivien writhed on the bed, her small voice crying out. Reddish blonde hair fanned around her head like a halo, and her pale skin was bathed in sweat. Shaladrea held her hand on one side and spoke to her in soothing tones. Torialvah held her hand on the other, his brows furrowed with trepidation. The Wolf stood in his place against the wall, his gaze impenetrable, and Lydia stood next to him, her small form pressed up beside his side.

The Magister rushed to Vivien, a spell at his lips. Tiny fae formed a series of runes that settled upon her arms to make a shimmering latticework design, enveloping the geas branded there like a pair of toxic gloves. He closed his eyes and concentrated, guided the fae to press deeper, deeper. Vivien stilled for a moment, almost as though waiting. The Magister continued. His spell had never made it this far before, not with these fae, and when they moved around the spell and began to disarm it, things appeared well for a moment.

Sherika hissed in warning and the Wolf tensed just as Vivien's eyes rolled back in her head. "Magister, you must stop!" The barbarian was suddenly at his side, a big hand on his shoulder. "Her heartbeat is slowing; it is too much for her."

Jor'aidan's shoulders slumped and he ceased the spell. The fae flitted away into the aether, leaving the elves and their dying behind. He knew the Council was still there, but he didn't care that they saw his weakness. He lay over the body of his daughter, ear pressed against her chest, listening for the heartbeat he hoped was still there. Then he just listened to it, shallow and thready for a while until it recovered.

He recalled something then. Vivien had done much the same thing when she rushed to the Wolf's side after their battle with the bears. And just now the Wolf had been able to hear her heartbeat. The man didn't even have to get that close.

How did he do that?

Who was he? What was he? And why was he so attuned to Vivien?

Chapter Twenty-Four
Wolf's Blood

Another day passed. And another. Her father continued to try and remove the spell, just as he promised he would. Each time left her more tired, weaker, but she preferred it over the nothingness he could have chosen. He was fighting for her, and that made Vivien want to fight for herself.

She found out how Sherika had managed to retrieve the Lady that night. The paw-prints in the snow outside on her balcony told the tale. The tir-reath had moved to the very end of the balcony, then ran as fast as she could before jumping onto the ledge and leaping out. Somehow, her front paws managed to find purchase on the railing of the Lady's balcony on the neighboring tower.

It had been an act of desperation, risking a horrible fall to certain doom. That, or the act of a great friend.

The pain would come and the Grand Magister took it away with a counter spell. It left her sickly and nauseous, but it was better than the sheer agony that threatened to leave her incomprehensible, pain that ultimately placed her into unconsciousness. The Lady never left her side, or the Wolf, or her father, or Lydia. Not even her estranged husband left her. Sherika remained a constant presence pressed against her side or warming her feet. The beast wouldn't leave, even to eat or drink, so both food and water had to be brought and set before her. Vivien would run her fingers through the thick fur and just focus on the feel of it, each strand of hair that joined the others to make something so luxurious.

One morning came, and Vivien could barely move. She couldn't eat any more, or drink, without vomiting it back up. In spite of the fire in the hearth and the blankets piled around and over her, the wintry chill outside the tower reached her, and she shivered. Only with Sherika pressed close on one side and the Wolf holding her hand on the other, would the shaking subside, and she would sleep. Pain would wake her, not pain from the spell, but from the gnawing in her guts. As a young girl, she once wondered what it felt like to be hungry like the poor human people she heard about in realms far away. She was sad to know now what it felt like, and hated that children starved to death on the streets when there was food aplenty in the world if one knew where to find it.

"Vivien. Vivien? Vivien, can you hear me?"

She awoke as though from the deepest of sleeps, like the ones a person has when they are healing from a grave wound or a terrible illness. The darkness weighed on her like a sodden winter cloak, pulling her down into murky depths.

"Vivien, I need you to wake up and look at me."

It was a wonderful voice, one that had become familiar over the past few months, a voice as deep as the ocean, one that reminded her of safety. She did as it bid her and opened her eyes to see her father leaning over her. Beside him was the Wolf.

The Magister whispered, "Vivien, I still have not given up." He pressed a fingertip to his lips, kissed it, and then pressed it to hers. "I don't want you to be afraid about what we are going to do today."

His image swam and she closed her eyes. She was so, so tired.

"Vivien," his voice was insistent, "tell me you won't be afraid."

Her voice sounded thick and sluggish. "I won't be afraid."

"Good, that's my Jashari. You are a true warrior." She felt his arms around her then, strong arms that she always ran to as a girl when she was sick or afraid. The blankets fell away and her body was instantly cold.

The deep voice spoke again, the Wolf's voice. "Here, lay her close to the fire."

The Lady's voice, "I have a blanket folded up there, one that will keep her off the stones."

The Magister lay her down. She felt the blaze of a fire to her left. She felt a soft warmth settle to her right, and then an objection. The Magister's voice sounded tired. "No Sherika, you must go. Come now, you must go."

The tir-reath growled and hissed.

"Magister, leave her there. She knows that her beloved hasn't much time left, and she wishes to spend every last moment of it at her side. Don't take that away from her. Let her stay," said the Wolf.

Then he was there beside her, between her and the fire. How the Wolf managed to be so close to it without going up in flames was beyond her. He leaned close. "Remember, don't be afraid. Your father is here with you, and the Lady."

"Wh...what is going to happen?"

"I am going to do what I told you I would."

She closed her eyes, and in her mind's eye, she smiled. *"Ahhh, you are going to save me?"*

His voice was distant. "I am going to save you."

"I just said that, silly man. I suppose I shall suffer it, but only because I told you I would already."

She could hardly hear the voice now, "I will see you on the other side..."

Elvish Jewel

Vivien found herself sitting at the bank of a stream nestled in a verdant valley. The cool, blue waters rushed over her bare feet and tiny silver fishes tickled the bottoms as they swam by. On the other side there were trees, and the wind rustled the leaves. The scent of wildflowers was heavy in the air, and when she looked behind her, there was a field filled with yellow, orange, and blue blossoms.

Tinkling laughter caught her attention and she looked up the stream. There, playing in the rushing waters, were two children. They appeared to be about eight or nine years old. The boy had his trousers rolled up to his knees and the girl had her dress pulled up and knotted at the side. In spite of these precautions, the children's clothes were wet, but they didn't give a care in the world.

Their laughter drifted through the air again, a sound that made her heart soar and brought a wide smile to her lips. In spite of the sun shining overhead in a cloudless sky, she was cold and she wrapped her arms around herself. She spied a crimson shawl laying in the grass and she placed it around her shoulders.

When Vivien looked back up again, a girl was sitting there in front of her. She knew it was the one from the stream even though the dress wasn't the same. The girl was engrossed in her work, tying together a string of blue wildflowers. Her small fingers manipulated the stems with ease, and before long, there was a long cord.

The girl finally looked up and Vivien's breath caught in her throat. Never in all her years had she ever seen a more beautiful child. Platinum, curly blonde hair framed a perfect face, and eyes were the color of storm clouds before a rain. Pink lips were a contrast to flawless, alabaster skin and the ears... the ears were not Elvish ears, but rounded like a human.

The girl held out the string. "Will you braid these in my hair?" The girl smiled as Vivien accepted the string and her beauty was so stunning, she thought she might weep. The child settled herself in Vivien's lap, and suddenly she was no longer chilled. Warmth suffused her where the girl touched, a warmth that went beyond simple contact.

The girl was a like a little bonfire, but Vivien didn't mind. She loved it.

Vivien braided the child's long hair, weaving the wildflowers through each plait. It was something she had always been very proficient at, and as a girl, all her friends would come and have their hair braided. When Vivien was finished, the child turned and the blue flowers accented the blue in stormy gray eyes that were, somehow, familiar. The child beamed, and with all the tenderness and love in the world, she wrapped her small arms around Vivien's neck.

Vivien felt warm, too warm, and took off the shawl. The children ran through the valley, and once at her side, they plopped down in the grass beside her. The girl instantly came to her side and nestled there. Even though the warmth was uncomfortable, Vivien instinctively placed an arm around her and held her close. The boy held something in his hands, a boat made of wood and fabric. He held it up for her to see, his green eyes alight with happiness, his cheeks plump with the smile on his lips.

"Look what I made!"

Vivien held out a hand and the boat was trustingly placed there. She turned it this way and that, made the appropriate sounds of a job well done.

"Well, Father helped me, but he says I did most of the work!"

Vivien grinned and his eyes sparkled with a gaiety that was contagious. "We are going to sail it down the stream," said the girl. "Will you play with us?"

"Of course I will, dear!"

Vivien rose, and the children walked with her to into the stream. She watched the boy proudly carrying his boat. His sun-streaked auburn hair was tied back at the nape of his neck, and his ears were tall and well-pointed like those of a high-born elf. Once in the middle of the water, he slowly set the boat down, and when it stayed afloat, he yipped with joy. "It floats! It floats!"

They followed the boat for as long as it could go, and when it got caught on some rocks, they picked it up and followed it some more. Vivien relished her time with the children, but it was hot, much hotter than she expected for a day like this with the breeze sweeping past every few moments, and the sun hiding behind white, fluffy clouds.

Finally they walked back to the place where Vivien had left her shawl. She bent to pick it up and it was hotter than ever. It was so uncomfortable, all she wanted to do was take every stitch of clothing off her body, throw them into the cool stream, and then don them again, dripping wet.

The children stood there for a moment, watching her. Their faces were happy, and Vivien was pleased she played a part in making them that way. Then, together, they moved forward and wrapped their arms around her waist. A joy she'd never felt before filled her heart, a joy so big, she felt she could burst. The children looked up at her, their beautiful faces everything she wanted to see until the end of her life. "We love you, M..."

Vivien surged into wakefulness. It was hot, so unbearably hot, like a fire was dancing across her skin. She opened her eyes and the first thing she saw was... BLOOD.

She screamed.

Blood covered her arms and hands– thick, red, and dark. The smell of it was rich in her nostrils, so rich she could taste it. Fear galloped through her body and she felt alive, more alive than she had in more days than she could remember. A voice whispered in her ear, a woman's voice, soothing like the rushing waters from her dream. "Vivien, do not be afraid."

Suddenly she remembered. *Oh yes, my father told me to not have fear. The Wolf said the same. I shouldn't afraid, but the blood is... everywhere... and it's... hot!*

If there was any water left in her, tears would have gathered at the corners of her eyes. For the first time ever, she even welcomed them there. She reached out a hand, and the thing she was looking for was still there. Sherika's thick fur was matted and sticky, but she was laying beside her, and it felt like she hadn't moved even an inch.

The Grand Magister spoke, his voice concerned. "Wolf, you look pale." He looked like he wanted to say more, but held his tongue, lowering his head in what looked like shame.

The reply was a deep growl. "I am not stopping until you tell me it's broken. The blood is being burned off by the spell. We need more."

It was then she felt it, fresh heat pouring over her belly. She looked beside her and saw the Lady of Moonlight and Love. The woman smoothed a cool hand over her forehead and nodded in encouragement. "Be strong, Vivien."

Fear gripped her again as she slowly turned to look on her other side. The Wolf was there. He had a long cut on the inside of his forearm and blood trickled from it at a steady flow. He held the wounded arm over her body in a macabre image that made her think of some sacrifice being made by a demon cult. She groaned in protest and tried to move, but her body was much too weak to do anything but writhe in place.

Lydia entered her line of vision, blocking her view of the Wolf. "Shhh, hush child. You must remain still."

She shook her head. "What is he doing? Why is he bleeding? Help him. Tell him to stop!"

Lydia put a forefinger to her lips. "Shhh, this is the only way."

"What?"

Shaladrea's voice was distant, sad, "The Wolf's blood is fighting the geas."

In spite of her overwhelming weakness, Vivien was speculative. "But how much more blood?"

Lydia's gaze grew sorrowful. "Until it is done."

In spite of light given only by the fire in the hearth, her eyes focused, and she saw him clearly. Hair like curtains of carved wood, his head was bowed. Her father was right, he was pale, with deep hollows under his eyes. He had slashed both forearms deeply, blood trickling freely from each mighty limb. The flow was like a hot rain, making her want to writhe away. Surely her skin would burn away, surely she would be so terribly wounded she would never heal. She cried out with the burning of it, yet the Wolf poured more of his life onto her with every passing second, letting thick streams flow onto her skin, burning so hot she imagined she could hear it sizzle.

The Magister watched in horror, his own face pale. "It is working?"

From the shadows behind the Wolf, Torialvah nodded. "Yes, I believe it is working."

The Wolf slapped his arms, clearing clots from the wounds and keeping the flow constant. Deep inside, Vivien could feel the spell fighting for permanence, linked to her and the tiny new soul inside of her. The faster he bled, the more the runes on her arms faded, but whenever it slowed, they grew darker again.

Her father's voice was a quiet wail. "Oh gods, it isn't enough!" She'd never heard him sound like that before, like he was losing something so precious, he couldn't bear it. It scared her.

Torialvah hissed malevolently, "It will be enough."

There was a slither of steel on leather. Lydia and the Lady both gasped in unison. Vivien opened her eyes again and saw her husband behind the kneeling Wolf. He savagely gripped curly chestnut strands of hair in one hand and pulled down. The barbarian stared up at the elvin lord, eyes flashing red, the bare steel of Tor's dagger pressed against his throat. Her father held his hands aloft, and glittering blue fae encased Tor so that he could no longer move. It was a scene that burned into her broken soul and would remain there forever.

The Wolf's eyes shifted back to dark and he nodded. "Yes, it will be enough." He abruptly leaned into the razor-sharp edge and violently swept his head to the side.

Vivien opened her mouth. She wanted to scream but nothing emerged. The Wolf slumped over her on powerful arms, blood coming from the uneven cut on the side of his neck and pouring in a pumping flow down upon her breasts. As she watched, the gushing deluge was already slowing and the wound closing. But she knew, everyone knew, it would not, could not, be fast enough to save him.

A stillness stole over the scene. Vivien looked into the Wolf's eyes. They were kind, and soft. Not dark or red, but blue as a summer sky with hints of gray. It was a happy color, and she wondered how they could be anything else. He smiled sadly, and she felt the weight of his emotion crash into her. He had told her he loved her the first moment he met her.

Elvish Jewel

Now, after all this, she understood the depth of it. Somehow, she could hear his heart, beating slower and slower, and she believed.

The stillness erupted as the runes across her arms cracked and shattered into motes of light. Vivien passed out and darkness reigned.

Chapter Twenty-Five
Freedom

Vivien awoke to an aged voice filled with irritation. "Just leave him there! He's not hurting anything where he is. And there's blood everywhere; we don't need the whole chamber bathed in it. Vivien and the six feet of floor surrounding her is quite enough!"

She blinked her eyes open to find the Lady seated beside her, a smile on her beautiful face. "I knew you would come around soon. I have some broth for you to sip, a recipe sent to me by your friend over at the hospice."

"Vivien frowned, slowly digesting what Shaladrea had said. "Who? Are you speaking of Mikarvan?"

She nodded. "Here, try it. I must say, it tastes pretty good."

"I SAID just leave him there! He weighs as much as three of you! He's fine where he is, you fools!"

Lydia tottled into view, her expression one of perplexity. Vivien frowned, wondering who she was shouting about.

The Lady rubbed her shoulder gently. "Come, drink Mikarvan's broth. It will bring you strength."

Vivien nodded and tried to sit up. Instantly she felt a stiffness in her joints, not just from deep inside, but on the surface of her skin. She raised one hand, and found it coated in a layer of crusty, old blood.

Her eyes flew to Shaladrea. "The Wolf? Where is he?"

The Lady pointed. "He is right there, at your side where he fell yesterday. He is recovering in deep sleep."

Vivien turned to find him collapsed between her and the fireplace. One big arm rested across her belly, and she could see that the wound traversing the length of it was healing nicely, just as his wounds always did.

She tensed. "Is Tor here?"

Noticing her shift in demeanor, the Lady slowly nodded. "He was here all night. When he realized the spell was broken, and that you would live, he left early this morning to see to some work at the forges."

Vivien only nodded. She felt apprehensive about something, but couldn't quite place her finger on it. She struggled to recall events from the day before, but they were elusive. Regardless, nothing had changed. Torialvah always had something more important than her to give his attention.

"Your students have been asking about you hourly. Once you have eaten and bathed, they may come in to visit if you choose."

"My students?"

The Lady smiled. "Yes, you know, the ones that have been flourishing under your guidance all these weeks. Even more, the warriors have also been here. You have left quite an impression on everyone."

Vivien frowned. "So all their work has come to a standstill? How long have I been incapacitated?"

"You have been abed for a little over a week. But I wouldn't say things have come to a standstill. You have quite the apprentice in young Master Tyrell. He has been keeping things afloat for you until your return."

She nodded. "Where is my father?"

The Lady chuckled. "He isn't as young as he often likes to believes he is. The only time he left your side was to speak to the council and consult his musty, old, arcane tomes. He wanted to wait for you to awaken, but he was so close to exhaustion, I made him sit on your bed. He remains there now, soundly sleeping.

The Lady moved aside and, indeed, there lay the Grand Magister of Rithalion, his robes spread around him in wild disarray.

The Lady picked up the bowl once more. "So, how about this broth? The longer we talk, the cooler it gets."

Vivien frowned. "I don't want to get sick after I drink it."

Shaladrea shook her head. "You should not get sick. It is often consumed by women in your condition and it helps even the ones who sicken easily."

Vivien placed a hand beside the thick arm still lying across her belly as if protecting the treasure within. Her voice was incredulous, and tears sprang to her eyes. "The child, he is still there. The Wolf saved us. How will I ever repay him for what he has done?"

"I don't believe he wishes for your debt, but I know, one day, the time will come that you will have the chance to serve him the way he has served you."

Vivien nodded and finally allowed Shaladrea to place the bowl to her lips. Indeed, just as she said it would be, the broth was good. She finished the entire bowl, and she was not sick.

Shaladrea's wives came to the chamber. One raised the Wolf's arm from overtop her and the other two helped lift Vivien from the blood-soaked blanket. Concern flooded her. The big man made no move, gave no reaction. She would have feared he was dead if not for the slow rise and fall of his back. They took her to the bathing chamber where two tubs of warm water had been prepared. They settled her within the first and the waters instantly became red, darkening with every moment.

"That… is a lot of blood," Vivien breathed.

"Yes, yes it was," agreed the Lady.

They helped Vivien out of the tub and into the second one. Here, the waters turned pink, but she remained within and her body and hair were lathered with scented soap and rinsed.

Suddenly, from the other room, they heard a roar. Vivien startled, but instantly knew who it was. Shaladrea left the bath chamber to see to the Wolf while her wives helped Vivien from the bath and wrapped her in towels. After she was dry, they slipped a soft nightgown on her and brushed out her hair. All the while, the Wolf's strident voice got calmer and calmer.

By the time Vivien was helped out of the bath chamber and into the bedroom, the Wolf was a man again instead of the animal so many people liked to claim he was. His body lost its tension when she entered, and his eyes banked into dark coals. His arms, chest, and thighs were caked in dried blood, and his muscular forearms still bore testimony of what he had done. A thick cloth was around his neck, and she wondered why it was there.

His legs buckled and he went to one knee. Shaladrea took one arm and it seemed to steady him. He nodded solemnly and came to his feet like a young colt. "It is good to see you well again, Vivien."

She nodded. "Likewise."

"Hot baths are being taken to your chamber now, Wolf," said Shaladrea. "They should be awaiting you when you get there."

He nodded. Looking far more ashamed than he should. "I am sorry if I disturbed your bath. I...I just didn't know where you were when I awakened. I was afraid..."

"It is all right," replied Vivien. "I understand. It wasn't disrupted; I was almost finished."

He nodded again.

"I hope you will come back later, when you are washed and fed."

"Maybe we can eat something together?" His tone was hopeful.

She smiled. "Yes, I would like that."

The Wolf left and her eyes followed him out of the room. There were dead spaces in her memory of the day before, and she wracked her mind trying to recall all that had happened. She hated not remembering. She attributed it to the human part of her heritage for elves had exemplary memories.

Vivien was helped over to her bed. The Grand Magister no longer occupied it, and the sheets were fresh. The Lady helped her lay down and placed the blankets over her. "Rest now. You need rest. I will tell the Wolf when you are ready for your meal with him."

Before Shaladrea could turn away, Vivien grabbed her wrist. "Wait..."

The Lady turned.

"You have...you have been a devoted friend, treated me like a daughter. It means more that you will ever know. Thank you."

The Lady bent to kiss her forehead. "It has been my honor, Vivien."

"I...I can't remember very much from yesterday. It's such a haze."

Her expression was gentle, but guarded, "You were very ill, and it was a long day. With time you will remember. Try not to worry about it, dear."

Vivien just nodded and watched the Lady leave the chamber. The place was bathed in silence. She felt a burst of loneliness and panic swept through her. She slowly sat up in the bed, her muscles protesting after so many days of abuse. She looked around...

There was only more silence.

Then she remembered something.

She placed a hand on her belly and rubbed it. She wasn't really alone. She smiled and lay back down. Her son was in there, a tiny seed, but still a force to be reckoned with. The geas had proved that. Her hope now was that he would survive the next few months. Pregnancies between humans and elves were too easily lost, something about the two races not being completely compatible.

Vivien curled around her belly in a protective embrace and was about to close her eyes when she felt something heavy leap up onto the bed and settle at her back. She smiled. It was Sherika. Of course she wasn't alone. She closed her eyes and it wasn't long before sleep overtook her.

It was much later when Vivien awoke. She tried to grasp the dream lingering in the recesses of her mind, wanting to remember it, but it was like tendrils of smoke that dissipated in the wind. She glanced around to see Betina there, and Kira, the Lady's first and second wives. They were busy placing her clothes and other belongings into a large canvas bag.

Vivien frowned. "What are you doing?"

"Shaladrea requested that we come to gather your things and move them into her chamber suite," said Betina.

"I...I don't understand. Why would she ask you to do that?"

The two women shared a glance. "She feels that you are too isolated over here and that you need supervision in your condition," said Kira.

Vivien narrowed her eyes. Something just didn't seem right. She remained thoughtful as she watched the two women for a moment, and then it came to her.

Elvish Jewel

"Has my husband been here today?"

The women shared another glance. "Yes, he came while you were resting. You were so tired, you didn't awaken," replied Betina.

"Did he visit with Shaladrea as well?"

Kira hesitantly nodded. "Yes, Mistress."

Vivien watched as the women completed their task, and when they were gone, she threw off the cover. Ire surged through her in waves. *How dare he come into my place and dictate where I live? When he has never bothered to be here with me? Why should he have any say at all as to where I keep myself?* The answer was easy to find, and she ground her teeth in frustration.

She no longer felt like she was in a place of comfort, but a prison. She had to leave. She had to be free.

Sherika was there before her name needed uttering. Vivien crawled to the side of the bed, donned her thick winter slippers, and slithered onto the tir-reath's back. The big feline padded silently over to the entry, and once there, Vivien took the furred, hooded cloak that hung beside it. She donned the cloak over her nightgown, fastening it in place at both and neck and waist. Vivien then leaned over and opened the door.

She lay back over Sherika's haunches as they descended the winding tower stairs, and when they were in the fortress proper, she shifted forward into her normal place close to the tir-reath's shoulders. They slunk along in the hallways until they came to the back doors that Vivien had used when she went seeking the Wolf in the Arena. Then they were free.

Sherika ran between empty practice fields covered in a layer of freshly fallen snow. The sun was setting, and shadows lengthened along the landscape. It was colder than Vivien realized it might be, the chilly air often finding a way to billow up under the cloak and nightgown. She was glad she thought to wear the slippers, because her feet were the warmest part of her.

Soon they entered the trees and Sherika darted among them like a ghost. By then Vivien's anger had died, but it left a void behind, an empty place that resonated with cold, bleak sadness. She finally gestured Sherika to stop beneath a large pine tree. The fallen needles made for a nice spot and Vivien slid down from her companion's back. Guilt instantly suffused her; Sherika was panting from a long run without rest.

Vivien sat down, leaning her back against the tree trunk, and gestured for Sherika to sit beside her. With a *whuff*, the feline obliged, curling herself at Vivien's side and placing her head in her lap. Fat tears rolled down Vivien's cheeks as she caressed the soft face, and Sherika purred in contentment.

"What would I ever do without you?"

Sherika rotated an ear at the sound of her voice and the purring intensified.

"I think...I think I would be unhappy, more so than I think I am right now. I think I would be lonely. I think that parts of me are alive because of you, and without them, they would be long dead. I think you are my light when I see none, my rain when there is only a barren wasteland. You are the best friend I have ever had. You are the keeper of my heart and a part of my soul. Without you, I would be only a shadow of myself."

Vivien looked beyond her place beneath the tree. The landscape glittered white beneath the light of the moon, and the wind rustled the limbs of the mighty pine. Her heart ached. "Yes, only a shadow," she whispered.

Vivien wrapped the cloak more tightly around herself, second guessing her decision to leave the shelter of the fortress at night in winter. However, she was in no hurry to go back. She wondered what they would do when they realized she was gone. She already knew that the Lady would be worried, and might blame herself for Vivien's departure. Her father would also worry, and maybe he would send a seeking spell to find her. Tor...Tor would just be his usual angry self and order someone else to find her.

Vivien raised a hand, and with the barest thought, tiny fae circled it in a sprinkling of golden light. Her lips curved into a smile, and her heart found a moment of peace. It was good to feel the magic again, to feel it without fear and pain. Tears sprang to her eyes anew, and she built a new resolve. Never, never would she allow anyone to cast a binding spell on her again.

The fae danced around her hand for a few moments longer before winking out. But the tears continued. She let them come and they slid down her cheeks. Her heart ached and a low keening issued from her throat. Sherika pressed closer in an offering of comfort.

Then she saw someone coming towards her across the landscape.

Sherika was instantly on alert, lifting her head and rolling her body into a low crouch. She made not a sound, the epitome of a perfect huntress. Vivien remained where she was, just watched the intruder as he got closer, and closer.

Sherika abruptly released her defensive stance and relaxed. Vivien knew who it was before she saw his face, and a fluttering sensation settled low in her belly. A few moments later the Wolf stopped to stand outside the cover of her tree. She just looked up and regarded him intently. The hours had restored his strength, and she wondered if anything could stop his mighty heart.

The barbarian gestured, "May I sit?"

Vivien nodded silently.

The big man went to his hands and knees and crawled beneath the tree, settling himself across from her. A few minutes passed before he spoke again. "Everyone is worried about you. Why are you out here?"

Vivien stared at him for a moment. He wore his wild hair tied back at the nape of his neck, a nice leather jerkin and leather pants, a thick winter cloak, and fur-lined boots that went to mid-calf. He wore the accoutrements of civility, but...

She blinked away her tears. "I know you are in servitude to my people, but you are the freest thing I have ever met. I want to feel free too, even if for just a little while."

The Wolf just stared back, searching her face. "I am not as free as you think."

The tears finally escaped and swept down her cheeks. "Please, just give me this."

He was up in a heartbeat and crouched beside her, one big hand cupping her face, his thumb wiping away her tears. "I will give you anything," he breathed.

Vivien looked into his eyes, colored storm-cloud blue, down the narrow bridge of his nose and to his lips surrounded by a neatly-shaven moustache and beard. His breath blew gently across her cheek, and she wondered where he would go after his service was over.

It was then she realized she never wanted him to go. She had found a friend in this man she had never had before except as a child, a companion, a trusted confidante. He moved closer and her heart thundered against her ribs, sensing his intent. He wanted to kiss her...

But then he stopped.

Somehow, she could sense the effort it took for him to do so. She also knew why. *He wants to do the right thing. This man they call an animal, this barbarian from the wilds, he wants to do the right thing by me. I respect that, cherish it even, but today, today I don't care about the right thing. Today I want to be free.*

Vivien hesitantly leaned forward and placed her face alongside that of the Wolf, felt his breath catch in his throat. She could hear his heart in his chest, the beating becoming faster. He turned his face, turned it just the smallest bit, and their lips touched.

She caught on fire. The flames sped along through her veins, licking at every nerve ending as it passed. It settled low in her belly, simmering there, waiting...

The Wolf didn't need any additional prompting. A flood-gate was opened.

His lips weren't a sweet caress, but they didn't devour her either. They gave what they took, insistent but uncertain, harkening of the hesitant, tender lover within. The fire in her belly flared upward and out, enveloping her in an inferno of sensation. His hands slipped inside her cloak and they were like brands through the fabric of her nightgown. His breath was hot, but she welcomed it, brought it closer with a hand that got entangled within his hair.

The kiss was like nothing she'd ever experienced before, like something she might never experience again, and she reveled in it. Much to her pleasure, the Wolf seemed to do the same. And after, he cradled her in his arms, her head on his chest, and they lay down together on the cushion of pine needles. She felt a moment of euphoria, felt acceptance without boundaries, security without feeling weak. They lay there for quite some time, and just listened to the snow fall.

Chapter Twenty-Six
Visitors

Horns blew, bagpipes blared, and drum-rolls rattled off of the stone walls of the buildings surrounding Castle Blacach. Ravn looked to his wife, his mother and father in law, and the brothers and sisters whose kinship he had in marriage. Everyone wore their finest clothes, in particular, Ravn himself, clad in the green patterned kilt his father used to wear when welcoming esteemed guests to the castle. On his hip he wore the badge of the Laird of Blacach, an ancient blood blade that had been in his family for generations.

Ravn leaned out of line to look at the far end where the guards stood with kilts and spears flying the family tartan. The man at arms stood proudly, saw Ravn looking, and gave the barest hint of a smile. Ravn was about to raise his hand to wave to Moray when he stopped, remembering another such time that he stood just like this in wait of visitors, about to do the very same thing.

A rush of loss abruptly swept over him as he remembered the proud face of his father and the beauty of his mother. His throat closed at the memory and his eyes watered. How he missed them, especially at times like these. They both should be standing there with him still. He glanced at Ròs, wanted to take her hand, but refrained. She had never been one to offer him any consolation, and had a tendency to tell him that he had no right to feelings such as these.

So Ravn just waited, his feelings of loss shuffling to the back of his mind. Soon SHE would be there, and sight of her always brought him joy. He remembered her vividly, and he'd dreamed of his moment for more years that he could count. But wait, that was a lie. He knew exactly how long it had been since he saw his friend last. Twelve years was a long time.

Ravn smiled, adjusted his tartan sash and stood tall as the convoy came through the cheering mob of people. At the periphery were elvin riders atop huge felines, each carrying longbows over their shoulders. Giant deer with large, branched racks walked with grace and dignity before beautifully carved carriages. At the forefront was the ambassador, an older gentleman wearing a hooded robe of gold trimmed burgundy. A beautifully designed circlet wrapped around his forehead and disappeared into silver hair that framed his face and rippled down his shoulders in waves. Twelve years had made Ravn into a man, but it had not touched the diplomat. His features, as always, were fine, with almond shaped eyes that shone with genuine mirth and goodness. Ravn remembered liking him despite the otherworldly air he carried around him like a cloak. The elf waved from the back of a great white stag, the antlers larger than any of the other deer in the procession.

When the white stag approached Ravn, the ambassador raised his hand and the procession behind him came to a stop. Ravn stepped forward as he dismounted and the two men stood there for a moment before both bowed. He and Ravn were the same height, but self-assured poise and confidence made the diplomat seem larger than life. Ravn smiled. "Welcome to Castle Blacach, Lord Magister! It is good to see you again after all these years."

The other man nodded, and replied in well-spoken Lairdstongue, "Indeed, it is Laird Blacach. And before any other words are spoken, I would like to express my deep condolences for the passing of your father and mother. They were good people, and the world is a sadder place without them in it."

Ravn blinked in surprise. Certainly he anticipated that this man would mention Liam's passing, but the kind words were beyond expectations. "Thank you, Magister. I feel better knowing that there are other people out there who believe as I do." Ravn then gestured to the convoy. "Please, my castle is prepared and waiting to accommodate all whom you have brought with you on your long journey. Let us make you comfortable and offer refreshment."

The Magister nodded. "Thank you, Laird. Your town and castle have seen much improvement!"

Ravn nodded, "Trade has brought wealth to my family. After the attack that cost me my father and mother, we invested in higher, thicker walls and towers, and more comfortable accommodations."

"It seems..." The Magister paused only a moment, "quite delightful." He raised his arm and the signal was noted by the first rider. He then made the same signal, and it traveled down the procession until it reached the end. Meanwhile, the door of the first carriage had opened. One of the carriage drivers stood by, offered a hand, but the young woman who stepped out graciously declined.

Ravn's eyes widened and his jaw almost dropped. He knew it was her, it had to be, but she looked so... different. He remembered this tiny weed of a girl who played with him around the castle and in the fields. Now she had grown into a beautiful woman. Her hair was the same color he remembered, a light chestnut brown that shone as though the sun was trapped in it. Her skin was pale, her figure small and lithe like the deer pulling the carriages. But when she stepped up, it was her eyes that really gave her away, colored an indescribable shade of green that seemed to encompass all other eye colors in one iris. Ravn struggled to breathe for a moment.

The Magister reached out a hand and she took it. "You remember my daughter?"

Ravn stared for a moment before composing himself. "Of course, Magister. How could I ever forget?" He turned back to the woman and gave a half bow. "My Lady, I hope your trip here was pleasant and uneventful."

She inclined her head. "Thank you, Laird Blacach. It was, but I am glad to be here now." Ravn torn his eyes off of her and turned back to the Magister. "Please, let me introduce you to my family. This is Ròs, my wife." He said a silent prayer as he put an arm around her back and urged her forward. Much to his relief, she stepped forward without balking and gave a slight curtsey. He would have liked her to say something, but when she did not, he moved to Ernan and Mòrag, who were very kind and welcoming.

Once introductions were over, Ravn instantly thought of his guests' comfort. "Please, come with me inside the castle. I will show you to your chambers myself." He offered his arm to the lady and she graciously accepted it.

"If you don't mind, I shall stay here and oversee as everyone disembarks, said the Magister. "But please, get my Jash'ari settled and perhaps send someone for me at the end."

"As you say Magister. Your wish shall be done." Ravn picked up one of the small trunks that had been deposited near them and turned back to the lady. "Please, come this way."

He began to lead his guest across the courtyard, not missing the scowl on Ròs' face as he left. He would probably have some kind of hell to pay later that night, but somehow, he couldn't find it in him to care. The light weight of Jash'ari's hand on his arm sent little shocks through it and all the way down to his toes. They entered the castle and he led her across the great hall towards the stairs leading to the east wing, where the best rooms were kept.

Finally they arrived at the chamber suite he had chosen for Jash'ari, the Magister, and their retinue. He opened the door and a small fire burned happily in the fireplace, already working to keep the chamber warm for the approaching evening. The sofa was covered in pillows, and a tray of freshly baked bread, cheese, and fruit sat before it. The manservant entered and deposited the two trunks he had carried up, then bowed. Before he could leave, Jash'ari put a hand on his arm and smiled. "Thank you."

The man smiled in return and bowed. "It is my pleasure, Lady."

When the door closed, Ravn just stood there and stared at her. Her gown was a lovely shade of cobalt, setting off the blue in her greenish eyes, and the color of her skin. He loved the way she had just made his manservant feel, like his work meant something to her. A flush crept across her cheeks. "What? What is it?"

"You are nothing like I remember, yet, so much more."

She gave a light laugh, one that he'd remember for the rest of his life. "You look different too, Laird. You are so..." she gestured to his person... "tall."

"It's Ravn," he corrected her with a smile. "To you it's always Ravn."

She nodded. "All right, Ravn." She walked across the chamber to the tray. "May I?"

His eyes widened in surprise. "Of course! It is there for you."

She put a hand to her chest. "For me? This is so nice. Thank you, Laird." She flushed when she realized her error, "I mean, Ravn."

He grinned. "I must say, your grasp of my language has increased. You speak it exceptionally well."

She picked up the bread and tore a piece off, beamed under the praise. "Thank you. I've been studying it since last we met, practicing it every night with my father. I get so rusty if I don't practice. It's the human part of me, I suppose." She gave him an impish wink.

Ravn blinked and a feeling of joy swept over him. "You...you did that for me?"

She gave another light laugh. "Yes, of course."

His chest had a strange fluttering sensation. "I...thank you. No one has ever done anything like that for me before."

Her brows furrowed slightly. "You have a wife. Surely she does things like this for you all the time. I didn't know you had married. Congratulations to you."

He paused for a moment, not quite knowing what to say. He wanted to tell her everything: his miserable life with Ròs, how she despised him, and how it would be a miracle if she ever did anything even remotely kind, much less learn another language. But he chose against it, wanting to keep their meeting light and carefree.

"Thank you. I believe it has been about three and a half years now."

The furrow still remained, telling him she wasn't entirely sold on the carefree. But she let it go and finally smiled again. "The bread is delicious. Who made it?"

"Isobeal, the daughter of our head cook made it. I shall tell her you like it."

"Please, allow me to tell her."

Ravn inclined his head. "As you wish."

Her tone became serious. "I know you have responsibilities now, and that you can't spend all your time with me. Please, go see to them, and when you can, maybe you can come talk with me."

Ravn walked over to her, and despite any protocol he might be breaking, he took her into his arms and embraced her like they did when they were children. "How I have missed you."

When her arms returned his embrace, his heart soared. "I have missed you too. I am so glad to be here today," she whispered.

He held her there for a few moments, then a few moments longer before he finally released her. "I will come to you all the chances I get. It's not every day a man gets to spend his time in the presence of an elvin princess."

She chuckled. "I'm not a princess."

He grinned widely. "You are to me."

Chapter Twenty-Seven
The Ride

Ròs' pale face was covered with a smattering of reddish blotches. "I see how you look at that elvin whore! Smiling and laughing and carrying on like you do is a disgrace. And yet you come to my bed at night and sniff around like a dog begging for table scraps."

Ravn reddened like his father used to when enraged, heard his heart in his ears, and felt a pressure behind his eyes. "You will not speak of her that way! Ever! Jash'ari has done nothing to deserve it. If you are angry, then abuse me, but never her!"

In spite of his proclamation, he glanced away, recognizing the truth of his actions, but not seeing the fault in it. Jash'ari's visit was one he may never experience again, and he wanted to cater to his guest as best he could before she was gone. Certainly she was his friend, but now that he was a man, there as an interest there. Truthfully there always had been, but Ròs had nothing to worry about. Soon Jash'ari would be gone, and she would one day be only a distant memory.

More anger swelled within him and he fought to keep his voice level, "And if you think I have such a wide-ranging wandering eye, perhaps you might consider sharing my bed a bit more often and–"

"Ha!" Ròs rounded on him, her long, thin frame trembling with rage, "Do you think I really want your cock thrusting into me, your seed seeping out of me like cold custard? You pompous, arrogant, weakling!"

Ravn's anger popped like a bubble and the familiar hopeless loneliness formed in its place. Ravn took that as his cue to turn and walk out of the room. He was unwilling to hear anymore. He had suffered her rage, month after month and year after year. He had remained faithful to his oath to her, saved her from certain death, and yet Ròs had never warmed to him or shown an ounce of kindness. His tall boots snapped on the cold stones of the rebuilt castle. Gone were the wooden palisades and weak walls of yesteryear. Coal money had brought prosperity to his people. The Liath had never returned, and the mines were working to fill carts and send them to distant Elvish lands. None of it, none, had brought him peace from his wife.

He approached her sweetly, openly, honestly, and even tall and proudly. Nothing he did had her show even the slightest interest in him. He took the stairs downward, for there was only one place he could relax, yet burn off excess energy. He emerged into the castle proper, walked across the great hall and out into the bailey. He then proceeded to the stables and was brought up short.

Jash'ari was there with the big white stag ridden by the Magister. She was petting him, checking his legs, and picking up each hoof to check underneath. He just watched her for a moment, taken in by the scene of the small elvin girl beside an animal so large. Finally she saw him and straightened. "Laird, I am sorry for my rudeness. I didn't see you there."

"Lady Jash'ari, it is all right. I could see you were working and I didn't wish to interrupt."

She patted the deer's neck. "His name is Farlo. He's a bit older than the others, so I come to check him daily and give him special treats." Her lips curved up into a mischievous smile. "In truth he is my favorite and is my special friend. Would you care to meet him?"

Ravn smiled. "I would love to, but the deer have been nervous around all of my stable hands."

She gestured him over. "Come."

Ravn slowly approached. The white stag lifted his head higher, but made no movement. Finally he stood beside Jash'ari. She took his hand and lay it over the soft white hide. He rubbed his hand along the back and side, happy to have her there beside him. The stag brought his head down to sniff at Ravn, and he took a chance and put a hand under the narrow chin.

"Here, give him this and he will love you forever."

Jash'ari dropped a few apple slices into his hand and he offered them to the stag. The great animal ate them delicately from his hand, and after, lay his chin on his shoulder before moving away to the vast paddock that housed the other deer and many of the horses belonging to Castle Blacach.

He turned to Jash'ari. "Thank you."

Her smile was vibrant. "I'm glad you like him. He seems to like you as well. It's isn't every day he puts his head on a man's shoulder."

"I came out for a ride. Would you care to accompany me?"

Her smile faded. "I'm afraid I've never ridden a horse, so I don't know all the cues." She looked up into his eyes. "I've met everyone in your stable. They seem so nice. I don't want to make anyone upset."

Ravn stared for a moment, wondering if she was talking about the stable hands. Really, there weren't that many... "You have met everyone?"

She nodded, "Well, yes. All the horses. They are wonderful creatures. I wish we had some where I live."

Ravn blinked and turned away. She spoke about the horses as though they were people. Of course, many times, he saw them that way as well, but it was strange coming from the mouth of someone else.

Ravn pitched his voice so as to be heard from within the barn. "Giles, if you can, please come."

A moment later a man emerged, followed by a girl approaching womanhood who looked to be about thirteen or fourteen summers. It was the man's daughter, who insisted on helping him in the stables. Ravn had questioned it a few times in his mind, but had never stopped her from coming because she never seemed to get in the way.

"Our guest needs a patient mount. She has never ridden before."

Giles nodded. "I know just the one." He regarded his Laird. "And who would you like today?"

"Bring me Storm. He needs the exercise."

Giles nodded. "Right you are, Laird."

The man turned around, looked like he was about to issue a command, but the girl was gone. He walked into the stable, and glancing at one another, Ravn and Jash'ari followed. He gestured to her gown, "Will you be comfortable?"

She nodded. "I believe so. I have light trousers on underneath."

"Why?"

"It is colder in these mountains," she said. Then she blushed and grinned. "And I'd hoped you would ask me to ride with you."

Ravn felt his heart soar, but just shook his head and chuckled. He had never met anyone like her, and he knew he would never meet another. She was rare, like the stone they sometimes found in the coal mines. Diamond.

They entered the stable and Ravn instantly noticed that there was a commotion going on near the rear where Storm was housed. They rushed to the scene to find Storm pawing at the wooden floor, ears pinned back, nostrils flaring. On the ground lay Giles. Ravn kneeled beside his hostler, and before he could issue a warning, Jash'ari had entered the open stall.

Ravn pulled Giles to safety as the young woman stood before the large, dappled gray stallion. She looked up at the beast, one hand outstretched in an offer of friendship. Fear surged through him, and every instinct told him to lunge inside, grab her around the waist, and pull her out. But, before he could gather his wits about him, Jash'ari was approaching the unruly horse.

And she spoke.

Her voice was like a swiftly flowing stream, fresh and sweet, as Elvish words tumbled from between her lips. For a moment she looked like some kind of delicate forest faery, light from the outside streaming through a broken board above her head, shining down upon her red-gold hair and giving it an ethereal glow.

Giles rose to stand beside him, his brown eyes wide. "Laird, I will grab his reins while you get the lady to safety!"

Ravn held up a staying hand and Giles quietly watched the interplay taking place right before their very eyes. Jash'ari continued to speak, her beautiful voice low and soothing. Storm had ceased his pawing, and his breaths were even. His ears pricked forward to hear every word the elvin girl had to say. Ravn tensed as she stepped towards the large horse, one hand grasping the reins, and the other laying gently on the shiny neck. But the horse remained calm, and allowed her to stroke him.

Finally he released the breath he'd been holding, and just as he was about to walk in, Jash'ari made a gesture towards the back of the stall and spoke, "Come, he is calm now. He won't hurt you."

Ravn watched as Giles' frightened daughter came to stand beside the elvin girl. He put a restraining hand on the man standing beside him, not wanting the hostler to cause the horse to startle and possibly crush the two small people in his stall.

"What is your name?"

"Neála, Milady."

Jash'ari smiled. "That's a pretty name. I like it very much. Would you like me to teach you something?"

The girl nodded. "Yes Milady."

"More importantly, do you trust me?"

Neála looked up into Jash'ari's face, hesitated briefly. "Yes, Milady."

"Take the reins and pet him just as I am."

Fear shone in the girl's eyes and the horse shifted nervously.

"Ooop, you said you trusted me, remember?"

"He doesn't like me."

"Nonsense, he doesn't know you well enough to like you or not."

"He seems to like you, Lady."

Jash'ari smiled. "He thinks he likes me, because I am speaking to him in his language."

Neála frowned. "His language is Elvish?"

Jash'ari chuckled. "No, of course not. I speak to him in my tongue. It doesn't matter what I say; all that matters is how I say it, with gentleness and confidence." She nodded towards the stallion. "Come, pet him. He loves to be petted. All beings such as this one adore honest affection."

Neála slowly reached out until her hand lay on his neck.

"Now, take the reins. Do not be afraid. Your fear makes him nervous. He doesn't understand you are afraid of him. Rather, he thinks you are afraid of something else that he, in turn, should be afraid of. Storm is not your enemy. Certainly, he is young and often facetious, but he is never your adversary. He was bred to be your friend. Treat him that way. Treat him the way you would a beloved comrade. That is what he lives for."

Neála looked up into Jash'ari's face and the elvin girl leaned forward, whispering words Ravn could barely hear. "I promise, I would never lie to you."

For the first time, Neála smiled. She reached up and took Storm's reins, and nothing happened. She slowly moved forward and the stallion moved with her until she was out of the stall and standing before Ravn. "Milord, here is your horse. I am sorry I caused such a commotion. I will do better next time." She handed him Storm's reins, gave him a small smile, and turned away.

Moved by her apology, he called out, "Neála."

The girl turned back.

"You did a great job."

She beamed at him, a beautiful smile that tugged at his heart. "Thank you, Laird."

A moment later Jash'ari came to stand beside him. She brushed off her blouse like nothing had happened. He stared at her until she looked up and grinned. Giles abruptly shouldered past him and enveloped her in a heartfelt embrace. "Thank you so much Milady! You have done me the greatest of services this day. I hope I can someday return the favor." He released her and bowed low, a bow one would give to someone of nobility. He then went after his daughter.

Ravn continued to stare. "You...you are amazing."

She stared back. "No, I am only myself."

He took her hand. "How do you know horses so well if you don't have any where you live?"

She shrugged. "I just know animals."

He stopped them before another stall and a black head appeared over the door. "This is Starla. She is my gentlest mare. She will be your mount." He handed her Storm's reins while he got the black horse ready, then lead her out of the stall. Once they were ready they rode out of the bailey and through the town. It was much bigger than it was in his father's time, for the coal mining had made it prosper, and some could even say it was a small city. People waved as they passed, happy people that bowed to their Laird with smiling faces. Ravn returned each wave and every smile, and Jash'ari did the same. The people loved her, the children following them in a small procession until they reached the outskirts. They then shouted and cavorted until their Laird and his elvin lady were out of sight.

"So how do you like her? Starla."

Jash'ari grinned. "She's wonderful. I love her already."

He grinned. "Do you think you can go faster?"

She gave him a mischievous grin. "Oh, yes. She is like my legs now. I can feel her every movement."

His expression became serious. "She is yours then. I want you to have her. She was made for you."

Her eyes widened. "What? No, I mean, I can't take her."

"Why not?"

"She...she would be lonely without her companions. She would be alone where I live, with no herd to make her feel safe and accepted."

Ravn considered this and lowered his head. "You are right. I wasn't thinking."

"But I love the gesture. You are good to me Laird Blacach."

"I...I just want you to remember me when you return home."

She pulled Starla to a stop and Ravn followed suit. She regarded him intently. "I have remembered you all these years. I have never stopped thinking about you."

Ravn looked to the path ahead, his voice husky with all the emotions she incited within him, "Nor I, you."

"Then you have nothing to worry about, Laird."

"He gave her a small smile. "Come, let's ride with the wind. Give Starla her head and she will carry you safely."

They kicked the horses into motion and they ran. They ran across the countryside and were free for a while. They reveled in the power beneath them, the wind in their hair, the sight of one another sharing a brief moment in time. And when they stopped, they slid off the horses' backs and let the animals rest and drink from the nearby stream. They lay in the grass, side-by-side, and talked to one another about silly things, things that wouldn't matter to any realm or kingdom, things that only young people talked about when they had nothing of import to say.

So, of course, Ravn never said the most important thing. The fact that, in his heart, he loved her. He loved her more than he loved life itself.

Chapter Twenty-Eight
Last Night

Her eyes were wide as he leaned over her. "Where did you learn to do that?"

He gave her a roguish grin. "I made it up myself."

He pulled her up and back into a standing position, then picked up her fallen blade. He presented it to her lengthwise, and bowed. "Milady, you are a good swordsman, and one day I pray we will meet again in the sparring arena."

Looking as magnificent as a queen in her sparring attire, she bowed back and accepted it, still slightly miffed at being so easily disarmed. "Thank you, Laird. Likewise."

Both sheathed their swords and looked at one another for a moment. He was the first to speak. "I shall miss you when you are gone."

She gave a sad smile. "Same."

They walked back to the castle, their feet heavy. Jash'ari would be leaving in the morning, and Ravn knew he may never see her again. The signing of the trade deal for coal had been a simple thing, but Ravn had drawn out minutiae as far as he dared, questioned every provision, and haggled like a shoemaker over every comma. He had done it to keep her here, as unfair as that may have been. Thoughts of visiting her in her homeland swirled about in his mind, but the trip would take several weeks, and he knew he shouldn't stay away from his people so long.

Once inside the castle they paused. Amidst the hustle of his staff preparing for the evening meal, they stood there for a moment. She was beautiful and her presence infused him like a heady perfume. Her hair was plaited and expertly coiled at the back of her head. He'd always wanted to ask her about how she did it, but never found the opportunity. They just took one another in, a moment in time that he would remember forever.

Finally Ravn gave a small bow. "I shall see you soon for supper my Lady."

She nodded before turning away. He watched her walk across the great hall before taking himself to his chamber suite, calling to have a bath poured as he made his way up the staircase. He had one ordered for Jash'ari as well, knowing she would enjoy the luxury before many days spent on the road. He passed his wife's chambers on the way to his own, and he pursed his lips. He hated the way Ròs spoke of other people, in particular, Jash'ari. It made him sick just to think about it, but he'd tried to soothe Ròs' ruffled feathers. He wasn't sure it did him any good, but efforts had been made.

A feast had been made for the departing elves, and after, the finest wine was taken out from the cellar. It was a great sight, elves and humans breaking bread and drinking with one another. Castle Blacach had accepted their guests with wholehearted aplomb, and the elves had been happy to stay. It was evident in the stories they began to tell one another, stories about two cultures that were vastly different, but accepted as a part of the people who had become friends.

Once he'd stayed the allotted time considered appropriate for a Laird, Ravn approached his friend. She was dressed in a gown, colored in varying shades of brown, beige, and gold. It felt drunk to look at her, and he tried to dismiss the rapid beating of his heart when she was near. He'd always noticed how apart from the rest of the elvin ladies she seemed to be, and he marveled at that. Jash'ari was such a dynamic person, he couldn't imagine anyone not wanting to be in her presence all the time.

Ravn gave a brief bow and held out his hand. "Will you accompany me to the balcony, my Lady?"

She cocked her head the side. "The balcony?"

"Indeed, it is my favorite place in the entire castle, but I've never had the chance to show it to you."

She placed her hand within his. "Of course, Laird. I would love to see it."

Ravn led her up the central staircase, past his chambers, and into the tunnel. He opened the door that led into the balcony chamber, a chamber that was kept meticulously clean.

Jash'ari looked around as she was led through, but gasped when she walked out with him onto the balcony. The balustrade was elaborately carved white marble with silvery streaks. The floor was made of the same, and it shone in the light of the full moon. She went to the edge and looked over, the moonlight laying gently over the rocky 'scape far below, and below that, the fields where they had gone riding a couple days ago. The stars formed a sparkling scarf across the sky and reflected perfectly in her eyes.

"This is beautiful!" She walked around the curved balustrade until she got to the end, where she looked over the stretch of lands belonging to Blacach Towne. Beyond that, which could not be seen in the darkness, were other villages that depended on Blacach castle for protection if there was ever an invading force, and every year the people paid the Laird with a portion of their crops. With money from mining, Ravn had put resources into the security of these villages, making them good places for people to want to come and live. They were growing rapidly, and he imagined that they might be as big as Blacach Towne within the next decade.

"Thank you. I had it made for Ròs about a year after our marriage." Jash'ari turned. "She must come out here all the time."

Ravn shook his head. "No, she never comes here." Ravn joined her at the balustrade. "The only feet that ever touch this marble are mine, and maybe the housekeeping staff that makes sure this place stays the way you see it now."

She was quiet for a moment. "I sense you are unhappy, my dear friend."

His shoulders slumped and he nodded. "Yes."

"I wish...I wish it was different. Your wife, Ròs, she is very blessed to have someone like you."

Every sharp word Ròs had ever uttered crowded into his head. "Humpf. Blessed?"

"Oh yes. The gods bless us with good partners in life who will stand by us: make us strong when we are weak, aid us in our difficult moments, and give us children whom we may share together."

Ravn gave a half grin. "Tell me who these gods are so that I may worship them as well."

She chuckled. "I too, will marry some day. My hope is that it will be a good match."

"You do not get to choose for yourself?"

She shook her head. "No. As the daughter of the Grand Magister, Elvish society dictates that I must marry according to my station."

Ravn nodded. "Then you understand. You know where your duty lies, and you will fulfill it."

"I am still young, much younger than you by Elvish standards. But, yes, one day I will fulfill my duty to my people."

He ground his teeth at the indignity of it, that a proud being like Jash'ari would be subject to the whims of others.

"Ravn?"

He looked up at her, pale skin offset by the warm brown gown she wore, her hair tumbling around her shoulders in gentle waves kissed by the moonlight to make it shine, her eyes regarding him with an intensity she'd never shown him before. "Yes?"

"You deserve to be happy."

His heart pounded. His skin felt far too tight. He stayed silent.

"Every man deserves happiness, and if that means finding it in unlikely places, then so be it."

He shook his head. "And remain true to any vows I've made?"

She shrugged. "Maybe. Vows to others are important, but you must also be true to yourself and live your life with some modicum of happiness. Life only lasts so long..."

Jash'ari abruptly stopped and turned away. Ravn could tell something was wrong. He regarded her for a moment before reaching out and taking her chin in his hand, gently bringing her eyes back to his.

"What is it?"

She remained silent, her eyes shimmering with unshed tears.

Ravn stepped close. "You can tell me."

"I...I will live a long time, much longer than you by at least three or four centuries. For me, life lasts so much longer than it does for you."

Ravn just stood there, looking down at her.

Her next words were a whisper. "So find happiness. Give it to yourself and to others. Do it while you have the life in you to do it."

The words came to his mouth before he had a chance to think about them. "Do I bring you happiness?"

Her gaze was intense. "Very much."

Ravn just stood there again, looking down at her. Her breath was sweet against his lips and smelled of the wine she'd drank before they left the dining hall. He was so close, he could see the flecks of golden brown near the centers of her green eyes, her hair where it swept off of her forehead to cascade down the side of her face. He swept it back behind her ear and rubbed a thumb over her cheek.

Then, without thinking, he leaned down and placed his lips over hers.

It was like a shock, the pulse traveling through him to reach every part of his body, all the way to his fingers and toes. It even went to his scalp, only fizzling out when it escaped through every hair on his head. It was a tame kiss, nothing like what he had seen people doing in the dark recesses of the taverns he frequented every once in a while in Blacach Towne to drink away his misery, but it reached into his very soul. It was like nothing he'd ever shared with Ròs even though they had been married for over three years. It was natural, it was giving, it was a reflection of himself. It was a reflection of her as well, young and inexperienced. She put a hand up to his face, her fingertips brushing gently over his skin to the place where their lips met...

...and that one touch was more intoxicating than any wine, draft, or ale. His senses spun and he leaned against the handy balustrade at his side, just to catch himself should he fall in a puddle at her feet.

But then it was over. Their lips parted and they looked into one another's eyes for several moments, moments in time where nothing existed but the two of them, moments that seemed to slow down and accommodate two people who may not see one another again for a very long time.

"No one has ever made me as happy as you do, Jash'ari."

She gave him a sad smile and he rubbed at the worry lines that formed between her brows. He frowned. "Why are you so sad?"

"I make you so happy, but I may never see you again."

His expression shifted into one of utmost seriousness. "My happiness doesn't hinge upon seeing you. It's knowing that you are alive in this world, and that you remember me."

She smiled, "I will always remember you."

Ravn hesitated, then pressed on, "If you were ever in danger, I would come fly to fight by your side, whatever the odds."

The elvin lady looked at him with mock seriousness. "I will hold you to that, Lord Blacach."

His senses still tingling with the power of her kiss, he nodded gravely, knowing that, as his love for her eclipsed the sun in his heart, he would happily die for her.

Chapter Twenty-Nine
Simrudian the Broken

Sim sobbed without tears. He had no tears. He had nothing left. Only the dry, wracking hate that moved him to shake, and cough, and want to cry. His feeble noises echoes off the dungeon walls in this vile, horrible city of nightmares.

Ignagamus watched impassively, sipping his drink.

Sim met his eyes only for a second, then the mountain of a man hurled the contents of his wine glass at him, slinging the cup high to low, and coating him with liquid. The low-elf recoiled and turned his head, but otherwise could not move. His wrists were bound by blistering iron cuffs, his ankles likewise, and by turning away he saved his eye but not the empty, bleeding socket. Everything, everything felt like it was on fire. The ice cold draught, made of the most potent sprits that could be distilled by men, sluiced down his naked chest and belly, catching in every cut, every stab, every open wound, burning as it mixed with old blood.

His hair had been burnt from his skull. His left eye had been gouged out with a dagger. His chest had been opened with the same blade in a dozen places, his nipples removed. His hands had been mauled by starved rats in tiny cages, the bones now exposed in many places. The chair he was locked to was padded with sharp points that imbedded in his skin as he sat there. His whole body had been beaten by fists, feet, and bars of iron. Of all his person, only his feet had been left untouched.

The sting of alcohol in his wounds made him writhe, pushing the spikes further into his backside, and the pain became a haze that robbed him of strength. He sagged forward, unable to move, or resist. They had all the information they asked for, weeks ago, while the rats chewed away on his fingers. Yet, they had not stopped.

Causing him pain was too much fun for them to stop.

Ignagamus, supreme tactician and general of the Iron Army had been there for it all. He was a man of immense size, with legs like tree trunks, arms that weighed a much as a child, and a torso that overflowed chairs. Inside the alcohol-fed flesh, there was a power that was utterly indomitable, but it was his soul that was his true weapon. He had watched and quaffed the flammable drinks without pause, but it did not dull his mind or wrack him with doubt. Ignagamus was a monster, and his flashing black eyes showed no remorse, no pity, and no care for anything or anyone but himself. He had not gained a sliver of joy watching Sim be reduced to a fleshy, quivering pile of nothing. He had just watched, bored, for he had inflicted far more exciting evils in his life before this.

The tactician stood, heaving his massive bulk upright and straining the seams of his gray leather jerkin and blue pants. The iron-riveted black boots almost groaned around his massive, distorted feet. He ran one hand through his greasy black hair, the cup falling from the other, baleful droplets spinning into the candlelight as it rang off of the stone floor. Silently, a servant caught it before it hit twice, filled it from the ever present cask of vile drink, and set it upon the table before withdrawing.

Sim glanced about, a hint of hope that the day's torture was done, but then the tactician spoke.

"Prepare him."

Cackling torturers came from behind, pulling the pins from the manacles and wrestling him, limp and unresisting to bend over the table, spilling the liquor. Strong hands held him, squeezing fresh blood from Sim's mangled fingers. He had no strength to struggle, but his heart began to pound in his chest. He hoped this was an end to his suffering.

Ignagamus turned and began to circle around him, his feet thudding like falling tombstones. He spoke again, his voice rumbling like a coming storm, "I am tired of you, elf. Tired of your people stealing our young men and women for your use. Tired of your closed borders. Tired of your spies. And now that I have all I need of you, I am letting you go."

Sim's heart raced at this. It must be a lie. It had to be a lie. But his feet ached for free roads and tall trees, for peace and life without pain. He yearned for the sun and the moon. He wanted his home. A feeble moan escaped him and he hated himself for it.

"But I tell you this," he spat the words, "know that my army is twenty thousand strong. Giants. Stone throwers. You saw it, and know the truth of my words." Sim heard the heavy *thunk* of a belt hitting the floor, "Now you can go hide the pain and shame that you have failed to stop me from inflicting upon you," He felt large, hard fingers tear open the seat of his ripped and tattered pants, "or you can go home in shame, knowing nothing you tell them will help them in the fight ahead, and knowing they will all see you belong to me."

Sim began screaming, for there was one more violation to endure before they tossed him out, half dressed, like a vagabond. They dumped him outside the city gates like he was nothing– for nothing was what he had become.

Can't it be over now? Can't it just be over?

For a while he just lay there without sound, not even a cry. But the cold of winter clawed at him, ate at him, pushed him to his knees. He had to move, to get away from this place. He took mouths of snow, broken teeth screaming in agony as it slowly melted down his throat and he continued to crawl. It was deep into winter, and no sane man traveled the roads.

Night settled in, and the moon reflected on the drifts on every side. He did not stop until he passed where two pine trees leaned together into an arch at the edge of the snow bound ruts. His heart beat a wordless hope as he found strength to come to his feet and dive into the drifts that stung his skin. He stumbled and fell, but though he left bloody handprints he could feel nothing in them. He tore forward like an animal, passing beneath the trunks and up onto a rocky hill. Stomach turning at the state of his shredded hands, Sim clawed at the snow under an overhang until he found the heavy leather pack he had secreted there days, maybe weeks before. He pried open the frozen flap and pulled forth the boots, thick vest, and heavy cloak. As the cloak unfurled around his shivering shoulders, a heavy weight fell free.

There, on the ground, a gleaming Elvish dagger mocked him in its sheath. He stared at it as if it were a snake, heart thumping.

Haven't you done enough? Couldn't it just be over now?

He shook himself from the thought and grabbed the weapon, slipping it into a belt retrieved from the pack. Inside he found that the water and food were frozen solid, but small skins of honey and tiny tree holly tea had not succumbed to the cold. He squeezed one into his mouth greedily, hardly remembering the sensation of sweetness, or the giddy rush that came to him as he sucked at the nipple of the small skin. He shouldered the pack, and staggered back to the road. Continuing his flight from the nightmare of–

They were on all sides, kicking and spitting on him, hooting and hollering. The tactician watched, bored, drinking that damnable liquor and not caring even a little–

He stumbled and fell, then stood and fell again. The crystals of ice were real, chilled his face and arms above the elbows, and he shook himself off and pressed onward. He trudged through the night, wrapped up against the cackling arrows of the wind and the thieving cold of the snow.

Dawn found him in an alcove by the road, huddled in a ragged lean-to built by some nameless human days before. Sim had managed to start a fire with a few pitiful logs, fingers finally coming back to life and howling like all the man-eating wolves in the world. The fire was hard to start even with the fire kit in the pack. Blood began to seep through bite marks that exposed bones.

He tried to weep, but no tears would come. He fell asleep with dry eyes and a hollow chest.

He came awake flailing. His heart pounded so fast no beat could be discerned, a painfully loud roar in his ears. The dusk forest was alive and angry at him. He snatched up his dagger in hands that refused to close. And he stumbled out of the tiny house of branches across the dead coals of the fire, pointing the gleaming tip in all directions.

Nothing. He saw nothing. Nothing but the gleaming dagger in his hand. It winked at him in the fading light.

Couldn't it be over?

His hands trembled until he stashed it away, and went back to his camp. He gathered his gear, then drank the water and ate the food that had thawed by the fire. He packed the skin with snow and slung it near his body to melt and squeezed another tea-and-honey pack into his mouth. It felt slimy, cloying on his tongue and he had to force himself to swallow it. His stomach shook, and his limbs had tremors, but he was able to move on. He voided himself the next day, and the pain was so intense he passed out. He awoke and continued. One day passed into the next, and then the next...

Mile after mile he walked, hour upon hour. He forced himself to go without sleep, knowing they would be there, in his dreams, cutting and kicking and screaming. The tactician would be there, watching with disinterest. He would remember and collapse, rising only after his body was cold and tired with freshly renewed horror. Every night they attached the mesh cages to his hands and the hungry rats inside would gnaw at his fingers.

Still he pressed on. Dagger whispering on his hip.

Wouldn't it be better? Wouldn't it? Couldn't it finally be over?

But it wasn't over.

Winter broke. The chill faded and the snows retreated. His feet took him to the top of a hill, and he cast glances back at the far shadows of deadly mountains.

His feet kept moving.

Later that week, he found another cache stashed under a rock that looked like an eagle. He opened it to find more food, clothes, water, and bits of tea-laced honey. He had run out of food two days before and he staggered toward the spot at as much of a run as he could muster. He used the dagger to cut through the melting snow, desperate to reach the entrance to the cave. He opened it up wide and crawled inside. He nestled in the tiny space, crawling far underground until the earth felt warm on every side. He finally slept, dreamless and at peace.

He awoke to some noise.

It is them. I know it is them.

He took out the dagger.

Wouldn't it be better? it asked, innocently.

He stayed in the cave, peeking past the snow at the entrance and seeing nothing. He had long since passed from the mountains into the thickly forested hills. No road marked his path, and a thin layer of fresh snow over the night had hidden his trail. He saw no one but he knew they were out there. He *knew*.

Please, wouldn't it be better?

When night fell he began again, a second cloak curved around his shoulders. He had barely endured the agony of pulling on the thick, fur-lined gloves. Once they were on, however, they hid the blood and bones, and he felt better. He pushed on for three days, trying to lose the torturers he knew were following. Rain began and was constant, a pressure that never left him as the last of the white cleanness was replaced by mud.

The next time he slept, the dreams were different. He awoke to a beautiful, serene day in the oldest of woods. The canopy of trees turned the rain into a light mist, screened the wind, and filtered the sun into a soft thing that gently touched the forest floor.

Oh gods, the dreams are real and this is the dream! I am still in the cage! The tactician is coming!

He screamed for three hours until he collapsed, exhausted. Face down in the mud, he saw his dropped dagger and it giggled in the light.

Wouldn't it be better if it were just all over now?

Sim roared and planted the dagger into a tree and ran from it, ran for all he was worth. Ran until he only walked, ran until he staggered, ran until he crawled. Until he passed out. For days.

One day he woke to realize he was too warm. He moved to let the second cloak fall from his shoulders, but the clasp was nearly impossible to manage. His screams echoed through the forest as he peeled the gloves from the wrecked ruins of his hands. He could see nothing through the black clots of blood, and he couldn't feel anything in his fingers anymore. It didn't matter. Nothing mattered. He laid down to die.

After what seemed like months on his feet, he just slept.

He awoke and found he was being carried. He was being carried back to the cell! It had all been for nothing! He voided himself, and the pain was as harsh and deep as ever. The tactician grumbled in his ear, *You belong to me.*

The dagger, miles behind, called faintly, *Wouldn't it have been better?*

He watched the ground slowly crawl past his face. He heard words, but they were alien to his ears. Dirt gave way to large, octagonal stones.

Those stones, they should mean something. Something...

Then he slept again.

He awoke from knives, and rats, and brutality to a comfortably spare room. He was in a soft bed, and light poured in through open windows. that let in the smell of pine and fresh grass. He lay on top of the blankets, white strips of linen covering him wherever he was hurt. His feet were wrapped, as were his hands. He looked at one, watching as tiny fae flew in lazy circles around them, crying glowing tears into the bandages.

He tried to sit up, but he couldn't.

His movement brought in a healer instantly. The brown-haired half-elf fluttered to his side, a sad smile on his face.

"It is good to see you awake. You have suffered greatly, but you are on the mend." He nodded with satisfaction and examined the fae as they continued to work. "You must try to stay still." The man looked into his eye, smoothing a gentle hand over his shoulder. "You are home now. You are safe."

Sim tried to speak, and it came out only as a croak, "Kil..."

The healer nodded, "Yes, he said you would ask for him," and disappeared into the hallway. Councilman Kilcahann, Lord of Discipline and Morality followed the healer when he returned. The pure elf, platinum-haired and ancient as time, came in and stood by Sim's bed, face stoic.

Sim croaked, "Kil..."

Kilcahann nodded, "I am here, Simrudian, my servant. I am here. What happened to you? What did you see?"

Sim shook his head, whispering. Kilcahann leaned closer, closer, seeking to catch his feeble words.

Then he heard them. "K...kill me."

Kilcahann recoiled, shaking his head "No! No, Sim, what happened?"

The once proud elvin spy spoke in a deadpan voice, his one eye reflecting the epitome of solemnity. "Spring is here. They are coming. They are coming! Please, kill me! Kill me!"

Chapter Thirty
War Council

Today the council chambers looked like the inside of a white rose opening as it went up into the empty flight of galleries. The massive chamber echoed with every movement, and no one spoke. She could sense the pall over the hearts of all assembled.

The last time Vivien had stood here, she and the Wolf were being judged. But now, her geas was removed and the Wolf's bonds had been struck from his arms by The Lord of Swords with the broken blade of Arisil. Now, they sat with the assembled council as honored guests without witnesses from the city. She felt a chill as she began to believe that this was a far more dangerous moment than the last. The high benches had been abandoned. Now a wide table surrounded by ornate chairs dominated the center of the chamber, only one left unfilled. In the center, a massive map of Rithalion and the environs demanded attention. Around it were the masters of their crafts, set to advise and consent on the proceedings... the war council. Among them were a few others, including herself and the Wolf. She took it for the honor it was.

Her husband, Lord of Ice and Steel was there as an esteemed member of the council. He all but ignored her, instead focusing on the map, his skin sallow and his dark hair plastered to his head with sweat. She looked to her father, who sat at the opposite side of the table to speak for the wizards of the city. He looked at her and tried to smile, but it was a forced effort. A chill came over her again and it would not leave as she looked from face to face, seeing little comfort and less hope. The warmage glanced at her partner, but his bearded face was stoic, giving away nothing.

Vivien looked at Torialvah again, stared at him for several moments. A realization began to creep over her, a memory that she had somehow kept squelched down deep inside of herself for all these weeks after the Wolf had saved her life. Unbidden images flashed through her mind

The Wolf kneels over her, the open gashes on his forearms dripping blood onto her naked torso.

Vivien put a hand to her forehead as Xadrian, Lord of Swords and Truth, stood from his seat and began to speak. His deep voice filled the empty space. "Our spy has returned at great personal cost. He bears a dire tiding; our enemy is on the march."

His words hung in the air like a descending blade. The reactions around the table varied, but none seemed surprised. Vivien felt her insides quiver and she gripped the child in her belly with a hand for comfort, but likewise there was a fire of determination. It put steel in her spine.

Vivien turned when she noticed the Wolf looking at her. His huge hand reached under the table to grip hers gently. It was so warm. She squeezed it and he gave a nod that said, *we can do this.*

The grip was comforting not just for what was playing out in the chamber before her, but for the images in her mind.

Torialvah stands behind the Wolf, a hand in his hair pulling his head back to expose his throat. Tor has a dagger pressed against it.

Swansee shifted in her seat uncomfortably. "How many are there?"

Xadrian opened his mouth, but it was Kilcahann who answered in a voice devoid of inflection or emotion. "At least twenty thousand."

Xadrian frowned. Vivien felt the flame in her flicker and burn so low, suddenly a tiny light in a massive void of hungry darkness. She gripped the Wolf's hand harder.

Oilariann stood as if addressing a full council chamber, "And how many soldiers can we field?"

The answer came from behind, a beautiful voice that fed the candles all around, making the place a little lighter. "Fifteen hundred." These words took the strength from him and he wobbled a bit on his feet, only held upright by pride and discipline.

A blue glow has enveloped Torialvah, but it doesn't stop the Wolf from leaning into Tor's blade and slicing his own neck.

Shaladrea almost floated into the chamber, pausing only for a moment as she saw the empty chair. "You are missing a member?"

Oilariann sat as Xadrian motioned to it and said, "Not anymore."

Shaladrea arced an eyebrow. "I was not invited."

Xadrian motioned again. "But you are expected."

She smiled sweetly at him. "Am I so predictable?"

Vivien startled as Torialvah's voice burst throughout the room, "Can we please continue? We face our total extermination!"

The rumbling voice that answered him took all eyes from Shaladrea as she sat down to focus on the Wolf. Vivien gripped his hand more tightly and chanced a look at him. *Yes, there it is, a thin white scar...*

"Human armies do not move like Elvish ones," he said. "The larger they are, the slower they will travel. They are chained to roads, to supply trains, and have to cut their ways into the forest."

Torialvah sneered, "What do you know of it?"

The Wolf frowned back, eyes building a banked glow. "Have you ever marched a human army?"

Kilcahann pounced upon those words. "Have you?"

The question was made to cause doubt in the human, but Vivian looked to the scar again. *He had to think he would die. He meant to die. For me.* She touched her belly. *For my child.*

Orinoco slapped the table, "Enough! How can there only be fifteen hundred soldiers to defend the city?"

Xadrian finally sat, steepling his fingers, as Vivien fought to control the sick feeling that overwhelmed her. "There are fifty thousand souls in Rithalion: men, women, children, full elves, lesser elves, and humans. It has been four hundred years since the end of the Civil War, and almost all of our soldiery has been born since. We have fifteen hundred that have fought in actual combat. The rest are youths in training, or old men who would not be fit to fight after the march. Another fifteen hundred. No more. Volunteers are being trained but–"

Torialvah snarled, "Then we call up conscripts! Anyone who can shoot a bow or hold a sword."

Again the Wolf spoke. "You do not want conscripts to fight this battle. Elfish lives take far too long to replace." He glanced at Vivien and frowned, somehow sensing something amiss. "Conscripts will die by the thousands."

Kilcahann, descending back into a black mood, barely gestured. "How many mages?"

Master Jor'aiden glanced at his daughter and then looked at the map to avoid all the eyes pleading for some number that would save them, a number that would not come, "Warmages? Fifty."

Oilariann gasped, "Fifty?"

Jor'aiden's brow darkened. "We do not force students to learn the arts of war. Most can defend themselves, but in the heat of battle they will act like a farmer given a sword. A few will rise to the occasion, most will die. We can spare twenty healers from the city. That gives us seventy mages total."

Swansee looked stricken, her beautiful features not just pale, but cursed. "How can so few stand against twenty thousand?"

Xadrian looked to the Wolf, who stood, grudgingly letting go of Vivien's hand well below the table. "We will not win with arrows or swords. We must fight with mobility and strategy."

Torialvah huffed. "You speak to us as if we were children."

The Wolf ignored the interruption and pointed to the map. "We meet them at The Fall."

Tor laughed without humor. "Two weeks march. No fortress. No defensible positions. Your suggestion is pointless." He let harsher words stink, unsaid, in the air.

The Wolf's eyes were brighter, but he ignored the bait. "Useless if you are fighting elves, but you are not. The Iron Army will be slowed by the forest. The place we have chosen is denser still. There is a massive meadow a mile across. The light makes the entry into the old growth forest like a wall from behind which the elves can sally and fire. The cliff above the lake to the east and the steep slope to the west will funnel them into that open space. It is the perfect place to meet them."

"And die." Kilcahann snapped. "They will have siege engines. Giants. Packs of killer dogs. My spy has seen them."

"That," Xadrian replied, grim but with a voice as steady as granite bedrock, "is why we will flank behind them. We will destroy their command structure, supplies, siege engines, and archers."

Kilcahann scoffed, "You can't still expect that demented plan to work? When you expected five thousand to come attack us it was improbable, now it is simply a waste of lives."

Torialvah frowned. "What plan? What lives?"

The Wolf sat, completely at ease as if discussing the weather. "We have a unit of warmages and soldiers trained to defend them unto death. We will circle the peak to the south through Pergatium and behind the human army. We will come up behind them and strike at their soft underbelly."

Vivien watched her husband's face drain of all color. Finally he exhaled and looked straight at her for the first time, and her blood turned cold. "This is what you have left my bed for? This? A plan to get the men you have been leading killed?"

Vivien gathered herself, knowing she was expected to make a reply. It was difficult, knowing what he had done, but forced her words to the subject at hand. She kept anger from her voice and sat proud and straight in her chair. "We have trained them. They have done far better than we ever expected. They work as a unit, and will inflict terrible damage."

Oilariann nodded sadly. "Xadrian had already informed the Council of the plan. We agree it is the best chance we have."

"Bah!" Vivien felt her heart shrink at Tor's exclamation. "If the march through the Doomed City does not kill them, they will certainly perish behind the enemy and be crushed like bugs."

Her eyes flashed, and she felt the words come from her lips between hard teeth, "The enemy will be two weeks from the coast and support. There are no farms there, no towns to raid. Still weeks from Rithalion, they will not find towns to raid or burn. As long as we destroy the supply caravan, the army will starve and die. We will ultimately win, no matter the rest."

Tor was barely listening. He made a dismissive gesture. "It hardly matters, I suppose, that this unit numbering...?"

"One hundred," she inserted in a monotone.

"...will die horribly." He sat back in his chair. "My forges have been working day and night. We have armor and weapons aplenty for four times the number of soldiers we have, a greater surplus once we lose a hundred to the folly of my foolish wife and her delusions of grandeur."

Vivien saw the Wolf's eyes go from a slow roar to a bright fire, though he barely moved. Many around the table had never seen his eyes glow thusly, and looked from one to another. She felt the opposite reaction inside herself, and coldness numbed the pain and doubt instantly. "Well if you are right, husband, you will be spared that foolishness any longer. I will be with that unit."

Exclamations ran around the room, but Tor was unmoved. "You are pregnant, and as such, not going. I forbid it."

"Forbid all you like. This is my unit. I trained them. I will be with them when we go to war."

She had to shut out her father's stricken face, the shock of elves all around, but then a hand touched her shoulder, and she turned to the calm face of the Wolf. *No. Not you, too. Anyone but you.*

But he did not berate her, council her, or doubt her. He simply asked, "Are you certain?"

Vivien considered it only a moment before asking defiantly. "If I am here safe in Rithalion and we fail, how long before the city is overrun?"

Shaladrea's tone was soft, and sad.. "The city is not meant to repel attack. It will fall in a day once they are here. My fortress will hold many, but it will eventually fall as well. Soldiers, siege engines, ladders, it does not matter. With twenty thousand troops they will cut us off and starve us in months."

Vivien looked into the crimson eyes of the big man, wishing, needing them to turn blue. "Death in battle or death of starvation. I will take the chance and defend my people, pregnant or not." Her stern determination cracked, just for a second.

The Wolf nodded, accepting her reasoning and silently pledging his support to her unto death. His eyes faded from bright to dark. She gave a small smile. He blinked, and the anger in them faded to a beautiful, stormy blue. He smiled back at her.

Tor's face was a mask of indifference, but his words were clipped. "This is insanity!"

Swansee nodded, "Perhaps, but the life of our city lies in the hands of the fifteen hundred soldiers, fifty warmages, and twenty healers. One hundred of those souls in the vanguard."

The situation laid bare, Orinoco nodded and leaned forward. "Then we must discuss fortifying the city, all the strong points therein, and the Lady of Moonlight's fortress, preparing supplies for the army that will meet the enemy, and those that remain behind."

Jor'aiden nodded, "How will the army travel? How long before they leave?"

Xadrian considered only a moment, "The Iron Army will plod along. It will take them five weeks to get to The Fall. Using tir-reath and reindeer for our main force, they can leave in four weeks and still have days to prepare the area. The swamp is treacherous, however. The vanguard will have to move on foot, and leave in two weeks at the very latest."

There was a silence as everyone considered. Into it a dagger of ice came from Torialvah. "You will die out there, Vivien!"

She swept her hair from her face, cursing the burning in her cheeks that betrayed the cauldron of turmoil inside her. "Then mayhap you had best come with the vanguard to protect me, husband."

He frowned. "I am not willing to die for this."

Her tone was one of sadness. "I know, you haven't been willing to die for me for a long time."

Chapter Thirty-One
What Was Lost

Vivien shifted restlessly and moaned. She was tired, but sleep was like the warbling song of the tiny sunset tanager, sweet and elusive. Her dreams were easier to come by, but also vague. Upon waking they were nearly impossible to recall; the only element she tended to remember was that they were intensely disturbing.

Instead of just laying there and having sleep come to her just before she needed to wake for the day, she decided to rise early. She donned a robe over her nightgown and padded down to the kitchens, where she found waiting kettles of freshly brewed tea. Mug in hand, she wandered around the fortress for a while, just taking in the activity of a place that would soon be at war. The thought was disturbing and fell in line with the images she recalled from her dreams.

Vivien returned her empty mug to the kitchens and grabbed the bag of scrap meat the staff would leave for her every day. She then climbed the tower steps back to her chambers. A mild ache gripped her lower abdomen for a few moments. It was a sensation she felt more often as of late and she ran a hand over her belly. It was still flat, but she imagined the roundness it would develop in the next three or four months as the child grew.

She entered the chamber suite and Sherika was patiently waiting. Vivien opened the bag and laid it out for her friend on the balcony. Sherika rubbed her head along Vivien's side before setting on the food with aplomb. Vivien couldn't help smiling as she went back inside, took off the robe, and sat on the ermine rug in front of the fireplace for a while. In spite of Sherika's presence, and the time she spent with the her apprentices, the soldiers, and the Wolf almost every day, she was lonely. She wondered how she was going to take care of a baby by herself, for she could no longer imagine Tor being there by her side as a husband or father.

And then there was the war and her part in it. She knew she was risking her life, but she risked the life of her unborn son as well. While there was a large part of her that wanted to keep him safe and just remain on the home-front, she knew how greatly needed she was out on the lines. It wasn't just about her or her son, it was about all the people of Rithalion.

Vivien rose from the toasty fire and dressed for the day. She thought about eating something but decided she wasn't very hungry. The ache in her belly had stolen her appetite, and thinking back on it, she hadn't eaten dinner the night before either. She attributed it to apprehension about the upcoming several days. Training was more intense than ever and the unit had practiced every possible scenario that could take place. These final days, the Wolf was looking for perfection. No mistakes could be made here in the comfort of Rithalion, with adequate sleep and full bellies, because out there, out in the middle of battle, stress caused men to make mistakes. If it was perfect now in perfect conditions, it was more likely that the operations could be executed the same way under strain. And if mistakes were made, well, maybe there wouldn't be as many.

Vivien grimaced as she donned her boots. Her belly cramped spasmodically, and she didn't feel very well. Sherika approached and put her head in her lap. Through their connection, Vivien could tell her friend wanted her to stay.

"Oh, Sherika, I can't stay today. I have a lot of work to do. If I am to go with them, I owe it to the men to be fit. I must train too." She caressed the top of her friend's head and the soft fur around her eyes. Sherika made a trilling sound, the one she used to try and get her way. Vivien chuckled. "Not this time, my friend."

She left the chamber and walked out to the practice fields. The nagging pain settled low in her belly, making it feel heavy, but she hoped it would go away once she got moving. When she got there she saw the unit was already at work, executing one of the strategies she and the Wolf had devised over the past several weeks. The mages cast with deadly accuracy, Tyrell at the forefront, just as they had agreed. If something happened, and she wasn't there to lead them, he would do so in her stead. The mages and soldiers obeyed him as well as they did her or the Wolf, and it was awesome to observe on this side as opposed to being in the middle of the fray.

So Vivien leaned against a wooden post for a while and just watched. It wasn't long before the familiar sounds of the unit at work faded into the background and her thoughts turned inward. Truth be told, she wasn't certain she was fit enough to be out on the field this day. The upper half of her inner thighs ached, and the cramping pain in her belly had worsened. It was only when she shifted to find a more comfortable position that she felt it...a wetness between her legs.

Alarm swept over her and she pressed a hand to her belly. Something was wrong, terribly wrong. Just as she turned to head back to the fortress, she heard someone call her name.

"Lady Vivien! Did you just see that? Did you see that maneuver? We executed it without a single mishap!"

She looked back to find that some of the soldiers were jogging over. She placed one hand against the post for support and tried to set aside the pain. "Yes, it was excellent work. You need to repeat it daily until it becomes a memory to your body. And then, when the time comes, and your mind is distracted by other things, your body will perform the task without thought dictating it."

The men circled her, all of them speaking excitedly about the operation. Vivien clenched at the post, hoping, praying to remain upright long enough for them to head back to the field. She felt a warm trickle down her inner thigh and her vision swam. *Just a few moments longer, just a few...*

"Vivien, are you all right? Vivien!" She had not heard him approach, but the Wolf caught her as her legs buckled.

She felt one arm curve around her back while the other swept beneath her legs. She gave an involuntary moan as she felt herself lifted up. All she could think was that she was afraid to get blood all over him. Her voice sounded strangely slurred. "Wolf, no. Please, put me down."

His voice rose over those of the other men, voices of confusion and concern. "Everyone, get back to work! Tyrell, have them execute the scatter maneuver again, but this time have them repel arrows, then iron, then a charge."

Vivien wrapped her arms around his neck as he carried her away at a quick pace, bit back another moan when she felt the cramping pain followed by a warm gush. "Wolf. Wolf!"

He looked down at her, his eyes dark. "You are ill. Let me get you back to your tower so you can rest."

Her tone held a hint of petulance. "Please, put me down. I can walk on my own."

He slowed his pace and frowned. "You almost fell standing in place. How can you walk? Just let me carry you; it won't take long."

She struggled. "No, set me down."

He slowed further. "Please, I want to help you."

"Just...I'll be fine. Just let me walk on my own."

His face moved through a series of pained expressions, but he obeyed her and stopped. She struggled until he released her and set her down.

It took most of her effort, but she stood there without falling, and she spoke without her voice wavering too much. "Please, go back to the unit. I'll be fine."

He just stood there, his arms held out from his sides and his chest rising and falling as though he was about to go into battle. His face was expressionless. "You will call if you have need of me."

She nodded. "All right."

Vivien then waited for him to turn around and start back to the fields. Once he was far enough away, she turned towards the fortress. She really didn't have that much further to go. With shaking hands, she slowly lifted her gown enough to view the top of her boots.

She swallowed back a cry to see they were red with blood.

She put one foot in front of the other and began to walk. It was harder that she thought because her entire body shook. All she wanted to do was slump to the ground and cry, but she wouldn't allow it yet. She needed to be safe behind the privacy of her own walls before falling apart.

Another painful wave hit her and she had to stop. She clutched at her belly and stood there, watched as dripping blood fell onto the grass beneath her feet. *Oh gods please help me...* Her head spun and her legs felt weak again. She toppled but managed to catch herself on hands and knees. The tears came, unbidden, as she allowed her reality to sweep over her.

Then she felt a warm arm wrap around her from behind, protecting, loving. She didn't look up, didn't want to know who was there.

His voice was a deep whisper in her ear, "Vivien, you are bleeding. Please, let me take you up to your tower."

She didn't resist as the Wolf picked her up again. She rested her head against his chest as he swiftly strode through the fortress. She could hear his heart thudding with power as he ran smoothly up the winding stairs, not into her tower, but the Lady's tower. He then took her through the main chamber and to the stairs that led down into the suite he shared with Lydia. Once there, he took her into his personal chamber and laid her on his bed.

She looked up at him through pain-filled eyes. "Why have you brought me here?"

"I didn't want you to be alone in your tower while I went to get you some help. Either the Lady or one of her wives is always in the chamber suite above. I will be back in but a brief moment."

She swallowed past the lump in her throat. "What if I want to be alone?"

He blinked. "You don't ever deserve to be alone, but if you desire it, I will leave. However, I won't do so until I know you have the help you need."

The Wolf left the room. She closed her eyes and curved around herself as another wave of pain gripped her. She cried pathetic tears into the bedcovers, and when it was over, she just lay there, trembling.

"Oh, my dear Vivien!" Shaladrea swept into the room and sat down beside her on the bed. She pulled Vivien close until she was in her lap, swept a comforting hand over her hair. "Master Healer Mikarvan arrived here a few days ago. I have called him and he will be here any minute."

Vivien wrapped her arms around the Lady's waist and lay there in her embrace. She saw the Wolf standing in the doorway, his expression one of great sadness. She closed her eyes for the briefest moment, but when she opened them again, he was gone.

The next morning Vivien opened her eyes to see Mikarvan slumped over in the chair beside the bed. His legs were propped up on the bedframe, arms crossed over his chest, blond hair falling over his face. He looked so serene sitting there, so unlike the man whom she'd seen the night before. That man had been so different than the young friend she'd always known, so knowledgeable, so confident.

It was that man who had delivered her stillborn son.

When it was done, and she was finally as comfortable as she was going to get, he had handed her the tiny child wrapped in a soft blanket provided by the Lady of Moonlight and Love. He was suddenly transformed back into the friend she'd known all her life, and he wrapped his arms around her. "Vivien, he's beautiful."

And Mikarvan was right. The child was more beautiful than she ever imagined he would be, and perfect in every tiny detail.

His voice was a whisper in her ear. "What is his name?"

Her eyes had overflowed with tears. How did he know she'd chosen one already? "I wanted to call him Gaelen."

"Then Gaelen is his name. It is a very nice one."

She bit her lip, feeling waves of sadness lap at her mind. "Is it?"

He placed a couple of fingers over the baby's head. "It suits him just right."

Vivien shook her head and brought herself back into the present. She continued to lay there, staring at him, wondering what it would have been like if elvin society who a half-elvin girl of her status married. Once, a long time ago, this man, then a boy, had been her only friend. They had hunted imaginary dragons together at the banks of the Fyresmee River that flowed in the gorge beneath the prison caverns. Mikarvan's father was the most renowned cartographer in Rithalion, and they had the best maps to use in their hunts. They always found their target...

Suddenly Mikarvan's feet were sliding off the bed. She startled and her gaze shifted to find golden brown eyes staring at her intently. "What do you see when you look at me so long?"

She inhaled sharply. Giving away her innermost thoughts would be useless and cause discomfort; she chose the safe route instead. "I see my best friend, the one who would have me when no one else would. I see the boy who saved me." Still painful, at least for her, but better than the rest.

Mikarvan sat forward in the chair and ran a hand across her forehead and into her hair. "I'm not certain I was the one who did the saving."

Vivien shifted, hoping to sit up, but a gush from between her legs stilled her. Seeing her look of alarm, Mikarvan rose and helped her up. "You will continue to pass blood for the next few days. It is normal after an event such as this."

She just sat there for a moment. Then, "I imagined I would feel more empty than this. Certainly, I feel something is missing but..."

Mikarvan just nodded. "Everything you are feeling is normal. And you are not alone. Almost every week at the sanatorium I have a woman come who is going through what you have."

There was another brief period of silence. "I didn't even know you were here until the Lady told me yesterday."

He nodded. "I have been chosen to lead the twenty healers accompanying the elvin forces when they leave Rithalion. We arrived a few days ago. I wanted to catch up with you, but I was so busy, and so were you." He frowned. "I'm sorry we had to meet like this."

More silence. Then, "To your knowledge, does Tor know about this?" she asked.

"I don't believe so. We wanted you to awaken first before sending the message."

Mikarvan must have seen something reflected in her eyes because he reached forward to envelop one of her hands in his. "Vivien, what is it?"

Her lower lip quivered. She didn't want to say it, but it was such a powerful force in her mind, she knew she had to. "I'm afraid. He will be so angry, more than he ever has been before. He will hate me."

He raised her hand to his lips and kissed it. "Vivien, listen to me. You have done nothing wrong. This happens all the time. Elves and humans, even partial humans, they aren't always very compatible. It makes for carrying children very difficult. Ultimately it works out, but it just takes some time, and unfortunately, some losses. Your husband knows this."

Vivien remained quiet.

Mikarvan leaned close and he spoke in a low voice. "Why are you so afraid of him?"

She shrugged, trying to make light of it. "It's just that he's been so angry with me. I've stayed here in spite of his wishes for me to come home. I work every day in the practice fields, and maybe I don't rest as I should."

Mikarvan shook his head. "Work does not cause miscarriage. Did you fall? Get hit?"

She shook her head.

"Those things *might* cause loss at the stage you were at, but not always because the baby is so protected by birth-water and the shell of your body. Really, there is nothing you could have done to prevent this. It just simply is, and you will move on. So will your husband."

Vivien nodded. Mikarvan gave her hand a squeeze and rose from beside the bed. "I am going to get us something to eat. I will return shortly. Shall I send someone in?"

"No, I really need some moments to myself, just to think about things."

"I understand. I will see you soon."

She nodded and watched the healer leave. She took a deep trembling breath and then let it out. While he was out she was sure he would give the word for a message to be sent to her husband. Mikarvan thought he was trying to help, but he didn't know Torialvah...

The winds whipped fiercely as Vivien watched Torialvah lay the tiny, shrouded form into the grave. His shoulders were hunched against the cold, and his crimson cloak waved like a bloody banner behind him. His words would have been lost if Vivien hadn't been listening for them.

"May the gods always grant a sunbeam to warm you, a moonbeam to charm you, a sheltering faery so nothing can harm you as you set upon your journey."

Vivien moved to crouch beside her husband and set a wreath of flowers beside the infant. "May flowers line your path and sunbeams light your day. May songbirds serenade you every step of your way. May rainbows arc overhead in a sky that's always blue, in my heart these are my fondest dreams for you."

Together they replaced the ground they had disturbed when they dug the grave, piling it on top of a boy that would never take his first breath, never run in the fields or bathe in the steams in and around Rithalion. An image suddenly streaked through Vivien's mind- a vision of a young boy and girl. *They were smiling, and their tinkling laughter filled the air...*

Then they were done, and the beautiful sound was borne away by the winds. A headstone would be placed at the grave on the morrow by Elrich, the stonemason. Over time, the rains would compact the dirt around the child, cocoon him within the place where all elves come from.

The two stood from the grave and walked down the hill, passing multitudes of other graves, some of them one on top of the other, for it was Rithalion's only burial ground.

Vivien stopped halfway to the bottom of the hill. She ached inside, and she was tired. When he noticed she was no longer beside him, Tor stopped as well and looked back. He shook his head, his features shifting into an expression of anger.

His voice was scathing. "You are despicable. If you had done what I'd told you to do, we wouldn't be here right now."

Vivien just stood there, eyes wide with shock. *Is he serious? Does he really believe that, just because I decided to not desert my work and come home, that I lost our baby?*

He saw the look of disbelief on her face and nodded. "Yes, I believe that you killed our son. All the spellcasting you persist in doing, all that running around with all those dirty soldiers in the middle of winter, with that hairy friend of yours that should still be in our prison cavern. It was your lack of guidance that caused you to get into trouble and have the binding geas placed on you, a geas not even the Grand Magister could remove, a geas that placed unnecessary strain upon the pregnancy." He balled his hands into fists. "You killed him, Vivien!"

She continued to stand there and just stare at him. She imagined she should cry, but she'd done all of that already, and there were simply no tears left, not for the ravings of a man who was proving to be an absolute lunatic. Spellcasting didn't kill children, or exercise, or the cold of winter.

But the geas....could he be right? Did the strain of its removal place too much stress on her unborn child?

Memories of that night flashed before her eyes: all the blood, the burning pain, the Wolf, and...and Torialvah.

The dagger glinted red in the firelight. It was pressed against the Wolf's throat, piercing the vulnerable flesh. A gush of thick, dark red blood poured over her in a crimson river that wouldn't stop flowing...

Her husband walked back up the hill in wide strides, closing the distance between them. Fear surged through her and she stumbled back. He caught her arm before she could fall and jerked her towards him.

He wrapped his other hand around her wrist. "You are a failure, Vivien. You always have been and always will be," he said gruffly. "And tomorrow I will be making that common knowledge by lodging a formal complaint with the Council."

Despite her fear, Vivien's response was immediate. "Make sure you make that complaint alongside your transgression, the one where you decided to murder a man in cold blood!"

His brows pulled together. "I never did that!" he snarled.

"You did! I watched it with my own eyes."

Realization dawned on him, "If you had watched close enough, you'd have seen the fool did it to himself."

"I was watching, and I saw your intent before my father stopped you with his spell. The fact that the Wolf finished what you started means nothing to me!" she spat.

His grip on her arm tightened, his blue eyes so pale they were almost white. They gazed at her without emotion, like she was nothing but a regular passerby on the street. His voice was a monotone, "I thought I could love you once. I was wrong."

The winds gusted again, sweeping into her hood and making it fall behind her. She just stared at him for a moment, her heart plummeting in her chest like a brick. It was one thing to think it, and another to actually hear it in the light of day. She had thought she could love him too, actually did love him for a while. She supposed it was a fault– loving people too much.

"Then let me go, Torialvah. Let me go." She was surprised by the strength she heard in her voice. In spite of the sadness, she heard it there, ringing in her ears. With every bit of energy left in her, she pulled back. Her wrist popped when she broke it free of his grip. She then swept past him and down the hill.

Vivien continued walking until she reached Sherika, who had waited for her even though the cat wanted to bound up the hill and come to her aid. Vivien showered the tir-reath with affection and praised her for her obedience, then mounted her. A gush between her legs made her groan; she must have pulled too hard against Torialvah.

As weakness shadowed Vivien's senses, her friend carried her safely back home, home not to a lonely house, but to a massive fortress on the edge of Rithalion, home to some of the people who loved her most.

Chapter Thirty-Two
A Piece of Happiness

Thunder rumbled in the distance, and the smell of approaching rain could be perceived through the open windows. Ravn stood there in the middle of the bedchamber, hands on his hips, and stared at his wife. "It's wrong of you to keep yourself from me so much. I mean, you've shared my bed how many times since the first time? Maybe ten? I'm your husband for gods' sake!"

Ròs turned to him, her blue eyes sparkling with rancor. "What? You are actually going to come in here and berate be for not meeting your standards for a perfect wife?"

"Perfect wife? Do you jest? You don't do anything even remotely wifely!"

She narrowed her eyes. "And the most wifely thing that comes to your mind is sex."

His voice was tight and he drew his lips into a thin line. "It is the most powerful thing that draws two people together, so yes, it comes to mind."

She walked across the room to her vanity and sat down before it. "You know how I feel about it with you."

He took a deep breath. "Yes, but I live my life hoping one day that may change. I desire you very much, I desire us. For there to be an us, Ròs."

Ròs looked at herself in the mirror, picked up the new jar of rouge she had recently purchased from town, and applied it to her lips. "Well I don't want to be pestered by you and your desire. Go find your rut elsewhere."

Ire swelled within him, an anger that had been foreign to him until he'd been forced to find other women to fill his bed. He hated having to do it, for he felt it was a breach of his marriage contract, a vow he took very seriously. But his wife refused him, night after night, week after week, month after month, until his desire for contact as so strong...

The thunder rumbled again, closer this time. "Yes, I recall you telling me that before."

Ravn watched as she dabbed at her eyes with a soft cloth, then turned this way and that in the mirror. She had filled out a bit over the years, but not much. Ròs was still a very slender woman, with small breasts, narrow hips, and a belly so flat it was almost concave. Her lank brown hair was most often raised away from her face in fancy combs, or bundled at the back of her head into a bun. Her face could often appear quite severe, especially with him, but every once in a while through the years he had seen her smile, truly smile, and she was beautiful.

He'd always wished she could smile that way for him.

Her eyes suddenly regarded him piercingly from the mirror. "Are you just going to stand there and stare at me? Just leave me alone Ravn. I don't want you. I never have."

He abruptly turned away, a rush of hurt sweeping through him. He opened the door and slammed it behind him, unmindful of who might hear it. He took the stairs downward two at a time until he reached the grand hall, walked swiftly through until he stepped outside.

Ravn stood there in the bailey, cold rain coming down in sheets, thunder sounding overhead. He ran across it to the stables, barely slowed at the door before rushing in and closing it behind him. He stood there in the semi darkness, his shirt plastered to his chest and his hair dripping wet. The comforting sounds of horses assailed his ears, the ones nearest him nickering softly in greeting.

It was then he realized it, a lantern lit nearby, breaking the darkness into pieces of long shadow. All of them should have been out at this hour and the ire swelled within him again. *Who has left a lantern lit in his barn? Unless...*

Ravn took the lantern down from the peg and moved deeper into the stable. Heads appeared over the stall doors as he passed, the mares he used to beget the next generation of foals he would sell to other Lairds who coveted them, the stallions he used to cover those mares, and the geldings he used to ride through town and on other business.

He slowed as he reached the back of the barn, heard a voice coming from the last stall, the one belonging to his old stallion, Storm. It was a sweet voice, the cadence rising and falling in a familiar tune. He heard a rhythmic brush stroke in accompaniment, and he thought that Storm was certainly the lucky one this evening.

He peered into the stall. Long, dark brown hair was plaited into a rope down her back, chemise stained, breeches littered with hay. Neála continued to sing and brush for a few moments before Storm gave him away and she turned around. She was startled to see him there, but her face brightened before she could tone it back to a more modest expression.

"Laird, I'm sorry, I didn't see you standing there. Do you have need of a horse tonight?"

He just stood there and looked at her. She was the feminine version of her father, and had taken over the stables when Giles became ill a couple years ago. She was only eighteen, but the man had taught her all he knew and she had earned her place as his successor. Throughout the years, Ravn had talked to her about the stable and the horses who lived there: foals, training, breaking mounts, new purchases. Always she was interested in every word he had to say, and her demeanor always seemed to beg him for more...

He hung the lantern on a nearby peg and stepped into the stall. Her eyes widened. "Laird?"

He raised a brow. "Have you seen the deplorable weather outside?"

"Well, yes. But rain doesn't always stop a man from doing what needs to be done if the situation warrants it." She continued with her brushing.

He nodded noncommittally and patted his dappled gray. "What has you out here at this hour in a storm like this?"

She shrugged. "Storm gets spooked by the thunder. I come here to soothe him."

He nodded again, a smile curving up his lips at the memory. "You once thought he didn't like you."

"Well, I was young and stupid then. I didn't know what I know now." She stopped and was quiet for a moment. "A young elvin Lady once helped me see beyond myself."

She looked up then, her brown eyes searching his. "I...I could see how much you loved her."

His brows furrowed momentarily, not realizing he'd been so transparent. "How did you know?"

Her voice became low. "It was the way you looked at her, the way you spoke, the way your hand would brush over hers." She chuckled. "Even at the age of thirteen I could see love when it hit me in the face."

He just nodded and looked away, looked at the wizened face of one of the his favorite horses in his stables. By no means was Storm an old horse, but he had a wisdom about him. He'd never been the same since the day Jash'ari had spoken to him and lay her hand on him.

Ravn stepped back and out of the stall, his mind roiling with memories. "Well, I should let you get back to your soothing then. It appears you are good at it, and I am certain Storm loves you for it."

Before he realized what was happening, Neála had followed him out and latched the door behind her. "You still haven't told me what brought you here, Laird." His eyes flicked beyond her to the front of the barn, where he suddenly felt it was best for him to go. But she stood in front of him...

She was about to say something more, he could see the indecision on her face. Instead she reached out a hand and plucked at the neckline of his shirt. "You are wet. The rain must be coming down pretty hard." She looked up at the sodden mess of his hair, seemed about to reach up to touch it as well, but stopped. "It makes your hair curl more than usual."

He chuckled. "It does at that."

Her hand dropped to his chest and rested there, her eyes looking up at him with a tenderness he wasn't used to seeing, even with the two women he had visited a couple times in one of the local taverns. He just stood there and regarded her intently, watched the pupils of her eyes dilate, her cheeks flush, and her tongue dart out to wet her lips. He breathed deeply, the pervading animal scent and her sweet, musky odor overcoming his senses. Without thinking he stepped closer until he looked down at her, his arm almost touching hers. He leaned down until their mouths were so close that...

Ravn stopped and swallowed heavily. *I shouldn't be doing this.* She was young, and in his employ. He'd promised himself he wouldn't bed any of the women working in the castle.

Neála's eyes searched his, her lips parted, her breathing much more rapid than it should be. "Laird?"

Ravn shook his head and stepped back. It pained him to do so, for the girl was pretty, much prettier than she ought to be after working in a stable all day. More than pretty, she was kind, and gentle, sweet... She deserved more than him. But she followed him back, her hand still on his chest. "Laird, please! Please let me be here for you."

He stopped and looked at her intensely. Was she implying what he thought she was? He reached out and put a hand around the back of her neck, drawing her closer, closer. He watched her eyes, looked for any sign of indecision, any sign that told him that he shouldn't do this.

There was none.

His lips met hers and he kissed her without further thought. Neála matched the gale of his passion, gripping his shirt in her fist and pulling him closer. Their mouths tasted one another in a dance of discovery, but finally calmed to a more tender caress. She was warm and wanting, drawing a moan of desire from the deepest parts of him. He wrapped an arm around her waist, felt her fit against him just right. Her curves, in all the right places, melded against him and it felt like she belonged in his arms, even if it was just for this night.

Storm put his head over the door and gave a hearty neigh, startling them both out of the moment. Neála laughed, pushing escaped raven locks behind one ear and blushing. Ravn smiled back as she took his hand and they walked to the ladder that led up into the hayloft.

Ravn remembered all the times they had spoken through the years, not just about horses, but about the flowers she liked, her favorite colors, her fear of stinging insects, and her love of the local songbirds that often made their nests in the barn rafters. She loved to ride onto the countryside when she needed to be alone with her thoughts, and it had reminded him so much of himself he couldn't help feeling a kinship with her. She had never met a man who could accept her for who she was, despite the dirty breeches, and he remembered feeling like there were so many people who were missing out on something wonderful.

They climbed up the ladder. Everything Ravn knew of her jumbled into his head at once as they crested the top and walked knee deep into fresh hay. Neála gave a sad smile and put a hand to his cheek.

"You are so deep in your own head. Don't be. Be here with me." She sank down into the hay and pulled gently at his hand to join her.

Ravn nodded and followed her down to lay beside her. The hay pricked through his shirt, and he smiled at the sensation. He remembered it from a time many years ago when...

"There you go again. Please, stay with me. I've wanted you here for a long time."

He rose up on his elbow, which was difficult since it wanted to sink a bit in the hay, but he looked down at her where she lay beside him. "What do you mean?"

She smiled then, a smile filled with joy, one filled with a bit of sadness, one filled with the past and the future. "I love you Ravn, Laird of Blacach. I have since the moment I first saw you, standing behind my father all those years ago when you first hired him to manage your stables."

And then he remembered. He recalled the peeked little face hiding behind Giles' legs when they met for the first time.

"That's a long time."

She nodded. "Indeed, it is. I wanted to impress you the day I went to get Storm out of his stall alone. I was certain it was over when the elvin Lady came in to calm him. She could have berated me, but instead she helped me. I think she knew; she knew I loved you, and she made me look so good in your eyes. I will never forget that day. She changed me forever."

Ravn chuckled, a rush of happiness sweeping through him at the thought of Jash'ari. "Yes, she has a way of doing that."

Neála looked at him for a moment. "You have such a beautiful smile when you think of her. One day I hope you will smile for me like that."

A solemnity washed over him, not missing that he had felt that very thing not so long ago when he was looking at Ròs. More than anything, he wanted his wife to be happy, even if it was without him.

Without any further thought, he leaned down to kiss her. He had no doubt that she would make him smile; Neála had that quality about her. And in the meantime, she would be happy with him, just as Ròs would be happy without him. And maybe, just maybe, he would find happiness too.

Chapter Thirty-Three
Elvish Army

Tyrell wandered through the palace of the Lady of Moonlight and Love, simply taking in the chaos. The War Council had met and the focus of the elvin people had moved from training to preparation. Instead of spending daylight on the practice field, the soldiers of the vanguard spent their mornings wrestling with attacks from other units, and their afternoons preparing. They were traveling on foot, and that meant sturdy boots, cloaks, and weapons and armor. The whole of the army was using this as the staging point, and the once poetically empty and hauntingly beautiful hallways were now filled with soldiers running, and practicing, and talking. The Lady had been storing dried and pickled food for years. No one had known why, but now it was proving invaluable to the barracked troops.

His steps lead him outside, away from the noise. He left by the smaller, rear gate to the ridge overlooking the practice grounds. Even now, there were men down there. Bows were being issued to every footman and rider in preparation for the battle, and for those less precise than others, practice was a must. A few were newly bonded with tir-reath and these soldiers were playing, and running, and riding the big battle cats into and out of the woods that surrounded the grounds. Some were even sparring together. They were not preparing for a fight because they were being paid, or because a king or priest willed it so. These elves of all purities of blood were preparing themselves to defend the lives of those they loved, and they had set their minds to war. This was the essence of the elvin people, along with cooperation and fierce determination. They felt their connection to one another and it made them like an army of brothers and sisters, far more powerful than any human brood.

Behind him, the small sally port in the gate opened, and he turned. There he was– the Wolf. Tyrell watched him sniff the air, eyes scanning in all directions. If possible, the Wolf had become more intense during practice. It was once men started to falter, when he would take them aside and build them up, that the unit started to love him. He asked much, and gave more in return. None doubted he would die for them, and so they would die for him.

He was dressed in Elvish clothing, and even put up his hood now in the customary fashion, but he was less elvin than a new husband won in any country and brought back to be a father to elvin children. He simply didn't fit in. The Wolf waved and Tyrell waved back. In truth, he still wasn't sure how he felt about the scarred man.

The Wolf turned to the door and offered a hand. The delicate fingers that took his were those of Vivien Valdera. Tyrell felt his heart flutter. The Lady of Moonlight and Love was perfection, and she glowed with a presence that blotted out all others when she was present. Vivien, however, was softer but no less brilliant.

Her hair was reddish-brown, but with golden highlights as though it had been kissed by the sun. Her eyes were gray, sometimes more green, sometimes more blue, and often flecked with brown. Her smile was honest and warming, her movements graceful and powerful. For a moment she saw only the Wolf, taking his arm and standing very close, but then she saw Tyrell. She said something to the big man Tyrell didn't catch and he nodded. In seconds the Wolf was gone, jogging down to the field alone.

Tyrell watched as Vivien approached. All elves were linked, weighted by the Elvish blood they shared, and could feel one another to some small degree. Tyrell knew he was better at it than most, and he could feel the deep well of sadness inside this accomplished warmage. He could hardly keep from taking her in his arms to give her what comfort he could. He lowered his hood, and gave a small bow in respect. She smiled and bowed back, then, much to his surprise, she took both his upper arms and pulled him close for a moment.

Tyrell's heart raced, and he returned the embrace and splayed his hands against her back. When they parted, her smile was a touch more genuine and it made his heart flutter again.

"How does the vanguard?"

He gave a sad smile. "They do well, but they worry about you. We all, every one of us, share your loss."

She nodded, face shadowed by her pain, "The healer said I should walk, so the Wolf and I came out to enjoy the spring morning."

Tyrell glanced down the slope where the Wolf was running free. "You seem to have lost your companion."

Vivien giggled, and the sound warmed him. "He is untamed. It is better for him to run, but I shall walk with you if you will have me."

Tyrell blinked for a moment, heart pounding as he offered his arm, "I would be honored."

She took his arm and they walked along the wall of the fortress, between the lofty heights of stone and the tall pines that marched down the slope. He felt at peace, but excited, alert but in a haze. He almost missed it when she asked, "How fare the mages in particular?"

Tyrell pursed his lips, "Jernell is still slow to react, and they are having trouble concentrating during the shield routines, but I think it is more nerves than ability. I have been hard on them, but they are becoming more apt. They are so used to acting alone, being in a mass of soldiers is distracting to them."

She nodded. "That can only be fixed by time, and we have none. We shall have to be vigilant."

"The problems crept in the moment they learned that they would be marching through the Doomed City."

They reached a winding stair set into the side of the hill, giving a wide view of the practice grounds from the north. Without much comment she angled toward the path, and they started downward. Tyrell could see her turning everything over in her mind until she finally spoke, "It can't be helped, but I have faith in us. I believe we will be successful and come home victorious."

Tyrell considered her words, and his reply was more pragmatic. "I pray we do."

Down on the field, the Wolf had borrowed a bow from one of the soldiers. He was known to be a middling shot, but the men forgave him. His power lay in his arms and legs, in his ferocity in battle. He made three shots and then handed the bow back to the owner. Then, like a dog, he scanned until he saw Vivien. Seeing her, he went back about his business.

"How have the mages taken to him, really?"

"An'drath?" he asked, watching the Wolf. "He is feared, and loved. The warmages know more than the soldiers that he can't be truly human. Yet, he is so without subtlety or guile they believe they can trust him."

She smiled at Tyrell warmly but he felt she was really smiling at the Wolf. "You can. I do."

Tyrell nodded, but kept his own council. The truth was, the massive human had always felt like a barely tamed animal, wild and unpredictable. However, the soldiers and mages admired his strength, his loyalty, and his ability. Tyrell and others felt something awry inside of the barbarian, but Lady Valdera trusted him, and if Vivien trusted him, it was good enough for Tyrell. For now.

They walked out onto the field, which had gone from a soupy mass in the winter to a hard packed ground as the dry spring had settled in. There had been no rain in weeks. Across the grounds, some soldiers exploded from the thick pines on the backs of massive cats. Wheeling across the south end of the grounds, they arced toward the center and Xadrian's lonely tent. Vivien gasped in delight and for a moment she was a young girl again, bubbling with excitement, "A group is bringing their new tir-reath in!"

Tyrell could feel her carefree excitement, and smiled at her. "Then let us meet them."

She did not run, not quite, but she managed a good pace as the riders came forward, their leader The Lord of Swords and Truth himself. The cats were kept at one side of the tent and he disembarked. He gave his mount a curt order, but then had to repeat himself when the tir-reath tried to follow him to the tent. Vivien giggled as he admonished the mount, then removed his helmet to greet the two mages. Within seconds, the animal had left its position again to follow the Commander, purring loudly. She tried to contain herself as the big grey and white spotted cat rubbed her shoulders against her master as he growled, "Fenella, Fenella, stop. Now–" She nearly bowled him over, "Now is not the time! Discipline! Discipline!"

The tir-reath was unmoved by his protests. Weighing in as much as three grown men, she would utterly dwarf Sherika– who was the smaller, more lithe variant of the same race. Fenella's long limbs held aloft a heavy body and all was covered in muscle. Her claws could rend chain links like paper, and they could carry a fully armored warrior at terrific speeds even in the densest wood. Sherika was slender and docile, while tir-reath bred for war were heavily muscled and far more aggressive. The tir-reath were amongst the least of the fae beasts, mortal and corporeal, but their connection to their riders was still a strong influence on them.

Xadrian frowned deeply at the beast, then made a disgusted sound and dropped his helmet on the empty table by his tent. Vivien's laughter was contagious, but Tyrell, mindful of the importance of the commander, managed to contain himself. "A new mount, Lord?"

The bald man's brows furrowed at Tyrell, but he nodded, "I have not had one in three hundred years, but when I entered the tir-reath den, Fenella came over to me with utter certainty. Can't get her to leave me alone."

And while he spoke, the cat gathered into a crouch, edged forward, and rubbed against Xadrian's leg. She sighed heavily as Vivien laughed. "Be at ease; she loves you Xadrian!"

His deadpan was total, "I would prefer respect and obedience."

Vivien clucked and held out her hand to Fenella. The warcat sniffed her and consented to be scratched over her ears. Tyrell watched the warmage visit love upon the mount, smiling at her gentleness and kindness. "She's an affectionate girl," he said, then realized he did not know of whom he was speaking. "Very sensitive."

Xadrian huffed, "Let us hope she is fearsome as well. The humans will be giving belly scratchings with axes and knives in a few weeks. We need to get all these soldiers–" He paused and addressed the crowd of soldiers and lounging warcats with a bellow, "MOUNT UP! FULL CIRCUIT! GO!", then returned to the conversation, "but we still haven't gotten them into armor. All of these cats were bonded as adults, so the connection is pretty weak, not like those taken from the litter as weanlings."

Tyrell nodded, but he was fascinated by the soldiers coming to mount their cats in a series of efficient actions. A few of the cats looked unhappy, but they left in more or less a large cloud, galloping and leaping into the stands that surrounded the practice yard, and then into the tree line, disappearing into the pines as they made to circle the fortress. Tyrell had never had a tir-reath, and wondered what it was like to ride one through the woods many times faster than an elf could run.

"Will they be ready?"

Xadrian dismissed the concern with a wave, "Ready enough as long as those with new cats don't ride into battle. What I'm worried about is the vanguard. Will *you* be ready?"

Vivien left Fenella to stand tall and proud before the commander, "We are ready."

The commander cast a baleful glance around the yard, "You only have a few days left."

Vivien nodded, strong and confident, "We *are* ready, and I thought the lot of them could use the last two days to prepare and to say farewell to family, friends and lovers. Sharpening a keen edge can only dull it."

He nodded. "Wise."

The reply she got made her beam, and Tyrell felt her like a man in winter feels the first summer sun. He felt himself calm and bask in her happiness.

The Wolf approached, a strangely serene look on his face, then he caught sight of Vivien's expression and smiled. *Like a dolt*, Tyrell thought, surprising himself.

A low screech shook everyone, but Vivien identified the source first.

"Good girl. Relax girl. He's a friend," she said soothingly, but Fenella's hair was standing straight at attention, her legs gathered for a pounce. Tyrell followed the cat's natural point as it's warning shriek became almost earsplitting. The Wolf stood his ground, but his hands circled into fists and he hunched over, ready for an attack with bright red eyes.

Xadrian marched between the two near the end of Fenella's nose, "FENELLA! DOWN!" Obediently, the cat plopped her massive hindquarters to the turf and stopped making noise, but her hair was still up, her eyes never leaving the barbarian. Xadrian shook his head,

"Probably never saw a full human before. I have much work to do with her."

Vivien finally moved from the angry animal and walked to the Wolf's side. Tyrell felt his insides churn with an uneasy anger. He looked at the oversized man more closely, considering the possibilities. Vivien took the Wolf's arm and smiled. "Everyone is beginning preparations and will be visiting with friends and family. I believe I will do the same. My father is still here, and of course Lydia and the Lady of Moonlight. Maybe even Mikarvan if he's not too busy."

The Wolf nodded, looking at her like there was no one else in the entire world. They turned and left.

Tyrell listened to Xadrian grumble at his cat as he rubbed her back into a state of calm. He then looked at the retreating leaders of his unit.

He considered the facts, darkly.

Chapter Thirty-Four
March Out of Mithalion

Mikarvan stood in the dark stairwell of Vivien's tower. He could still barely believe the turn of events that placed him there. Never in his wildest thoughts would he have imagined that she would be going to war with only one hundred men and women to try and save Elvish lands from human encroachment. Even when she became a warmage, he never imagined it. Even when she became one of the highest ranking warmages in her class, he never imagined it.

Who in their right mind did such a thing? Who in their right mind allowed such a thing?

Mikarvan didn't know all the intricacies of their battle plan. He was sure it had been deliberated a thousand times over. But it didn't stop him from feeling like it was a fools mission, and that he might never see her again. The possibility made him feel like his insides would break.

So there he was, standing in the darkness outside her chamber suite, wanting to tell her all the things he'd ever wanted to tell her but couldn't.

Mikarvan walked the few remaining stairs to the door and stopped again before knocking. *What should I say to the woman that I want to pull into the nearest closet, close the door, and lock her in to keep her out of harm's way? What should I say to the woman I've loved since the moment I saw her when we were children?*

He was about to knock on the door when it suddenly opened. Vivien stood there, cloak in hand. Her eyes widened and she put a hand to her chest. "Gods Mikarvan, you scared me!"

He shouldered his way into the room, suddenly wanting to be out of the hallway, and closed the door behind him. Her sudden proximity was disarming; they stood so close that his arm bushed against hers. His tone was husky, "I'm sorry, I didn't mean to."

She looked up at him, her gaze questioning. "Wh...what is it? Is something wrong?"

He regarded her intently. "You are leaving on a desperate mission. I came to see you off."

"I...I tried finding you yesterday. Everyone seemed to think they knew where you were, and when I got there, you had already left. The cycle repeated three or four times before I finally had to give up."

He put a hand on her upper arm and rubbed it with his thumb through the fabric of her blouse, his mind wandering to the soft skin beneath. "I didn't know you were looking for me." He thought he felt her tremble minutely. "And please– never, never give up on me."

Vivien trembled again. It was hard to miss, and she stumbled over her words. "I...I'm sorry. I didn't mean to. I mean, I didn't really. I just...I had something that I...I needed to do, and..."

This woman, she is all I've ever wanted, and she is standing right here before me, about to head into...

Mikarvan stepped closer. She reflexively took a step back and his hand dropped from her arm. Her eyes stayed locked onto his as he followed her back, back, back into the dimly lit chamber. She had a look about her he'd never seen before, one he couldn't quite describe, one that stirred him.

She stopped when the back of her legs hit the bed. He closed to within inches of her and she just stared into the wall of his chest.

Aching to peer into her soul, his voice was a deep whisper, "Vivien, please look at me."

She gave a heavy swallow, almost seemed afraid to do what he asked. His heart thundered in his chest and his body felt charged in a way it had never been before. Slowly she gazed back up into his face, and he looked into eyes that shone sea green in the small bit of light cast by the nearby lantern.

Mikarvan placed a hand against the side of her face, leaned in until his forehead rested against hers. He had done it once before, when they were much, much younger. It was springtime and they were standing at the far banks of the Fyresmee River, Vivien not yet engaged to the indomitable Lord of Ice and Steel. They had both been so happy then, so much more carefree. The world was open to them, and ripe for the taking. He wanted to ask her to marry him. If she had been the daughter of any other man in Rithalion, she could have been his wife. He remembered leaning in, closer, and closer, and closer...

Anguish suddenly reflected on Vivien's face and she lay a hand on his chest. "Mika, I...I never really..." Tears came to her eyes before she could stop them and her lips trembled. "I was sad that I couldn't tell you goodbye."

He moved his hand to her chin and tilted her head up. He heard her rapid breathing and it stirred him deep inside. *By the gods, I want her.* Vivien closed her eyes as his lips descended to hers. It was nothing like the chaste kiss they had shared that day at the river.

This one stole his breath away.

He wrapped one arm around her waist and the other went to the back of her head, his fingers sliding over the braids she had woven into her hair. He deepened the kiss and she opened her mouth to let him in, her hands running over the contours of his chest, down to his hips, and then back up gain. And just when he thought he was going to starve for air, he released her lips and gazed at her with a fierce intensity. "Do not say goodbye to me. Ever."

"Mikarvan..."

He put a finger to her lips. "I haven't heard you call me Mika for a long time."

The tears finally spilled. "I'm sorry, I didn't mean to; it just came out. I'll try not..."

"Shhh. I always liked it when you called me that. You are the only one who has."

He then kissed her again. It was different this time, sweet and tender. His lips played over hers, and his tongue teased her until she reciprocated in kind.

Then he pushed her back.

A rush of alarm swept over her face, but his arms caught her just before she hit the mattress and he lay beside her. He kissed her and her lips were like the sweetest wine; he could taste of them all day. He had kissed many women in the past several decades, but none of them were like this!

"Mika. Mika, wait." He stopped to look at her, his breaths ragged and uneven. His insides clenched spasmodically, almost painfully. "We can't do this."

He swept a strand of hair from her face and whispered, "Why not?"

"Torialvah."

A rush of anger swept through him and his voice was rougher than he intended it to be. "Your husband is a damn fool. I heard about his formal complaint to the Council."

He saw the shame reflected in her eyes before she turned her face away. Another surge of anger gripped him. *She's thinking about how bad a wife she's been to that bastard while I can't imagine living my life without her in it!*

"Vivien!"

She turned to look at him, her body stiffening with his tone. He instantly regretted it, and imagined mayhap she'd heard it much too often with her husband. Sadness stole over him, dampening his anger. He caressed her face then, starting at her hairline, then down the bridge of her nose to the tip, then down further to the swell of her lips.

His voice was a whisper again. "Vivien, I love you. I am in love with you. I always have and I always will be. I don't care about your Lord. I only care about you and me." He kissed her again, softly, gently. "You are going away today. My entire being fears for you. I don't want to let you go, but I know you must. I heard about what you said in the Council Chamber."

She only nodded, relaxing in the softness of his caress.

His warm breath swept over her lips. "I never want to take your identity from you, always want you to do what makes you happy in this world. He kissed her again, this time more insistent. "I want you Vivien. I've always wanted you, even before I kissed you that day at the river."

Her voice was breathy, "You remember that?"

He chuckled. "How could I ever forget?"

Mikarvan wrapped his arms around her, his lips taking hers like there was no tomorrow. His hands took her hips and pulled her into him, so that, even through the layers of their clothing his hardness pressed against her, announcing his physical need. He worked at the laces of her tunic, pulled it off, and then opened the neckline of her blouse. He pulled down her camisole...and she gasped.

He suckled at her breast, pulling at the nipple and circling it with his tongue. She shuddered and he gripped her tighter, reveling in the softness of her skin, the feel of her fingers in his hair, the pressure of her hips pushing against him, and just the scent of her, a scent he never wanted to forget as long as he lived. He worked at the buckle to her belt, and slipped his hand down along her belly and into her damp curls. She gasped again and arched her back. Mikarvan hovered over her, stroked her, looked down at her with adoring solemnity. He gave her acceptance, release, no small amount of the love he felt for her every day.

He wanted her, ached for her, but not more than two weeks ago she had lost a child. He wouldn't risk her. She was still in mourning, whether she realized it or not, and he didn't need to complicate things for her during such a delicate time. So he just kissed her, caressed her, and loved her until the first signs of dawn entered though the opening to the balcony. He then helped her get dressed again: handed her boots, sword, and cloak. They patted Sherika, and he promised to keep the tir-reath with him while Vivien was gone. He walked with her down from the tower and into the fortress proper. There she left him and she walked alone to the front gate where the rest of the one hundred had gathered.

And to the one man whom he knew would give his life for hers if need be, the man they called the Wolf.

With dawn's early light streaming in through the open door of the balcony, Mikarvan silently helped her don the clothes she would be wearing for days on end on the road. Vivien had chosen her most comfortable pants and tunic, and a second set was in her travel pack. Her favorite boots would also go, and her sword, the one given to her by the Lord of Swords and Truth years ago when she became accomplished with it. She never left home without it in spite of her ability with magic. One never knew when one would need a trusty steel blade at her side in the thick of a fight.

Finally he settled the dark green cloak over her shoulders, clasping it to the shoulder pads of her vest, then reached back and placed the hood over her head. After, he just stood there for a moment before grabbing her travel pack and hefting it over his shoulder.

He grimaced. "This is heavy."

She smiled widely. "I know. That's what all those days of jogging around the field were for."

"Well, I can at least carry it down the stairs for you."

She nodded and patted Sherika's head again. "I will miss her so much. Thank you for keeping her for me."

He shrugged. "I can only do so because she likes me so much. I must say, she chooses well." He winked and smiled.

Vivien huffed. "You are such a rogue."

"I know. You've told me on several occasions in the past. A man never really changes my dear, only becomes better at what he does best."

She chuckled and bent to hug Sherika a few times. When she was ready she noticed that he was fussing with one of the straps on her bag. "What is it?"

"It's nothing. It was just twisted up. I fixed it." He reached out a hand. "I'd best get you downstairs; the rest of the vanguard is probably waiting."

She nodded and took his hand, allowing him to lead her down the winding tower stairs. Once they entered the fortress proper, he reluctantly released her hand and gave her the travel pack. "Godspeed to you, and may the sun always shine upon you."

She nodded, "And to you as well."

With a heavy heart, she turned and walked through the fortress. The place was unusually quiet and she imagined everyone had made their way to the courtyard. She turned a corner and saw the unit there, all men but for three women spellcasters. All nodded solemnly as she passed them on her way to the front and she returned the gesture. She felt something hitting against her right elbow and turned to look. She frowned when she saw something hanging from her pack, but when she stopped and got a closer look, her eyes widened with astonishment. There, carved in perfect detail, was a sunset tanager in flight.

Vivien blinked away the tears that threatened, remembering Mikarvan fussing with the strap of her pack. It was a stunning gift, one thought out and executed several days ago. When they were young, she and Mikarvan would walk along the river. Birds lived in abundance near the great water source, many of which were beautiful sunset tanagers. On the days they saw the most of these scarlet and gold colored birds, good things tended to happen, and so they became a good luck charm.

She continued to walk, this time with her head held much higher, towards the massive gate that slowly began to open. She saw the Wolf just ahead, his large frame a stark contrast to the more slender shaped elvin men that surrounded him. He looked down the line of soldiers and mages, and when he saw her, he seemed to relax slightly.

The Wolf's voice was a bellow, "Everyone in formation! Now!"

Vivien slid her pack off her shoulders, and for the sake of time, the Wolf helped her don her armor. Once properly clad, she placed her belt back around her waist, slipped her sheathed blade on it, then buckled it securely. She picked up the pack again, clasping the small tanager in her hand.

"Everyone, ready! March!"

Beside the Wolf, Vivien walked at the forefront of the eighty six soldiers and twelve mages they would be leading into battle. This spring was the driest the elves could ever remember. The grasses were brown and crackled underfoot. The vanguard, traveling by foot, was dressed in light armor plates of bright steel, carrying axes, hammers, and unadorned shields, accompanied by packs groaning with food, supplies, and water. They were suddenly grateful for the months of marching, carrying, and running that the Wolf had made them do.

Hundreds had gathered to see them off, but the pennants waved weakly in the light morning breeze, and the crowd stared at them as though they were at a funeral. They were off to defend the city far from home, but word had gotten out that these were the first to leave and face a force many times their number, the force of a vicious and implacable foe. Not only that, but the path of those that marched lead through the Doomed City. It cast a pall over the crowd, and it began to sink into the soldiers, soaking them to the bone like a cold rain.

They continued down the road, feet hitting the huge octagonal stones in almost utter silence. Vivien cast a worried glance back at the men, then to the human beside her. The barbarian's face was stoic, but his brow was furrowing into a dangerous expression.

She inhaled a trembling breath and her heart ached. *They don't think we are coming back.*

Ahead, a beautiful reviewing platform had been erected. There, the leaders of Rithalion had assembled, many with the same look of fated determination on their faces. The elders held no illusions of their chances.

The Lady of Moonlight and Love stood there as well, trying to look hopeful as she waved to the troops. Next to her, The Lord of Swords and Truth stood, a fierce frown on his usually stoic face. In a flurry of motion, he drew Arisil from its sheath and held the broken blade above his head in a silent salute. In reply, the Wolf snatched the newly-forged Elvish axe slung across his back and swung it in a glittering arc before holding it above his head.

And then the barbarian howled.

It was a cold and clear sound, bursting above them all and echoing into every soul. Xadrian, shocking the elders, howled back from the stage. The Wolf howled again, and Vivien joined in with a sound that expressed the determination she felt resting in her heart.

Before long, the whole vanguard was howling defiantly into the sky as they lifted steel weapons in clenched fists. The elves on all sides replied, a rumble of voice that began low, then gathered into a single call in a voice thousands strong.

"La'athai! La'athai! La'athai!" *Wolves. Wolves. Wolves.*

Their feet marched more forcefully. Their backs became straight. Vivien howled for a second time, and the troops responded in kind. In a few steps, the Wolf called for a run. The troops secured their weapons and began to move with renewed vigor, an enthusiasm, a hunger for victory.

The crowd cheered louder, "La'athai! La'athai! La'athai!"

And as easy as a simple salute with a broken blade, the vanguard did not leave the city under a cloud of tears. They departed with defiance, not crawling towards doom, but ready and eager for a hunt. They would forever be Wolves. They would fight as a fearsome pack and bring terror to the enemies of the elvin people.

Chapter Thirty-Five
The Contract

Ròs swept past and brusquely entered the chamber, barely taking note of him as she went to her vanity. She sat and removed her modest cap and lace hair decoration, then undid the braid that made up her hair. Ravn entered behind and closed the door, just stood there until she decided to grace him with her attention. She finally rolled her eyes. "What is it? Can't you see I'm busy?"

Ravn stepped forward, "Wife, I have come to discuss someone–"

Ròs interrupted him, used the tone most calculated to cause chills. It spoke of thrown objects and broken gifts. "Ahh, I think I know what this is. You are here to tell me you are having your whore displace me, yes?"

Ravn felt his ire rise in a tide of emotion. "She is not a whore. Her name is Neála."

Ròs arched a brow and closed her eyes as she began to draw the ivory tined brush through her hair. The sound it made was that of a far off farmer reaping grain. "I do not care to hear the whore's name spoken in my presence."

Ravn gathered his hands into fists, but took a deep breath and relaxed them. He stepped directly behind his wife and placed gentle hands on her shoulders, "Ròs–"

Her eyes snapped open. "Get your hands off of me!" she hissed. "I will not have a whoremonger touching me." Ravn felt as if he had been slapped. He straightened stiffly and backed away from her as she continued with her brushing. Her voice took on a light, carefree tone. "You humped that bitch, and you kept away from me. There is absolutely no reason why you should be standing before me now, discussing her, unless you mean to displace me."

Ravn growled, "I have not come to have her displace you. You are my wife, and I would never do such a thing. You know that, so stop spouting idiocy."

Ròs stopped brushing her hair and looked at him through wide eyes. In all the years of their marriage, he'd never spoken to her that way. The expression on her face was one he'd never encountered before, making him wonder what she was thinking.

"Then why ARE you here, husband?"

Ravn set his face in stone and spoke plainly. "She carries my child."

ROSS ЄROSS

Ròs stiffened in her seat. In the full length mirror he had bought her for their wedding, he could see her face go deathly pale with only burning red spots on her cheeks. She licked her lips like a lizard. Her hands shook as she set the silver backed brush down on the white pine table, making it clatter a little as it touched.

"Kill her and burn the offspring before it breathes."

Ravn could barely believe what he had just heard, words he'd never imagined hearing anyone speak. His heartbeat sounded in his ears like a war drum as he fought his fury and concentrated on the back of Ròs' head until he could trust himself to utter a single word.

"No."

Ròs stared at him in the mirror as if the act of glaring at his reflection could shatter him. "Unless you lied to me and really are looking to supplant me."

The accusation struck him again, but he remained impassive.

Ròs suddenly rose from the seat and lunged towards him, screaming. She struck out at him, hitting him across the face once, twice, and almost a third time before Ravn grabbed her wrist and held it up, nearly lifting her off the ground with the force of it. She slapped at him ineffectually with her other hand, curses leaping from her mouth to find the soft underbelly of his heart. He moved to the side with her, and once he knew it was safe, cast her onto the bed.

Ròs began to weep, rubbing at her wrist. "And now I see you clearly, faithless husband. Now that you have no more need of me, you cast me off. You spit on everything my family has done for you as you abandon me, soiled and used." Her eyes widened. "Or kill me! Will you kill me?"

Ravn felt the blood drain from his face. He closed his eyes as her words tore at him. When he opened his eyes, she was not the bitter woman weeping at him now, but the scared little girl in the carriage, the trembling waif surrounded by vicious creatures bathed in the blood of his mother and father. His heart ached and he had to admit he still loved her.

"No."

"What, then?"

"You are my wife, bound to me by sacred ceremony and oath before the gods. You shall remain here as my wife. Neála is the mother of my child. She will come and be here as my lover."

Ròs frowned and shook hair from her face as she gathered herself and stood on the other side of the bed. "So I am to be shamed? Is that it? You spurn my bed and my body?"

Dumbstruck, Ravn just stood there a moment before composing himself. "We have been married for years. You have never welcomed me into your arms or your bed. Your family knows this. Our people know this. You even told me to find acceptance elsewhere."

Ròs folded her arms and turned away, hiding her tear-streaked face. "Then I suppose I shall have to wear the mantle of bad wife you drape around me like a funeral shroud. Never can the grand Laird Blacach be sullied by the rumors he is an undeserving husband."

Ravn set his jaw and swallowed sharp words. He had tried so hard. He had tried and failed to love this woman for years. Nothing he did was good enough, and his touch was repulsive to her. He yearned for her, wished for her appreciation and kindness. All she had ever done was deny his worth and even the basic beginnings of friendship and trust. But maybe, maybe it could start right here.

He tried for a soft, even tone, "I have loved you for more than half my life, Ròs, but I need something back. Neála gives me the love and affection I crave... that I *need*. I owe her a place in my life because of the place she has in my heart. I do not seek to shame you, but to give you the freedom from me that you desire, have always desired."

The reply that bounced off of the wall was full of thorns. "So it is your way or divorce, then?"

Ravn sighed. "I want you in my life, but I have other responsibilities now that also require my dedication."

Ròs sniffed. "If you and I ever reconcile, there is a bond already broken. The whore bears your seed first and her child will inherit Blacach, not mine."

Ravn drew himself up to his full height, knowing that this would come up. "I will not have the child live without a name, but I shall draw a decree keeping the babe from the line of succession. If we ever have children, yours will inherit. If not, then it will pass to your family."

The words were a kindness. The plan selfless. Ravn watched Ròs' face twist into a horrible mask of vile hate and went cold. *What madness did I cause to drive a woman to be like this?*

"No!" Ròs shouted, "You will find a way to nullify it. You will go back on your word."

Ravn reeled at her attack. "Am I that man? Do I not honor my oaths?"

Her next words slipped into his ribs like a thin knife. "Like your marriage vows?"

Ravn winced and looked away. Tears came to his eyes. He knew the god of his forefathers, the spirits of his parents, were looking down with disappointment. His love for his elvin Lady, his love for Neála– neither had been reasons to discard his wedding vows. He should have found a way to placate his wife, to woo and win her. Everything he had tried had failed, but his vows did not give him release from finding her needs and filling them.

The room rang with silence. Ròs folded her arms and smiled triumphantly.

Ravn's eyes scanned the room. Richly appointed with warm woods and thick carpets, it had was filled with tokens of love and adoration that had fallen on deaf ears and blind eyes. It was a tomb decorated with riches to keep the death of their marriage comfortable in the afterlife.

He thought of Neála. He had spent the last three years basking in her affection and he had shared himself with her as well. Now, she glowed with pregnancy. Simple, poor, unlanded and untitled, she had given her all to him in every way. She deserved a life of ease for bearing his burdens, and for taking on his sadness as her own.

"In ancient times..." He started to speak, then stopped. Half formed thoughts buzzed in his head and he looked down to his hands, thick with calluses not from labor, but from practice with weapons of war. "In ancient times men proved their love by venturing into the wilderness." He closed his big hands into fists, "There are stories and tales that outlive men by hundreds of years. Their lovers would give them a task, and they would go forth to complete it as a token of their dedication." He looked to his wife. "I request that you give me such a task."

Ròs frowned. "A bargain?"

"A test." He replied. "Give me a test to prove I can keep my word or die in the attempt."

Ròs nodded. "A quest, then."

Ravn nodded back.

Ròs walked to the other side of the room and over to her desk. She took a taper and lit it from a candle on the wall, then transferred the flame to the wax column on top to produce light enough for her to produce parchment, ink and quill from the first drawer. She began to write.

"You shall go forth into the world with no men at arms or guards of any kind. You will find and defeat the most powerful creature you can find."

Ravn walked behind her and looked over her shoulder. "What kind of creature?"

Ròs shrugged. "The creature that is as strong as your will, as dangerous as your love is pure. So deadly that only the power of your oath would ever have to fight such a thing."

"A Liath? A hydra? A giant?"

Ròs continued to write in her perfect, curvy hand on the paper. "I will not give you an end to your quest. Simply bring back the heart of whatever you can hunt and kill. You will not return empty handed. Your devotion will be measured by what the heart belonged to. One way," she finished with a flourish, "or the other."

She started to turn but Ravn placed an unyielding hand on her shoulder. Ròs went stiff and she set the paper back on the desktop.

"Write also that Neála will be given twenty gold coins from our vaults every month, and then her child after her until death." Ròs flinched but nodded, starting to write. "She will not be harmed, and if she or her child meet with any kind of foul end, I will return and visit vengeance upon you for it. And if not me, then the gods in my stead."

Ròs' face twisted as she wrote. "And since you seek to disinherit the child anyway, that shall be written here as well."

Ravn nodded and let her go.

Ròs finished the addition and wrote 'SO I VOW' at the bottom of the page. She turned to her husband, not with a quill, but with the small blade used to sharpen them.

Ravn presented his left hand. Ròs pricked his thumb with the knife and pressed it to the paper. Her eyes glittered like blue ice in the firelight. "This is not a contract, but an oath. It cannot be broken. Signed in blood, it can't be burned, drowned, buried, or ripped and tossed to the wind. The blood will keep it alive as long as you are."

She let go of his hand, but Ravn grabbed hers before she could move away. "I believe there is an oath there for you, too."

She glared at him flintily, but relented. She pricked her thumb and pressed it to the paper, then cast fine sand across it to keep the whole from smudging.

Ravn nodded. "I leave in the morning."

"Want to hump your whore one, last time?"

Ravn leaned in to put his face so close to Ròs' that he could kiss her. "Your indifference is more attractive than your hate. Do you want me in *your* bed?" Ròs shook her head, perhaps sensing she had gone too far. "Then let me find my peace. My quest will end your fears, both of our fears."

Ravn turned to leave the room, glanced back before shutting the door. He saw his wife pouring over the paper contract, signed in their blood.

Chapter Thirty-Six
The Challenge

ergatium was a place of broken dreams and murdered families. The city was a place of unburied bodies and the impact point of a shattered nation. The dragon elves, humbled and twisted by baleful curses, had fled into the mountains to the west. They had summoned dragons to rend the rock, unleashing the Forgotten Lake and Clefting River from their banks, flooding the valley and killing tens of thousands. Always a place of floods, the mass murder had tainted the entire swamp that had been created by the deluge.

Three and a half days of hard marching had brought them there, and after the La'athai cleared the forest, they watched the afternoon sun shine down upon the broken, rotted trees swimming in the fetid waters of their old homeland.

Vivien examined it with barely suppressed trepidation. Standing beside her, Tyrell could feel her tremble a little, and did not fault her in the least. His own heart shrank from the place. Yet the Wolf stood defiant before the mists that smelled of corpses.

"We are in luck. The dry season has drained the waters greatly. We will make good time," he said.

Tyrell looked again at the stinking morass of half drowned ground paths and then back to the Wolf. He was comforted that Vivien looked as shocked and incredulous as he felt. She leaned close to the big man, "Wolf, are you sure we can cross…this?"

He nodded, "Yes, but not at night. Never travel at night unless you have no choice. One misstep and the swamp will swallow you whole. We should camp here."

Vivien gave the order, and two pairs traveled no more than a hundred feet before finding a flat piece of ground for the hundred soldiers and mages to settle. Finding dry wood was no problem, but clearing fire pits took some time to dig. The last thing they needed was a wildfire from a blown ember. The season was so dry, and it was a constant worry. Canvas tents were raised a little while later, water passed around and food combined to make more palatable meals.

Men were picked, and these grumbled as they went to watch first around the camp. The rest set shields, many now painted with a vague wolf's head, next to their tents. They gratefully dropped heavy axes and hammers next into groups leaning against each other to form small pyramids of hafts. Armored plates, hot even in the cool air, were shucked next. Dressed only in armor padding they sat next to the fires and joked while in bare feet, grateful for the few extra hours of rest. They took some of their precious supply of green tobacco leaves from their packs and pushed them into spare water skins, topping them with a little water, preparing to repel leeches during the travel.

Tyrell checked on them all, walking from campfire to campfire, then each paired set of watchmen before coming to where the Wolf and Vivien were speaking softly. Tyrell frowned, his stomach tightening at the sight. The Wolf was always relaxed, yet ready to fight. The human was curling to pounce, or striking, simply waiting for something to kill him. Vivien, however sat next to him on the ground leaning toward him and smiling as if this were a simple jaunt into the woods with friends. Tyrell took a calming breath. The two of them spoke so easily together, and Tyrell caught snippets of a past he desperately wished she would share with him instead. It was as if she could not sense the wrongness of the barbarian even as she opened herself to the man.

Tyrell chewed on that, for maybe that was the crux of it: she spoke of endless adventures with a childhood friend, walking in the woods with her father, and her lessons as a young and lonely mage at the college. The Wolf, however, never spoke of himself. He simply listened to everything she had to say and only asked an occasional question. He acted as if she was his whole world, never existing before or without her. It was so damned transparent, he couldn't believe she would be taken in.

Tyrell took a few more moments of this before approaching the two and lowering his hood. "Excuse me. I was wondering if it will be necessary to go into Pergatium itself?"

The name of the city cast a pall over both of them, and all the men in earshot. The Wolf frowned and shook his head as if shooing a fly. "I hope not. It is more dangerous than the rest by far."

Those honest words hung in the air as the sun set behind far away mountains. Darkness was coming fast but for the lonely fires, an obscured moon, and the brightest of stars. Vivien cleared her throat and stood. "In that case, I might as well take some time to take my nightly walk around the encampment."

Tyrell nodded. "I already took the walk without you, but I don't mind going again."

She gave him a silly pout, one she had no idea would affected him like it did, making his heart stutter in his chest. "You went without me?"

He barely managed a recovery before giving a mock bow. "My apologies Mistress, but I saw you were busy..." he indicated offhandedly to the Wolf.

She chuckled. "It was an early stop tonight. You could have waited or just interrupted. We weren't discussing anything important."

She began walking and Tyrell glanced back at the Wolf before falling in beside her. The big man paid them no heed and had already turned to his pack, a piece of wood, and a fist sized stone. Tyrell quietly walked beside Vivien as she moved from fire to fire, talking with each of the men there before moving on to the next one. He watched how the men responded to her, how their eyes lit up when she approached, and how they sincerely appreciated her presence. He loved how she made efforts to learn all the soldier's names, and that she would take all their jokes in stride.

This woman will be a great leader one day. She will lead men, many men, and they will want to follow her because they love her. The thought almost stopped Tyrell in his tracks because he suddenly knew why he'd seen the Grand Magister watching his daughter so closely as of late. It wasn't because the man thought she was frail due to life's unfortunate circumstances. It was because he knew she was strong and would one day take his place.

Tyrell caught up with her at the next fire. It was larger than the others and several men sat there, their tents pitched close together. He walked in the middle of some friendly banter, a bit of joshing back and forth between Vivien and the men.

Vivien planted her hands on her hips. "And what was that comment for, Gregor? What exactly did you mean by it?"

The other men guffawed and slapped the offending man on the back. "Awww, now what do you go and say that for?" said one. Tyrell glanced at her to see that her eyes were bright and her stance had become a bit defensive.

Gregor gave a wide smile. "I mean exactly what I said. Without your magic, I don't think you would never be able to hold your own in battle."

Her eyes flashed. "Really?"

He nodded. "Really."

Silence reigned, not just around this fire, but the surrounding fires that had heard Gregor's proclamation. Vivien seemed to deliberate for a moment before responding again.

She spoke in a low voice. "Tyrell, please go get my sword."

He issued a small half-bow. "Right away, Mistress."

He almost ran back to her fire, his mind sweeping over the possibilities of what was about to happen. He had seen the sword before; she kept it sheathed at her side beneath her long tunic. The Wolf looked up as he went to Vivien's belongings, said nothing as Tyrell picked up the sword and rushed away again. Vivien stood as he had left her, and when she accepted the sheathed blade from his hands, he saw steely determination in her eyes.

The men just sat there and watched her, nervous grins on their faces.

Her voice rang out for everyone in the vicinity to hear. "Pick your best swordsman."

A few of the men chuckled. "You can't be serious," said one.

Her eyes flashed. "I am deadly serious."

The men chuckled again, but this time not so loudly. No one offered a name.

"I say, choose your best swordsman."

The men all started looking beyond her shoulder. First one, then many of the others began to point.

Tyrell turned when Vivien did. Behind them stood the Wolf.

The big man looked around blankly at all the leveled fingers. "What?"

Tyrell watched Vivien smile like a cat watches a tasty morsel scamper into a clear spot beyond the tall grass. "Get your sword, my friend."

The Wolf shook his head. "I have my axe."

"Oi!" a voice called, and a sheathed sword came from out of the crowd of men.

The Wolf caught it easily. He stared at it like it was a foreign thing and started to ask a question. That was when Vivien placed the tip of her blade against his right breast. But for the crackle of the fire and the sounds of bugs and frogs from the fens beyond, there was no sound.

"These blades are sharp," he said.

Vivien smiled. "I can play if you can."

Tyrell gasped, for the Wolf blinked, and his eyes became a stormy gray for a brief instant. "I can play, Lady Elf."

Vivien gave a quizzical look, throwing off her thrust just an instant, enough for the Wolf to twist to the side so the forward rush of the blade missed him. He batted the flat of the blade away with his hand and retreated. Vivien came at him, but the Wolf freed his sword from the sheath and threw the holder at his opponent. The La'athai began to cheer. The soldiers for the Wolf, the mages for Vivien. Bets were made swiftly.

Tyrell knew the warmage, and she was bright beyond most men's capability. She had watched the unit train for weeks, and seen the Wolf fight on many occasions. He could see her dissecting the barbarian, calculating his movements. The Wolf stood easily, sword held delicately, but his muscles were bunched for motion.

He smiled. "So, are you proficient with that thing?"

Again, Vivien stuttered in her advance. Then she lunged, feinting a stab that turned into an upward cut. The Wolf batted the attacks aside with his blade, setting them both to ringing. Tyrell gasped and the men fell silent but for some groaning from gamblers. She was *fast.*

She smiled grimly. "I was trained by the Lord of Swords himself."

The Wolf countered with a series of powerful cuts: high, low, high, middle, then from the other side before she turned the tables and stopped retreating to push forward with a series of cuts of her own. The swords called like bells into the evening air.

The Wolf was intent. "I was trained by an old man-at-arms. So how good a student were you?"

She feinted an advance and the Wolf reached to where she should have been, seeking to place his powerful hands on her. Leaning forward, he was off balance when the flat of her blade slapped down on his shoulder. He ducked his head as the sword moved sideways to cut, and again he rolled under the blade as it moved across him.

She grunted, "I was an excellent student," and executed a series of cuts. Each met the Wolf's steel but he had to give ground before the flurry of blows. His face was mask of concentration as the blurry blade seemed to come from everywhere at once. The mages cheered and howled to see the display, but there was a flash of steel and suddenly the Wolf was right next to Vivien, a big hand coming around to grapple her.

"I was middling," he said with a smile.

Tyrell gave a shout, but she had already smashed her foot into her opponent's instep and escaped his grasp while he growled in pain. They circled again, wary. Tyrell's heart leapt to see her avoid him, but there was a nagging doubt in his mind. Again they came together, force and finesse. She expertly kept him at a distance, catching powerful blade on the base, the strongest part of her blade. She flicked her sword forward, instinctually knowing where every weak point in his defense could be found. Every time, the Wolf's sword was there just in time.

Their faces had become grimaces of effort, but as Tyrell watched, he saw the emotion in their eyes. They were facing one another with razor-sharp, Elvish steel. They trusted one another so implicitly the thought of disaster didn't even enter their minds. They weren't fighting, not really, they were...loving. The thought dropped a stone into his soul, muddying it into a pained mess.

Vivien backed away, but the Wolf ate up the distance. Their swords rang for minute after minute. Tyrell saw her flagging. The Wolf retreated and Vivien followed, but then he was there, passing his sword along hers to lock them together, blades and crosspieces. She realized her mistake an instant too late. He lunged forward, almost bringing their bodies into contact. He wrenched her sword and hand over her head, bending her backward enough to take her off balance and opening her to attack. His free hand wrapped protectively around her waist and pulled her even closer. Tyrell ground his teeth as the two just stood there for a moment, she with hands above her head, bent backward, and he over her. She was utterly at his mercy as he cradled her gently in his arms.

But her face showed an expression of shock brought on by some unknown thought. "Wh...where did you learn that?"

The Wolf smiled roguishly, their faces only inches apart. "I made it up."

Vivien's face drained of all color and her free hand reached out and traced his jawline. The Wolf blinked, then shook his head as his features fell. He gently lifted her to her feet and unlocked the blades. Men were laughing, or groaning, as they exchanged coins.

"Hold!" The Wolf barked, "She would have split any three of you down the middle without even breaking a sweat. Grab your weapons. Basic exercises. All of you. Now!"

The La'athai groaned but made to move and gather their tools to go through the collection of strikes and blocks they knew from their first weeks with weapons in their hands. One mage collected his sword from the Wolf. Tyrell watched Lady Valdera wipe off her sword absently and sheath it as if in a dream. Her student set his jaw and stalked over to the barbarian.

"You fool!" he hissed, "You weakened her in front of the men!"

The Wolf turned and seemed to grow in stature, looming over him with eyes that were flickering into a deep glow. "She fought better than any of you ever have. And I don't think I excluded you in the basic exercises. Grab your weapon and practice."

"Are you even listening?"

The Wolf's eyes grew brighter, "After your exercises, grab your gear. You will stand a double post at guard."

The half-elf sneered, glittering motes collecting around his hands as he unconsciously called fae to his aid, "You insufferable–" The Wolf's eyes were like suns in his face, and his huge hands formed into mighty fists.

"Tyrell!" Vivien's whip-like tone lashed the fae back into the aether and robbed him of his head full of hot coals.

"Mistress, he–"

"Tyrell!" she snapped, now close enough he could see the dangerous glitter of her eyes. "You have your orders."

Chest aching under her harsh gaze, he pleaded, "He embarrassed you!"

"*You* are embarrassing me, and yourself. It was a friendly spar. Nothing more. Now move to your duties."

Tyrell bobbed his head and mumbled apologies to her before moving on to collect his sword. As he walked away, he heard her speak to the Wolf. "Thank you for humoring me. I am going to eat and get some rest before tomorrow."

Tyrell rushed through his exercises, the other La'athai avoiding looking at him as much as they glared at Gregor, considering their restful evening stolen because of his mouth. Then, with his body aching, Tyrell slapped on his armor and relieved the guard who stood nearest Vivien's tent.

He stood there half the night watching the beautiful warmage stare sadly into her campfire before being relieved by the next guard.

She sat there in the solitude of her tent, staring out the flap at the fire. The strands and layers twisted and cavorted about one another in a sensual dance, the colors shifting from golden yellow, to deep orange, and then to crimson red. The last reminded her of the Wolf's eyes when they burned at their brightest, but today, during their mock battle, their color had been nothing like the dark embers she was accustomed to.

They had been the color of a blue sky under threat of an approaching storm.

She shook her head for what seemed like the hundredth time and the same litany rang through her mind. *No, it can't be. He's dead. He's been dead so long now.* Tears sprang to her eyes, silly tears that she fiercely wiped away with the back of her hand, stubborn tears that kept coming even though she had mourned already.

Vivien's ears perked at some sounds she heard to her left where the Wolf's tent was pitched. A bit of shuffling here and there, and then he came into her field of vision and knelt beside the fire. She simply stared at him for a while, taking in his masculine form: the width of his shoulders, his lean waist, tendrils of curling hair falling alongside his face.

She breathed deeply of the night air, suddenly wishing she was back in Rithalion again. She closed her eyes and remembered the long ago past. In many ways, it was a happy one, for she never had want of anything, never hungered, never hadn't a place for shelter. Her father took her on many of his diplomatic missions into the northern hills and mountains where the human Lords lived in their majestic cliff-side castles.

It was during that time she'd learned Lairdstongue, a language she'd forgotten over the years since the last time she had visited there. She had taught herself the language from a book she'd found at the college, and it was the same one she'd given the Wolf when he first came to Rithalion.

The Wolf. *How in the world could he have known those words? Was he a diviner? Had he somehow plucked them from her innermost mind? For he certainly couldn't have been there to hear them.* But it was more than just his words; it had been his actions too, actions that rushed back to her as he tipped her backward over his knee...

A shadow moved itself between her and the fire. She waited for it to pass, and when it didn't she looked up to see the Wolf staring down at her. They remained like that for a moment before he spoke, "May we speak?"

She nodded. "Of course." Her voice sounded small, even to her ears. "I will come out there. The fire is nice."

He nodded and stood aside, waited for her to sit before seating himself. He watched her from dark eyes for a few moments. "Vivien, I am sorry I hurt you. I did not mean to. Please tell me how I can make this right."

She was thoughtful. "You didn't do anything wrong."

He raised a skeptical brow.

"I just had a memory, that's all." She turned to gaze into the fire. "I told you that Mikarvan was my only friend when I was younger. That's not entirely true. There was also this boy, a human boy."

The Wolf was quiet.

"I only met him twice, but he was my friend all the same. The first time, I was no more than fifteen summers old, and the second time, twenty-seven. He was...he was part of a world that fascinated me beyond belief, a world I would dream about for decades." Her voice became wistful. "Sometimes I still do."

The Wolf's eyes gleamed in the firelight.

"I remember running through the castle and across the countryside. We hid in the stables and fell asleep until the captain of the guard found us in one of the stalls. The boy's mother had been so worried, but instead of beating him, she just held him close. And then you want to know what she did?"

Vivien looked up at the Wolf. His face was impassive, his storm-grey eyes reflecting the orange glow of the firelight. Her voice was a broken whisper as she spoke past the burning lump in her throat. "She took an elvin girl she'd never met before and held her close too. Her arms were strong, and her chest soft and warm. She smelled of lavender."

She blinked and a tear slid down her cheek. The Wolf's finger was there to catch it before it rolled off her jaw. She looked into the fire again.

"The years passed. I couldn't wait to see him again one day, and when I finally did, he wasn't a boy anymore. The roundness of youth had been replaced by lean muscle, and his jaw was defined. But his smile...his smile was the same.

"We didn't run through the castle anymore, but we ran across the countryside on the backs of the best horses in his stable. We walked through the villages and I could see how much the people who lived there loved him by the smiles they cast us as we passed."

Vivien's gaze became haunted and her tone hushed. "I never saw him again after that."

She shook her head free of the memory and turned back to the Wolf. She gave him a sad smile. "Sometimes I still think of him, and in my mind he is still that young man standing with me on the marble balcony of his mountain-side castle."

For a while there was just silence and the crackling of the fire. The Wolf's voice was a low rumble, "I'm sorry for what I did to make you remember painful things."

She gave him a bittersweet smile. "No, don't feel sorry. My friend is important to me and deserves to be remembered."

The Wolf blinked in what seemed like a flash of surprise and his eyes searched her face intently before he finally nodded.

"I hope," Vivien paused, searching for the words she wanted to say, "I hope that the time he lived was good, and that he found happiness."

He stared at her for a moment, then rose. "We have a long day ahead of us tomorrow. We should get some sleep."

She just nodded and watched him walk to his tent. He turned to look at her before he finally lifted the flap and entered. She stared again into the fire, remembering the long ago past. She didn't know how long she sat there before heading into her own tent to find sleep that would be difficult to capture.

Chapter Thirty-Seven
Pergatium

Vivien sat on the side of the hill overlooking the stream. It was a beautiful day, and the sun shone between great, white puffy clouds that soared in a sea of blue. A flock of geese honked down at her as they flew past, their perfect vee-formation broken by the one on the end, who flew too far behind. The breeze swept the hair from her face and she took a deep breath of the mild lilac scent.

In the water there was a boy, his trousers folded up to his knees, his damp red-blond hair shining in the sun. He knelt before a small object moving and bobbing along atop the waters and she recognized it as a small boat. She smiled. Yes, it was the one he'd worked so hard on, the one he'd made with his father.

It wasn't long before he was plucking the boat from the waters and running up the hill. She saw the smile in his eyes before his lips curved up into a roguish grin. He settled onto the grass beside her and set the boat in her lap.

"See here," he pointed. "she needs a bit of repair. Do you think Papa will help?" His grey-green eyes squinted to look at her through the sun's rays.

"Of course he will. You have only to ask."

A melancholy seemed to sweep over him then, and he looked down. "He loves me, but he doesn't have to."

Vivien felt an ache deep inside. "No, he doesn't have to. But he does, and that is what makes it even more special."

He nodded. "Do you think he loves me as much as he does Sister?"

Vivien reached out and caressed his hair. "Yes, I believe he does."

He nodded again.

Vivien was thoughtful "How do you feel about Sister? Are you upset about her?"

The boy looked up at her again, his eyes wide. "Oh no. I love her. She is everything to me."

Vivien blinked, not expecting such a heartfelt response.

He continued, "Once, when I still lived in the dark, I had a brother. He left me and I was all alone." He twisted a strand of grass around his forefinger. "Then, one day Sister came. I wasn't alone anymore. She lit up the darkness even before I came to live in the light." He looked up at

ROSS &ROSS

Vivien. "I never want to be without Sister, and if I'm ever upset with her, I remember how much I love her, and it goes away."

Vivien stared at the boy sitting before her. Shock settled into her mind, for she had never heard anything like it before...

She jerked into wakefulness, and the foul stench was the first thing she perceived. Vivien opened her eyes and felt like she was going to fall out of her harness when she lurched to the side, her heart pounding against her ribs. The green snake just ignored her and slithered past. The smooth scaled body rubbed against her arm and she shuddered. *Only a week left, and we can leave this hideous place behind. Only one week.*

She unhooked the harness and carefully made her way down out of the tree. Glancing around the vicinity, she saw others doing the same. The Wolf had taught them how to weave harnesses out of ropes to hang themselves up high in the trees. Leeches as long as an arm would come from the water at night and seek out blood. Vivien had seen them questing about at the base of the trees and reaching blindly in the air for the soldiers and mages. That meant they had to move from one copse of half rotted trees to another, finding enough perches for them all night after night. When they couldn't, they huddled together in groups, fires built high and tents rigged into walls between branches, watchmen vigilant as the blood suckers came looking for a meal that would kill anyone they fed upon from blood loss. On those nights no one slept deeply, and awakened every time a boneless predator was cleft into twain.

Vivien had wondered a time or two why the Wolf had ever learned to make such a contraption. *Where was he from that he had to learn to sleep in trees with a harness?*

Groaning against the growing sickness in her stomach, she went over to her travel pack, looked it over before handling it just in case there was another slithery surprise awaiting her, then opened it to extract her water skin. She then moved slowly away from the rest of the group to find some privacy. Over the past fourteen days it had become a morning ritual. As she walked, the nausea mounted. It was the smell of the place, reminiscent of rotting flesh, and knowledge of the creepy denizens that lurked just beneath the surface of the murky waters.

It wasn't long before she was forced to stop. Vivien doubled over and vomited into the cesspool, retching over and over until her sides ached. One hand on the rotting stump beside her, she closed her eyes and sank to a crouch, struggling to keep her clothing as free from the nastiness as she could. The men thought she had swamp fever. She was wont to agree with them, only she didn't have a fever, just this sickness every morning and many other times throughout the day. She moaned and cried a little,

268

uncorked the water-skin and took a sip. She rinsed her mouth of the foulness and spat it out.

She was slow to recover, but finally decided she was ready to head back to the others. She opened her eyes...only to find herself faced with something from out of her worst nightmares. It was gruesome to behold, something that would haunt her even after this day. It was a man staring up at her from the swamp waters. The discolored flesh was sunken around the skull, the eyes dark pits filled with slime, the mouth open in a perpetual cry.

Vivien screamed. She rose and almost fell, screaming again in terror. She stumbled back, back, back, and when she looked down, she saw another man, and another. They were all dead, and she was surrounded by them. She screamed a third time...

"Vivien! Vivien, what is it?" She felt a pair of hands on her shoulders spinning her around. Tyrell pulled her close and held her tight against his chest. "Shhh, it all right. You are all right. We are all here now."

She wrapped her arms around his waist and pressed her face into the crook of his arm. "They are dead! They are all dead!"

Tyrell put a hand on the back of her head and stroked her hair. "Shhh, I know they are, but it's all right." He held her until her shuddering finally stopped, and when she had collected herself enough, she saw that the rest of the unit had gathered. A pall covered the area, for the reality of what they were looking at was a difficult one to comprehend.

It was the bodies of some of the elves who had perished when Pergatium was flooded hundreds of years before.

Vivien heard him coming, and when she turned her face from Tyrell's chest she saw him ready for battle. Wearing nothing but his breeches, boots, and scars, he carried his rock and rope coil, as well as his Elvish waraxe. Loose hair flowing down his back, eyes blazing like rubies, he was a fearsome sight. Despite herself, she wanted to flee from Tyrell's arms and press herself against the Wolf.

She was taken away from the thought as Tyrell's arms tightened. His voice buzzed like angry wasps, "It is an elf, *was* an elf, long dead."

The Wolf's reply was cold, instant. "Stab it in the head."

Vivien recoiled and Tyrell snapped, "That is one of our people! They deserve a burial."

"Was," the Wolf said leadenly. "It *was* one of your people. If you try to dig a grave here, it will fill with water as you shovel. Whatever he or she deserved, they will not get it. And sometimes," he looked into Vivien's eyes, his own now dark rubies in the morning light, "sometimes they come back."

Her stomach rebelled and her gorge rose again. She fought it down and closed her eyes. "Tyrell, have the men do as he says."

The sound of it might have been worse than watching. She left Tyrell's arms, which clung to her as if not wanting her to go, and let them to their work. When they were finished, the soldiers went back to their tasks. It was morning, and they had to move.

She felt a large hand on her upper arm and she blinked. The Wolf stood grimly beside her. "I was up early and I scouted the way. The land bridge I knew of here is gone."

Tyrell frowned. "Gone?"

The Wolf nodded, "The land masses shift and change in the tides of rain and whims of the gods. There must have been a storm that washed it away. I checked the depth and it is too deep to wade. If we try to swim it, we will get sick from the tainted water."

He frowned in a certain way, equal parts fear, frustration, and consideration. It tickled another memory and Vivien stepped away from him.

The Wolf's brow contracted and he shook his head, "I could not have known–"

Vivien felt her insides twist, knowing he could not understand what was in her heart. "Stop," she snapped. "The Iron Army is almost upon us. We must push forward. Is there another way?"

He shrugged, holding up a weighted rope with the log tied to it as a buoy. "I can test the depth of new paths, but it will take time."

Tyrell made a disgusted noise. "Oh gods, please send us a guide for our guide so we know where we are going!"

The Wolf glared at him. "There is one road left, but…"

Vivien waited a moment then crossed her arms. "And?"

The barbarian seemed to shrink. "It lies through Pergatium."

Vivien felt the word hit her with the weight of doom. Tyrell recoiled, "You are mad!"

Those three words entered her head, three simple words that burned her with the echoed sentiment of her husband back at the war council. She steeled herself, clamped down on her rebelling stomach, and cut the air in front of Tyrell with her hand like a knife. "Enough! How many days water does each man have?"

"Seven days," Tyrell said, clear as to who's fault he felt this was.

She looked to the Wolf. "How far if we go through the Doomed City?"

"Seven days," he whispered, his face pale.

"Then we march through," she said. "Break camp. Tell the men."

Tyrell cast a nasty glance at the Wolf, then hurried off to obey. Vivien was left alone with the barbarian, whose shoulders hunched under the weight of his thoughts. He moved stiffly to his tent and struggled into his padding and armor plates. Vivien fought the trembling of her body, tried not to be vulnerable, tried not to be weak.

"Wolf?" He looked at her, his eyes glinting in the morning light fighting through the dark mists. "I need you. I need you to be strong."

She could see her words reach into him. She could see them light something inside his soul. They weighed upon him, burning off the doubts and fears. He crushed his eyes shut, gritting his teeth with monumental effort. She feared him for a moment, feared the terrible strain he was under, but then he calmed, he opened his eyes, and he was the man that stood before her during the ambush upon the caravan so many months ago. Wild. Indomitable. A wolf. His eyes glowed slightly even in the daylight.

He slowly nodded.

She wanted to reach out to him, to pull him into a hug and offer him comfort, but she couldn't. She didn't have the strength to fight his demons and her own. But her heart ached, and she wanted to be close to him, "Wolf, what… what is it?"

He shook his head, again slowly.

She frowned. "Assemble the men."

The elves had descended from the safety of the trees, bolting food and drinking gulps of precious water. She went to her belongings and dressed quickly, grimacing at the still wet padding and heavy armor plates. She took a moment to grasp Mikarvan's tanager in her hand, praying to whatever god listened for safe passage through the Doomed City.

Properly attired, everyone shouldered packs so much lighter from lack of food and water. Each took the water skins of soaked tobacco leaves and squirted the solution down their pants and boots to keep away the leeches that infested the place. They looked toward her and she put on a brave face for them. They looked to the Wolf, and he simply burned at them like a wounded animal.

She sighed, set her jaw, and nodded. It may be cruel to push any man until he was like this, but if they lived, it would be worth it to them both and the rest of the pack. The Wolf had needed pushing. She had pushed. It was what had to be. "Lead on."

The Wolf had been keeping a hard pace, forcing the elves faster than they would like into the depths of the swamp. Now, however, at the nod from Vivien, he scanned the broken ground of the fen and took off at a run even in his steel armor. The men were startled, then scrambled to keep up. Tyrell appeared, carrying the Wolf's half empty pack and rope buoy.

"Convenient that he forgot this. Should I leave it?"

Vivien stared at him, feeling ire rise to cover the surging emotions inside of her. "I think you should carry it, Tyrell."

And she left him behind, seeking to get ahead to catch sight of the Wolf, but never quite able to push herself fast enough to reach the front of the pack.

The La'athai were panting heavily within the hour. The paths before had been carefully chosen, as clear of standing water as they could be in this place. Now, the Wolf chose straight lines and hard ground. His axe was a thin blade, made for war, and he still knew that in his current state. He did not cut down the foliage in his way, and leapt or shouldered aside heavier logs that had fallen to cut off their path. She was able to submerge her dreams and doubts in the constant misery of moving through the awful place, though she constantly jumped when the odd branch or half submerged rock looked for just a second like a limb or skull.

They finally caught up to him an hour after noon. The La'athai collapsed to a man on the wide ground, and Vivien staggered into the center of the group and sat heavily, joints aching. The pace was wearing down the men, and she had to rein in the wild human before some began to collapse from exhaustion. She went to stand and realized that the thin coating of vines and grasses under her were in regular patterns. They sought life from between thick cobbles and, in fact, they were not in a clearing, but on some kind of floor. On all sides, walls lay like broken teeth, barely over the level of the ground as they rose from the forgotten foundation. At some point they had entered the Doomed City, and had been running atop its corpse. At the edge of this foundation, near the water, the Wolf panted from atop not a rock, but an old broken pillar as he looked out beyond.

She approached him, lifting the straps of her pack where they cut into her shoulders. She formed her question and made to speak, but forgot them immediately. Just on the other side of the water was Pergatium.

She had not yet been born when this was a place of beauty. Wide buildings constructed of ancient stones, linked by flying walkways and raised platforms. She had found leather-bound texts that were made all the more tragic by knowing that the grand manses, the delicate bridges, and beautiful archways had been reduced to this. Yet, she had never comprehended how complete the destruction was.

The water had not washed away the city as she had always thought. It had broken it. Nature was not reclaiming the bones of the city rotting in the swamp. It was devouring it. Hallways that went nowhere were curtained by vines with sharp thorns. Wide bridges were murdered abruptly in mid-flight, hanging with no end to their path. The buildings that once held families of elves now echoed with the sound of dripping water and were furnished only in lichens and less palatable growing things. This had been a place that had provided rice for consumption and export, fish for the table, animal skins, rare woods, and medicinal herbs now only found in conservatories and collections.

Vivien felt her control crack, and she tamped down on it hard. There was still the bowshot of water to cross. "Is it safe?"

The Wolf looked at her, eyes still banked into low coals, and she ached to see the glow there did not fade while he looked at her. Without a word, he stood and leapt downward into the water. It was only calf deep, but she saw a few leeches splash out of the water and land on his muscled arms. She started to call to him, but she watched the slimy things latch on to his skin, then flail madly as if burned, and fall harmlessly into the water.

Men gathered around as he continued to slosh, deeper and deeper. The brown water was churned black as his feet disturbed the mud at the bottom. He choked up on his axe to hold it directly under the head, and pressed onward without pause. Ahead of him, bubbles flitted like gnats to the surface, but still he moved onward. Vivien, the La'athai, everyone held their breath as the water came to his waist and he did not falter.

Behind her, chatter buzzed.

"Can we cross that? Will we have to?"

"I'm not crossing that."

"That's too deep."

"He said as long as you don't have open cuts or swallow it..."

"He can survive arrows in his back. Maybe he doesn't even get sick!"

"Wait. What's that?"

And, indeed, the bubbles continued. They had seen them many times. Weeds rotting, a log underwater that was settling, fish fighting– it could be hundreds of innocent things. The Wolf stopped. Then he tripped, or the water got deep, or–

Whatever the reason, the Wolf went under the water with a splash.

Vivien felt the fae stir on all sides, and was shocked to find she was calling them. She gathered them and held them for some reason she could not name, not knowing if he was truly in trouble, not sure what to do if he was. Moments passed, and then some more. He was gone. *He was gone and not coming back!* She leapt the low wall and splashed into the edge of the water, heart racing.

The word came from deep inside her, and even as she heard it coming she could not stop it from being desperate, needful, and alone, "Wolf!"

Then the water far ahead rippled. Then it churned. Then the Wolf, eyes ablaze like the brightest of lanterns broke the surface and roared. He shook his axe at the sky in one hand, and a rotted branch in the other. He gasped, coughed, shook black droplets from his head, and panted.

Vivien's caught her breath and she nearly laughed with relief. The Wolf cast one measuring glance back and then continued his slog to the far shore. The water got shallower, his progress easier. He stepped up onto the stone foundation of the other side and tossed the branch away with disgust. He motioned the others to follow.

Vivien began walking, her stomach again lurching as the corpselike fingers of the water reached into every place she had. Shorter than the Wolf, she had to remove her pack and hold it over her head lest the water taint her skins and food. The churned water stank of excrement and rot, and she dared not stop when she hit the tangled branches and logs that had tripped the Wolf. The rest of the La'athai followed suit, soldiers especially careful since the bowstrings and arrows in their packs would be ruined by the water. Tyrell was last, holding two packs awkwardly and glowering.

She got to the other side and relished the water draining from her, but then felt the telltale squirm of living things near her skin. She shucked her armor and padding as the Wolf patrolled the road into the city, foregoing modesty to expose herself in her smallclothes and douse the few leeches that had latched on with more tobacco water, causing them to squirm and let go.

The Wolf circled around the large plaza, pausing at one lonely bush in the corner, a relic of a more civilized time, to rip at it meaninglessly. Then he continued his path around to where the rest were exiting the water, each repeating her ritual to strip almost naked and get rid of the parasites. Where the leeches had latched they left little fingernail sized welts that bled. They took out their kits and spread powdered crab shell on the wounds to clot them quickly.

Vivien approached the Wolf, but if anything, he had retreated even deeper into his animal nature. She stopped a few steps from him and sadly wondered if he even remembered her behind those bright, glowing eyes. He held out a hand filled with small, green leaves. She took them gingerly, looking at the bundle curiously.

His voice was low, harsh, like speaking was an effort, "Raspberry leaves. Mother gave us tea made from them when we were sick. Maybe now you can begin to feel better."

Those rough words made tears come to her eyes. *He is in there. He thinks of me.* "Th...thank you."

She looked down at his feet and saw the branch he had discarded when he exited the water. It was not a branch at all, rather, it was rotting, shrunken, leathery and black. It was an arm severed by a blade. She thought about all the branches and logs she had bumped into under the water.

"Sometimes," he said gravely, *"they come back."*

She turned to the soldiers, who were even now sitting down and breaking out wax paper wrapped bundles of food, "Clean yourself of leeches! Eat at a march. Prepare to move."

The Wolf nodded and began down the wide boulevard lined with wild trees poking through the stones, heavy vines cloaking doorways, and empty homes open to the sky. She bundled the leaves into her pack and set off after him, determined to not let him so far ahead all alone ever again.

Chapter Thirty-Eight
Spirits Never Truly Die

They traveled all day and into the night, finally taking refuge in the upper story of a dilapidated building, part of which was still standing despite centuries of erosion. The roof had long since rotted away, but the stairs kept them out of the reach of the giant leeches, and what was left of the walls gave them some sense of safety.

Vivien slept fitfully, only falling asleep when she saw the glowing eyes of the Wolf watching over them all from the top of the stairs, and waking to the same. Someone had gathered wood during the night, but it was wet. Her stomach began to roil, so she gathered some fae and applied them to the wood, where they danced and cavorted, turning water into steam and then wood into a bright fire. She took out her metal trail cup and dumped in some raspberry leaves with her water. It was soon steaming and she sipped gingerly. It was not the most pleasant taste, but her stomach did settle. She hoped she would not become feverish from whatever swamp malady had her, but at least the Wolf had given her a way to survive the nausea.

She considered him as he scanned the streets beyond and she moved over to him. The previous day had beaten her muscles and strained her joints, but he looked fresh, tireless, new.

She came near and sipped some more. "Thank you. It is working."

He nodded, watching still, axe in hand.

"Have you slept?"

He shook his head.

"You must sleep, Wolf."

He looked at her with those glowing eyes and said without emotion or inflection, "No. Not safe yet."

She felt dread again, and hoped he was wrong.

The sun rose and the men broke camp. It was hotter this day than the one before, and the constantly wet and sweaty armor was beginning to chafe through the padding. The boots smelled horrible– they never felt dry, and their hair and bodies were grimy from lack of bathing.

Still, they arose and ate, drank some of their meager supply of water, and marched down into the streets. It was becoming clear that this place had always been a wet one, and the main road was for dry days, while the rest of the city would fly overhead. Some elves would spend days above it all, with homes built above to save them from rising waters or slithering things. It was sprawling, like the gorge, and built along the needs of nature to thrive in an inhospitable place.

Vivien tried to consider these things, for considering the Wolf was more and more of a worry. He was more hunched, sniffing the air and moving as if he expected attack any second. He stopped at a black mark in the lee of a decrepit pile of stones that was once a temple. He stared at it a long time, then moved on as she approached.

It was a horrible stick figure, frozen in a state of terror. What could have been hands were held up in vain to stop the doom that had descended. The thing was caked in soot, as well as the stone on all sides. It had been burned by something so harsh nothing dared grow in the mark even to this day.

Tyrell motioned the men to follow the Wolf and paused by her. He shook his head. "That's...that's an unseleighe."

The word brought a few more warmages from the line of moving La'athai. They looked in amazement at the thing.

"An unseleighe? How?"

"It's a greater unseleighe. An unbound spirit."

"Why is it here?"

"It could have been left from the war?"

"So long? If they are here we are in real danger."

"They might infest this place? But look at it. It's been dead decades, maybe a century."

"You think that's why An'drath is afraid?"

"Who could have killed it?"

"Not who, what," Vivien said, looking ahead to the retreating back of the barbarian. "That kind of fire only comes from a dragon." She looked to them all, feeling her own fear mirrored in each and every one of them, "Get to your positions. Be ready. And let's hope we don't see any more."

Vivien hurried to the front of the column. As she did, the boulevard took two dozen steps up to a raised plaza. She took the steps two at a time until she stood next to the Wolf. The La'athai pooled behind him, mouths wide in shock.

Unseleighe were spread like droplets from a discarded cup, radiating out from a huge building to the west. They were broken, dismembered, and burned. Dead, but not dead, gone, but locked there for eternity. In the center of the square, statues to the gods, the Deep Green and the Mother of Light among them, lay in the center. Across them was a massive skeletal shape, easily seventy feet long. The wings were sprawled to either side, the bones having been picked clean over decades, maybe even a century or more. The horned skull lay blasphemously across the statues, maw agape.

Elvish Jewel

Fear raced through Vivien without pause, and she saw the Wolf tremble. His eyes burned like red suns in his skull, anger keeping him to his task despite fear that bubbled out of him like swamp gas. He stared at the beast. And he waited.

Tyrell came forward and dropped his pack next to the Wolf. Vivien expected him to jump, but he paid it no mind. All his attention was on the monstrous skeleton. Then Tyrell saw the winged spirit, and breathed out, "What is it?"

Vivien's eyes traced backward to the destroyed doors to the tall, rotting edifice behind. It was too familiar to be coincidence, and more of what she had read came to her mind. "That is the college of magic. It is the epicenter of the battle between the dragon elves and ourselves." She took one step forward and faltered. "It is said that, during the battle, the masters of the fae and the conjurers of dragons summoned not just lesser spirits, but those whose names were written in ancient tomes, creatures that had never been tamed. These are some of the fae, and that is one of the dragons."

Tyrell shook his head. "Well, it is dead. Why are we standing here staring at it as though it is going to get up and eat us alive?"

Vivien glanced at the Wolf, who still stared at the thing. "Death means something different to these creatures. They are all but immortal; they could only be returned to the aether by the strongest of magic, or the most powerful of weapons. They were bound by words captured in times long forgotten." She shrugged. "However, this one seems to be quite dead."

Vivien glanced back as she was bumped from behind by the jostling of the men wanting to get a better look, then looked back at the remains. She just stood there for a moment, staring. *Such a proud, majestic beast lying there broken and alone.* She took a step forward, but a huge hand snatched her wrist and hung on. She turned to the Wolf.

He shook his head emphatically. "No. It is not dead."

A shudder swept through the men. Vivien felt herself tremble, but when she looked back to the dragon, she detected no movement, nothing that would tell her it lived beyond death. *He's so beautiful, lying there. So still, like one of the statues lying around the place. His scales look like they might be smooth to the touch.* She blinked at the strange thought, for the beast's hide was long rotted away. She steeled herself and looked back at the Wolf. "I want to see."

The glow in his eyes faltered. "Please don't do this."

She looked back to the dragon, lying there so forlorn. "Let me go, Wolf." Her hand began to tingle from the strength of his grip. "I *need* to see."

His eyes flickered. "Please, trust me."

Vivien frowned. "You must trust me too."

He narrowed his eyes and dropped her hand almost like it was a hot brand. He looked away from her, but not before she saw his eyes flare to life, burning with an intensity she'd never seen before. His lips pressed into a thin line, he glared across the stones of the plaza, and clenched his fists. Vivien stepped away from the Wolf and moved forward a bit, then some more. It wasn't until she was several paces away before she realized he was following her. She continued forward, took another step and entered the plaza. She made her way past the first carbonized figure, this one a seleighe. She examined it, seeing the horror and loss frozen forever on its burned face. She looked back to the dragon, and it had not moved. She pushed down on her fear. *You aren't a child anymore, Vivien. Be strong!*

She drew herself up and continued on. Behind her the Wolf followed, and behind him, the La'athai watched. She was almost to the skeleton, weaving between the blackened bodies, coming ever closer, closer, and then felt a dread weight sweep over her, a negativity, a depression. She shook her head. *What am I doing here? Why am I so far from home on a mission that is probably going to kill all these men, one that will probably kill me too? We can't do this.*

Vivien didn't realize she'd slowed to a stop until she felt the Wolf's arm brush against hers as he stopped beside her. She looked up at him, and he must have seen some of her thoughts reflected in her eyes, for he visibly recoiled. Some of his anger seemed to fall away and his brows furrowed. "What is it?"

She shook her head. "I...I don't know. I just suddenly feel like–" She stopped then, not wanting to say it.

He stared at her. "Yes, I feel it too. It's the pall of the dragon. You have to fight it."

Her eyes widened. "He has that kind of power, even in death?"

The Wolf nodded. "He isn't dead."

"How do you know?"

He frowned, shrugged angrily.

She stared at her friend for a moment. She got the strange feeling that he was keeping silent to hide some truth from her. "All right, then let's have a quick look before heading back to the others."

He frowned, nearly pleading. "Vivien, have you not heard what I've said?" But she had already stepped away from him and continued towards the massive bones that jutted to the sky. She heard him muttering to himself in his tongue, but she moved ever closer. One of the ribs was broken, and pieces of it lay on the ground beside one foreleg. She walked around the massive chest, and over to the skull. The maw was open wide and she imagined what all those rows of sharp teeth could do in life. Her foot connected with something on the ground and she looked down. It was a broken blade with runes scrawled over the shining surface. Before she could say something, the Wolf bent to pick it up. The blade shook. The Wolf was trembling.

Vivien turned from where they had come. The men still stood where they had left them, watching. The weight on her mind lifted and she shook it, feeling for a moment like she was waking from a terrible dream. She looked to the bones, suddenly feeling an endless rage churning within. "Wolf, I'm sorry I have kept us here. I'm ready to go back when..." She stalled when she turned back to see him standing there, sword blade shoved into his belt. He had cut his palm, and blood dripped from his hand.

Alarmed, she moved to get back to his side when she stumbled on a broken piece from one of the statues. She toppled forward into the Wolf, and he just managed to keep them both from falling by putting out his injured hand and catching himself against the enormous jaw. Blood smeared over the bone. It glittered evilly and steamed.

His recoil was instant, and so was the transformation.

Right before their very eyes, the dragon began to change. Like the pieces of a jigsaw moving at the speed of a tir-reath at a full run, they fell into place, starting from the place where the Wolf had touched it. She gasped and stumbled back, and the Wolf did the same, taking hold of her hand and clasping it tight.

Within moments the massive dragon lay before them in all of its monstrous glory. His scales shimmered in the late day sun in shades of crimson, ginger, and gold. The maw was no longer rimmed with just teeth. It was an entrance to hell with spiny growths deeper in, pointed down the gullet to make sure nothing that was swallowed could ever escape.

Oh gods...

The Wolf pulled at Vivien's hand, but she stood rooted in place. She looked into a red eye that glittered with hatred. "It's alive," she whispered breathlessly. "Oh gods, it's ALIVE!"

The Wolf pulled Vivien away from the head, around the forelegs and to the side. She was hit with it again, the terrible pall. *Why am I even trying to leave this place? Why? Just to enter a battle we can never win, only at the end of an iron sword?*

The Wolf, his face a rictus of pain, took her arms and turned her towards him. "Vivien, you have to fight it! Tramp it down; use all you've got!"

She looked up into his dark eyes and nodded. Tears trickled down her cheeks even as she held back her sobs. She looked over at the dragon, and her eyes widened with shock. Over the area where the rib was broken, the skin was flayed open as though from a mighty strike. Inside the wound was a crystalline mass the color of rubies. It glistened in the paltry sunlight that entered through the gaping hole. At the center of the mass there was an empty space where thick ropes she recognized as arteries connected to... nothing.

She just stood there agape. It took her a moment to finally recognize what she was looking at. Or rather, what she wasn't looking at. The heart. The heart was missing. The Wolf pulled at her again, this time more insistent. "Please, Vivien..."

She nodded, fighting the overwhelming feelings of despair that washed over her yet again. With no small amount of effort she moved through the forest of statues with him towards where the men waited. Suddenly, there was a strange, pregnant pause and the air around the dragon distorted in a mighty roar that was not heard, but felt. It vibrated the ground with deafening silence, scattered leaves and dirt from the maw. Vivien reached out a desperate hand and latched onto the arm of the Goddess of the Moon. At the edge of the plaza, La'athai stumbled from the burst, covering their faces from the rush of sheer will that tossed dirt like a sudden storm. When the blast faded, a churning pain in her stomach hit Vivien hard. She fell to her knees, grabbing herself, and a pathetic groan escaped her.

The Wolf put an arm around her shoulders. "Vivien..."

It was then she heard a voice scream her name. She looked up to see Tyrell, face in anguish, running towards them with two other mages right behind. The wind of pure will started again. It was a roar that reached into the soul. It made everything small, powerless, rendered everything that heard it into prey. Across the stone street, La'athai braced themselves against the onslaught or were tossed down the stairs like twigs. Tyrell and the mages leaned forward as if against a violent current. Their clothes and hair whipped as if about to rip from their bodies. They had to fight for every step.

Vivien felt no such push. She gathered herself to stand, the Wolf beside her, and just as she was about to move, the pain came again. She doubled over and the Wolf put his arms around her. He held her there for the briefest moment before they were also caught in an unendurable force. They found themselves crushed against the statues and, in the opposite direction of the others, pulled back through the copse of stone legs towards the dragon.

Vivien's thoughts spun and fear surged through her. She and the Wolf were dragged, slowly, slowly back, not toward the gaping maw, which was dripping bloody saliva, but towards the center, toward the open chest that shone wet with blood. They grasped upon the feet of gods, seeking to delay their fate. The inexorable force pulled stronger, a tongue that trapped them and pried their fingers from god to god as they fought for handholds. The Wolf screamed, an auditory counterpoint to the soundless pulling, a sound that reflected the battle they fought.

She looked through the forest of divinity, saw that the two mages had fallen, but that Tyrell still persevered. However, that was short lived. He covered his face to protect it from flying detritus and lost his balance. His feet slipped from under him and he rolled all the way back into several soldiers, sending them all sprawling down the stairs.

It was then Vivien's strength began to flag. Days of slogging through a nasty swamp coupled with daily stomach expulsions had taken their toll. She screamed as she slid back, away from the Wolf, away from the handholds she desperately tried to clutch onto. She looked toward the head of the fell beast. More saliva dripped from the open mouth and steaming blood ran from a dozen deep lacerations across its hide. The eyes, though, the eyes glowed like blazing pyres.

Vivien screamed again as she slipped further and further, her legs now past the statues and flailing as if she dangled over a cliff. The hungry wind pulled harder, but somehow, she found purchase. She heard the Wolf snarl in frustration as she hung on for dear life. It was only moments before she felt her grip begin to slip. *Oh gods, please save me. Please...*

She screamed as her hands broke away from their precious hold–

And fists that could bend iron bars snatched her in midair.

Vivien looked into the face of her fierce comrade. Somehow, he was no longer being dragged with her; the pull had released him from its death hold. He was being battered, bashed in the forest of stone, and still he held on. In that moment, as the Wolf fought for her life yet again, something surged within her and arrived at the fore of her mind. It was something she had been resisting for so many weeks, months, however long they had been in proximity. It defied reason, it defied everything, but still it was like a gale from the mightiest storm, fierce. It frightened her a little, but it also liberated her.

Blood from his wound seeped from their joined hands, coating their palms and robbing their grip of traction. Try though they might, inexorably, their hands began to slip, and she felt inevitability cloaking her like the fresh dirt of a grave. She scrabbled at his hands, hoping, praying the pull would just miraculously let her go like it had the Wolf. Her guts gave another painful twist and she screamed...

The Wolf roared as first one hand came free of his, and then, as he tried to grab her, the other. She skidded toward the empty dragon chest and she saw it all: the droplets of blood, the swaying meat, the pulsing mass of organs. Instinct surged through her and she spun toward certain doom, suddenly felt power flow through her like she had never known. She felt fae from far and wide screech toward her hands as she held them up, a glowing bulwark that halted her progress. Glowing fae formed the barrier, crumbling at the edges as they disintegrated and fell like ash in the wind. She called more, and more, but the momentary respite slowly dissolved under the titanic will of the elder dragon. Death was coming for her. Worse than death. She only had time for one last thing.

Vivien turned, unwilling and unable to die without speaking a final truth. It was too late, far too late, but at least it could be said. At least it could see the light of the sun and live for a moment before being swallowed. She turned to the Wolf. His face was dirty, unkempt, filled with utter loss and despair. She gave the golden piece of honesty to him, setting it free to fly to him. Words, so small, but holding all the truth she had been avoiding for months.

"Wolf!" She hesitated only the briefest moment. "Wolf, I love you!"

The angry, red light of his eyes faded, leaving behind two eyes that were perfect stormy blue. She smiled sadly, the shield crumbled, and she was pulled toward an indescribable doom in the chest of a dragon that had been a pile of bones only minutes before.

His eyes blazed again, glowing with the power of the forge of his soul, a blue that bathed the area in defiant brightness. His face constricted and he roared– roared not like a wolf, but like a dragon.

It was a roar that shook the entire city.

The force let go of her, and a shadow flashed overhead. The Wolf propelled himself with a thrust of his mighty legs, soaring above her and colliding with the empty socket of flesh like a boulder. The entire dragon shook, and the unheard sound changed timbre. Vivien watched in awe as the Wolf roared again. She heard a tearing of cloth, then he brandished the hilt-less blade from the belt around his waist. He plunged it into the meat to his elbows, grappling against gods only knew what. He hung from the body, planting his feet into the breach, snarling and heaving, veins standing out on arms that shook with the strain.

The phantom calls became panicked, strained, pleading. Still the Wolf heaved, his entire body pulling and pushing, his teeth gritting into a mask of death and determination. He roared and she felt the ripple of emotion like the pall, but instead it was determined, triumphant, indomitable.

Elvish Jewel

There was a crack like a thunderclap, and the barbarian fell free, landing hard on his back. A deluge of dragon blood splattered to the ground joined with the ring of a fallen blade. She caught sight of two halves of the massive spine, half cut, and half pulled apart by a power beyond reason.

The whole body of the dragon shifted. The scales became dull. The light from its eyes flickered and slowly died.

The pain in Vivien's guts fled as if it had never been. In the silence, she stood shakily. She heard her voice, small against the quiet. "Wolf?"

She turned and he was there, covered in steaming blood, uncivilized, untamed, unafraid. His chest still heaved, his legs and arms trembled. Still he stood. His chest piece had slipped, exposing the little white scar where he had tried to kill himself to save her and her baby.

She regarded him and hesitated...

The Wolf, expression unreadable, opened his arms and she threw herself into them. They closed around her, welcoming her to him. She didn't care that he was bathed in stinking, hot, crimson, she pressed herself close and accepted his mess as her own. Under the cloying aroma of dragon blood, his woodsy, spicy scent was still there and it filled her with a sense of safety. He held her tightly while offering protection and comfort as her body trembled. He asked nothing of her, demanded nothing, but she gave back in return. She could relax and be weak for a moment without being thought of as helpless, indolent, or fragile. She listened to his heart slow from a harsh frenzy into a lazy thump, and she felt somehow complete.

It was then she heard someone, or *someones*, cheering. The sound got louder and louder, and she recognized it as the La'athai. Within moments the men surrounded them, their happy voices lifted to the sky. Hands were patting her and the Wolf, hands filled with acceptance. These soldiers and mages... they saw her standing there in an embrace with a human, the Wolf, and they didn't care. All they cared to do was cheer for them.

The La'athai tightened their circle around them, howling to the sky. The Wolf grinned and Vivien returned the sentiment. Tyrell watched from the periphery, his expression bathed in profound sadness. Finally, she had an inkling as to the reason for his sharpness towards the barbarian. She broke away from the Wolf, hoped to approach her second in command, but she caught sight of the bright, broken blade that the Wolf had picked up before the fight with the dragon, the one he'd used to sever the enormous spine. She retrieved it out of the pool of ichor, watching in amazement as blood beaded across its surface and ran off without the slightest trace. Where she touched it, the dragon's remains squeezed from her fingers as if escaping the silvery sheen of the steel. She admired the engraved scrollwork, then caught her breath in recognition.

The men quieted as Vivien spoke, "This is the rest of the blade belonging to the Lord of Swords and Truth's sword, Arisil."

The Wolf nodded, his blue glowing eyes dimming to the barest flicker.

Vivien considered it again, then the Wolf. There was a story there, one that needed to be told. "How did it come to be here?"

Again he nodded slowly, knowing what was in her mind. "After the battle."

She gave him a ghost of a smile, feeling him as if he were an elf. "After the battle, then." She directed her attention to the La'athai. "Behold the blade of Arisil!" She held it aloft and her voice rose. "This is an omen for our upcoming battle! Let us rest for the night and then make haste; the destiny of our people awaits!"

Chapter Thirty-Nine
Two Hearts Beating

Loneliness pressed upon him as he wandered. One month passed into the next, and then the next. Autumn took bounty from the land and made hunting and foraging difficult. Hunger became a mainstay. More months came and went. Winter brought increased scarcity and chilled him to the bone. Though his horse died in the cold, Ravn did not stop and seek shelter throughout the rest of the season. Hunger dogged his every footstep, as well as voracious timber wolves that kept him half awake and wary even in the darkest hours of the night.

Spring brought heavy rains. Wetness pervaded his entire being and the very moment he finally became dry, more rains ensued. His boots were perpetually damp, and his feet itched and burned, sloughing off layers of skin that died while he walked. A group of malcontents accosted him one day. The first to come close lost his head to a strike he never saw coming. The rest decided Ravn had no possessions worth fighting for, and it was a stroke of luck. Until he took food and water from the dead bandit, he had not eaten in days and wasn't sure he had the strength for even one more stroke.

In spite of his unresolved plight, Ravn persevered. He had faced starvation, bandits, and wolves, but nothing with a heart he could take home to his estranged wife and claim her trust, love and devotion. There was a time, so long ago only an elf could remember, that monstrous and fantastical beasts were thick upon the land. Now those lands lay quiet as the elves had tamed it thousands of years before. The great, wandering tribes of giants, the troops of trolls, and packs of goblins were found less often in the region. Still, he searched, never losing hope, and took refuge in his mind.

Homesickness reigned. Ravn remembered hearty meals and the warmth of the hearth. He longed for the peace and silence of the kirk, and the camaraderie of the guards as they sparred in the courtyard. He missed the solidarity of his faithful horses, the devotion of his castle staff, and the passion of Neála, who loved him. He even missed his wife, though he was certain she wished he'd never been born to be given to her in unwanted wedlock. He came to a stop in the rain, wolf-skin cloak sluicing water off of him as thunder rolled angrily.

Laird, I have always loved you like a son. You are the finest warrior I have ever seen. Please don't do this, Moray had said. It had begun a bitter fight with his oldest and most loyal retainer. *Then so be it Laird, but when you are desperate, look to the warlock in the swamps near the lowland bog alongside the falls, The Tears of Infinity. I have no trust of magic, but he has been there longer than your forefather's castle has stood. Maybe he can lead you to what you seek.*

"Is the warlock to be trusted?" Ravn started, realizing he had spoken aloud to the memory.

No, Laird. I would not trust one such as he.

Ravn sank to his knees on the cold, wet ground. The rain instantly soaked through his kilt and chilled his skin. His heart trembled, for he was lost in the world and in his heart. The cloak he had brought had fallen apart. His beard and hair were hacked off by the edge of his dagger. His skin was taut and his muscles were rangy and devoid of fat. His clothes were likewise threadbare, his family tartan black with grime. His shining armor and sword had begun to rust. He looked like a beggar knight, and he felt a measure of self-loathing. Even if he found a heart, who would love him as the gaunt, hollow-eyed phantom he had become? He looked at the ground. *What would it be like to just lie down and not move?*

NO.

Ravn lurched backwards. The denial had reverberated inside him but the voice was… was…

"Father?!" The Laird Blacach could hear his heart in his ears as he spun around. "Father?!"

But he had seen his father dead, killed by the Liath. Tears came unbidden and unwanted. Ravn gnashed his teeth and pressed his palms into his eyes until the darkness swirled with ghosts and stars sparkled across the blackness.

Moray's words came back to him. *How long will you be gone, Laird?*

A supernatural calm came over him as his own answer echoed in his head and out of his mouth, "I swear by all the gods, I would wander the wild homeless for a hundred years if it meant earning true and enduring love."

The calm drained from him, leaving him without comfort or company. He was tired, empty, and alone, but he was standing. He put one foot in front of the other. Where innocence or heart could not survive, cold determination would suffice.

He faced upward, icy drops slapping his face for his weakness. His tears mixed with those from the sky and he opened his heart to any that would hear it.

"Gods, all gods of love and hope, please...please. I just need this to be over."

Still it rained. Thunder rolled.

He lowered his face, nodding. "So be it."

He marched onward, with no clear path available, the thunder above becoming more and more constant without relieving the darkness with momentary light. He began to feel a pattern, a rhythm that was only broken by strikes from far off lightning. It was a rolling thud, like a massive hammer, like a heartbeat, like…

…footsteps.

Steel was in his hand. The rain acted as thick lace in every direction, turning the gloom of the day into nearly complete darkness. He heard the footsteps, knew that they were near and belonged to something huge. He could see nothing, had no idea in which direction his destiny lay. He spun, cursing his breath for coming hot and fast, blotting out the sounds he needed to hear. Now he could sense the thud and the squish as tons of weight displaced rain softened mud. It was coming closer, closer.

Ravn ran five steps to the north, then to the west. *East*? Nothing. The constant crash of the rain to earth deadened any fine sensitivity to his ears. What the rain didn't rob him of, the frantic beating of his heart did.

The footsteps stopped.

Ravn gathered himself to spring, but had no idea which direction to move. He heard a wet, annoyed snuffling.

Lightning flashed, and Ravn found himself face to face with a mountain giant. It's club was already moving to crush him.

The Laird flung himself to the side, skidding through mud on his shoulder as the massive club smashed where he had stood. It left a crater to dry earth as mud splashed like water away from the impact. Ravn shook his head, certain that his moment's disorientation would cost him his life. Somehow, it did not. He lifted his sword, a tiny sliver of metal to ward off almost a ton of aged oak club, but the attack did not focus on him. The thirty foot tall monstrosity used a club in the other hand to hit the same patch of ground again. The awesome display froze him in his place for a moment more, but again it did not turn to him.

The brute was manlike, but far more muscled than tales of the flabby forest cousins. The ugly, ropy muscles were stacked on the body like the overstuffed balls children kicked around the fields. The joints were massive, and the body sloped from gargantuan feet to thinner shoulders with two heads perched atop. One head swept around, clearly searching for him and snuffling through a snotty nose. The other peered at the ground, poking the spot where he had stood with its club. Then it listened, then sniffed the air. It took a step toward him.

It was *smelling* him.

The rain intensified, and Ravn could barely make out the outline of the massive beast. If it had worse sight, it could hardly see his comparatively tiny form at all. Using the smallest movements he dared, he got his feet under him. He pulled his makeshift cloak, made from the skins of hungry wolves, and dropped it to the ground. His grip tightened on his sword and he squelched away from the spot where he had slid, thankful the rain was now a constant chatter on the ground as both heads jerked like birds to catch phantoms of his passing.

He circled it slowly, and it smelled the air. He had almost gotten behind when it roared from both mouths, a sound that hit like a punch and loosened his bladder. One right head then brought its club down almost on the cloak, then smashed again and again to finally hit it and throwing up splashes of mud. The left head, however, stopped the moment he felt the warm line of piss course down his thighs and trickle over his boots. It was sniffing, and turning toward him.

Thinking quickly, he tore the purse from his belt. It contained twenty silver and ten gold coins he had never spent out in the wilds. He lobbed it between the creature's legs as it lifted the right hand club from the mangled cloak. The purse hit the man sized piece of dry earth and split open. The high pitched tinkle of coins spilling brought the creature fully back around and it began smashing the dirt with both clubs like a blacksmith punishing a red hot bar.

Ravn did not pause. He leapt forward, sword held low and across his body. The left head turned just as he planted with his right foot and as his left came forward he swung the rusty steel up and right, every muscle and his weight behind the cutting edge in one desperate hit. The sword bit into the most upper part of the thing's inner thigh and cleft deeply into the meat.

The sword came away cleanly with a twist that opened the wound and Ravn dove completely through the arch of the creature's legs. As he slid through mud his pack strap snapped and tumbled free. It took a stumbling step towards where he was and smashed the ground. Then again. Ravn scrambled away as it began hitting the ground randomly, roaring in rage as its lifeblood poured from the deep gash and spoiled the ground. It went down to one knee and continued to hammer the ground with strike after strike, then the left head began sweeping the ground in a wide half circle around it. Ravn leapt away, but the edge of the club clipped him in the breastplate, ringing like a bell and sending him sprawling, sword tumbling off into the rain.

The left head looked toward where he had been, but it took several moments for it to catch the attention of the right head, and struggle to its feet. Ravn scuttled backwards on his backside as it took faltering steps forward, trailing the injured leg. It was facing slightly the wrong way, but began slapping the ground again, sending liquefied sod flying. The clouds above let forth a horrific crash of lightning, and in the light, Ravn and the left head of the two headed giant saw cleanly into each other's eyes. Ravn flipped himself and began to slip and slide, trying to gain traction. The giant tried to walk, but the injured leg buckled, still gushing blood like a swelled stream. The creature let go of the right club and put the hand down to keep from going to its faces in the mud. The left lashed out at him again, but the club fell short. The strike did not hit dry dirt. It struck again, but it was far more of a tap.

Ravn stood and watched as the mighty creature continued to slow and turn pale. Eyes bright with rage became dull and glassy. The right head's mouth was slack and drooled uncontrollably. The left made a roar that only exited as a growl. Suddenly Ravn felt the deep dent in his armor where the club had clipped him as it began to throb and seize up, the muscles tightening with pain. He hissed and doubled over.

He looked up as the creature wheezed as if from a marathon run. It could not get enough air, and once mighty limbs that could powder stone now twitched feebly. It watched him with eyes that could barely see, gasping as the blood pumped in weak rivulets down its thigh. Ravn felt an immense guilt as the creature stopped breathing, on its back and staring into an angry, uncaring sky with sightless eyes.

Tears came to him as he forced himself to stand despite the pain. He hobbled to where his pack had been crushed by the giant's feet and found his hatchet was miraculously intact. Then he returned to the body, huffing as his ribs ground against one another as he hacked, and hacked and hacked through a cage of bone with bars thicker than a man's wrist.

He thought about Neála. He thought about his wife. For the first time he had doubts about his grand, epic quest, now that the cost of it had been a life. *Only a giant, but still? Would he have murdered even a dog to make Ròs happy? And now that he had done this for his wife, should he not do it for Neála too?* But she had no need of bloody tribute, even though she deserved it far more.

With sickening sounds he butchered the carcass until he exposed the stinking organs inside. Then he saw them. Two hearts.

Ravn closed his eyes, but there a perfect set of green eyes was smiling at him. They were happiness and joy, friendship he had known since he was a boy. He had no heart for her, and that realization made him cold and empty even in this moment of triumph. For a second he considered packing up both hearts and running south straight into Elvish lands. He could find her and give them to her.

His elvin princess.

He shook off the dream. She wasn't really a princess, but a prestigious sorceress. She had always said her fate was determined by the needs of her people. She would never, could never, have a simple man as her mate. She would be disappointed in him for this, saddened by death being required to prove the love he had inside. She would cry if she knew. He stared into the sky and felt the rain beat down on his face. He loved Neála. He loved his wife. But in that moment, kneeling on the broken body of his prey, he remembered how much he loved Jash'ari too. Nothing his father or mother had ever said prepared him for a soul pulled in two directions, let alone three. He knew he had to let the elvin lady go, but even after all these years apart, he knew he could not entirely do so. As such, he hid the thoughts of her deep inside, and simply cherished his memory of her.

But when his heart beat, the sound it made was her name.

Ravn repaired his leather pack and collected his bloody prizes into it. He found his sword and shook off what was impossible. He had done something worthy of song; he had saved his marriage and saved Neála and the child they had together. Now he could finally live happy.

Now he could go home.

Chapter Forty
Calm Before the Storm

They waited, but only because they had to. It was a tense time, the men tired from their trek, but not enough for them to remain still. They paced the camp like wild tir-reath, their eyes wide and alert.

After another week of travel through the swamp, they had finally come to solid ground yesterday around midday. The La'athai had wanted to celebrate with a fire, but the Wolf frowned at them until they gave up the idea. Vivien wanted to give in, for they all needed something warm and bright after weeks in the swamp, but the knowledge that the humans had to be near meant there was no other answer. They had, however, moved out of the valley enough to leave the fetid stink of the swamp behind. That is, until they realized it was soaked into every article of clothing they had.

To a man, and even a few women, they stripped down to their smallclothes for the night, hanging padded gambesons on branches to air out, and boots left upturned so putrid feet could breathe. Vivien busied herself likewise, but she aired herself out in the privacy of her tent. She uncorked a small bottle of scented oil, rubbed down her skin, and then scraped off the excess with a short hooked metal rod made for such a onerous task. She recoiled as the gathering line of oil she removed came away black. Afterwards she sighed contentedly and rolled out her blankets into a pallet and, without bothering to dress, lay down. She had yet to make her rounds for the night to check on the men, but after weeks of waking at every sound and sleeping in rope harnesses off of the ground, the simple earth covered in blankets was pure luxury.

Vivien heard the Wolf giving orders softly to groups of soldiers and she reflected over the past several days. After the fight with the dragon, the La'athai had walked across the rest of Pergatium, stopping at the edge of the swamp. They took up residence in another structure, just high enough to keep them safe from nocturnal visitors who might want to devour them in the night.

Regardless, Vivien did receive a visitor. She had wondered if he would come to her, especially in light of a declaration made under the most intense of duress, one made with the understanding that death was inevitable. Once everyone was asleep, the Wolf had padded over to her on the lightest of feet. In spite of her fatigue, she was laying there awake, looking up at a sea of stars. She'd raised herself up onto an elbow as he situated himself beside her on the floor, his eyes reflecting blue in the light of the pale full moon.

They regarded one another for a moment. Then, with a hesitancy he'd never shown before, the Wolf reached out and put his hand into the mass of her hair where it lay over her shoulder. He rubbed it between his fingers, a smile tugging at the corner of his mouth.

His voice was a low whisper, "What you said today means very much to me."

She just lay there, watching him, her heart thumping against her ribs. In spite of all the time they had spent together: making battle plans, practicing, and discussing tactical errors, he had never given her the feeling he gave her at that moment. She sensed a rawness about him, coupled with passion, that simmered just beneath the surface. She knew it could overwhelm her in its power, and it both frightened and excited her at the same time.

She bit at her lower lip in anticipation, not knowing what to say, not certain she needed to say anything at all for events to unfold as they would. The action caught his attention. Her heart leapt into her throat as he stared, no longer at her eyes, but at her mouth. He leaned forward, closer and closer until she could feel his breath against her face.

A warm sensation crawled through her, down her torso to settle into the pit of her belly. It roiled recklessly, bending her into gentle knots that folded in and out. He paused then, his lips so close to hers she could almost feel them against hers.

"I want to kiss you Vivien," he breathed.

Her senses exploded.

All of a sudden she could see the lines around his eyes, hear the snoring of the men as they slept paces away, smell the presence of the swamp beyond their camp, taste the travel rations she had eaten before settling down for the night, and feel the textured wool of the blankets beneath her. But more than all of those things, she sensed a connection between her and the man before her, one that stretched beyond space, beyond time...

His hand tightened in her hair and his breathing was ragged. "Please tell me you want me to."

Her eyes flew open. Was he asking her permission? She'd never had a man do that before!

He brushed his lips against the side of her face in a gentle nuzzle. An ache settled low into her pelvis, one that made her yearn to reach out and crush herself against his muscular body. She didn't know what to say, so she didn't say anything at all.

Instead, Vivien pressed her lips gently against his. Memories of the last kiss they'd shared cavorted through her mind for the briefest of moments before the reality of this one swept in.

No longer was he the hesitant tender lover.

His lips were like a brand against hers, hot and insistent. They pressed hard, moving over hers with an intensity that spoke of longing and desire, making her yearn for more. He gave to her in spades, parting her lips with his tongue, giving all he had and taking no more than she could give. He moved his body closer, took his hand from her hair and moved it down to the small of her back. He pressed her closer with an urgency, a hunger that she felt with every movement of his mouth against hers.

Vivien trembled. Never had she felt a man so deeply. She could feel his passion, and that he reined it in, keeping himself in check. For the briefest moment, she wondered what he would feel like unharnessed...

And then it was over. The Wolf pulled away, his eyes closed. His hands ran up her arms and cupped her face as he pressed his forehead against hers. "I love you Vivien. I will never let you go again."

It was with those words that he left, rising quietly and padding back over to his own sleeping pallet that lay somewhere among the other men. She was left feeling a bit of confusion, for she didn't recall when he'd ever been forced to let her go.

Vivien's thoughts returned to the present. She didn't hear the Wolf's voice anymore, and for that matter, she didn't hear anyone's. She must have drifted off for a while, and she wasn't surprised. Fatigue had been a constant companion throughout their ordeal in the swamp, not to mention, sickness every morning upon waking, and other times during the day when she least expected it. She'd lost quite a bit of weight; she could tell by the fit of her trousers around her thighs. The strange thing was that they were the same around her waist, if not slightly tighter. She wondered about this, and it made her nervous about that kind of sickness she could have caught that would cause her belly to become so distended. Unfortunately, without a single healer among them, she could do nothing but wait it out.

Vivien closed her eyes, again thinking of the Wolf. He hadn't come searching for her in the night except that once, but during the day she would catch him looking for her. He had always done that before, but now it seemed to be different. They would share a glance, nothing more, but he would smile. It sounded crazy, but those smiles, they were catching. She would smile too, and they would do this back and forth all through the day. The men noticed, and they were happier too. Everyone was smiling in spite of the horrid conditions they trekked through, in spite of what they were moving towards. And for the first time in her life, Vivien felt an acceptance she'd never had in all her one hundred thirty-five years. She felt it from a bunch of soldiers and some misfit mages she shared nothing in common with but a desire to fight for their homeland...and the Wolf.

She supposed that was enough.

She drifted. It was so nice to know she was surrounded by people who cared so much about her, maybe even loved her. They had become a family, and she waited for the end of every day so that she could stop and talk to every one of them. Her body started. Oh yes, she had forgotten to visit the men! She needed to get up and do that!

Suddenly, the Wolf was there, eyes glowing blue like twin moons. He was smiling at her, but somehow, it reminded her of a young man she had known almost a century ago. He was floating over her, and she knew he was there to love her. She had a thousand objections, but it was joyful acquiescence that came to her lips. She spread her legs and felt his weight press down on her, comforting and gentle. She gasped and sighed as she reached for his hair, pulling it back from his rugged face so she could bathe in the light from his eyes. He leaned in for a kiss–

"Vivien."

She startled awake. He was still there, but instead of lying over her, he bowed over her from the side. She blinked and looked down at herself. She was certain she had fallen asleep on top of her blankets, but one was pulled around her soft curves to spare her modesty. She looked back to him. In a tent cloaked in darkness, his eyes were a dim blue glow. She really saw nothing else but the outline of his face and the rest of his body.

"Vivien, we must make ready. We heard a tir-reath attack somewhere up the mountain. They are coming."

She jolted at the news, and a surge swept through her. She nodded her understanding and he made to stand. "Wolf, wait!"

He knelt back down beside her, regarding her intensely. Her gaze searched his, suddenly not knowing what she wanted to say, or if she did, not knowing how to say it. But he did. The Wolf brushed a gentle hand over her cheek, sweeping errant strands of her hair back from her face. The he curved his hand around the back of her neck and pulled her forward.

His kiss was a loving caress, tender and sweet across her lips. It was almost like he was teasing her as he allowed his mouth to play over hers, gently squeezing and then pulling away, as though exploring the contours of her lips. She reciprocated, and luxuriated in the moment they allowed themselves to share, a moment among the few they had experienced together over the brief time they had known one another. She brought a hand up to his face, ran it along a beard that had grown longer than it should, a beard streaked with bits of silver. She brought a thumb to where their lips met and she heard him give a sharp inhale.

For a moment time seemed to stand still. There was no eminent battle, no war to fight. They weren't surrounded by men who might all be dead on the morrow, in a place she'd never been before. She never wanted this moment to end, a moment that included just the two of them in an embrace of the likes she'd never shared with anyone before. Love surged through her, followed by the peace she'd been searching for their entire journey thus far. What would be would be. And that was the all of it. If it was her time to pass into the realm of Mehg'mehl, then so be it. But she wouldn't pass into that place of death without a fight.

They finally broke apart. The Wolf lingered for a moment longer, silent. Then he kissed her on the forehead, rose, and walked out of the tent. Vivien got up from the pallet and donned her padding, dry but still crusted and foul with odor. She strapped down the breastplate, vambracers and greaves. Her sword and belt came next, a comforting weight. Her deep green cloak, now patchy and stained from her time in the Doomed City was last. Every part was another bit of her identity as an elvin warmage. Out of habit she raised her hood as she left her tent, her heart beating with forced calm. All around, men were striking camp, gulping down all but the last of their rations and the last few gulps of water. The travel packs were taken to the lonely bushes holding onto the side of the grassy hill and left there with a sense of finality. They would be back for them, or they would not. All they would need would be in their smaller pouches, quivers, and sheaths.

Vivien set her pack with the others upon the hillside, but before leaving it, she took a soft cord from inside it. She then took Mika's tanager and threaded the cord through it, twice, then wrapped the cord around her wrist. She made a knot, pulled it tight with her teeth, and admired its new place. Now Mika could be with her through the battle, and she could have the good luck he intended for her to have.

Half the soldiers slung their shields and weapons. They strung bows and knocked arrows. Among them, the Wolf moved like a towering presence, watching them but saying nothing. Vivien began walking among them, the need to see them all suddenly overwhelming. The first man she approached, she put down her hood. It was Gregor. He noticed the action and his eyes widened with the realization of it. He removed his helm and kneeled.

"My Lady, I will do you proud on the battlefield this day!"

She smiled and lay a hand on his shoulder. "I have no doubt you will, Gregor. Peace be upon you."

The man stood and she turned to the next man, and then the next, calling each by name and touching him either on the arm, hand, or shoulder. Before long they had formed a line, each man waiting to be greeted by her, standing with helm held under one arm and sword in the other. Vivien's heart swelled with the honor of such an action. At the end she reached her mages. Each of them stood there, hoods lowered. As a unit they all bowed. She approached each one and bowed over them, her forehead touching the crown of each head. At the end, when she reached Tyrell, she paused.

Vivien bowed over him. "If I should fall, don't forget your duty."

The man rose and regarded her with conviction. "I may have let you down in the past, but not this day."

Vivien nodded. "I know you won't. You are a good soldier and a good friend."

He shook his head. "I have not been a good friend, Mistress. But one day, I will be."

Vivien smiled and placed a hand on his face before turning away. She was taken aback to see the Wolf standing there behind her, waiting. He stood like all the other soldiers had been, only he had no helm. He proceeded to kneel before her, head lowered over the broken blade known as Arisil.

Her heart skipped a beat and she held her breath. The entire encampment was silent, every man and woman watching. Vivien slowly stepped forward, praying he would get back up and stand before her as an equal. *Oh gods, what is he doing?*

Then she was standing before him. She barely hesitated before reaching out and splaying her open palms upon his forehead. "May the road rise to meet you. May the wind always be at your back. May the sunshine warm upon your face, and storms besiege your enemies. And until we meet again, may the gods hold you in the palms of their hands."

The Wolf then rose and the encampment cheered. "*An'drath! Jashi! An'drath! Jashi! An'drath! Elthari Jashi!*"

Elthari Jashi, the new name the men had chosen to call her. Elvish Jewel.

Chapter Forty-One
Battle Preparations

Tir-reath moved faster than anything the humans had brought to bear. The enemy simply plodded across the land, demolishing everything in their path. Twenty thousand strong pounded the dry ground into flat earth with hard soled boots. They had brought everything reported: iron parts for siege engines in massive carts, packs of vicious dogs, and four forest giants far to the rear, controlled by human trainers. And, of course, the legions of humans, with their marching that sounded like thunder. These were neither conscripts, nor farmers. They were trained soldiers, and moved with a soldier's purpose. They could not hide, and didn't bother to try.

Xadrian's scouts had met enemy outriders miles away. He had immediately alerted the enemy to his presence by ordering his mounted scouts to demolish all outriders in a storm of fangs and teeth. The bodies were left to be found by the army, with trails any fool could follow back to this place. They were heading directly for his force, the Lord of Swords didn't even need to bait any further. They had to know that the Elvish city could not field anywhere near the numbers of the Iron Army. They came on like a group that meant to crush all opposition, and just might.

Xadrian had three days to prepare. He made use of the time in every way, everywhere he could. Fifteen hundred soldiers, forty mages, and twenty healers devised the best defense they could, turning the forest into their stronghold. Arrows were made by the thousands, all with sharp bodkin points brought from Torialvah's stores. Their bowstrings were freshly waxed. Men had been instructed to eat their fill. No one knew when they would get another chance.

The elves had a manic optimism. Nothing else would do. Everyone had to know they would likely die here, but they couldn't. If they failed, their city would surely perish.

Jor'aiden, the Grand Magister, came from deeper in the forest, standing next to Xadrian and looking upon the swaying grass on the forested hillside. He was normally the most serene of elves, but now he fidgeted in the breastplate Xadrian had insisted he wear.

The warmage frowned. Then shrugged slightly. Then shook his head almost imperceptibly. Xadrian knew what he was looking for, decided to ignore it.

The Lord of Swords cleared his throat. "You haven't fought since Pergatium, have you?"

The Grand Magister shook his head. "It won't be like that."

"It will be enough like that."

"We both lost a lot of children. Grandchildren. I lost my..." He swallowed hard, "...my wife."

"I remember your first wife. She was a brave warrior, one of the finest." Xadrian frowned, not taking his eyes off of the hilltop. "She fought with me. When she went, it was quick."

The Magister blinked back tears. "You did tell me, and I thank you for that."

"We all learned the limits of our mortality, of who we could protect, in those days."

This drew a look of skeptical surprise. "I thought you were supposed to be uplifting, Commander?"

The return look was cold. "You are supposed to be the smartest of us. Would lying help?"

They looked at each other frankly. Xadrian sighed, "You still feel her." It was a statement.

Jor'aiden's control wavered, but he remained impassive. "I do. Vivien lives."

Xadrian rewarded him with a rare smile. "Then there is hope."

"The dangerous part is yet to come."

Xadrian's smile fled into a knowing frown. "No. The dangerous part is now, before the fighting begins, when fear rots into cowardice. Once battle is joined, we will be unyielding."

"I hope you are right."

The commander placed a hand on his friend's shoulder. "You make magic. I make war. Trust me to know in this."

At the sound of a footstep, the two turned. Torialvah, resplendent in the finest armor his forges could muster, stiffly walked toward them. The Magister and he exchanged barbed looks. "All the arrowheads have been affixed, all the weapons sharpened and dispensed. We have three spears for every man along the tree line. All the armor is being worn. I don't know what more we can do."

Eyes caught by movement on the hilltop, the Magister turned. "They are here."

Torialvah hissed, "By the Deep Green."

"Good," Xadrian growled, "now it begins."

The humans had arrived long before midday, as Xadrian had expected. They must have camped just a few miles away and meant to begin their march into the forest with the most daylight they could manage. Inside the old growth, even broad daylight would be a twilight without Elvish eyes, and their movements would be hampered. The huge force crested the hill a half mile beyond the old forest edge. Just on the outside of the tree line, one hundred soldiers were waiting for them. As the Iron Army bellowed through trumpets and made signal to arrange themselves, the one hundred scampered back into the tree line. They had to be careful. The edge of the forest received a great deal of light. The inside was easier to traverse, but the few dozen yards to the edge was a thick tangle of brush that the elves had made ready. Hidden in the brush were deep trenches to twist ankles and break enemy formations. There were cut logs sharpened into points, turning the first twenty feet into a hedgehog maze of stabbing wood, undetectable by those outside. They had turned it into a killing field, and the human army would discover this to their sorrow.

Horns blasted into the daylight, and standards were raised. The crawl of the humans felt endless, and Xadrian stood motionless as he watched them array themselves for battle. For hours they marshaled over the hilltop. They pulled their giants to the rear, their soldiers to the front, archers just behind. Dogs were brought up. Heavily armored men on horses set to one flank. They covered the grassy hill.

The mage peered quizzically. "They are setting up one tent. There is a wagon of barrels. Some kind of ammunition?"

A shake of the head. "No. Our spy reported that their general consumes an enormous amount of spirits, the strongest stuff ever distilled. He keeps the supply near him as a man would a lover. He is never without the stuff. He is our true enemy. If he is putting up his tent, then they will attack soon."

Finally, just past noon, the squares of men stopped moving, facing the forest. For several heartbeats there was nothing but stillness. Then another horn blared.

The packmasters in the very front unleashed their dogs. Easily a hundred dogs came, snarling and barking, eager for the blood they had been trained since birth to crave. They howled, driven to near madness by their training, and they flew on legs far more swiftly than any footsoldier could follow. They weren't animals, they were weapons beaten into sharp shapes by unholy men. Each had been fitted with a sharp collar and thin chain coats lay on their backs to deflect any haphazard sword strike. They came closer, closer. They would slip past the defenders' improvements to the terrain and hunt them in the brush.

Xadrian frowned, watching them come down the slope. Torialvah loosened his sword. The Magister stood utterly still. All around him,

Xadrian could hear the elves in the branches, on the forest floor, and mounted on their tir-reath hold their collective breath.

The dogs suddenly started hopping as if the ground were made of fire. They sniffed wildly, suddenly unhinged, and bolted away from the elves, away from the forest, and away from their angry masters.

Jor'aiden let out a breath. Xadrian chuckled and slapped him on the back.

Torialvah sniffed. "And what was that?"

Xadrian gave him an appraising look. For a man with much attention to detail, he was surprisingly unaware. "Fifteen hundred tir-reath produce an amazing amount of urine. We had them coating that field for three days."

"And?"

"In the wild tir-reath hunt wolves," Jor'aiden grudgingly answered, "wolves, pigs, foxes, deer, and…dogs. They are terrified of the scent."

Torialvah took a deep breath, his voice even. "And what now?"

Xadrian unhooked his helmet from his belt and slipped the padding onto his head and pulled it on. "Now let's hope they march on us so that we can kill them all."

Above, another blow of the horn alerted the footmen. Legions jockeyed into position and came in a front nearly a quarter mile across. Xadrian whistled, pulling in units from the flanks to reinforce the center. His opponent was rumored to be a master tactician, and he had broken their spy. He knew he faced less than two thousand behind the face of the old growth forest. He was going to try to punch a hole in the center of their formation and scatter the army to mop up survivors.

He's going to try.

Elves were born to the forest. It was part of them. It was eternal and so were they. Even the lesser elves felt the connection, and it brought peace and tranquility when called upon. But not now. The La'athai had blended in to the light forest, gathering stained cloaks around them and all but disappearing into the brush. Yet Vivien could feel a nervous energy infusing the place. The La'athai waited, not patiently.

The Wolf, quieter than any could believe, had scouted forward, ranging ahead like his namesake. He had spent years of his life in the woods, and had used those skills to hunt for his food. Compared to a rabbit, a sage grouse, or a deer, humans were easy prey. He had gone since he knew what he was looking for, and seemed the most likely to survive if he came to trouble.

Still, Vivien waited his return with trepidation. She remembered the feel of his hair slipping between her fingers as she plaited it. It hadn't taken her as long as it would many others, for she had become a master at the craft as a young girl. Before long, the Wolf sported at least twenty plaits in his long hair, and these she had swept up into three sections and tied back at the nape of his neck.

For a moment he'd looked at her, his gaze fathomless, then disappeared into the forest.

Her stomach suddenly clenched spasmodically, and the familiar sickness swept over her. With small movements she took her mug out of a large pouch, then the waterskin from her belt. She filled it, replaced the skin, then concentrated for a moment. Fiery fae swirled around the cup, bringing it to a hot steaming boil in seconds. Then she searched in the pouch again and brought out a square of cloth. She opened the depleted bundle, and there lay the wilted remains of the raspberry leaves she had left from the march through the remaining swamp. She smiled, remembering that the Wolf who, even when so distraught, had taken a few moments to gather them for her. She steeped the leaves in the cloth for a few minutes, then sipped hot beverage, waiting for the medicinal properties to work.

The men continued to wait. Even the low-elves drew upon their better nature, seeking peace while their thoughts swarmed with chaos. They sought to wait without succumbing to fear. Vivien saw some of the men fidget, or sweat nervously. Some checked their tiny packs over and over, some counted their meager supply of arrows, others held their weapons, making deals with the steel to keep them safe, some spoke to the gods. She felt for them, for the cold fingers of dread were nesting in her belly as well. She had trained for decades to be a warmage, and yet the fear was always there.

Horns blared into the sky, echoing down the mountain and across the swamp, now miles downhill. Men stirred from their spots, looking to her. She scanned the forest, looking for any telltale signs of his arrival, but when she did not, she went back to sipping her tea. The men settled back to their waiting, never knowing how her stomach clenched or how her heart fluttered. It was the coming battle: the flash of iron fangs, the sounds of agony, and the blood. But it was also him. She wished to see him, have him safely returned from his scouting mission. She breathed deeply, letting go of the future and the past to reside in that exact moment. She too, drew on her Elvishness, and she found some serenity for her mind.

Her heart, however, called for the Wolf.

More trumpets blew from far above. Calmly, she drank the last of the tea and tapped the dregs of spent leaves from the vessel. She tied it to her belt and waited. She could feel the men draw from her calm, and suddenly the gruff, stoic Lord of Swords and Truth made so much more sense to her.

More trumpets, and a far off call that was so much like falling rain. But it was not. It was the roar of tens of thousands involved in a charge. Every soldier, every mage, clenched fists as they listened. They no longer sat at rest, but sat in wait, waiting and hoping to pounce at any second. Yet minute after minute crawled by. Men looked to her and shifted from place to place, unable to contain the nervous energy of knowing their countrymen were fighting, and likely dying, and yet they sat here in hiding.

Vivien closed her eyes, shutting them all out as she waited in her own spot. She worried at the tanager in her hand, smoothed her thumb over the contours, wondered how Mikarvan was, and her father. She ignored the pressure of the men, of the far off battle, of the gnawing fear and uncertainty and–

He was there.

She opened her eyes, searching among the trees. The Wolf jogged into the clearing, his chest rising and falling with each breath. He appeared unhurt and gave the customary hand signal for safety. The La'athai melted out of their hiding places and gathered around him. He hunkered down and began to draw on a patch of dirt. Vivien moved next to him, feeling the heat of his skin, smelling his familiar woodsy odor.

As was his custom, he forewent all pleasantries. "They are less than a mile distant, so keep quiet. This line," he indicated, "is a caravan of supplies the likes of which I have never seen." He marked another line. "This is the closest we can get to the line of wagons. The army has made a road as it marched, and the wagons can't leave it. They are trapped. Here," he marked an X, "is a troupe of five hundred men. They are still armed and armored, but no archers. They are setting up tents. I think they are an emergency reserve and just there to watch over the caravan."

Tyrell shook his head, his eyes wide. "Five to one? And they are waiting for us?"

Vivien frowned, "No. They are prepared, but not for us."

Some of the men smiled like predators.

The Wolf marked another X. "I could see the tip of a tent just over the top of the hill. That will be their commander's tent. And here," a large circle at the far rear of the wagon train, "these are the camp followers: whores, armorers, tradesmen. They will run, not fight."

Vivien scanned the lines, fear and uncertainty bleeding away as she imagined the actual layout. "We must destroy the carts of food and supplies. Once those are gone, they cannot feed their soldiers. The army will wither."

The Wolf pointed at the command tent. "And we decapitate the army. Remove the commanders, and it will dissolve into chaos."

Vivien set her jaw. "Wagons first."

The Wolf nodded. "Agreed. A small group takes the carts. Ten men. The rest will engage the rear guard."

Vivien shook her head. "Ten soldiers will not do enough damage fast enough. Two mages should go with them. The rest face the five hundred."

The Wolf looked up at her, his eyes a stormy blue. He nodded to her and stood. "Good, now we just need a commander with that wagon team."

Vivien's heart sank as she considered those words, then steeled herself. She felt the fight coming, knew it would come. She frowned fiercely as walls rose up inside of her, preparing for the argument. She had to be with the main assault force. It was her place, her duty. She took a deep breath and prepared for him to push back hard. "Tyrell should lead the wagon team."

The Wolf nodded. "That is what I was thinking. He can direct the other two mages." He turned to the second in command. "Sir, pick your team."

Vivien made to argue, then realized there was none to make. She looked up at the barbarian, and he smiled at her. "The charge of the eighty seven would not survive without you, Lady Warmage."

She heard him say it, and felt his sincerity. She reacted to his fierceness and was infected by it. "Tyrell, name your men!"

"Yes, Mistress!" Tyrell was already moving, "We will need arrows. Everyone needs to give. We will need quivers from at least a third of the men."

An uncommon certainty flooded through her. "You heard him; hand them over. Everyone, half your arrows to the wagon team."

The Wolf grabbed Tyrell and pointed to the map. He tapped it with his axe. "Get to the edge of the heavy brush here and wait. When we charge the five hundred, hit the carts and don't stop until..."

Tyrell gave a deep inhale and looked up at the Wolf.

Vivien laid a hand on his shoulder. "If you destroy the carts, Rithalion lives. If you do not, it dies. No matter what happens to us, you must destroy their supplies. The life of our city hinges on you and your team."

Tyrell looked at her, and for a moment his mask of calm determination slipped. His eyes glistened with tears. "Be safe, Mistress."

She smiled reassuringly. "You are the important one, here. Save our people." Then she moved to the side. "Charging team to the elm tree here! Form up on the elm!"

Men jostled about in a frenzy to hand over arrows, quivers, and spare bowstrings to the names of those Tyrell called to order. Meanwhile, the Wolf briefed those men on where they were going to go, and what they needed to do. Then, after all was said and done, the thirteen parted from the rest of the force, heading through the trees to their designated location.

Tyrell turned once to look back. He caught her gaze and gave her a salute before he was hidden among the trees. The Wolf approached and stood beside her as the rest of the men walked out of sight.

His voice was pitched low. "He is worried about you."

She nodded.

"He is in love with you."

She started and looked up at him.

His gaze was impassive. "You don't know?"

"I began to suspect in Pergatium."

The Wolf looked away and gave a small smile.

She was quiet for a moment. "So you are not?"

He frowned. "Am I not what?"

"Worried about me."

The Wolf glanced back at the men, then pitched his voice lower, "When my heart beats, it speaks your name. It is a fierce name, a proud name, full of power. If I must, I will have it beat its last than have you come to any harm, but if my love has to make you weaker to embrace you, what good is it to you?"

His words reached in and flooded her with emotions she could scarcely understand. She managed to keep them from her face in front of the La'athai but she smiled, "Very good, An'drath."

"You are deserving no less," he smiled impishly, "Elthari Jashi."

She wanted to hug him, hold him, but this was not the time. "Let us hunt."

He only nodded.

Chapter Forty-Two
Summer's Curse

ate spring fled before the flaming sword of summer. The heat beat down on him like a recitation of his sins. His head swam with it. After a few days he discarded the dented breastplate, but it wasn't enough as his thick, northern clothes acted like an oven. After a few weeks the black, green, and lavender mark on his chest from the giant's club faded. He could breathe again, and that alone kept him moving. But he could never drink enough, never find rest, and the bag flapping at his side drew a constant cloud of large, black flies that droned on and on.

For the first few weeks he had tried to take the hearts and dry them by the fire, but the rains during the last two weeks of spring had frustrated him. Flies had gathered on the meat by morning, and he had been forced to seal them in the bag and redouble his speed to return home. He was unable to hunt, and ate and drank only what he could gather on his journey. Springs and streams were enough until the rains abated and the heat began in earnest. He ate less and less.

Every night he hung the precious meat high in the branch of a tree to ward off predators, and every morning climbed to fetch it, waving the flies away, before continuing to follow the path of the sun to his mountain home. The outside of the bag was always slimy to the touch now, and foulness dripped from the stitches. He dared not open the bag, for the smell of rot was pungent. He had no brandy or whiskey to preserve the things, and his anxiety grew every day that the hearts might be too bad off to identify when he returned to his family's home.

He entered the Forlorn Hills, and looked down into the valley that held the bog. According to legend, five hundred years past, the elves had fought a war. Against whom, he wasn't sure and elves never spoke of it. His eyes trailed down the slope to the huge depression where Broken Lake used to be. The war had destroyed it somehow, and he shuddered at the implications. The lake was fed by two rivers, but now they deposited a miserly tithe into a pool that was more of a bend in their flow before traveling northward to race down into the swamp. He found one of the sparse trees in this area. He hung the bag, wiping the foulness from the bottom off of his hand onto his blackened family tartan, settled down, and slept.

The next morning he clambered up the tree and retrieved the bag. As he descended the bag bounced against the trunk and the stitches in the bottom gave way. He lurched to catch the precious hearts and fell to the ground. Pain flared across his shoulders and back, the world spun and stuttered before his eyes. He groaned and swatted at the choking cloud of flies that surrounded him and he swatted them away from his mouth and nose. It took a long time for him to sit up. When he did he looked to where the hearts had fallen.

He screamed in agony, his soul rent into tatters.

The weeks of heat had done their work. There were not two massive hearts but a single puddle of muscle dissolving into a black mess. It was crawling with maggots and lay there, mocking his pain, his misery, and all his broken hopes.

He had no thoughts. He simply sat on the ground and wept.

...when you are desperate, then look to the warlock in the swamps near the lowland bog alongside the falls called The Tears of Infinity.

Ravn looked over his shoulder, seeing the rising peak that marked the Lairdlands, a home forbidden to him without at least one prize. He looked down to the drained lakebed.

It was no longer just about marriage, or love. His people needed him. He was their laird, and they depended on him and his judgment in many ways. He may be able to give up on himself, but not his wife, not Neála, and not upon his people.

He stood and walked downhill leaving the leather bag and the rotted pile to the vermin.

Depression weighed upon him with the ferocity of a mountain lion. More than ever he thought of Neála and the child she had already borne. He thought of the names he liked, and if he would ever have the chance to give one of them to the child.

In the distance Ravn saw the corpse of the lake. He approached it, too tired for proper caution. The heat of the day beat upon him, and if the giant had not destroyed his cloak, he would surely have discarded it. His stomach growled again and he ignored it. He had managed to find a straight sapling and carved it into a simple spear with his dagger, but nothing edible presented itself. He leaned heavily on it with every step. Ravn pressed onward, for it was the only thing he could allow himself to do. In his mind echoed, *look to the warlock in the swamps near the lowland bog alongside the falls called The Tears of Infinity.*

He wandered through the abandoned village that once thrived on the shores. The homes looked to be carved from massive shells, but on closer inspection they were simply cunningly crafted to appear this way. Still the sparse vegetation had yet to make a sizable dent in the small number of homes, even after what had to be centuries.

Elvish Jewel

Ravn stepped from the streets onto the lake bed, seeing the oddly rounded rocks that formed a strange landscape where the grass grew abundantly but not tall. The lake was all but dry, the rivers that poured into it never filling any but the lowest depressions. He reached the flowing water as fast as he could and drank until he couldn't anymore, then filled his waterskins. Around him were the scenes of broken dreams and abandoned hopes. Ancient boats lay as fragments of wood and brass in the dirt, skeletons of a long dead life.

He paused for hours until he had speared a few small fish, then broke off pieces of a derelict boat to burn so he could cook them. He could barely wait for the fish to be prepared, but when he began eating he found his shrunken stomach wanted to rebel at the portions he had made. He packed the rest in a cloth and stored it for later.

With no boat and no bridges, he followed the flow of the rivers that joined and ran northward. It was only a hundred feet across, but deep. The rivers exited the dry bed strangely, through a gap in the hill that looked like it had been dug out by some titanic child pulling their hand through mud. The flow had eroded the banks, creating a path beside the water that was thankfully in the shade. Once upon it, he could see for miles along the length. It was clearly not a natural formation, and ran perfectly north at a uniform depth clefting a little from flat areas, and huge chunks out of higher ground. It was not long before he was walking through the heart of some hills that folded over him like the hands of a trap. As the hills grew larger it seemed some unknown force had pressed their hands into the ground, pulling apart the rock and soil to create the river through angry force. He walked for days, sleeping on the ground and surviving on fish cooked over fires built from whatever detritus had been washed on the shores of the river.

Finally, after a week of slow progress on tired legs, he was drawn by the sounds of a far away cheer that heralded the falls. Knowing they were there did not prepare him for what he found. He had seen waterfalls before, but this was both beautiful and terrible.

The waterfall was not tall, not grandiose, but it was as if a dagger had been drawn across the world. The side of a mountain had been carved out, and the river ran straight through it. The crystal clear water exited the other side and fell thirty feet to the floor below, where it became a green churned pool. The pool looked unhealthy. The land beyond was worse.

Ravn stood in awe, a terrible weight settling into his stomach. Mist rose from the soggy mass in a stinking miasma. Trees, dead and alive, all watched him and swayed in the breeze as if reaching with unwanted touches. Broken logs and choking vines were everywhere. Born and bred to the forested mountains, he had no idea a place like this could even exist. He waited, and watched, but he saw no movement not accounted for by the choking wind, but he did see paths that wandered out of the swamp along the tops of the sparse archipelagos of land. They all lead to the base of the cliff below. The short cliff face was exposed strata of rock, each eaten away at different rates by the rushing flow.

Ravn drank one last time from the river, made sure his skins were filled, and tossed down his makeshift spear. His boots had never been made for climbing, and he was glad for the easy surface. Yet, he was mindful of his weakness and fatigue. The falls pummeled him with sound as he descended, one foot and hand hold at a time. He was near the bottom and had gotten into a comfortable pattern when his left foot looked for purchase and found nothing. He leaned back to see and his right hand slipped, dumping him twelve feet onto the turf with a resounding crash.

He gasped and wheezed, unable to catch his breath. He couldn't draw in air, and fought to do so. Then it came, a deep shuddering release that filled his lungs. He gulped in the air gratefully, then relaxed upon the stone to inventory his pains. He did not get the chance.

"So, you will live. Interesting."

If Ravn could, he would have reacted. Fear. Surprise. Shock. He just lay there as pain intruded on his numbness. With all of his limbs feeling like lead, the burning pain in his ankle and the sharp pain in the back of his head, he just lay there.

The figure was darkly cloaked. Stains had settled into the rich robes, robbing them of riots of color and turning them into muted browns and blacks. It was threadbare, and the hood deep with shadow. The hands that poked from the sleeves were long, and delicate, but the knuckles were knobby, the skin stretched tightly against the bone. They flapped lowly at him as the silken voice purred, "Poor, dying thing. All broken on my doorstep. Shall I save it? Or shall I roast it over my fire and eat it?"

Ravn lurched to his feet, ripping his rusty sword from its sheath and lunged at the–

It was not there.

Almost faster than he could comprehend, the thing was behind him, holding a dagger of chipped obsidian to his throat.

The voice slithered along Ravn's ear, "Oh, the little bird has talons? Well, little bird, why did you come all this way to die?"

Ravn exploded into action. He grabbed the knife wrist with one hand and pushed his body back, putting the warlock off balance. As fast as he was, the creature could not keep from being flipped over Ravn's shoulder onto the stone floor. Ravn yanked the wrist in his hand to full extension, and placed his sword alongside it, pointing at the warlock's armpit, and thereby, his heart and lungs. All the pressure, all the hurt, disappointment and pain woke some kind of animal in him, and he growled menacingly. But what emerged was not formless, it was a word.

"Love."

The warlock paused there, held on the ground. The hood had fallen back to expose the perfect mouth and chin, almost Elvish in their design. His head moved to the side as if to cock an ear. "Love? Love you say?"

Ravn sheathed his sword and hauled the warlock to his feet. "I have sworn by blood to bring back the heart of a mightiest creature I could find. I will hunt it, slay it, and return with its heart."

"A quest?" The warlock backed away from the mountain laird, flicking the dagger and making it disappear up his sleeve. His hood had fallen back down, obscuring all expression. "You are a fool. Go back to where you came."

Raven felt his teeth creak in his skull as he spat words through them. "I need you to tell me where to find a mighty beast, and a way to preserve the heart so that I might climb the mountain to my home with it."

Moments trickled by, the falls behind continuing to pour bright emeralds, sapphires, and diamonds of water into the murky pool below. "I will tell you, but you will surly die."

Ravn frowned. "So be it."

Again the warlock considered, "I was right, you are intriguing. Come into my cave. I will feed you and allow you to rest. You cannot traverse the swamp at night. It is far too big for you to kill and it is always hungry." Then, without waiting reply, he disappeared into the cave, moving without hint of age or infirmity.

Ravn followed stiffly, breathing heavily as his body sought to calm itself after such a short, frantic fight. His guide disappeared ahead, but after months on the road, the climb, and fall, the laird's legs were wobbly and there was only one way to go. The walls were hung with elaborate chandeliers containing glowing stones. They were beautiful and delicate, so at odds with the crude spikes hammered into the walls and ceiling to hold them. They glowed dimly, and seemed to strengthen the shadows rather than provide real light. The sound of the waterfall receded the further he walked.

He came to a rug adorned with Elvish patterns intricately woven into the surface. It was ancient, stained almost to the point where the designs could not be seen. A man and a woman were there, in love. She hung above him, suspended in the sky like a faery with the moonlight bent into wings. Pale fae danced around her. The man was made of tree bark and leaves. He raised his hands to her in supplication. A pack of wolves at his feet howled a hymn to her. A dragon watched him closely from a cave, maybe ready to pounce. It was dark, and eerie, with hidden things in the forest watching them both with bated breath. He shook off the otherworldly feeling and pressed onward.

The hung rug shifted easily and he entered the main chamber, itself as disturbing as the door to it.

The cavern hall opened up and space flung off in all directions. All manner of thing was here, shelves of books, tables and chairs from rich houses, and clothes hung from lines and on suspended poles. More chandeliers, giving light too puny to even scratch the back wall of the place, reflected from mirrors, plates, and off of a city of glass tubing on one table. Tapestries hung from lines strung on spikes to guard against imagined faces written in eroded rock walls. Dominating the chamber was a massive altar, several feet thick, and carved in ancient runes that swam before his eyes. Before it a small fire burned, but the air was not smoky, and he wondered where it let out. Stalactites hung from the ceiling, and made Ravn feel like he was in the maw of a great beast about to be chewed.

The hooded man appeared from around a blanket, carrying a plate of food and a decanter of red wine. He guided Ravn to a seat by a small side table, set the food down, and stood back silently.

Ravn had not seen real food in months, and once he sat he realized that he had not yet. There was dried fish, dried meat, as well as some kind of plant cleaned of the roots, dirt, and leaves. The only prepared thing was a small wheel of pan fried bread with a chunk missing. Still, he had eaten worse, and took a chunk of bread and placed it in his mouth. The warlock did the same, popping the bit of bread stolen from the small loaf into the blackness occupied by his face.

"We are bound now, man of the mountains. You are my guest. I can bring you no harm, and you may not harm me. This is written in laws as old as time and dire fate will descend upon anyone who breaks this law of hospitality. It will offend the gods, all gods, yours and mine."

Ravn paused in chewing, thought about spitting out the rough bread, but swallowed anyway. He nodded.

The warlock nodded and took a seat, this chair as random and beautiful as all the others. "So, you are here for love?"

Ravn nodded again, and peeled the dried fish from the bone. It came away in large flakes, and he ate it. The food was simple to see, but spiced in exotic ways. As it hit his stomach, Ravn realized a voracious need, and began eating it gratefully.

"Love is not better than life, boy."

The laird let the form of address pass. "Life without love is hollow. I have lived it, and I will have such an emptiness no more."

"Even if it kills you?"

Ravn nodded, chewing on the surprisingly tender dried venison. "Even so."

"Well, I may be able to help. But I have a need as well." Ravn stopped, mid-chew, watching the warlock closely. The slippery voice chuckled from in the darkness. "Nothing is free, barbarian."

"My people are civilized."

The warlock stood and walked up the sloping, melted looking rocks to behind another curtain. "Spoken like someone who has never seen civilization."

Ravn frowned and took a long drink from the decanter. He had three long gulps before he realized it was not wine, but salty, spicy, and tasted of anise. He lowered it. "What is this drink?"

The reply was carefree, "It is juice of a swamp fruit."

Ravn did not believe him, yet it was not blood, at least not the blood of a man. He ate more and felt his great hunger finally sated. Even the earthy plants rejuvenated him and he relaxed in the chair, grateful to not be squatting in the dirt or perched on a bug filled log.

The warlock reappeared, carrying a shallow bowl carefully in one hand, and his obsidian knife in another. He approached Ravn slowly, and then held out the knife. Ravn took it, then looked at him quizzically.

"I cannot harm you human, but I have a price for my help. Perhaps ingredient is a better word. I need blood for your love quest." Ravn steeled himself, stood and placed his hand over the bowl of oily liquid. He put the blade to his palm. The warlock huffed and sighed, "A simple drop will do, barbarian."

Ravn paused, then nodded, removing the blade, but it had already left a shallow cut. He squeezed the heel of his palm and a drop of his life fell into the bowl. It flared to life, sprouting green flames like a torch and Ravn dropped the knife. He looked down, confused, and could not connect how the obsidian knife had left his hand and broken on the floor. He sat heavily. His mouth was dry, he took another gulp of juice. It did not help.

The warlock took the bowl to the altar and peered into it, making strange gestures. "Can it be? *Shanta maree, ustawa dracororis?*"

Ravn started. "You speak Elvish?"

"Do you?"

Ravn shook his head. "A few words."

"Just as well." A gasp, "You did not lie, barbarian. She is lovely. Such wonderful green eyes."

"Ròs..." He couldn't think, "my wife... has blue eyes..."

"Oh, I know." The warlock sounded delighted. He walked slowly to his chair opposite and sat down, leaving the burning bowl behind. "You did not lie to me, human. You are in love. The truest kind. Fraught with pain, loss, hurt, and struggle. But love."

Ravn nodded but couldn't move. *So tired.*

"So very, very, intriguing…"

Ravn came awake instantly. His body thrumming with life and energy. His aches and pains were gone. He looked to his palm and the thin cut was gone as if never there. Before him stood the warlock, holding out an Elvish-made backpack.

"Food, water, blankets, what could be salvaged from your... possessions."

Ravn stood, uncertain. "You will help me?"

"I already have, human." The faceless voice chuckled. "And if I'm right, I have helped me as well."

"My quest?"

The warlock nodded. "Go one day to the west. There you will find the ruins of a small Elvish city. There is a road. Follow it to the ruins of Pergatium, cursed by war since long before your grandfather's, grand-father's, grandfather's grandfather walked under the sun and moon. There is a massive building at the center of the city that still stands tall, but half the height of when it was whole."

"How will I find the beast?"

"Oh, it will find you," the hooded man said knowingly. "Now I have fed you, and healed you, and pointed your way. The time for your quest is now."

"But the heart? The last hearts I won rotted."

"This heart cannot rot. Win it and take it to your one, true love."

Ravn saw his plate and decanter had been taken away. The fire had burned down to nearly nothing. Many more items had moved slightly while he slept, and he began to wonder for how long. He shook his head to clear it. "Th- thank you."

The warlock stood back, hands hidden in his folded sleeves. "Not yet, human. Not yet."

Ravn nodded, but was uncertain. He left the cave and waterfall behind, shocked to find it was the dawn of a new day. Behind him the warlock stood like a specter, refusing him re-admittance to the cave. Yet he nodded to the strange fellow, who shooed him on his way.

And Ravn began west.

Chapter Forty-Three
The Forest Fortress

The human soldiers came in a tide, a straight line of doom joined into a square locked by shields. Xadrian had expected no different. Had hoped no different. His force could harry and harass the humans all the way to Rithalion. There was no way the opposing general could leave them here. The elves would have to be rooted out before he could proceed.

The enemy marched closer, feet moving in unison to shake the very ground. The elves watched in silence behind the face of the forest, giving them nothing. Xadrian could feel them on every side: his countrymen, his soldiers, his people.

The enemy came closer, he could smell their fetid, half rotten stink from days on the road with no baths and no rest. Each man began wading through the knee high grass, ignoring the spicy tang of the tir-reath urine. They did not know the ground had been prepared for them as well. Xadrian was certain that their commanders did not care.

The Lord of Swords felt his mouth go dry, for they were about to care. *They were about to care a great deal.*

The first line took one step, another, and then another. But for the last step it was as if the ground fell away. It had not, but water fae had been summoned by the warmages three days previously. They had been tasked with pulling the water from the depths of the ground, pushing it into the topsoil, turning the half a bowshot in front of the forest into a quagmire masked by the waving grasses. The first line went down to their knees in the mud. The men behind could not stop, and tumbled over them. The next line did the same before the formation could even think to halt.

Xadrian eyed the huge man watching from a wooden throne. He was drinking from a mug drawn from a barrel at his side. His posture was uncaring, unbothered. He flapped one large hand ahead. Trumpets sounded and the faltering line was ordered to charge again. The men ahead were pushed over, and those that came behind walked upon them. As men fell, more were trod upon, creating a carpet of bodies drowning in the mud. A few broke ranks, tossing down shields and swords to claw through the rear lines. Some were cut down immediately. Others were cut down as they exited the rear of the now messy and irregular formation. One man fought his way free and made it two hundred paces toward the woods, fleeing for his life, when a mounted knight rode him down and speared him in the lower back. They left him, pinned there to slowly die, screaming.

The Tactician waved his hands again and flags waved. Trumpets blared. The unit of five hundred cavalry wheeled in a huge fan and set out south to where the ground became more steep. Xadrian whistled, And a hundred elves mounted on tir-reath bolted for the south, shadowing the cavalry heavy horsemen.

Back at the forest edge, the soldiers began putting their shields down into the mud, more were passed up from those behind, creating slippery bridges for the feet of the men. It proved as ineffective as the tactician's need for advancement was voracious. But it stripped the front ranks of their shields, and bunched up the rear lines of men upon them. Xadrian whistled.

Arrows from all levels of the forest flew with deadly accuracy. They came from the brush at ground level, the branches of the trees, and the treetops like a cloud of wasps. The first few ranks dissolved, falling into mud and muck as more horns blared and archers all across the rear lines of the enemy let fly with arrow after arrow. Thousands at a time leapt into the air, and Xadrian winced as he felt elvin souls wink out, their fires extinguished. The arrows kept coming as they flew into the trees, but fired blindly, few found their mark. Elves took cover behind the boles of ancient trees. More trumpets pushed the foot soldiers faster into the muck, their own feet chewing their numbers as men died in the press to reach the woods. They came to the edge of the mire, thirty feet from the forest, and clambered onto the hard soil.

Xadrian gave another, three part whistle.

From deeper in the forest, Jor'aiden lead the warmages who all let fly with fae of the air and wind. Invisible hands molded the sky like clay, shifting currents to point downward in a vertical sheer. Clouds of arrows turned midflight, pointing downward in a deadly shower. It took many moments, and thousands of arrows, before the trumpets called to stop the archers, but by then, the five thousand men that had been dispatched to spearhead the attack on the forest were largely destroyed, cut down by the sky-darkening arrows of five hundred archers and the muck created by the fae. On the hill, Xadrian saw his counterpart pick up a uniformed man with one hand, slapping him until the body did not move, and drop it like he was discarding an article of ripped clothing. He motioned and more trumpets blared. The rear lines pulled back, a fraction of their former strength, and Xadrian caught the relayed whistle of the tir-reath far down the line. They knew their orders, and he knew what would happen.

The knights would end up running around the elf-fashioned mire and then ride straight up to the forest. They would breach the thick brush at the edge and find the sharpened stakes that would puncture the breasts of their horses and stab at the legs of the riders. Dressed in heavy armor, many would still make it through, and the smart ones would follow in the cleared paths of those that went first. Maybe they would shout as they gained the eerie darkness under the towering canopy of the old growth forest.

Xadrian smiled, for he could imagine one of them looking up into the branches, eyes still dazzled from the sunlight. It would be a network of blobs and shadows for a few moments, but as it cleared, he would see elves. Rank upon rank of elves mounted on heavily armored tir-reath which, in turn, were on branches, makeshift platforms, and hidden in the sparse bushes beyond the edge of the wood. The human might get a chance to raise an alarm, but likely not. Then the armored cats would pounce, and the first few dozen would be dead. The rest would try to enter the fray immediately, and find more stakes braced to impale them, snares meant to trip the horses and throw the riders, and one hundred tir-reath ready to pick them off as they fought free of the heavy brush.

Another hour passed as the huge army languidly reasserted itself, sending thirteen thousand men in huge blocks, ready to smash through the front of the brush ramparts. Xadrian waited, and waited. Around him the elves buzzed with activity. Wounds were tended. Those that could not fight were taken from the front. Arrows were replenished from stores.

More trumpets blared, and Xadrian shook away thoughts of the distant battle and looked to the field. The impromptu moat of mud was all but full of corpses. Still the Tactician kept back his giants, opting instead to send his footmen forward, hoping that his cavalry would break through further down the line and clear enough defenders from this section of forest to make an easy entrance to the old growth.

Xadrian called again, and as the horns blared for the massive fist of foot-soldiers to move forward, tir-reath stole from behind the screen of green to the north, another hundred men and mounts who found their spot near the lake and waited. The Lord of Swords and Truth saw them, and unsheathed the broken Arisil. The wave of enemy soldiers raised their shields and stepped upon the bodies of their comrades. He raised his sword and whistled. Arrows stormed from the woods again, seeking tender flesh behind raised shields and under heavy iron.

The Lord pointed at a nearby archer and a whistling arrow was launched into the air. It could be heard for miles, and wailed into the air until it fell to earth. Elves abandoned their places and retreated to the edge of the brush. While this happened, the second group of mounted elves burst through a hole in the traps two miles away. They rushed across logs disguised by squares of grassy sod that had been laid across the morass.

They arced uphill, galloping at a full run. Armored men pushed on, but found the same traps as the mounted knights. With the press of men behind, many were impaled by their comrades, or pushed into snares. The clean, organized lines of battle were rendered into utter chaos by twenty paces of dense foliage.

Those that made it through were not set for battle, and staggered into darkness. Then they saw light. It lay in the hands of the Grand Magister. It illuminated hundreds of bowmen, swordsmen, and mages ready for the disorganized huddle of men.

Xadrian muttered a growl, "Welcome to our home."

Then the intruders died in storms of ice, lightning, steel, and blood.

The human commanders saw the racing tir-reath too late. They flitted across the battlefield, but not for the footmen assaulting the forest, nor the thousand men guarding the front of the general and his tent. They dove in to the archers. Cats and elves fought all comers like animals. Dressed in no armor, with only the simplest of hand weapons, the elves cut the bowmen down with abandon. Some of the archers tried to fight, wielding short swords or firing panicked shots with their bows. They left a bloody smear littered with bodies and body parts.

The tactician ordered a retreat, and like a man retrieving a mangled hand from the mouth of a bear, the army made a turn around. The tir-reath fled their slaughter, leaving twenty elves, eighteen tir-reath, and two thousand humans dead in their wake.

Xadrian wiped at his forehead, more annoyed than alarmed at the blood he found. The Grand Magister joined him at the hole in the brush, slumping against the tree and panting hard. All around, wounded elves were being tended. Humans were being put out of their misery.

He dismissed the last of the fae from his hands and closed his eyes. "How long?"

Xadrian frowned. He took a waterskin from his belt and downed three long gulps. It washed the harsh claws from his throat and handed it to Jor'aiden. "An hour since they breached the forest. If we are lucky, hours. If not, they will come back to crush us."

"But we have routed them?"

Xadrian affixed the mage with serious eyes, voice pitched low. "They have covered the moat, they have knocked holes in the brush. When they come next, they will punch right through us."

Jor'aiden looked into his eyes, and knew that he spoke truth.

The tactician was gesturing wildly. An armored man was arguing with him from the back of his horse. The huge man pulled his subordinate from the horse and poured a full mug of his caustic drink into the slits of the helmet. The huge tactician went into his tent, retrieved a candle and touched it to the gasping, writhing man's helmet. It burst into flames. He struggled to remove it, but did not manage it before he died.

More horns sounded. Xadrian frowned. "Now we sell ourselves dearly."

Jor'aiden reached out and grabbed the commander's arm. "Do you smell that? Burning!"

"He lit one of his men on fire."

"No!" Jor'aiden shook his head, a smile on his face. "It is wood smoke."

Xadrian thought quickly. "They are burning the wagon train. If we can smell it... Get a mage to push the wind the other way."

Jor'aiden summoned no other, for none could perform the summoning but him. Though tired from the day of fighting and casting, he still reached deeper and deeper for energy. This did not require just power, but finesse. He called up an ancient name not spoken in over a century, feeling his heart quail and pain lash across his mind as he did so. He went to his knees as the unbound spirit answered, materializing from the aether. Xadrian cursed.

The greater seleighe was there, and not. Made of glass that dissolved and reformed, it was mist and lightning, rain and thunder. Power thrummed across it, giving it the impression of massive clouds racing across the sky, pregnant with mighty winds and heavy hail.

YOU HAVE CALLED UPON MY PACT.

Jor'aiden gasped, holding his chest as the power needed to call the seleighe stole from his very life. "Go and move the wind, sound, and smoke from over the hill away from the attacking humans."

SUCH A SIMPLE THING?

"It is what I ask." the Magister was panting, pale.

I WILL HONOR THIS, GROUND BOUND THING.

And it dissolved, gone to carry out its task.

Xadrian knelt over the mage, feeling his thready heartbeat. "Healer! Get a healer here!"

The old soldier never got a chance to give comforting words, but heard Jor'aiden's before he passed into unconsciousness. "Please, be safe my dear daughter, my little jewel."

Xadrian looked through the hole in the brush and saw the humans had turned again. They were coming.

Chapter Forty-Four
Carts and Giants

Eighty-six elves and one human came from the forest, making no sound. Vivien placed all extraneous thoughts, all fears, into tiny boxes and shoved them away deep into her mind. This was her calling, and she would stand tall while doing it. Everything was so vibrant, so significant. From the shushing of the grass against their boots, to the smell of sweat, and faint tinge of swamp that followed them, the chatter of the five hundred men ahead, and the smell of their cooking fires. She saw and felt it all as she called fae from the aether to her side.

The elves jogged lightly, saving themselves from more effort than they had to expend. There would be effort enough shortly. The human soldiers ahead were sleeping, sitting, or eating, thankful to be away from the fighting, and stealing what comfort they could while the world dissolved into blood over the hill. The elves were spotted a bowshot out, and the whole tiny camp dissolved into action. Vivien saw one man run from relieving himself paces from camp and snatch a signal horn from the pole of his tent.

"Gregor! Horn!" she called.

The gangly low-elf raised his bow, separated from the pack, went to one knee, and shot an arrow high into the air. The note of warning had barely begun when it was cut short. Then, a whistle of an angry ghost filled the air on all sides, rising from over the hill, arcing up and changing pitch as it reached its apex and came down. The enemy was forming up, but some soldiers, lacking discipline, charged the elves, yelling wildly.

The Wolf barked. "Halt! Archers, loose!"

The La'athai stopped in formation. Elves spread to either side, Gregor joining their ranks, and all of them fired as fast as they could, knocking over half-dressed humans into the grass and then setting a withering hail into the forming force. They had only a few shafts each, the rest given to–

Vivien glanced back and gasped.

As the Wolf had predicted, the baggage handlers were fleeing from Tyrell's small force. The soldiers were plying their bows with speed, only pausing as the warmages cupped glowing hands around the heads. Then a tiny inferno with wings would grab onto the ammunition, and ride it into the carts where it was placed.

Fire fae.

Strictly speaking, they were not unseleighe, yet they were still viewed as dangerously close by the college and Council. However, for this job they were ideal. Each arrow carried them to their target where the little, mischievous things would dance along the contents of the wagon until it was merrily ablaze. But there were hundreds of carts, and the strain of summoning so many–

The Wolf's call shocked her. "MAKE READY FOR FAULT!"

Vivien turned and saw the humans were making a ragged block and advancing. The soldiers expended the last of their arrows and hurried back to their formation, readying axes and hammers. They joined into the line taking shields from their slings and gathering into position. The soldiers ringed the warmages in every direction and prepared to protect them with their lives. The Wolf took out his thick-bladed dagger and held it before Vivien.

She stole a single look into his eyes, then touched a finger to the metal. She felt the fae surge through her more powerful than ever before, like drinking from a stream that suddenly became a rushing river. The Wolf nodded, handed the *Storm* charged dagger to her and turned. Front and in the center, he raised his axe and bellowed, "READY FOR... SHIELDS!"

The humans tossed the damned cloth sacks of iron filings from their belts. The elves had drilled over and over for this. They raised their shields above in a roof, angling them away from the mages in the center. The hurled bundles exploded on the upraised wood, and streams of black dust fell from them onto the outer soldiers in the formation. Finally, they flung the shields away from the center. Vivien ran the charged dagger over herself, the magnetized blade growing fuzzy with black dust as she collected stray particles, then passed it to the soldiers nearest her to do the same. The other wizards followed suit, and in moments all elvin mages and soldiers were clean and clear of the black iron.

The humans came in at a jog. Vivien watched them spread out so their line far exceeded that of the La'athai, threatening to envelop and crush them from either side.

Vivien called out, "READY FOR SCARECROW!"

The Wolf bellowed, "READY FOR FAULT!"

The Wolf howled. The La'athai howled. The humans raised their weapons for the first, momentum driven strike. The lines were two steps from each other when the Wolf called, "FAULT AND STRIKE!"

The whole body of elves took one step back as the humans tried to make their first attack, wasting their momentum on empty air, then stepped back forward, hitting the front line hard. Screams and shouts

ELVISH JEWEL

filled the air, and the wide line of humans began to fold in on either side, seeking to whittle at the ranks of the elves.

Vivien called out again, "SCARECROW!"

Fae leapt from the grass at the calls of the warmages. They sucked the long blades into tightly packed limbs and gangly thin torsos. These grass-men then set upon the attackers on the flanks. Swords hit the grass and stuck in the ropelike compact bodies as the grass-men pushed, hit, and grabbed at weapons.

The front group was static, acting as a wall and allowing the human soldiers to break upon them in a wave. The axes and hammers crushed the enemy armor, sheared through limbs, and hooked down shields so that others could strike at unprotected bodies.

Vivien called another command, "SNOWGLARE!"

Into the slowed flanking troops, mages cast shards of ice. Where they hit, the sharp blades exploded, leaving frosted armor and mangled limbs. One man appeared to be in charge, calling orders from the rear of the formation. Unkempt, unshaven, and missing his helm, he looked at the edge of panic. Vivien felt the fae come from the aether and settle into her hand. She projected the spear of ice directly into his face, catching him in the open mouth and dropping him immediately. The reaction was immediate. The human soldiers began to resist advancing. A few in the rear threw down their weapons and ran, and the fighters in the center front began swinging wildly like trapped animals.

Elves fell, but they kept their formation, closing ranks and lifting shields to accept incoming strikes without pause.

"BELLOWS LEFT!" Vivien called,

The warmages concentrated, summoning fae of the wind to sweep across the closest lines of enemy soldiers. It caused many to stumble, caught their shields and flung them open to attack.

The Wolf did not waste the opportunity, "SRIKE AND ADVANCE!"

Fifty men went down in a second, and the elves began burrowing into the enemy formation, reaping as they went. Without a commander, the human formation began to disintegrate. They fought less as a unit than as a mob. Yet now the elves were surrounded. The Wolf caught her eye, his face strained.

The whole world slowed there. Elves on the edges of the formation turned to face the new threats, but he knew his passion and ferocity had led to a grave error. She smiled at him, for she felt incomparable joy as she shouted the next order.

"FIREFROST!"

The mages again called on fae at home in the wintery north. They touched soldiers on every side and the weapons held were surrounded by tiny blue halos. Where they struck, cold followed. Humans fell, shivering, to be dispatched easily. The Wolf howled mightily, and three men cowered before him as his mighty arm hewed every enemy within reach, shattering shields and cleaving through armor. He picked up an iron sword from the ground in his free hand, and he began reaving with skill and ferocity unmatched.

The juggernaut of five hundred were now only two hundred standing. The rear guard of the human army had decided they had seen enough of the La'athai. The enemy broke, some scattering for the woods, some for the cliffs near the lake, but the great majority went toward the safety of their numbers over the hill.

The elves panted, and counted their numbers, looking back over the sea of fallen men that surrounded them. It was a terrible thing to behold because, more than the fact that they were the enemy, they were people. They were people who had families who waited for them back home, wherever home was. They had once had hopes and dreams that were now smattered onto a bloody battlefield. It was the most terrible thing about war, the wanton destruction of people, good people who wanted to live their lives and be happy.

Vivien counted ten missing from the elves still standing and gasped. Ten fallen elves was a blow, but it chould have been so much worse. She looked to the Wolf, saw where he had received cuts that were already closing, and then past him to the hundred or so fleeing humans already halfway up the hill.

Her eyes widened. "Oh gods! They are going to alert the rest of the army!"

The Wolf reflexively turned and saw the men fleeing, then back to Tyrell's group, who had moved down the line, firing carts. "Will they be done?"

Vivien shook her head. "We can't take that chance!"

The Wolf raised his now notched and scratched axe. "Up! Up! We must move!"

The La'athai responded, coming to their feet with grim faces. Vivien felt the same tiredness, but they had to stop those men, or at least delay the counterattack that was sure to follow. Weary men joined into formation and they began to jog. Vivien felt an ache in her legs that simply would not end, a hollowness that ate at her very being. She set her face into a mask of determination and pushed on. The Wolf would never flag, but the men would see her and be inspired to dig deeper. She felt her stomach roil and she begged silently, *Not now. Gods, not now.* But her gut held, and they peaked over the ridge as the Wolf pulled away.

What they found was chaos.

The field had been trampled all the way to the old growth forest. The grassy hillside was smeared with blood. Thousands of humans were marching on the edge of the brush, seeking to push through. A pack of tir-reath were wheeling away from a scattering of thousands of archers that were knocked like tenpins in their wake. Less than a hundred feet away a tent sat primly while men surged around it to get away. There was a small band of humans on horseback even now orienting themselves on the elves.

A huge man, easily the Wolf's height but twice as wide in chest and gut, was bellowing orders.

The Wolf raised his axe, but Vivien reached out and grabbed it, "Wait! Hold!"

The Wolf's eyes drank in her face, and she almost felt like he touched her. He nodded. "Hold for charge!"

The elves raised their shields as the ten armored men on horseback accepted long spears from young boys nearby and brought themselves into a line.

From behind suddenly paltry steel-banded wood, one of the elves panted. "What are we doing?"

The Wolf growled, "Holding the line."

Vivien began to pull the fae from the aether. It was complex, since she needed two different kinds, one powerful and offensive, the others nurturing and many. Vaguely, she heard the soldier again. "They will tear right through us."

The Wolf's voice was dangerous. "Run and I will cut you down myself. Vivien says hold, we hold."

The horses were spurred into a gallop, hooves eating turf in huge gulps. She could hear her heart beating in her ears as she captured the fae and directed the nurturing spirits of air all around. She took deep breaths, concentrating, concentrating... The ground began to shake with the pounding of the run of the horses. The iron points on the spears glinted evilly. She raised her hands. On all sides, she thought she could hear elves praying.

The spears were only a dozen feet away when she brought her hands together, discharging the furious fae of the storm. A thunderclap echoed out, one so loud that nine of the ten steeds bucked and tried to turn, sprawling in a big mess of arms and legs. The last reared, but the rider held on for dear life as his spear bounced uselessly onto the ground.

The fae of the sky had created a bubble-like shield around the horsemen, keeping the brunt of the sound from the reaching the human army. The Wolf wasted no time, and sprang forward to pull the one remaining knight from his horse, hacking downward into the breastplate and splitting it open. The other elves swarmed forward and dispatched the rest on the ground. The Wolf tried to free his axe and couldn't, so he took the fallen knight's iron sword and hefted it. Ahead, the trumpeter continued to blare orders onto the hillside.

Less than a bowshot downhill, the handlers, struggling with fists full of heavy chain, were dragging the giants in a slow circle to face the La'athai.

Below, men were turning their forces around, stopping their assault on the forest to return to their commanders. Vivien rallied the elves into formation, but the Wolf ranged on, passing in front of the tent where adolescent boys holding signaling flags dropped them and ran. Only the man blowing the battle horn stayed to blow on.

He passed by a wooden throne, a table loaded with a keg and drinking mug, and the front of a pavilion. As he passed the opening, a dark shape shot forth like a hurled boulder. The two, Wolf and Tactician, went down and rolled on the turf. They came to their feet locked in each other's arms. They strained and gasped, feet churning the grassy ground as they heaved against each other with strength few men could dream of. Muscles strained, teeth bared, the two titans roared at one another with rage barely in check. Vivien gasped as the Tactician got one hand around the Wolf's throat and began to squeeze.

The warmage glanced at the coming giants, saw all the elves were watching the Wolf. She made to call out an order, but then focused again on the battle, the one where her heart was breaking as the Wolf was slowly bent backward, unable to get air. He needed her, but so did the men. These were her men, and she could not leave. She saw the lusty look of triumph on the Tactician's face as the Wolf was pushed to his knees.

Then the Wolf shifted. One hand grasped the hand holding his throat and twisted to the side. The Tactician lunged forward uncontrollably, but the Wolf held on to one thumb. It was wrenched nastily, and the Tactician screamed as he fell to his face.

The La'athai cheered. Vivien felt she could breathe again and moved the formation to face the first giant being brought towards them. She glanced back to see a gasping Wolf wasting no time to stomp on the Tactician's elbow, eliciting a wet snap as it suddenly hung loose like the limb of a rag doll. The big man turned over screaming, and the Wolf brought his whole weight down on the opposing knee to break it cleanly. Then, shaking his head as if to clear it, he walked to the horn blower, yanked the huge ivory instrument from the man's hands, smashed it on the ground, and handed the mouthpiece back to the stunned soldier.

There was a shout and Vivien turned back to find that the first giant was upon them.

Elvish Jewel

Three times the height of an elf, and many times the width, reeking of its own excrement, the huge mountain of muscle and fat came on. It's legs were thick, and the head pointed and smaller than was proportional. Beneath the stringy beard and huge rolls of fat that acted as protection during a fight, the skin was thick as any heavy leather and bore the scars of brutal treatment. Dull, animalistic creatures, giants lived in solitude except to mate in the wild. This one had been bred only to fight and eat. One of the handlers pulled at a rope running alongside the chain to release the collar with an audible snap, the creature came to life. It raised a massive tree shorn into a crude club and roared.

She raised her hands, fighting weariness as she called upon the fae, "FROSTFIRE!"

The other mages wavered, wobbled on their feet as spears of ice slammed into the giant with horrible effect. Bright blood exploded from where the icy daggers hit. The thing roared again, a bestial sound that rattled their bones, but it kept coming. Every seemingly lazy step on feet shaped like cut logs bringing it closer, faster than Vivien could believe. She fought to contact the fae, fought to sound calm, fought to give the order,

"FROSTFIRE!"

More ice flew forth and the creature recoiled as its front became a forest of icy spines. Yet it did not stop. It raised the massive tree trunk club and then brought it down on the front line of La'athai and their raised shields. Three men in a line were crushed by the impact that caused the ground to shudder. Two mages went to their knees, exhausted. The giant roared again, a trumpet that rattled trees in the far off forest line.

It was answered.

The Wolf sprinted from the left, eyes blazing red in the daylight, roaring from his soul with the voice of a dragon enraged. The dull creature looked to the sky, but the attack came low. Stolen sword in both hands, he swung it with the minimal grace bloodlust would allow. His strike took the thing in the back of the knee. It trumpeted in pain and staggered to one knee as the other collapsed. Without pause, the Wolf dodged back from a blindly sweeping hand, scooped a fallen La'athai hammer from the ground, and then charged.

Vivien didn't realize she was yelling until she heard her own voice, "TORCHLIGHT!"

But of the remaining mages, only she and one other cupped their hands and let loose with a blinding light that flowed like water and spat into the giant's eyes. Still, the thing recoiled, blinking stupidly and bellowing. The Wolf, hammer in hand, used the icy blades stuck in the giant's front like a ladder. The beast slapped at the Wolf as one would swat an insect, making contact and flattening him against the thing's chest. The barbarian cried out, then heaved himself to the next set of ice spikes, leaving a telltale swath of blood behind. Yet he pushed past the pain, scaling to the shoulders without pause and without fear.

The creature recoiled, and the big man struggled to keep his feet, but he entwined his left hand in the giant's hair and raised the hammer like the judgment of an angry god. The steel fell, once, twice, three times. Vivien felt new life fill her as he struck again and again. The creature's voice gained a gurgling quality, it wavered, and then fell over backwards. The Wolf rode it's shoulders to the ground and rolled clear.

Vivien kept her feet as men sprawled on every side of her, utterly exhausted. The sight of the indomitable man, even holding his side where an ice knife had broken through his armor, filled her with such life she felt invincible. The Wolf grabbed an axe from one of the elvin dead and jogged over to her. She embraced him and he held her as if it were the last thing they might ever do.

Vivien looked about and saw stricken faces, another giant coming, the massive army turning from the forest below to face her dwindling force. They could not abandon the tired and wounded. There was nowhere to run or hide. She pulled from him, looking into eyes fading from blood to blue.

"What now, Enchantress?"

She nodded at him. They had always known it could come to this, "We fight until we can fight no longer."

He nodded, hefting the axe. Behind him the next giant roared. She watched his eyes swirl from blue to blood red and begin to dance with vengeful fire. Then they began to burn blue. It was then she understood that his love for her did not replace his anger, it just burned so much brighter.

His voice had a hint of something, something deeper and more resonant, "They will find killing us harder than they might imagine."

She smiled as the world came to murder them from every side, "I'd like to believe so."

Chapter Forty-Five
Simrudian the Free

His hands had never healed, but they had left him his feet. He had used those feet.

The feet had carried him out of the infirmary, through the woods, across the swamp, past the dragon bones and into the hills. His head constantly whispered with dark tidings. He had stopped sweating the day before, and his skin felt tight, hot, and dry as parchment. His hands throbbed with pain, and closed eyes meant relived horrors, but his feet had carried him.

He had been robbed of his peace, his serenity, his very Elvishness. He wanted to get them back.

Food had run out two weeks before. Water a week later. Now his feet moved with almost automatic need. He pushed onward, ever onward. What parts of his hands weren't screaming in pain, or numb and dead, felt tiny squiggling he dared not check upon underneath the gloves. He had trained for a decade on how to disappear, to track, to shadow, and he followed the trail of the vanguard.

The flanking force of elves had left the safety of the woods long before he arrived. Some were firing a train of wagons almost a mile long. The other had engaged a huge group of humans and sent them scattering. The elves were chasing that huge, bearded human at their front. Sim caught the telltale flutter of pennants on a pavilion just over the crest of the hill. His world was blotted out but for those red and blue birds flapping in the wind on top of the tent poles. It was there. *HE was there.*

Sim staggered up the slope, drawing his only companion from his belt. It had whispered for weeks. Now it was silent, the steel edge breathing heavily as his limbs shook. He licked filthy, chapped lips and pushed onward, hearing his own breath come in ragged gasps. He fell to his knees and lost sight of the pavilion. He stood. He fell to his knees again. He stood. Horns blared, panicked and bright in the afternoon light. He heard horses screaming. Still he climbed the hill.

He fell completely, catching himself on his poor, mangled hands. Pain shot through him and black swirling dots shot through with shooting lights swam in front of his eyes. He grit his teeth and stifled a scream. On the ground in front of his face, the gloves had split across the backs of his hands. Fat flies and white maggots spilled forth, the stench of rot filling his nostrils.

He felt something snap as pain washed over him, leaving his body as corpse flies buzzed around his head, looking for another piece of him to feast upon. He began to laugh.

Is it like this, then?

The knife finally answered. *Of course it is. You have known what you were looking for this whole time.*

"Yes," he growled, "like this."

The world swam as he stood. His eyes felt gummy as he tried to blink and failed, then forced them closed and then pried them open. He was walking, walking on perfect feet.

There was a roar above. The horn had stopped and he didn't remember when. He staggered, faster and faster, up the slope. He came over the crest of the hill, screened from the world by the tent. He circled to the left, and nearly tripped over the long bar at the front of a cart. His heart, already fast and thready, began to beat in his ears as he saw keg after keg of the vile drink that the Tactician downed like water. It was never far from him, and they were piled high and deep. He wondered how many there were.

Twenty, silly. You know that. Concentrate.

We are busy with other matters, the knife replied.

Sim drew the dagger, spilling more maggots from his gloves. He had to look, he couldn't feel the handle. He tried to grip it tightly, but his hand couldn't manage more than a limp hold.

Dammit.

It will suffice, the blade promised and winked at him.

He nodded and crept around the cart on weak legs.

There should have been servants, guards, the captains and generals meant to lead the massive swell of men. No one waited around the front of the pavilion. Sim glanced behind him, expecting an ambush, but there was nothing but the long stretch down the hill to where the wagons formed a long, burning snake. But there were soldiers coming. No...elves. Some were helping others, trying to run but burdened by the exhausted or the dead. He ignored them.

He crept back around and elves were facing a giant. Ice flew in cloudy shards. There was noise. So much noise. He ignored it. Bodies were spread along the far side of the tent. None. None were HIM.

Sim slipped around the cart, across the front of the tent, and ducked in, blade held weakly.

The inside was lit only by a few candles in a stand, and his eyes refused to adjust. He shook his head, the strange overfull feeling sloshing back and forth. He heard laughter.

"So, one of you has come for me?"

Elvish Jewel

THAT VOICE.

Sim blinked, and the room revealed itself. There was a mammoth bed, assembled of timber brought from far away. A huge table was spread with maps. On the table there was also a tapped barrel of the foul drink the owner was known for. A thick carpet covered the floor. A stand bore untouched armor that never got worn, a helmet never donned. He was not The Warrior. He was The Tactician. He lay on the floor to the side of the table, one arm and one leg swelling to three times their normally gargantuan size.

He was broken. Beaten. Even now he smiled grimly at Sim, gritting teeth against his pain. Sim took one dead hand and pushed off his hood, letting it fall.

The Tactician hissed and smiled, eyes dark and dead even now, "So, it is you. Have you come for your dignity?"

No.

"Is that what you have come for, elf? For all the little bits of you I took?" He gasped, breathed heavily, and shifted onto his remaining working arm. "Well, you can't have it. I took your bits, elf. I took them and they are mine."

No. Sim began to widely circle the Tactician on unsteady feet.

He looked Sim up and down frankly, taking in the swamp stained clothing, his shaking limbs, his stooped, hunted stance. "And you are unable to reclaim them anyway. Come near me and I will crush you even with one hand."

No. Sim looked at the Tactician absently, then to the dagger, for a moment unsure how the two fit together.

The big, greasy, black haired man smiled ruefully through his pain. "Come on, then. Try to take your dignity back. But you know, and I know, that even after I am dead I will live in your soul. I will live there for all time."

Sim felt his heart begin to beat irregularly.

The knife was sad, *Even now you can feel fear? Wouldn't it be better?*

"Come on!"

Sim felt the knife twist and he looked at it. His weak grip had allowed it to dip toward the canvas wall of the tent. It pulled him, moved him away from the sprawled, broken man.

"Come on!" The Tactician shouted, a command. "Come here and let me have you again before I throttle you to death!"

Sim wasn't listening. Instead he watched the knife fly lazily in his hand, drawing lines that were not there, guiding him. Suggesting to him. On impulse he thrust it into the wall and drew it to the side. A huge gash opened at the razor's touch, exposing the cart of spirits beyond.

"What? Are you mad?"

Mad? Yes I am mad. More angry than I can live with.

The tip of the knife sunk into the end slats of a barrel, *Yes. It would be better.*

Sim took as good a grip as he could manage in both hands and shoved the knife where it wanted to go, between the boards. He shoved against it with his weight, digging it into the wood.

The Tactician roared with rage, "STOP THAT! STOP THAT! THOSE ARE MINE!"

The knife penetrated, and Sim yanked it to the side. A finger sized hole was splintered away, and foul, choking liquor was unleashed across him in a flood.

He sputtered and his eyes stung.

"Fool! What do you hope to accomplish by spilling my drink?"

Sim blinked and turned back to the Tactician, then saw the lone barrel on top of his table next to the candle holder.

Drink.

Sim staggered away. The Tactician lunged for him, but was far too weak, to hurt to catch him. Sim slowly circled the table and reached around the keg. He turned the tap slowly, letting a stream escape. It traveled along the grain of the wood, puddling and soaking into maps and papers, plans and lists, until it found the edge of the table and began to piss off the side.

The Tactician saw the stream of liquid and lunged for it despite the pain. He caught it in his mouth and lapped it from the air greedily. It poured down his chin and soaked his shirt, spattering the carpet all around him. As he took in as much as he could manage, Sim dropped the dagger to the table, staggered slowly around, and sat in the Tactician's chair.

The stream still falling, the leader of the Iron Army looked to Sim, wiping his face. "You have shown me a kindness. And now I will kill you quickly." And he grabbed Sim's perfect foot inside of a swamp stained boot.

Isn't it better for it to be over?

Sim said, "Yes."

And he knocked the burning candles over onto the liquor soaked papers.

The fire leapt across the table, down the stream.

"NO!" The Tactician roared.

"Yes." Sim whispered.

The fire enveloped the Tactician. He roared as he flopped with broken arm and leg. Then he screamed. Then he squealed.

Elvish Jewel

Like a living thing, the fire engulfed the soaked carpet, the walls, the bed, the cart and the pierced barrel. Long before the liquid inside began to leak out and send the fire to spread like an army of the damned, the flames caught Sim's impregnated clothing. It raced up and down him, but he couldn't feel anything, not anymore. No fear, no pain, no doubt or hate.

He felt nothing, and found his peace.

The casks of liquor began to breech and spewed flames like teakettles of boiling oil.

The raging fire, uncaring of elves or humans, spread through the dry grass.

Chapter Forty-Six
Fire and Escape

Vivien and the Wolf looked downhill and saw that the vast bulk of the army was turning around, units sloppily moving now that each unit was not receiving directions from any one commander. They started to march toward the tiny knot of La'athai, abandoning the units already being slaughtered inside the forest wall.

The about facing was shoddy, the formation ragged. There were no trumpets to make sure of timing. Yet they managed a turn of twelve thousand men and began heading uphill. Without the spotters on the hill, blowing horns to keep the army moving where it needed, it had become a huge, dumb beast unable to see.

Fae, born of air and sky, rippled out of the greenery like pure vengeance. They swept up and down the line of men. Humans swung at them with iron weapons, only one making contact and dissolving the poor thing in a tiny thunderclap. The rest made their circuit, up and down and back, becoming angrier storm clouds with every passing second. The tiny clouds let loose with flickering spears of lightning, bolts arcing from one to another and causing them to shake and fall. That was when arrows began coming out of the forest like a horizontal hail. Men died behind by the dozens, and the portion of the army lurching away had no way to know it. Then the arrows stopped.

A cry went out from far at the bottom of the hill, the shrill shriek of a thousand tir-reath screeching at once. Mounted elves exploded through the foliage, launched by furred long legs full of corded muscle. They landed in the midst of the soldiers, lashing about with tooth and claw, riders swinging hammers to great effect against iron armor. As the humans tried to rally to the hundreds of enemies in their midst, fae were sent from inside the forest, ripping into them with ice, storm, and thorns. The ranks crumbled, humans died *en masse.*

Tyrell and his group of twelve appeared over the ridge. Vivien shouted and waved them over. The giant was closing, burdened by the eight handlers jockeying it into position with chains. Behind it, two more lumbered in.

"Carts are fired." Tyrell reported, pale and drawn.

The Wolf hefted his hammer and glanced over the La'athai and the incoming giant. "All of them?"

He smiled wolfishly. "Every one."

Vivien smiled and checked on the incoming legions of men. They heard the battle behind them, and some were turning to face the tir-reath. More of the battle-cats were emerging to fight now, joined quickly by a few hundred more from the tree line to the north, speeding in to flank the rear of the formation.

Tyrell jumped and pointed. "Unseleighe dancing!"

Vivien turned and the pavilion at the top of the hill was a raging conflagration. As she watched, the ropes tying down the barrels stacked sideways in the wagon snapped, and the flaming barrels rolled off, gaining speed and leaving trails of fire as they went downhill toward the enemy ranks. The men moved to give way to the flaming barrels, some starting to veer to one side or the other.

Vivien gasped, "Wolf! The La'athai could make it through!"

The Wolf glanced, then frowned. "The giant is almost upon us."

Tyrell, his face with a sheen of sweat from the effort of calling so many fae, ordered someone to get all the wounded on their feet, then turned. "I will hold the giant. Take the men and go."

The Wolf shook his head. "Not your place. I will hold off the giant. Get the men and move. NOW."

Tyrell saluted grimly and moved to obey. The La'athai were exhausted, some broken, and many of the mages barely able to keep their feet. Soldiers closed around the wounded and weary, moving to the center of the group.

The Wolf watched the giant coming, blood trickling down his side. A deep growl began in his chest, and she could see him stoking his internal forge for battle. Vivien could hear his heart, literally hear his heart, pounding in his chest like a call to the end of the world. His massive fist tightened around his borrowed hammer, knuckles popping under the pressure. The human soldiers released the collar and ran. The giant that faced them bellowed. The Wolf roared back.

He glanced at Vivien, then aimed his red glowing eyes back at the towering thing, "Run, and I will protect you!"

She felt her own heart slow, then begin to ramp in rhythm as her soul reached out to the spirits of the forest. She waved the La'athai into motion, "No. Attack, and I will fight alongside you."

The giant smashed its club into the ground, shaking the soil and swaying the two of them in challenge. The Wolf looked at her, red eyes burning into blue, flashing in time with the pumping of his lifeblood, "I love you."

"I know," she replied. She raised her hands to the heavens and sprites of storm and thunder came to her wordless call. She dug deeper than her skill allowed and fed her magic with her very life, felt it seep through her fingers as she cast.

The barbarian roared and charged. Tiny leaves swirled from far off trees and danced around her fingers. They swirled around her, and before long it was like a maelstrom. Her heart began to sync in time with the Wolf's. Vivien flung the fae from her fingertips.

Wolf and Jewel fought as one.

The Wolf came in and the giant raised its club. Vivien's hurled thorns hit under its raised arm like an army of stinging gnats. It ignored the tiny things and swung the club down. The Wolf flung himself to the side, rolling to his feet as the tree trunk crashed into the ground, splintering the end with the impact. Vivien drew on more fae, hurling them in handfuls into the giant's knees. The giant dragged the club across the ground in a vicious swing. Wolf leapt desperately, the club clipping one foot and spinning him into a heap out of the air.

Vivien called and cast, called and cast. She peppered the thing's stomach, and neck. She felt her strength ebbing, waning as she fed her calls with energy from her soul. But already she'd cast far more than she ever had before, and even in the thick of the battle, she wondered about it.

The creature raised one hand and brought it down like a child crushing a bug. The Wolf got to his feet as the appendage came down. He raised his hands and the sheer weight smashed into him, bringing him down onto his back. His trembling arms began to fail as the giant roared again and leaned down, down, down onto the supine barbarian. Vivien cast one more handful of thorns into the giant's arm, the one pressing down on the Wolf. The Giant leaned down harder, harder. Its hand collapsed finally his resistant arms and thudded into the center of the Wolf's chest. Blood shot from the hole in his side and the steel plate deformed.

Three more barrels came rolling by, cutting her off from the giant and spooking the others to fight their handlers and flee.

Vivien ignored the smoke, ignored the shouts of the men down slope. She had to ignore the pained, reddened face of the Wolf as the life was crushed from him inch by inch. She brought her hands together, and called the fae in the thorns.

The creature jerked, then again, then lurched up and off of the Wolf, who gasped and inhaled like a man emerging from a crushing rock pile. The beast roared in pain, lifted its left arm, and exposed the bloody mess of a half-grown blackberry tree. It had dug into the skin, with unnaturally long thorns that rent the flesh. Blood flowed freely as it whined loudly and pawed at the branches. The Wolf scrambled to his feet and the giant fixated on him, raising a hand to swat him when the thorns in its knee sprouted to life, tearing flesh and dropping it to the ground.

The beast roared, but Vivien barely heard. Darkness swirled in her vision and the world was becoming fuzzy and distant. She shook, but continued to pour energy into the fae, creating clusters of hard wood and thorns in the thing's belly. She'd never been able to harness power like this. Until this moment, it had been beyond her ability to do so. Only the Grand Magister had the capacity to instruct the fae to create life, and at such a rapid rate.

In truth, she didn't know how she'd done it.

The Wolf grabbed his dropped hammer, unsteady on his feet. The giant pawed at him, and Vivien sprouted the tree in his right elbow. The giant was a fountain of blood, screaming piteously and causing the other two to hasten their retreat directly into and through the human legions, scattering them like drifts of bloody autumn leaves.

The giant kept its knees as the Wolf circled it wearily. He lined up his shot carefully, then brought the head of the hammer around in a two handed grip into the giant's spine. There was a crunch like a pillar being severed, and the creature flopped forward and lay still.

Vivien let go of the fae and took notice of the world again. She could see nothing past the plumes of black smoke that erupted everywhere from the grassy hillside. She could barely even see the Wolf, or the mass of the fleeing legion coming her way. The La'athai were somewhere below, but she couldn't see any way to reach them without being cut down by enemy soldiers.

The Wolf's voice rang out clearly, but it wasn't a bellowed command. It was a desperate plea. "Vivien, run! Run! I will catch up!"

She wanted to stay by his side, but she trusted him and obeyed.

She staggered east, across the line of advancing men. The fastest of them were already fleeing past her as she called on spirits of the wind to make holes in lines of fire. She forded the first line easily, the second less so. Soon, she feared the swath of flames would be too great for her to keep at bay.

A human lurched out of the thickening smoke and yelled at her, swinging his iron sword. She drew her own blade and the ring of steel rent the air. Her strength was flagging, but she blocked the next blow and the next. Her reserves were at their limit. The human smiled, but didn't see the twin red orbs coming out of the smoke. He never felt the hammer blow that crushed his helmet and killed him. The Wolf crouched over the fallen body, gasping and bleeding.

Vivien made to go to him, but he waved her off. "Flee! Flee!" Then he turned and met another panicked soldier, caving in his chestplate with one strike and reducing him to a wheezing mass.

Her sword tumbled from numb fingers and she ran. Her desire for life, the gnashing teeth of the fire, gave her the ability to run even as her vision swam. Eastward she flew, toward the lake and the very eastern arm of the only thing that meant safety to her tired mind. The forest.

Chapter Forty-Seven
Leap of Faith

Her feet had wings as she turned and sprinted into the forest. The crackling was just behind her, heat seeking to envelope her in a fatal embrace that she ran to escape. Fatigue weighed on her, but fear kept her moving. The smoke was the worst, burning her lungs and making her hack and cough. She chanced a look behind her, hoping to see the Wolf there, but she was greeted only by the sight of orange flames leaping from the trees, scorched branches falling to land where her feet had just trod. The fire was so fast, faster than anything she'd thought imaginable, as dry scrub along the forest floor caught aflame, fueling the sweeping inferno above.

Oh gods, how did this happen? She supposed it could have been rather easy. They had called a lot of fire fae that day, and any one of the fires they created could have leapt from its place and begun this deadly swath of destruction. Guilt overwhelmed her, made her stumble and stop. *This could be my fault...*

Within moments the flames were surrounding her, but Vivien paid them no heed. She called upon her magic once again and air fae swept through, a cool wind that battered against the conflagration. She then called upon the water fae, a desperate choice, for her energy was flagging rapidly. The customary rains of spring had never arrived. While that had been a boon in the swamp, it was a terrible part of what was happening now. This fire would never have come so far so fast if the vegetation had been filled with the fluids needed for growth and life.

But there was a water source near, a lake. She'd been there a couple times as a young girl. *But it wasn't just any lake...*

Vivien called. She called again and again, called for all she was worth. In spite of the awesome power she'd rallied when faced with the giants, her energy flagged. The popping, cracking sound of burning wood surrounded her, and her heart beat a staccato rhythm in her chest. She coughed again and her eyes stung with the thick smoke all around. She barely managed to leap out of the way as a fiery branch landed beside her and, tired beyond measure, she collapsed into a heap on the ground and just lay there.

It was hot. She coughed again and her sides ached.

"Vivien!"

She looked up at the sound of her name and tried to see through the smoke.

"Vivien? Where are you? Vivien?"

"Wolf?" she croaked. The coughing worsened and she closed her eyes. It was hard to breathe and she gasped for air.

Suddenly he was there, kneeling over her and talking in her ear above the sound of the fire. "Vivien, I need you to get up. You can do it!"

She rose to her feet and together they ran. The Wolf's legs were much longer than hers, but he moved only as fast as she could. They fled more swiftly together than she could alone; he lifted her over the things that lay in their path, and he practically carried her when she was beset by coughing that somehow had no affect on him whatsoever.

Before long they were in front of the flames again. In spite of all it took her to keep running, she began to breathe a bit more easily and regained her feet. They moved further and further ahead, and for the first time since she'd seen the fire, hope surged through her. Maybe they could escape it after all.

Suddenly the Wolf faltered and he hissed an expletive under his breath in the language of his forebears. She glanced up at him and then to where he was looking. Her heart skipped a beat and her breaths stopped.

The land stopped.

Hand in hand, Vivien and the Wolf moved forward, and when the land ended, they stood at a precipice. They looked over the edge...down the craggy cliff face to a shimmering blue lake. The elves spoke of it often, and referred to it as the Lake of Dreams, or Dreaming Lake. Looking at it now, Vivien could see why it had that name, for the center was shrouded in mist. However, unlike other days, they could see a bit beyond the fog, and the reality was awesome in the most terrifying sense, beautiful and dangerous.

In the center of Dreaming Lake, shrouded within a layer of mist, was a circular waterfall.

In spite of the raging fire behind them, Vivien could pick out the sound of the massive falls that fell into a hole half the size of a small town. From this height, the lake looked calm, almost pristine, but she could imagine the mighty pull of the water just before the falls.

She looked at the Wolf. "I...I've never seen it this way before. It's always been shrouded in fog."

He nodded. "The falls are awesome to behold."

"You have been here before?"

"Yes, a few times, but never below the falls."

Vivien looked into the forest behind them, and the Wolf followed suit. The fire was coming. She looked left and right, took in the jagged outline of the cliff face, the fire coming closer and closer on both sides.

There was no going back. The only path was downward. It was a long drop.

Oh gods, we survived the battle only for it to come to this? Fear coursed through her while terrible fatigue weighed like a winter cloak sodden with swamp water that stank like years of unwashed feet. Fae that customarily arrived without her having to think of them were glaringly absent. Her throat closed and a painful lump sat there, unmoving, impeding each inhale.

The Wolf left her side to walk along the cliffside. Tendrils of curling hair had escaped the braids, and they framed his rugged face as he looked down to the lake waiting below. Vivien closed her eyes and concentrated. She closed out the fire, closed out her fear, closed out the world around her. She sought out her inner self, found her center, and began to call. It was difficult, more than it ever been before. Even when she was a yearling novice it wasn't this hard to call upon her magic, and with each moment that passed, what little bit of energy she had left was drained away. Once, before the battle, before men died, before the giants, she could have saved herself and the Wolf.

Now...now she was nothing but a withered husk.

The Wolf was suddenly back by her side, removing his gauntlets and discarding them on the ground. "Vivien, come with me over here. I think I've found a good place."

She furrowed her brows. "What?"

He took her arm and led her to a place not far away along the cliffside and pointed down. "This is a good place for us to climb down."

She stared at him, eyes wide. "What do you mean, 'us'? I can't climb down that. I will fall!"

The Wolf shook his head. "I know you can't climb it. I will carry you."

"How?"

"On my back."

She stared at him like he was a crazy man. The escarpment was at least a quarter mile to the bottom. How could he carry her so far? Certainly he was big, and he was strong. But now he was also tired, just like she was.

CRACK! Vivien jumped as a massive limb fell from the canopy above and landed just behind them. Within moments the fire would be upon them and all of this would be over. In truth, if she had to choose her death, she preferred going up in flames to falling and being dashed upon the rocks.

"Vivien!"

She turned to look back at the Wolf. He had already lowered himself over the cliff face, his feet and hands having adequate purchase on the craggy surface. He reached out a hand. "Do you trust me?"

For the briefest of moments, time seemed to stop. His eyes, once colored a dark red, were now a stormy blue. They regarded her with the utmost of confidence, tinged with a look of hope. He repeated the words, "Vivien, do you trust me?"

She felt the heat at her back, the flames reaching to devour her. By the gods, she did trust him. She believed in this man like she had none other her entire life but her father. She grasped his hand and she stepped from the cliffside and onto his back. She wrapped her legs around his waist and her arms around his neck, and when she was ready, he descended.

The Wolf's head had just cleared the ridge as flames surged over it.

Like a herd of wild horses, Vivien's heart thundered in her chest. She squeezed her eyes tightly shut and focused on the flex and pull of his muscles as he made the climb down. In truth, she'd never placed her life in the hands of another individual as much as she had this day, and the reality was more frightening than she cared to contemplate. But contemplate it she did as they hung thirteen hundred feet over a lake that had a giant maw that would easily eat them alive if they floated anywhere near it, with a massive wildfire that raged overhead.

The Wolf descended, step by agonizing step. Their armor plates shrieked as they rubbed against one another. Within the first few hundred feet she could sense his tiredness, not just by his lack of words, but the trembling of his arms and legs. It got worse as they continued, and she ached for him, wished she could relieve him of his burden. But of all the many things Vivien could do, she could not climb a cliff face. Maybe, one day, if they lived, the Wolf could teach her.

She prayed they would live.

Until those moments, hanging over Dreaming Lake, she'd never realized how much her father would want to see her again. Out of all her brothers and sisters, she was the only one who still lived with him. The others were long gone, either living in a distant city, or perished in Pergatium. Mikarvan would want to see her, and Lydia, and the Lady of Moonlight. If any of their men and women had survived the fire, they would want to see her. Maybe even more, they would want to see the hulking human who had led them.

Elvish Jewel

The Wolf stopped. He looked from side to side, moved one hand here, another one there, hoping to find adequate holds. Suddenly, one foot slid over the crumbling rock, causing him to lose purchase. She gripped him tight as they slid down, down, down, until his feet and hands finally caught again. And when they stopped, his chest rose and fell heavily with every breath.

She trembled against his back, and guilt rushed through her like a river. She caressed the side of his face. "Wolf, let me go. Without my burden, you can make it to the bottom."

"What? No! I will make it with you right there! I asked you if you trusted me. I would never have asked you that if I questioned my ability to do this," he said.

She nodded. "I know. But what we believe we can do and what we can actually do are two different things."

"Vivien, I can do this! You placed your faith in me. Please."

She was silent for a moment, then nodded. "All right."

The Wolf continued, rocks skittering down the cliff face as he moved. Vivien kept her grip on him as tight as possible. As they got closer to the lake, they could hear the roar of the falls more distinctly. The blue waters shimmered far below, became white as they tumbled into the orifice at the center.

The Wolf paused, catching his breath. "In the Lairdlands, there are stories about places like this, stories I heard as a young boy growing up. They say that they are eyes into the pit of the world, and that if you descend into them, you will have knowledge of everything."

"Do you believe that?"

The Wolf chuckled. "I don't believe much of anything anymore. Those were just tales."

She nodded and was quiet as she worked at the buckles of her armor.

"But I do believe one thing," he said.

"What's that?"

"That I love you, and that I will never let you go."

Vivien unfastened the last buckle and shrugged out of the grimy upper armor her husband and his men had labored so hard to fashion. It slipped away and the Wolf looked down as it splashed into the waters below.

"I'll have to work at keeping you around a bit longer then." She began to work at his upper armor, her fingers nimbly moving over the buckles.

His voice sounded strained. "Th...that's a good idea. Thank you." He slipped again, hissing as he struggled for traction along the sheer rock face, his hands leaving a trail of blood behind. The sight made a trill of pain travel through her, and she fumbled, making her wonder if she should reach down into her boot to unsheathe the dagger waiting there and just cut the damned armor off.

Finally it was done. The Wolf's chest plate slipped away and he gave a great sigh of relief. She untied his padding, wincing at the blood soaking the side of it, taking it away before starting on hers. When it was done, all that was left was the armor and padding still on their legs, the short brais they each wore, his linen undertunic, and her chemise and mamillare. She pressed close to his sweaty back riddled with multitudes of scars and bulky with muscle, reveled in the warmth of it despite of the sun beating down on them. It was then she realized how close they had come to the lake, and the Wolf stopped moving.

"What's wrong?"

He hesitated. "We have run out of rock to climb down. My feet feel nothing there when I try to descend."

She wanted to look down and under, but dared not. She didn't want to unbalance him and make him lose his hold. As she'd removed their upper armor, she'd been meticulously careful of that, and it was the reason why she never took the armor off her legs.

He looked from side to side his knuckles white under the strain of holding on to one place. His palms and fingers were shredded, and strangely, had yet to heal the way most of his wounds tended to do. For that matter, neither had the deep lacerations he had on his arms from their battle with the giants, and the stab wound to his side...

"Well, we can't hang around forever. The drop is not far from here," she said.

He nodded. "All right. You go first. I will follow immediately after."

She nodded, and without further thought, let go. She tumbled from the Wolf's back and into the lake. When the cool waters enveloped her it was like a shock, for she hadn't felt waters like these for weeks. Even better, they washed away all of the nastiness that remained from that foul swamp. What was bad was that she instantly felt a current.

She crested the surface, and seeing that she was far enough away, the Wolf dropped before she could issue her warning.

Oh gods...

Vivien began to swim against the current, towards the Wolf, and towards the rocks that she saw in the distance. What made it difficult was that her feet did not touch the bottom. The Wolf surfaced and she shouted.

"Wolf!"

He turned towards her voice. "Vivien, there is a current pulling towards the falls! We need to get out of the lake."

"Do your feet touch bottom?"

"No."

Her heart sank. "I'm swimming towards you. Try to swim towards the shore."

For several minutes it seemed like they made progress. They took off their leg armor and padding, managed to swim past the cliff face that they had been climbing down and beneath it towards the rocky beach in the distance. It was slow, but it was progress. Unfortunately, they were also tired. Casting spells, fighting multitudes of men, casting more spells, fighting giants, running through a burning forest, climbing down a sheer rock face, and holding on for dear life had taken all the energy they had.

Vivien finally caught up to the Wolf. His face was pale, and his chest rose and fell like a bellows. It was easy to see he was suffering. Looking down into the clear waters, she saw a plume of blood from the injury to his side. She instinctively placed a hand over it. Oh gods, he was bleeding out...

The battle with the current began to turn against them, and before they knew it, they had been swept beyond the escarpment and back out into the lake. The Wolf pulled her close, his teeth chattering against the water's chill, and she wrapped an arm around his neck, her other hand held ineffectually against the deep wound in his side.

He wasn't warm anymore, not like she was used to feeling, and she knew there was something terribly wrong. She looked into his eyes and saw fear there, fear like she'd seen in the swamp before they went into Pergatium. She took deep trembling breaths, closed her eyes and put her head on his chest. She heard his heart beating, and she remembered when he'd told her it beat only for her.

She felt a hand alongside her face, followed by a deep voice speaking into her ear. "Vivien."

She looked up and into his eyes.

He didn't say anything more. He just kissed her. His lips worked over hers in a rough caress, his moustache and beard scraping against her upper lip and chin. He knew it had to be uncomfortable, but he didn't hold anything back and she didn't want him to. They tread water as they floated towards the falls, locked in an embrace she never wanted to end. The roar filled her ears and her heart pounded a hundred beats per minute as they crept ever closer.

Finally the Wolf pulled away. He gripped her hand tightly in his and his expression was one of conviction. His voice rose over the falls, "We are going to live through this. I had a dream of it."

She simply nodded.

"Hold onto my hand. Whatever you do, don't let go."

She nodded again. They were there, at the falls. The pull was so strong.

ROSS ℰROSS

"Say the words. Tell me you won't let go!"

In spite of the water spraying on her face, she felt warm tears. Her voice was a shout, "I won't let go! I won't ever let you go!"

And then they fell.

Chapter Forty-Eight
The Heart

Ravn entered the city of Pergatium not knowing its name, but being able to feel the history there. It lay, discarded in the foul wetness of the swamp, crumbling buildings echoing with violence and loss. He might have wandered without purpose, but all the streets looked like they were heading to a particular place. They radiated out like spokes on a wheel, slowly sinking into the marsh like men drowning in slow motion.

The whole of the swamp smelled like death, and though rejuvenated by his stay with the warlock, he felt very small and helpless against the backdrop of loss. Even the birds avoided landing anywhere here. The snakes and rats were enormous, and the leeches that came out at night even more so. Worse, he felt like there were things watching him with unseen eyes, every moment. Once in the city, he found raspberry bushes here and there, from some unknown source and fighting to live in the dirt piled in the corners of the streets. They gave him some hope for life as he walked past decaying homes on raised streets of dirty stone.

He climbed the stairs to the main square, rusted sword in his hand as his instincts screamed of danger. "*Oh, it will find you,*" the warlock had said. So far there was nothing but an unnatural stillness. But at the top of the stairs, he found no living thing, only a field of death.

In the center of the square a series of grand statues stood. Maybe they were kings, maybe deities, but they were all elves. Around them were nonsensical nightmares that stood like men, but were not. Some looked like bundles of wood or stone, others like cobbled together collections of all the insects that haunt children's' dreams. Others looked like armored men, or expressions of fire and war. They had all been burned black by some horrible force, rendered into carbon statues caught in their last moments of pain... from something.

Ravn traced the cones of black scoring that scarred the concrete for untold number of years, following them back to the broken, yawning passage that led to the towering building the warlock had described. The sun was high and beat down angrily upon him, and the inside was an impenetrable blackness. Ravn's body wanted to tremble, to allow the smallest bit of his fear to escape, but he refused. Though his heart pounded in his chest, he refused to give in to his emotion. This was his chance, his last chance, to live in peace with the women he loved. If, instead, death was the end, it was better than the uncertainty and pain he

ROSS EROSS

had now. So he put one foot in front of the other, entering the building with no expectation to ever leave.

When he went inside, he was struck dumb with wonder.

The swamp had invaded even here, with vines and plants growing in every place they could wherever daylight shone. At the very entrance was a scene of violence confirmed. Two elves were locked in a struggle for all time. Rendered black by the same strange fire, they were unchanged. One lay on his back, holding onto the blade that pierced him. The other, a female in carbon blackened armor, thrust into her enemy's chest with a longsword. Of all the things they carried, only the sword remained unrusted and unburnt. The blade was covered in delicate, Elvish script. The grip was wrapped in some strange leather, and the hilt inlayed with rubies and amethysts. Ravn yearned to touch it, but held back. The burned and hardened faces were masks of death. This was the last strike in a mighty battle that had rung with its futility.

Suddenly Ravn felt his stomach give way into a pit. He may never find the heart he needed. He may never get to return to his wife or his lover except as a dog with his tail between his legs. And who would love him, then?

Ravn turned away to see that the combatants were by a little stone wall that turned out to be a fallen statue. It had once been massive, bigger than the ones outside in the square. It was broken at the ankles, and the arms lay separate from the body. One hand held a book, and the other, a dozen feet away, held a staff topped by a dragon. Ravn marveled at the skill of the artist, for he had captured a look of defiant confidence on the face of the statue he had never seen equaled. He raised his tarnished sword before him and continued onward.

Ravn went up a flight of stairs to the main floor. Inside, the same glowing chandeliers from the warlock's cave made islands of brightness in the vast gloom. Stairs were everywhere, some collapsed while others leapt up to different levels or onto balconies. There were shelves and desks, though many had been split or burned or decayed into rubble.

The shelves were a virtual maze. He moved left and right, almost at random, walking quietly on the corpses of moldering books and rotted carpets. The place smelled of mold and the papery decay of uncountable numbers of tomes and scrolls. Something else, something dry and terrifying, lay beneath, but he shoved it aside. The scent of rotting knowledge was everywhere, and darkness pressed in on all sides the moment he was clear of any of the islands of light. He felt doubly watched, and the pervasive fear had become a strange kind of noise in his soul. Yet there was nothing there, no insects or mice, birds or rats.

Everything alive had fled this place. He passed shelf after shelf of ramshackle books spilling from broken wooden leaves onto the floor.

And there was no beast from which he could claim a heart.

Ravn reached the far end of the shelves, and felt like he reentered the swamp. Huge windows, bigger than any door he had ever seen, dominated the wall. They had long since shattered and the pieces scattered into the dirt underfoot. Plants had blown in and taken root. What had probably been a sitting space to read books in the brightness of natural light was instead a conservatory, with growing green things everywhere. On the wall, haloed by vines, he saw an oval of movement. He raised his sword, and so did the image. He crept forward to find a bronze mirror, polished to a high sheen. Inside of it, Ravn could finally see himself.

He was disheveled, broken, dirty. His hair was tangled and matted, his beard even more so. He had come all this way only to fail. There was no beast here, no heart, no hope. Tears began to stream from his eyes in a flow that would not stop.

He reached out one hand and placed it on the cold surface of the mirror. He hung his head and wept. For all his adult life, he had garnered respect, power, money, and success. But without love to balance it all, he felt without a center, without a core.

He wiped his tears on his sleeve, sword still in hand, and saw more movement in the mirror. He peered into its depths, looking, looking. And then eyes emerged, laughing eyes, green eyes. He saw a beautiful face, and with it, a more beautiful soul filled with kindness, compassion, and love.

The face of Jash'ari smiled at him and he couldn't breathe.

He finally exhaled and spoke a truth he said aloud, one that rattled his soul, "I am in love with you, have always been in love with you. I wish you could be by my side, have always wished it, even as a young boy. I...I wish you could choose me the way I have chosen you even though we are apart. I..."

Suddenly there was a sound, a sliding slither of sound that made his skin crawl. He spun just as a long shadow appeared on an upper balcony and leapt toward him. He raised his sword, but as the wings extended and the beast descended, he felt smaller, and smaller, and smaller.

The creature landed, shaking the stones underfoot and causing balanced objects across the huge chamber to topple. It was covered in scales the color of a roaring fire. It towered over him but brought its pointed face down to his height, golden-red eyes glittering cruelly. It was massive and his heart quailed in his chest. He felt invisible hands take his fragile soul and begin twisting it, squeezing the fear from him like juice from a fruit. Ravn staggered under the assault, blinking away the dust in his eyes. The creature looked like it was grinning at him, grinning at the torture it would inflict.

He felt a word so old and so powerful it could never be fully spoken, only mewled by voices that could not encompass the word– Dragon.

Ravn's knees buckled and he fell to a kneel. The monstrosity raised to its full height and trumpeted in triumph, then brought a slavering mouth back down to him. Soul pummeled, heart fluttering, Ravn recognized the look in the beast's eyes. It was the look that Ròs had every time she banished him from her bedchamber...*He's pathetic.*

Ravn had no hope. He had no courage. He had only fear and humiliation and pain. The creature turned its head to the side to bring its mouth in for a vertical bite that would sever his body from his head and shins. The mountain Laird threw every bit of his broken heart into one strike. It came in from the left, across his body and he screamed as his heart rent asunder with the strength needed to make it. The old, rusted, mountain steel of his people crashed against the face of the horrific beast. Crashed...and shattered.

Ravn stared dumbly at the broken hilt in his hand. The beast recoiled in surprise, then pawed at its face to find no blood, not the slightest wound. It gazed at him. The red-gold eyes began to glow like lamps in the murk of the library.

Will broken, Ravn turned to flee through a window. The dragon snatched him it is mouth. He felt the teeth tear through his clothes and skin, but it did not rend his flesh. Instead of biting him in two, it hurled him back into the library. The Laird landed hard and rolled into a bookcase that topped onto him. He lay there, stunned by the pain of his own continued breath.

For a moment he lay there, trembling and hoping the thing would just go away. But then a set of claws scraped across the wood and flipped the heavy case off of him as a man might move fallen leaves. He was grabbed once more and hurled over more bookcases to crash into another and fall into the space between. The dragon roared, and again he felt hands tear at his heart, causing nauseating pain as despair raked over him. His sides ached, his back crackled as the joints in his spine popped in protest of movement, but hiding was not an option. He had to rise, he had to flee. He staggered into the maze of bookcases.

Shelves flew by on either side as he chose turns at random. He heard the thing leaping above from one balcony to another, the massive weight cracking the stones and casually shoving statues and debris aside. Ravn dared not look up, but caught sight of a fallen bookcase from above, making a tunnel ahead across two standing. Ignoring his pain, he raced towards it. He skidded to a stop beneath it, but immediately the ground shook as the beast landed, legs straddling his aisle. It's tooth-filled maw tossed the lintel bookcase to the side and a long tail came from along the denuded passage and slapped him. The breath whooshed out of his chest as he rolled head over heels to the end of the aisle.

He landed and saw flashing light, felt pieces of himself shift painfully as parts of him died under the assault upon his spirit. He heard a deep intake of breath and some latent instinct made him scrabble to his hands and knees, flinging himself out of the aisle and over a toppled desk.

The inferno unleashed behind him was too hot for words. It blasted the aisle he had been in, flashing sodden paper to smoke instantly. The wood, the rock, everything caught in the path did not burn. It incinerated. Ravn gave the wreckage only a glance as he scrambled away to see it was not aflame. It had already burned thoroughly. It was no longer fuel; it was blackened carbon that sent thick, choking clouds up in great billowing masses like the escape of damned souls.

Ravn took the first turn as the dragon landed to examine what should have been his funeral pyre. He heard it paw at the carbon, looking for him, then chirp cheerfully and leap to another aisle.

Ravn skidded to a slow halt and listened. Choking smoke clawed at his lungs and filled the library, cutting his visibility to close to nothing. He could hear the dragon leaping from place to place, hunting him precisely as a cat does a mouse in a barn. He posed no threat. He was beneath notice and beneath contempt. He had struck it hard enough to shatter steel and had not put even a scratch upon it. It was hunting him to be cruel. For sport.

It was *enjoying* this.

The Laird ripped his sleeve and wrapped his face with the cloth, knowing any cough would have the beast down upon him. He scurried quietly and quickly, making for the steps down to the front doors. Praying, hoping, the image of green eyes in his mind would give him the strength he needed to persevere.

He made it to the edge of the steps when the weight of the dragon landing behind him made him fall. From his back, he looked up at the mighty beast. It radiated smug satisfaction and shoved him with one wing, almost casually, down the steps. It relished his tumble to the floor below. Ravn stood to run and it pumped its wings, just once, the blast of wind toppling him over the fallen statue and sending him into the charred remains of the two elvin combatants at the bottom. They disintegrated into chunks, their eternal conflict finally ended. The amethyst decorated sword clattered next to him and Ravn snatched at it, for all the good it would do.

The beast called to him roughly, and tiredly Ravn got to his feet. Hopeless inferiority washed over him again, but he felt his insides finally,

finally, become numb to the torture. It was all over. He was dead. He faced a life of dishonor and an afterlife where he would never hold his child, meet his ancestors, hold the women he loved. It brought a strange peace into his being, a clarity he had never known. There was a silence inside him. A terrible calm that became the calling of a storm. The beast trilled at him, urging him to run.

Ravn felt an animal awake inside. As old as humanity, as hard as stone, and as fierce as any being alive, it began to burn in him. The dragon trilled again, angrily.

Ravn feigned left and the beast shot a short spurt of fire ahead of him. He mocked right, and another line of hot death blocked his path. He started to leap the fallen statue to charge and the dragon buffeted him with wind made by its wings, pushing him back. Ravn did not fight it. Sword in hand, he got his aching feet underneath him and sprinted for the open doors to the city beyond.

The dragon made a screech of delight and shot after him. Ravn exited the smoky darkness of the library and into the glaring light of the world. He turned. The beast was likewise dazzled. Low to the ground, running on all fours it could only have glimpsed the tiny human as he struck. It was not a blow of fear and trepidation. It was not made of courage, or wrath. It was every part of Ravn's being focused into the only thing he had left, the only force that kept him on his feet, the only thing that could bring him so far and still fight. Ravn dug into the depths of his soul to where love resided, the love he had for his life, his people, his realm, for laughing green eyes. He brought the ancient blade around in a glittering arc.

The dragon bowled into him like a collapsing wall. He was thrown to the side with every limb hurting. He slid to a stop and looked to see the glittering sword he had claimed shorn a foot from the base. He glanced at the beast that had slid across the square and come to rest by the statues. The head made pained gasps for air it could not breathe. The body tumbled uselessly betwixt the two, the glittering blade had broken, but it had rent the thing's armor, had reached deep into the flesh, and severed the spine.

Ravn stood slowly, pain the only indication he still lived. Numbed hands still held the broken sword as he limped, inexorably, toward the dying body of the dragon. Despair and loss flooded over him like a wind, whipping at him with gale force, but he continued to move. He was a null, a void in the chaos. The creature had taken his courage, and his pride, it had reduced him to nothing like a piece of wood ground into dust against a rock. Now, only his determination remained. Only the driving need to be done. Those, and the green eyes that haunted so many moments of his life.

Elvish Jewel

Gloom flooded over him like a rushing river. Ravn took step after step, allowing it to flow through him like a fish does the water. It was part of him, and he moved against the current to the body of the thing. He saw the shining blade there, oozing red as it jittered with each labored breath. The Laird looked to the dragon's face, and saw not defeat, but raw hatred. It pummeled him with unseen hands of misery. He turned back to the body and raised the shortened blade for a final stroke.

He slashed and the beast did not scream, but it hit him with the pain of the blow. He felt the razor sharp tear as if it had pierced his own chest. The creeping numbness in the limbs, the horror of the steel scraping against his spine. He felt it all.

Ravn screamed, but he struck again. And again.

Bones parted and he felt as if they were pulled from his own chest as he hacked away meat to expose the bright muscle beneath. Blood flowed over him, coating him in boiling hot crimson. The organs twitched and jumped. Deep inside two lungs moved the whole mass like a pair of desperate bellows. But there, right before him, was the beating heart the size of two of his heads.

The first blow nearly killed Ravn as he felt it land. Blood pumped across his face. It was salty, hot, and tasted of anise. The second blow was easier. The third easier still. The dragon gave one last push at his mind as he tore the beating muscle free of the shattered cage of bone. Ravn screamed in agony as he wrenched the muscle into his arms.

He stumbled and blackness reigned.

Ravn came to out of terrible nightmares into the coolness of night, but he felt fevered. The eight chambered heart was in his hands, hot as a cauldron from the fire. The dragon possessed a coiled spirit that still clawed at him. The body may be dead, but the dragon was still there. However, in his hands, now only half the size, was the heart of the beast. Wicked whispers mauling his mind, he shrugged off his battered pack, placed the heart into the sack the warlock had given him and turned to go.

He caught sight of the broken hilt of the sword, and picked it up to fill his own sheath without much feeling. His body felt less battered, but his spirit was raw and flayed open. He gave one last glance at the dragon's head. The eyes flashed menacingly before once again returning to death.

For a moment, Ravn considered striking off north, into Elvish lands, finding the Jewel who lived there, and giving her the magnificent heart. But she would live like the moon, above and eternal, and he would live only as dust beneath her feet long before she aged a day. The thought of bringing her such pain squeezed cold tears from his eyes, the last of his innocence escaping his soul.

Ravn felt no triumph, no remorse. He felt nothing but weariness. Yet, he had his prize. And now he would take it home, complete his oath, and live with what peace and love he could find.

He left the Doomed City, hoping to never return.

Chapter Forty-Nine
The Underwater Cavern

Falling. A terrible sensation. A sensation one often feels when one is going to sleep, when all of the muscles in the body suddenly tense and release. Vivien had fallen before. It was a ritual test she had to endure during her training as a mage. She never really understood it since her fear of falling remained after.

Impact. Another terrible sensation. A sensation one feels after falling, when all of the muscles of the body brace to be hit, and when they are, besieged by pain of varying degrees based upon the height of the fall.

Vivien supposed this fall, and the resulting impact, could have been much, much worse.

Amid the crystal blue waters of Dreaming Lake, Vivien hit bottom just to find that she was in another lake. Beside her, the Wolf, with all his weight, fell deeper. His hand was ripped from hers, and if she hadn't been underwater, she might have screamed. Luckily for her, she knew how to swim, and was quite proficient with years of bathing in the Fyresmee River. In spite of the shock of the impact, she managed to hold her breath, continued to hold it, and continued longer, looking for him amidst the millions of tiny bubbles that wanted to obstruct her view.

Wolf, where are you? Gods, please show him to me! Please!

And then he was there, a giant hulk lifelessly floating, his undertunic and brais billowing around him. She propelled herself over to his side, saw the wound along the left side of his face that told her he'd hit his head on a rock at some point during his fall or upon impact. She was astounded that the same thing had not happened to her. His lips were parted slightly and she knew he was dying.

Until now, nothing had been able to kill her invincible companion. But drowning certainly would.

No. No, no, no. You can't die, not now. We've been through too much, and I hardly know you. She touched his face, his eyelids, his lips. *Please! You can't die!*

Fear surged through her, fear like she'd never felt before. It was painful, gut-wrenching, agonizing. And she screamed....

Water entered her mouth and nose, drowning her as certainly as it did the Wolf. She struggled, choking as it entered her lungs and began to settle there.

As her body shuddered, Vivien did what she did best and called to the fae. She knew she had nothing left within her; all her energy had been depleted long ago. So, without thinking about it, she took what was around her. The energy produced by the falls was great, and within the blink of an eye, air fae were there. They surrounded her body, pushing out the water until she was enveloped in a bubble. Vivien coughed, sputtered, and vomited what had entered her stomach and lungs, then desperately grabbed the Wolf.

Vivien called again, telling the fae what she needed done. Her eyes rolled back in her head and the fae began to swim in a tight circle that enveloped her and the Wolf. Some broke away and entered her mouth. Faster and faster they spun and Vivien placed her lips over the Wolf's.

She kissed him– deeply, passionately. The fae spun tighter and tighter, and looking out through the bubbles, all she could see was a wall of shimmering silver. Slowly, she drew the Wolf in. Slowly, ever so slowly. And when he entered, his clothes were dry again. His hair, his skin, all was dry. She took her lips away, and when the fae flew out of his mouth, they cavorted about her, lovingly touching her face, her hair, her neck and chest. Vivien cradled the Wolf in her arms and when he took his first breath, she smiled.

The rest of the fae came flying out of his mouth to join the others that continued to spin around them. The Wolf opened his eyes, and when they finally focused on her, they reflected all of the love he left.

"I thought I'd lost you," she whispered.

He looked all around them, at the wall of silver, at the fae that danced along the periphery. "Wh...where are we?"

"We are below the falls."

"This...this is magnificent." He looked back at her, reached out to cup her face. "YOU are magnificent."

She smiled sadly. "We only have so much time left. The fae can't stay forever. When they leave us, we must navigate our way to the surface and find a safe place to get out of the lake."

He nodded, and not long after, the fae began to dissipate. The wall of silver broke away, and all that remained was a bubble. Outside it they could see the world outside it beneath the water of the falls. It was dark, darker than she remembered. She frowned and realized they had sunk deeper into the lake. Fishes of all shapes and sizes swam around them, their silvery scales highlighted only when they turned just right in the paltry light shining down from the surface.

She turned to the Wolf. "We have sunk deep." He put a hand to his temple and she saw the concern reflected in his eyes before he turned away. He withdrew his hand and when he saw the blood on his fingertips he shook his head silently.

Vivien just looked out of the bubble, one she knew would break any moment. She took in the openness around them, the fishes, the sandy bottom below, the rocky wall to their right...

She felt it before it happened. "Hold your breath!"

The bubble broke with an audible POP! and the two were once more submerged into the cool waters. Right away she could feel the pull, a suction pulling her down. She grabbed onto the Wolf and looked him in the eyes, urging him to keep holding his breath. If they were being pulled down, it was because there was an air space to fill. As opposed to fighting the pull and trying to make their way up, the better course at this point was to get to the place where the current was trying to take them.

They needed to reach it as soon as possible.

Vivien grasped the Wolf's hand and dove down, down deeper into the lake. She squinted her eyes, scoured the rocky wall before them. It was then she saw it. She put a hand on the Wolf's arm and pointed. He nodded and, lungs beginning to burn for air, propelled themselves towards the opening.

Vivien was a strong swimmer. The Wolf was even stronger. Within moments they were at the opening and being swept inside. They found themselves being carried along by a current, every once in a while bumping against a wall smooth from eons of erosion. Vivien began to reach her endurance, and her lungs burned to take a breath.

And then she couldn't hold it anymore.

Vivien gave a sudden kick upward. Up, up, up she went and her sight began to dim at the periphery. She kicked with all her might, her arms pulling at the water...

And then she breathed in. Water flooded her mouth, into her airway, and then into her lungs. She felt a pair of massive arms around her chest and under her arms. They pulled her up some more. And then some more. And then there was only darkness.

Vivien awoke to cold, damp cold. She coughed, shivered, and rose up onto her elbows. It was pitch black. She could see nothing but the few luminescent mosses that scattered the walls. Water lapped around her legs and waist, and overtop her backside was a heavy weight. She reached beside her, and when she felt that the Wolf was alive, she relaxed. As long as he was there with her, she felt that she could get through anything.

"Vivien?" His voice was thick and slurred.

She put a hand on his arm. "Yes?"

He was silent as he pulled the rest of his body out of the water and stood up. She could barely see the outline of him in the paltry greenish light cast by the cave mosses, but it was better than nothing. He came back to her and helped her out of the water. Now that she was waking up, it was colder than she'd originally realized, and her teeth chattered.

The Wolf put an arm around her and pulled her close against his side.

"I can't believe we made it," she whispered.

He pulled her around to face him, and even though she could hardly see his face, she knew he was looking into her eyes. "I can. I told you we would. My dreams told me so."

His words lifted her a bit and she glanced around in the darkness. "We need warmth, and a place to rest."

He nodded. "Stay here and I'll find a good spot."

He made to leave her side and a sudden, irrational fear swept through her. "Wait! Why can't I go with you?"

He put a hand against her face. "I'm not leaving the chamber. I'll still be right here."

She nodded and he moved away into the deep darkness of the cave. She felt silly for behaving that way. She'd never been so needy before, and she hated the feeling. She was a warmage, after all, trained to kill or be killed. She'd survived the being killed part, but mayhap there was a cost to surviving such a thing.

Vivien stumbled in place and finally hunkered down to play with the laces of her boots. They were full of water, and her feet cried out at the abuse they had suffered this day. She didn't know how long she and the Wolf had lay there at the water's edge, but fatigue pummeled at her and she felt terrible. She fell back on her backside, and when nothing was there to catch her, she tumbled onto her back and just lay there looking up at the cave ceiling. She gasped in wonder when it looked like she as looking up at a sky full of green stars. She wondered how the La'athai fared, and if they had made it back to the rest of the Elvish army. She missed their presence and it made an ache in the center of her chest. She placed a hand over top of it and...

"Vivien?" She startled when she heard the Wolf speaking so close. "I found a good place for us to rest."

She took the hand he offered, rose from the ground, and tiredly followed him back into the recesses of the cave. He walked up to a small alcove and gestured her inside. "Here, this place isn't so rocky, and when we light a fire, the walls will keep in some of the heat."

Vivien nodded and stepped inside, briefly feeling along the walls to get a good idea of size. There was ample space for her, the Wolf, and a couple other big men like him if the need arose. "Good idea. I like it."

"I am going to go and find some kindling. This time I'm leaving the chamber, but I'm not going far."

She nodded, feeling silly that he had to say that. Somehow, she was glad he did.

He chuckled. "I'm just too tired, having problems keeping my legs under me."

"Then I should help you."

"No, no, I want you to stay here. You can barely walk either. Trust me when I say I'll be right back."

She nodded and just stood there as he walked away, wondering how in the hell he could see without the light of some kind of candle or torch. She placed her back against the nearest wall and sank to the floor. She was bone chillingly cold, but still her eyes blinked shut. Whenever they closed, she could once again see the cavern ceiling shining with a smattering of green stars...

Vivien heard the crackling and popping of burning branches, felt the heat against her skin, smelled it as it consumed the forest around her. She shouted for the rest of the La'athai, hoping they could hear her. She ran as fast as she could...

She awoke with a start, opened her eyes and found herself laying before a small fire. It happily danced in a pit built from mismatched rocks of varying sizes. She sat up and the Wolf's arm slid away from her shoulder to lie at her hip. She glanced behind her to see him restfully sleeping. Gingerly she checked his side for the deep puncture wound he had gained in battle. His chest was heavily bruised, and numerous cuts covered his arms and legs, but the deep gash was finally closed, and she exhaled in relief. She stared at him a moment, not sure she'd seen him so peaceful before, and was happy to see him that way. She then turned to the fire. It was dying low. She was about to rise to try and look for something when she spied a small heap of driftwood lying close by. She picked a piece from the pile and fed the lackluster flames, flinching when they rose high for a moment to hungrily feed on her fresh offering.

Vivien just sat there and stared into the flames. The fatigue was still there, but not like it was. The Wolf had been busy while she slept, gathering the rocks and the driftwood, starting the fire, and then removing the boots and stockings from her feet and setting them close by to dry. The dagger she'd kept in her boot was also there. She scooted a little closer to the fire, holding her hands out to the flames to absorb more of the heat. She knew she could lay back down next to the Wolf and get better warmth, but she was afraid the motion would just wake him. *Best to just stay here and...*

"You are the most beautiful woman I have ever seen."

She turned to the sound of his voice and saw him staring at her, wide awake. She smiled. "Why do you say so?"

"Because I have seen inside your soul, and what lies there is amazing."

He spoke the words with such fervor, she was tempted to believe him. "And what is it you see?"

"I see a woman who loves just the way she fights, with a ferocity I have never seen before. I see someone who thinks of her father with every decision she makes, someone who caters to children and the elderly and makes them feel important, someone who kneels to her animal companion and treats her like she is an equal. I see someone who goes to her tent late every night because she wants to talk to the men and women she would lead into battle." The Wolf hesitated for a moment, indecision shining in his eyes. "I see someone who took an unkempt, disfigured human from the wilds and made him feel like a man again."

Vivien just stared at him, moved by his words in a way she'd never been moved before. She bowed her head, not certain she deserved all of the adoration he expressed in those words.

"Vivien, look at me."

She slowly looked back up at him, almost afraid of what he might say next.

"I am telling you the truth. I swear to you, I will never tell you a falsehood. Ever."

She just sat there, not knowing what to say, not knowing if anything needed to be said.

He held out his arm. "Please come lay back down. You are still tired. I am tired. We need more rest before we can figure out a way out of here."

She regarded him solemnly. Undeterred, he motioned her over again. Finally she rose to her hands and knees and crawled over to him. He pulled her close, situated her against his side and wrapped his arm securely around her. His warmth was a candle compared to the bonfire he had always been, but it was there and it felt like it was all for her. Within moments her eyelids were heavy and sleep was close behind.

Chapter Fifty
The Laird

Vivien hunkered down beside the Wolf at the river's edge. By the light of the torch standing nearby, they could see the silvery fishes swimming beneath the water's surface. "So do you think you can catch one?"

He slowly turned to look at her, a sparkle in his stormy blue eyes. "Is that a challenge?"

She blinked and looked at him. "No, of course not. I mean, I can't catch one, not the way you propose."

"Well, how would you go about doing it?"

"I would need a spear. That's the way I was taught, with a spear, not my bare hands. I just find your...uh...method... fascinating, and unlikely to succeed."

He grinned wolfishly. "So it IS a challenge."

She shrugged. "If you say so." The Wolf placed his hands just over the water and became very still. He waited, and waited, and waited. Then he waited some more. She wondered how he could keep that position so long without moving. Then, faster than the blink of an eye, he reached into the river and withdrew his hands.

Vivien smiled and shook her head as the Wolf presented the flapping fish to her for her inspection. "Impressive. However, I have grave doubts you can do it a second time."

"What?" His tone was incredulous.

She sniffed, enjoying the play back and forth. "That was just a lucky catch."

The Wolf chuckled. "Fine, I will catch a one for you too. But only because I love you so much."

Vivien took the fish from his hands and brought it over to the alcove. She proceeded to cut off the head, gutted it, and scaled it. She then skewered it on a crooked stick and positioned it over the fire. The flames licked at it for a few moments before the aroma of succulent flesh was soon permeating the air. The Wolf entered not long after with two more fish in his hands. She raised her brows, but said nothing. She knew he would catch more than just the one; it was simply his nature to do so.

Vivien took the skewer from the fire and held it out to him. He stared at her for a moment before he seemed to realize she wanted him to take it. "No, you eat. I will take one of the others."

She frowned. "But I had you in mind when I cooked it."

Slowly he reached out and took it. He continued to stare at her as she swiftly beheaded and gutted the other two fish, watched as she scaled and filleted them and put them over the fire. She looked at him from across the flames. He seemed so uncertain now, so different than the warrior she saw on the battlefield.

"Where I come from, as a warrior and a hunter, I am expected to make sure that my woman and my children are fed before myself. It is something I do gladly."

Vivien stared at him. The Wolf had never before spoken of where he was from. "Where I am from, if a woman prepares and cooks something for someone, they are bound to take it. They are not required to eat, but it honors her if they do so."

The Wolf raised the skewer to his mouth and took a big bite of the fish. She saw his body relax even if he didn't consciously feel it. Even though she was hungry, he needed the nourishment so much more than she did. Within moments the fish was gone and she smiled.

The Wolf returned the gesture and shook his head. "How do you do that?"

She gave him a second skewer and cocked her head to the side. "How do I do what?"

"How do you make me feel like..." He stopped before saying more.

"Feel like what?" she pressed.

"How do you make me feel like I mean more to you than you mean to yourself?"

She just sat there for a moment and then gave a shrug. "I am who I am, no more, no less."

He nodded. "Yes, and that is a great thing."

For a while they ate, then just sat there and stared into the fire. Every once in a while she glanced up and looked at him. The wound to his temple and face was slow to heal, and it concerned her. He saw her regarding him and curved his lips into a grin.

"What it is about me that has you staring so intently?"

Vivien pursed her lips. "I could ask you the same thing half the time."

He chuckled under his breath.

"But it is the wound on your head and face that worries me so much. Usually you are so quick to heal. Not so much this time."

He nodded. "Yes, I noticed that."

"I would like to take a look at it."

The Wolf paused only for a moment, then nodded. He stood and came to her side of the fire. Vivien shifted to face him as he sat back down, leaned forward to get a good look at the wound. It was red around the periphery, and when she touched it, she felt him flinch without ever moving. A part of it disappeared beneath the weeks of hair growth at his jaw and chin, and she couldn't suppress her frown.

"What is it?" he asked.

"I...I think you should shave your beard."

"Why?"

"I believe that the wound is festering beneath it and that it is getting infected. That might be why it's not healing."

He was thoughtful for a moment. He then extracted his dagger from his boot and handed it to her, hilt first. "I think mine might be sharper than yours."

Vivien took the blade and looked him in his storm-gray eyes as she set carefully to work. She'd never shaved a man's face before, so he had to instruct her at certain spots. With each small move of the dagger she pulled away chunks of hair and set them beside her. The dagger was sharper than hers had ever been, and it cut the hair so close to his face, the skin was smooth. She was afraid she'd accidentally cut him, but somehow she never did.

Finally she sat back to view her handiwork. Her heart suddenly stuttered in her chest, and her mind spiraled into a vortex. She opened her mouth, but no words emerged, and her eyes widened more with each passing moment. The Wolf saw that there was something wrong, something terribly wrong, and his face paled. He even seemed to know what it might be.

He reached out a hand. "Vivien..."

Quicker than she thought possible, she scuttled back out of his reach, hitting her shoulder against the wall of the alcove. Her heart hammered against her ribs, it was hard to breathe, and in the periphery of her vision she saw a shimmering halo.

Oh gods...it can't be. It just can't. She blinked her eyes, once, then twice, then three times. *I can't have been talking to a dead man all these months.*

On hands and knees, the Wolf slowly approached her like she was a cornered animal. His hands were open, his eyes pleading, "Vivien, please talk to me."

She shook her head back and forth, kicked out at the apparition coming towards her. Finally her words came, and she brandished the Wolf's dagger between them. "Keep away from me. Keep away!" Tears began to stream down her face, tears so prolific she thought she might drown in them. Agony tore through her like a scythe and she was reliving his loss all over again.

"Vivien, just let me explain. Let me tell you..."

Her voice was raw, spoken with a heart shredded to tiny bits and left to die on the barren wasteland of her soul. "No! Shut up! You don't get to talk! You have taken *HIS* form! How could you do that? What are you? No! Don't answer that. I don't care!"

Vivien rose, the dagger still between them, backing towards the alcove entrance. And then, once she got there, she turned and ran. She ran, and right away she realized her error. It was black as pitch. She ran as fast as she could, as far as she could.

And then it was over.

A pair of thick, muscled arms tackled her from behind, wrapped around her and held her close against a solid wall of chest. Somehow, like she could on the battlefield, she heard his heart beating. His voice was deep in her ear, the same voice she remembered from almost a century ago, a voice she'd been hearing since the Wolf first told her he loved her after she and the Lady were ambushed. "Vivien, stop! It is me, your friend. I know it's difficult to believe, but it's the truth."

Vivien allowed herself to go limp and just hung there in his embrace, breathing deeply. He felt so real standing there behind her. *How could he be a ghost? How could he be anything undead when he felt so terribly warm all the time?*

"I'm going to pick you up and take you back to the alcove."

He waited a moment before carrying out his statement, making sure she had time to process it in her befuddled mind. When he swept her up in his arms, the tears came anew, memories from the past crowding into her thoughts to squeeze out all others. A part of her just wanted to take one of the torches and leave, leave to find her own way out of the cavern system alone. But then there was the other part of her that wanted to listen to her heart...

The Wolf carried her back to the alcove in silence. She'd run further than she thought she had, and she found an odd peace in that fact. The feel of his arms beneath her was comforting, and by the time they had made it back, she had calmed a bit. He set her down at the entry and waited behind her until she walked inside. He then followed and just stood there, giving her distance.

Vivien turned around to look up at him. It was his face, a face she'd fallen in love with as a young girl, a face that eventually haunted her dreams when she was older. It was his eyes. She should have recognized them right from the start. But then, she couldn't have, because only recently had they been the storm-cloud blue she saw now.

She watched him standing there, looking at her, guarding the entry so she wouldn't run out again like a complete and utter fool. She wanted to tell him she wouldn't, opened her mouth to say it. Her voice made it past the painful lump in her throat, but the words didn't come out as she intended.

"Ravn? Is it really you?"

Chapter Fifty-One
Homecoming

Ravn entered the lands of his people a week before, but still he walked along, alone. He had accepted help from his generous people; food, shelter, even a trim of his wild beard. None had known him, his tartan fallen to rags weeks ago, modesty covered only by the length of his ragged shirt. He gave his name to no one. He was nothing but a wandering rogue, but they accepted him and showed him kindness anyway. He remembered each of their names so he might make gifts to them if he returned home. Perhaps it was the glittering hilt that bade them, but regardless they had done him a great service, allowing him to return to humankind slowly. He still felt his soul fractured by the marauding will of the dragon, but for now the breaks were knitting with every step toward his wife and his love.

The bundle containing the heart he clutched to his chest. He imagined he could feel it beat languidly, but whenever he checked it there was no movement. The warlock had not lied, though much smaller it still glistened and was as fresh as when he had carved it out of the hideous beast.

The rutted dirt became gravel paths, and went from wandering along valleys and ridgelines to a constant rise. He kept his eyes on his feet. One boot sole had come loose, and flapped in the dirt. The other had a rent that let air and water across his naked toes. One step after another. Soul quieting from the terrible pain, his animal side lessening the closer he came. Up and up along the road to his home.

He smelled cooking fires and heard animals fenced in on either side, but still he watched his feet. He could smell the soil of fertile fields that grew grain and oats for the city that bore his name, but he only saw his steps in the dirt. Dogs barked ahead. The sun fell to the horizon and bells ahead called the faithful to the kirk, but still he did not look. He could not. He dared not. It could all be an illusion, a delusion, a dream. Instead he concentrated on walking. Walking. He smelled food and his empty stomach grumbled but he pressed on. The only certainty was that the road had to end. That his home was ahead somewhere and he would one day see it.

"Halt!" a voice commanded in the language of his people.

Ravn stopped, numbness thrumming through him. He wavered as if drunk.

The voice was unsure of what the owner had found, but it was aged, and practiced, and knew what to ask. "State your name!"

Words burbled from Ravn like a mantra, for they were the words he'd been using every time he made a stop at a village or a town, "I am nobody special. I..." He paused. The voice was familiar.

"Well sir, Nobody Special is welcome in this city..." There was suddenly a change, a moment of magic wonder. "My liege?"

Ravn looked up to see he had passed the first line of buildings outside Blacach Towne. The man before him had aged badly, face etched with worry. Now, however, the old, balding, man-at-arms dropped the targe from his arm and let go of his sword. Moray rushed forward to embrace him fiercely. "I knew you would return! I walked these roads every night looking for you, for I knew you would return! There is no living thing that can kill you, my dear Laird!"

Ravn nearly collapsed into the embrace, but the outpouring of human contact shocked him, revitalized him, brought him back to the place where he stood. He was at the edge of Blacach. He was home.

He began to cry, then began to laugh. The two men separated and looked at one another. Tears streamed freely from their eyes and they embraced again. Moray jumped as if scalded and broke away long enough to take a bottle of raspberry brandy from his pouch and hand it over. Ravn drank greedily and felt himself infused. His retainer waited patiently until the bottle was lowered, then took the back of Ravn's head in his hand to bring him close again.

"Thank you, Moray."

The old man smiled at Ravn honestly, for there was more than a bottle of wine in that gratitude. There were years of training, honest advice, kindness, and firmness. "I never did aught for you that you did not repay tenfold, Master. But thank all the gods you are home."

Ravn took another long pull, careful for so much brandy on his empty stomach, but feeling the deep need for it nonetheless. "I have walked farther than most men ever will, and I swear on my wife's love I will never to be that far from home ever again."

"Aye, a damn fool thing it was, too." Moray frowned. "No one knew why you left. One of the handmaidens said she found a contract in your wife's chambers..."

Ravn nodded, confirming it all. "Neála?"

Moray stood agape. "Yours was the son she bore!"

Ravn's head spun, *a son*! "They are–?"

"Even just rumors that he was yours kept him in the graces of every castle servant. Both mother and son are hale and healthy. He has your look, Master. You must see them!"

Ravn felt joy spread through him, but his oath still tore at his soul. "No, not yet. I have to go to Ròs first."

"But... your wife has a price for your return?"

Ravn lifted the bag, still clutched in one hand that refused to let it go, "I brought her the heart of a dragon."

Moray's face drained of color and his eyes were wide. "Master?"

"A dragon, Moray! The mightiest creature to walk the world. Her contract is fulfilled, my oath discharged. Neála and the boy will be safe for all time under the protection of the castle and my love." The two men embraced again, only parting slowly. Ravn returned the bottle, "I must get to my chambers and present this to my wife."

"Come! You do not look yourself, and I can get you easily into the castle. You can wash and change in my quarters. I will come with you to–"

"No, Moray." Ravn stood straight on feet that burned, set shoulders that ached. He felt the wounds on his heart finally closing, his old self returning. He scratched his long beard. "Get me to your room to clean myself, but tell no one who I am. Small skill it will take, none will know me like this. This must be a surprise to Ròs so she cannot deny or delay. I will return, triumphant, and earn my lover and son."

Finally, finally, both men felt like their world was right again. Ravn would have love, and a family. Moray would have the beloved Laird he had helped raise as his own.

Everything would be happiness from now until the end of time. For even in sadness, they would all have one another and sadness cannot even scratch that kind of joy.

Chapter Fifty-Two
Dreaming

They didn't walk as far as they could have. They knew they were still recovering from wounds received in battle and the aftermath, that they needed extra rest from all they had endured. So when they found a suitable place they stopped.

But it wasn't just suitable, it was extraordinary. It was a chamber separated from the main cavern. In the center was a pool of water, a pool that was as clear as any water Vivien had ever seen, so clear that she could almost see the bottom. But what made the chamber so different was the mosses that grew there, not the typical green ones they had been seeing throughout the rest of the cavern, but ones that glowed yellow, orange and pink. They were prolific, and covered the walls and floor. It felt nice to walk on something other than hard stone.

Conversation had been paltry throughout the day after her revelation. Vivien wasn't sure what to say. She'd stared at his back as he led them through the cave system, wondering what she should call him now that she knew his true name. He'd look back at her from time to time, his eyes reflecting the sadness he felt. She'd wished she could help him, but she just didn't know how to do it, and she felt the same sadness.

Vivien saw his wounds healing slowly and breathed more easily. The wounds were pink and raw, but closed. That, at least, was something.

Vivien went to go and gather pieces of driftwood from along the river while he fished. When they were finished, they met back at the spot they had chosen. With her strength returning, she called the fire fae and flames were soon burning in the makeshift pit he had built. She took the spear of fish he brought and they both worked to prepare and cook them. They ate and drank water taken from out of the clear pool, boiled in a small depression in the cavern floor.

All was done in silence.

Finally they just sat there and watched the flames leap and cavort together in the firepit. Vivien added another piece of driftwood, a larger one than the rest, and the fire blazed hotter and higher. On her side of the fire, hidden from the Wolf, she allowed her tears to fall. Suppressed feelings washed over her and she mourned the loss of one of the greatest friendships she'd ever had. If she separated Ravn from the Wolf, two.

Behind the wall of flames, she finally spoke, her voice much more broken than she preferred for it to be. "Why didn't you tell me it was you?"

But for the crackling of the flames, silence reigned for several moments. "At first I didn't realize I should. By the time my senses came to me, and I realized I was deceiving you, I didn't know how to."

"You didn't trust me."

"No! That's not it."

"Then what is it, Wolf?" She shook her head. "I'm sorry. RAVN."

"I...I wasn't Ravn anymore. I was Nobody. I'd spent decades wandering throughout the wilderness, stopping at villages and towns now and again. The people there, after a while they didn't even seem to see me anymore. I was lonely. It was a loneliness that can scarcely be imagined.

"When I saved you in the ambush, I was Nobody. You gave me a name. I gladly took it. I still want it. I want it because it is the name YOU gave to me."

Her throat burned with suppressed sobs and her voice was a whisper. "But it's not your real name."

Somehow he heard her. "It is now."

She blinked at the tears and they fell in warm rivulets down her face. Her chest ached and she could barely speak. "When you closed your eyes, did you dream about me?"

She stopped breathing when she heard his low voice, one filled with the pain and agony of a hundred years. It shook as he spoke. "Every day and every night."

Vivien pulled her legs up to her chest and wrapped her arms around them. She buried her face in her arms and wept. She cried piteously and the sobs wracked her body, making her shudder with each inhale. Moments stretched into several minutes, but when she finally stopped and looked up over her forearms, she saw Ravn standing there.

It was a sight she'd wanted to see as long as she'd thought he was gone. His stained long tunic was tucked into brais that reached only to mid-thigh, and his leather boots had seen more than their fair share of weathering. His hair was down and lay around his shoulders but for a few braids she had plaited before she shaved his beard. His chest rose and fell with each breath, his arms hanging at his sides, hands clenched into fists. He looked ready to go into battle despite his lack of armor and weaponry.

Vivien stood from her place. She trembled as he slowly approached, his eyes regarding her intently. When he finally stood before her, he raised a hand to her face and swept his thumb beneath her eye. He hesitated before speaking. "Did you dream about me too?"

She took a deep breath and whispered, "All the time."

In a single motion he closed the distance between them and wrapped his other arm around her waist. His lips covered hers in a searing kiss that stole her breath away. She closed her eyes, and let the power of it sweep over her. She ran her hands over his chest, up to his neck and down again, her fingertips taking in every contour. She wanted to feel him, all of him, make sure he was really there. The feel of him was heady, and his lips crushed against hers stirred her deep inside.

She pulled away, looked up into stormy eyes dark with passion. "Ravn, I can't believe it's really you," she breathed. "I can't believe I'm feeling you here, now, after thinking you were gone from this world."

He kissed her forehead, then one cheek and the other before coming back to her mouth. "Believe it, Vivien. I'm right here. I never left."

He kissed her again and the tingle of it rushed through her like a wild river that had no end. She brought a hand to his face, caressed his cheek with her fingertips, and like she had done once before, she gently touched their locked lips.

He gave a swift inhale and pulled her closer. His body was hard against hers, and warmer than she had felt it since they'd arrived at the cavern. She moaned against his lips and he inhaled again, his hands moving to her hips to press her ever closer...

Vivien abruptly pulled away and the Wolf let his hands drop. She felt drunk as she went to the low-burning fire and placed another piece of wood on top. She watched as the flames licked at it, looked up to see him watching her with a predatory intensity he'd never exhibited with her before. Suddenly there weren't just flames in the firepit. They were sweeping through her, touching every part of her and setting her ablaze.

With all the restraint she owned, she sat down. If only she could catch her breath. "I feel like I'm in a dream, and that when I wake up, you will be gone again." The chamber spun a bit and she closed her eyes. She took a drink of the water they had boiled, and then another. He sat beside her, a warm presence that dominated the entire room...

And he couldn't seem to take his eyes, or his hands, off her.

It was a brush of his hand down her arm, a fingertip swiping a tendril of hair away from her face, a thumb across her cheek. "So you came for me?" he asked.

She turned to him and nodded.

"But when you heard I was gone, you went on without me? You lived your life?"

She regarded him intently, thinking back. She thought of her studies, her husband, everything. She shook her head. "No, not really. Every step in my life has brought me here, to this place."

"But they say the heart goes on."

She nodded. "Sometimes it does. Did yours?"

His eyes left hers to look down at her lips. "Just like you, I experienced other loves. But no, it never left you."

"I wanted you to be happy. I'm glad you were able to have that, if even just a while."

He looked back up into her eyes. "For that I am eternally grateful to you." Again he reached up to touch her face, but this time he let his hand slide down the curve of her neck, to the hemline of her chemise, and then to the swell of her breast. "I am no dream, Vivien."

She gave a small gasp and trembled minutely. He had never been so blatant before, never touched her with such intent. Her head spun and she was about to move away, but his hand around her wrist stopped her. "Vivien wait..."

She paused, remembering speaking those words to him when he'd given her news the battle had started. His hand moved to caress her palm, then threaded his fingers through hers. "I want to kiss you. I want to touch you." His eyes searched hers and his voice shook. "Please tell me you want me to."

Time seemed to stand still. She wanted to speak, but the dream had taken over. The Wolf leaned in, closer and closer, but it wasn't the Wolf. The Wolf had never been so brazen. It was Ravn, but a much older Ravn with the body of the man she knew as the Wolf. He was RavnWolf.

He placed his face alongside hers, much as she had once done to him as they sat beneath a pine tree in the middle of winter in snowfall. His breath was warm beside her lips, teasing. She took the cue and emulated his actions from all those weeks ago, brushed her lips against his.

Ravn's eyes twinkled and she felt him smile against her lips as he gently pushed her back, back down onto the mossy cave floor. She wrapped her arms around his neck as he kissed her again...

Vivien dreamed. She was in a cave illuminated by the glow of thousands of mosses that blanketed the walls and floor. There was a fire that burned close by. Even though she wore only chemise, mamillare, and brais, it was warm, and her skin glistened with a sheen of sweat. The man before her was someone she'd dreamed of before, only much older, his face rugged and worn by the ravages of time, his body thickly muscled with a century of hardship and scarred by his trials. But his eyes, his eyes were the same, and they spoke of the eons he had waited to be here, in this dream, at this time.

She knew him as Ravn. She knew him as the Wolf.

Her mind said she shouldn't be dreaming about him. Even though her husband had publically denounced her, she was still married, and the dictates of her society frowned upon elves of her status taking human lovers. If she'd been born a pure elf, their union would be encouraged, but she was only a half.

But today she didn't care. She wanted to dream of him.

Crouched beside it, she placed another piece of wood on the fire and the flames glowed brightly. She felt him kneel behind her, his legs on either side of hers, and felt the heat of him before he touched her. His hands started at her shoulders and ran down her arms, clasping her hands and raising them to rest in the thick strands of his hair. He brought his hands back down the inside of her arms and down her sides as he kissed the curve of her neck below her ear. She shivered, the sensation like a tiny electric shock that sent every part of her on edge.

His voice was deep, "I have loved you since the day I met you."

She smiled. "But you were just a boy."

He shrugged. "I still loved you."

"How is that?"

"I loved you the way a boy loves a girl. And when I grew older, I loved you the way a man loves a woman." He kissed her neck again. "Shall I show you?"

He didn't wait for an answer. His hands left her sides, went beneath her chemise to move up over her belly, along her torso and to the swell of her breasts. Her breath hitched in her throat as his deft fingers found the end of the cloth that bound them and began to unwind it, his lips kissing and sucking gently at the flesh of her neck.

The cloth dropped and she felt his body's response, a hardness against her back that made an ache settle deep into her belly. His hands swept over her breasts, his thumbs finding the nipples and circling them lazily. She lay her head back on his chest and closed her eyes, reveling in his touch, and hoping it would continue.

RavnWolf took one hand from her breasts, swept it downward to slip within the confines of her brais. She gasped and slumped back against him as his fingers swept over her womanhood, briefly caressing her there before bringing them out and leaving a damp trail back up to her breasts.

By the gods, she'd never wanted a man as much as she did this one. His lips were again at her ear. "Have I shown you enough?" he whispered.

She said nothing as her chest rose and fell in response to his ministrations, her body longing for his touch. She didn't need words to answer him.

Vivien pulled away from his grip and slowly stood. The chemise dropped away as she turned and looked down at him where he knelt, wondered briefly what he saw when his eyes roamed over her body clad only in warrior's brais. He rose to stand beside her, standing at least a foot taller, probably more. She noticed the desire in his eyes, his muscular chest rising and falling, the fullness of his brais. She smiled to herself. Two can play this game.

Vivien set her hands on his chest. RavnWolf moved to embrace her, but she moved her hands to circle is wrists and pulled them down to his sides. She saw the look of surprise pass over his face before she went back to his chest. She swept her hands across the contours through the fabric of his long tunic before she spoke.

"Please kneel."

RavnWolf briefly hesitated before doing as she asked. Once he was on his knees, she took the sides of the tunic and slowly drew it over his head. He lifted his arms to help her, and once it was off, he looked up at her through eyes smoldering with passion.

Vivien looked down at him, stepped closer until her breasts were before his face. He brought his hands to her legs, slid them up to embrace her backside before putting his mouth over one nipple. The suckling sensation was like a pulse that traveled through her body and down to her groin. An ache settled deep inside her belly and she gave an involuntary whimper. She ran her fingers through his hair, and he groaned against her breast. He grabbed the brais and pulled them down over her hips and legs. He then took his lips from her breast and sunk down until he was even with her womanhood, gripped her hips in both hands, and pulled her forward.

His tongue was like a shock. She arched her back and threw back her head, her hands pulling at his hair. Each stroke made her legs shake and a warmth engulfed that place. When he stopped, he rose back up and just stared at her through eyes that looked like they wanted to devour her. She had the instinctual urge to flee, but instead she stood firm.

Her voice was a whisper, "Stand back up."

He rose to tower over her, and she wavered. It was a game, and he was very good at it. He was also very tall, so tall she'd needed to ask him to kneel to take is tunic off. She looked at the wall of his chest, bare but for the hair that covered it, hair that trailed down his midsection to disappear into the waistline of his brais. In a more delicate fashion than the one he had used for her, she brought her hands to the front of the brais and untied the drawstring that held them tight. She pulled them wide and then simply let them fall.

Vivien took in the sight of him. RavnWolf reached for her, but she put a hand on his chest and he dropped his arms. Her fingertips trailed down to his navel, then lower to his erection. When her hand wrapped around him, he barely suppressed the moan that came from deep in his throat and his hands clenched into fists. She rubbed her hand along his shaft, squeezing at the base and relaxing towards the tip.

It wasn't long before he'd had enough.

RavnWolf stepped close and enveloped her in his arms. Vivien released him and clasped her hands around the back of his neck as he pulled them down onto the mossy ground. His lips locked onto hers in a fierce embrace while his hand slid between her legs. She closed her eyes and arched her back when his fingers plunged inside, whimpering against his lips. The sound elicited a groan and he pushed them deeper and faster. She whimpered again and shook her head.

He stopped and withdrew his hand, put a knee between her legs and gently spread them apart. He took both her hands in his and raised them over her head. He released her lips and she opened her eyes to see him looking down at her. His breathing was fast and heavy, his brow beaded with sweat.

His deep voice was rough with passion. "I want you Vivien." He squeezed her hands in his. "Please tell me you want me too."

She looked up at him, and this time, used words to tell him. "I want you Ravn." Her voice shook with emotion. "I've always wanted you."

His eyes locked onto hers, he removed his knee and slowly positioned himself over her. His shaft was warm and thick at her entrance, and when he hesitated, she shifted beneath him. His eyes blazed and he pushed inside her, slowly at first, and then faster. She released one of her hands and brought it to his face, caressed a scar across one cheek, one on his forehead above his right eye, and then the most recent one on his neck. He brought his lips to hers and kissed her tenderly as he pressed deeper. She wrapped her legs around his backside and matched him, arching against him with each thrust until he cried out. She climaxed with him, and when it was finished, he held her there for what seemed like hours, placing soft kisses on her. Only later, he slid off of her and lay on his back.

RavnWolf then pulled her close and cradled her tightly against him like he never wanted to let her go.

Chapter Fifty-Three
Out of the Cavern

avn walked in a dream. It was dark, and the cavern walls shifted and wavered in the torchlight. The woman walking before him was clad in only a pair of brais and a mamillare. Her waist was small, hips and thighs a gentle curve, her upper arms more muscular than he remembered. Her long, golden brown hair lay over her back and shone in the torchlight. She looked back at him every once in a while, and his heart would stutter for a moment. Her lips curved up into a smile and her eyes danced.

She is simply the most beautiful thing I've ever seen in my life. How did she come to be here with me? In this dark, chilly cave without anything to wear but smallclothes and boots? *He frowned for a moment as he struggled to remember.* Oh yes, we fell in the lake. *He thought harder, the dream falling away a bit more.* How did we get in a lake?

He left his thoughts behind as she turned again, the torchlight illuminating the delicate lines of her face. The ones around her mouth and eyes were most prominent, and when she smiled again, he felt his heart melt.

He wanted the dream to last forever. Jash'ari had haunted his quiet moments of rest, decade after decade after decade. She never changed, her beauty ageless and immune to the ravages of time. Even when awake, he could see her in his mind's eye, her voice whispering to him in the winds as they rustled through the leaves, and her soft laughter in the burbling of mountain streams.

His elvin princess had been his rock, the place he always went to when he had nothing left. So when he finally saw her again after one hundred years...

Ravn blinked awake. His feet fumbled and he caught himself against the cave wall, torchlight cavorting about the narrow passageway. Confused, he glanced around, saw Vivien walking in the darkness ahead. Alarm swept through him. "Vivien, stop! Wait for me to catch up!"

Startled by the sound of his voice, she stumbled and went down.

Heart in his throat, Ravn rushed towards her. He blinked away the miasma surrounding his mind, dropped the ad hoc torch and went to his knees when he reached her side. Vivien looked up at him through pain-filled eyes. Her knees were a bloody mess, scraped by the uneven rocky floor.

He swallowed heavily, placed his hands over her wounded knees without touching them. "When we get back to the river, we will wash them off."

She looked around her then, her eyes widening as if, she too, was awaking from a dream. She spoke in a tremulous voice, "How did we lose it?"

"I...I don't know." He looked back and forth, trying to remember their steps and knowing he could not. So much was cloudy, fuzzy.

She simply nodded.

"Here, let me help you up." Ravn rose and offered her his hand.

Vivien took it, trembled as she rose. "I feel so groggy, like I've slept for a couple of days."

Ravn pursed his lips and said nothing. He bent to retrieve the torch and held it aloft, thinking. *It might be something in the air of the cave, something that fogs the mind.* "Keep hold of my hand and don't worry. I will find the river before you know it."

She put a hand to her forehead and gave a deep sigh. "I have a headache. I hope it goes away soon."

He squeezed her hand. "Let's get moving. I will walk as slow as you need."

Ravn proceeded forward, torch held before them. He fretted about their course away from the river, and considered turning back. But then, he didn't know how far they had come, and for how long. So he moved forward, hoping to find a side passage that might give him some indication that might take him to the right path.

She shivered. "The silence, it is dreadful."

Ravn nodded. "Talk to me."

She flashed a tired smile. "About what?"

"Everything. Anything. Something happy."

They walked for quite some time. They talked, mostly about memories they shared together in their younger years. He knew she was curious about his 'death' but she didn't bring it up. He was grateful, for it was a terrible story best told where sunlight could enter the wound and help take the poison out. He also knew that she wondered what he'd done with himself for the past several decades. Many of those years were difficult, but the ones that weren't, he told her a bit about as they moved along. So much of his past was a tapestry of loneliness and death. In the light of this woman woven of light and life, he felt like a heavy, earth bound thing. Vivien stumbled every once in a while, and he would be sure she never reached the floor. She would look at him, an apology written across her face, and he wondered what she had to apologize for. He imagined it might have something to do with her estranged husband, whom he enjoyed damning to the hells. He liked to think the Liath might find the arrogant lord there, but that was where he stopped. The image of his father and mother laying dead came to mind and he struggled to let his anger go. He wouldn't wish the Liath on anyone.

Finally they reached a cross passage. He held the torch high and waited, waited, waited. And then he saw it, the slightest shift of the flames. "We go down here," he pointed down the side passage.

Vivien just nodded and followed without question. She had become quiet, and he saw her wincing in pain every once in a while. But it wasn't just her knees. She had a hand over her belly, which was slightly distended despite the fact they hadn't eaten much. He worried for her, wanted to pick up the pace to get back to the river. But he didn't think she would be able to handle it, not with the level of discomfort he noticed.

And it just seemed to get worse.

When they got tired enough, they stopped and slept in one another's arms. They didn't know if it was day or night; time simply had no meaning in this place. When they woke they walked some more, thirst and hunger their constant companions. He prayed for the river as Vivien stopped more and more often in the passageway, overcome with some pain she felt deep inside.

Ravn put a hand in her shoulder. "Jash'ari..." He hesitated. The name meant 'little jewel', and her father used to use it when she was much younger. But now she was an adult, and she wasn't so little anymore. "...Jashi, what is wrong? What pain is this?"

She shook her head. "I don't know. It's low in my belly, and deep."

Alarm swept through him. "Did you get hit in the battle?"

She shook her head. "No."

"What kind of pain is it?"

"It's an ache. A terrible ache."

Ravn's shoulders tensed. He had some knowledge of sewing wounds or setting breaks, but nothing like this. "It's not hunger pain?"

"I feel that too. But this one is much lower."

"Are you bleeding?"

"No."

He nodded. "Do you want me to carry you?"

She frowned. "Of course not! I will get to be too heavy."

He forced a smirk past his worry. "You underestimate me, but I will accede to your wishes."

They continued to walk, passed one side passage, and another. These he tested just like before, but ended up staying along their current path. He didn't know how long they moved, only that it was a long time and Vivien was getting slower and slower.

They slept again. It was cold and damp. Vivien trembled in his arms in spite of his warmth, moaning in her sleep with whatever pain plagued her. He hated feeling so helpless, a condition he'd been experiencing so much with her as of recent. Ravn gathered more wood from the riverside several times each day, and Vivien dried it with magic. Then he would bundle it together and she would light it to make another torch.

They walked. And walked. And walked. They came to another cross passage, and it was then he heard it.

Rushing water.

Vivien heard it too, and her demeanor instantly improved. They hurried down the passage, the flow of water getting louder and louder. They saw another fork in the passage ahead, and it was then they paused. Even without seeing it, they could tell the river moved much too fast.

Ravn turned to Vivien. "It's finally rained."

She nodded. "Let's see how high it is."

His gaze was intense. "Stay next to me?"

She slipped her hand in his. "Some days I am strong. Today is not one of those days. I would like to hold your hand so you can help me when I need it."

"My strength is yours." He smiled. "I always love holding your hand."

Together they moved towards the crossing, and when they reached it, they stepped into a massive chamber. Bisecting it was the engorged river, flowing at breakneck pace. Instead of the clear waters he remembered, it was muddy. Floating within was all kinds of detritus, including branches from trees, small shrubs, and the bloated carcasses of beavers, raccoons, and even small deer.

Ravn led them into the cavern and they walked beside the river. They were thirsty, but didn't dare drink from it, and the fish were long gone, hiding from the rushing current. Finally they stopped to rest. Nearby was a deep indentation in the cavern floor, one that had filled with some of the grimy water. Just like she had done before on their first night in the cavern system, Vivien called the fire fae and they boiled the water. It took a while, but the debris settled to the bottom to leave a clear layer on top. They drank slowly, relishing the feel of the water coursing down their throats, and then they slept in spite of the pain of hunger.

The next day they continued to follow the river. Much to their relief, it also seemed to be receding. Things were being deposited along the banks, and the stench of some of those things was a bit strong. They had not become ill, but the thought of drinking again from the river turned their stomachs. Unfortunately, they might not have a choice.

They walked another day, and another. Hunger gnawed at their insides, and it reminded Ravn of other days best left forgotten. Alone, he suffered the pain as one out of many in his life, but he hated that Vivien suffered, for he didn't believe she'd ever known hunger like this. But she hardly complained, at least out loud. It was only in her sleep, which was fitful to say the least, and not spoken in words, but incoherent moans accompanied by tears. He just held her close and tried to warm her.

And then they were there. The river seemed to just flow through the cavern wall, but a few feet higher, and they could see another hole through which a shaft of light came through. All they had to do was climb up there.

Ravn turned to Vivien. "You think you can make it?"

She smiled, the most radiant thing he'd seen in days, and nodded. This time, the path was a simpler one. Even though the rock was easy to traverse, Vivien shook as she climbed, her body having reached its limit days ago. The air became warmer as they ascended, and once they were at the top, Ravn took her hand and they looked out.

The place was something from out of a dream. The waterfall below them cascaded down the remaining cliff face and into a glistening pool. All around one side were rocks, but on the other was a forest. The trees stretched for a few miles, and when Ravn looked out beyond, his eyes widened.

Where once there had been a vast canopy of trees was now a charred waste.

Vivien made a sound in her throat and he turned to see the agony written across her face. He enveloped her thin frame in an embrace and she shuddered. "They are gone. Everyone is gone."

"You don't know that."

"You think they survived? I am afraid to believe."

"I know. But we shouldn't assume anything until we are faced with proof." He squeezed her hand, but feared the same.

She nodded and glanced, her eyes widening when she saw it, a rugged path leading down the side of the cliff. Ravn held her hand as they walked, kept her on her feet as best he could on the uneven, shifting terrain. He breathed easier once they reached the bottom, and once at the pool, walked around it to the calmer side near the forest. There, they set up camp. Vivien made the fire while he caught fishes for the first time in days. Just like in the cave, they gutted and scaled the fish together, and then cooked them.

"Eat slowly. Your stomach will rebel otherwise," he cautioned.

She nodded and gave a small smile. "I do know some things."

He regarded her for a moment. "I know you do, but hopefully not from firsthand experience."

She looked abashed. "I...you're right. I'm sorry."

He frowned and moved from his place across the fire to hunker beside her. "Why? Why sorry?"

"You were trying to help, and you're right, I've never known starvation before." She looked up at him through pain filled eyes. "I'm sorry you have, Ravn."

He cupped her face in his hand and leaned close. "I never want you to be sorry, not for something like this. You are the strongest, most capable person I have ever known. It is all right for you to tell me the things you know about, even if I turn around and tell you I might know more." He searched her face. "I respect you for who you are, the things you've learned in your life."

Vivien reached out to touch his face and he closed his eyes, reveling in her touch. He leaned forward and kissed her, the first one they had shared since that day in the cavern filled with pink mosses.

Images suddenly swept through his mind, arousing ones that made him inhale sharply. Then he remembered bits and pieces of the dreams he'd had, dreams of passion beyond his wildest aspirations.

They suddenly heard a hiss and looked up to see that the fish was finished cooking. It had begun to scorch on one side and a piece had fallen into the fire.

Vivien removed her meal and brought it close to blow on it. "Oh no, we can't have that. You belong in my belly."

Ravn just smiled and watched her from the corner of his eye. She seemed a bit appreciative of the diversion, and he supposed he couldn't blame her. They were both hurt and raw. The dragon, the battle, and his revelation had come with little pause between. They ate slowly and then rested before eating again. The cavern had taken a horrible toll on them both. Ravn figured they had spent about a week in the bowels of the earth before they found their way out. They had been a bit thin before their ordeal, but now he looked close to sickly, Vivien even more so. Where once there had been gentle curves, there was now just skin and bones. He'd watched her adjust the mamillare as they traveled, wrapping it tighter and tighter. The drawstring on her brais barely kept the cloth over her hips and she'd pulled them up over and over again as they walked. Her lackluster hair lay in a messy braid over one shoulder, and her skin was streaked with dirt.

"It's a warm day. Why don't we bathe in the pool? I saw some soapwort while I was fishing. I can wash your hair."

She looked at him with uncertainty and he chuckled. "What are you worried about? It's not like I've never seen you nude before."

She nodded. "Yes, I know. I just didn't want to..." She stopped and looked away.

He chuckled again. "I do not take your nudity as an invitation, or a promise." His demeanor then shifted into one of seriousness. "I would never lie to you."

She looked back at him, her lower lip under her teeth, and his heart melted. "Only if I can wash your hair too."

He blinked, "What?"

She smiled. "I'll do it only if I can wash your hair. It looks terrible."

This time he laughed. He stood and held out a hand. "Come on, we can wash our clothes at the same time. Well, whatever clothing we have."

"The boots too?"

He smiled at her, and it was a smile that went down to his bones, "Gods yes! Especially the boots. Every time you take yours off I think my nose is going to fall off my face!"

"Ravn! I daresay, the stench from your boots is infinitely more abysmal than the one from mine!"

"Well, we have no judges here, so we will simply have to agree to disagree."

She shrugged. "Fine. But one day I think I'll be able to prove it."

He grinned. "I look forward to that day."

Chapter Fifty-Four
The Vanguard

In the paltry light of a new dawn, the Grand Magister watched as the army prepared for the days travel. The tents were quickly brought down and folded away, cooking fires put out, the wounded placed on stretchers to be carried. Throughout the night the rains had been kept at bay, but now that daylight had arrived, a sprinkling here and there could be felt. A part of him hoped that it would be a better day than yesterday, which saw a downpour for several hours. He supposed it was a good thing though, for it certainly had stopped any remaining fire that may have survived the first rainfall that took place the day after the enemy had retreated, a retreat that had secured a victory for Elvish forces.

Jor'aiden knew he should be happy. Rithalion was safe for at least another two years while the Iron Coast amassed another army. And actually, for a while he WAS happy, for he could feel his daughter and knew that, even though she and the Wolf had not returned with the vanguard, that she was still alive out there somewhere. But then, late in the afternoon a couple days ago, that had changed.

He had felt her life wink out, just like so many of his other children.

Jor'aiden didn't realize he was screaming until Xadrian was standing there, talking his shoulders in his hands and shaking him. "Magister! Magister what is it? Is it Vivien?"

Jor'aiden fell to his knees. His soul sought hers, searched and searched. Gut she was simply...gone.

He screamed again, clenched his hands into fists and raised them into the air. "Noooo! Vivien, no! I love you, please come back to me, please don't be gone from me! I need you so much, please come back! Viviennnnn!"

The Lord of Swords and Truth had followed him down to the ground, his expression one of turmoil. The man loved her, truly loved her like she was one of his own. He'd trained her to be a fighter, trained her in the ways of a good swordsman. Vivien was slowly becoming a master...

But not anymore.

Jor'aiden sobbed into his hands, felt Xadrian put his arms around him to hold him close. The contact made him feel like he wasn't the only man on earth, and that someone cared. It made him feel like he could keep crying. So he did. He sobbed piteously, like a man broken so deeply, it could be felt by any who came near. He didn't bother to hide, hiding was for the young who had their entire lives spread before them. But he, the Grand Magister, was an old man. He had nothing to hide. He wailed for the world, so that all could know his agony, and that he had nothing left. Nothing but his tears and his heart broken into thousands of tiny shards that bit into the force that kept him alive.

And then, when he was done, he cried some more. He cried until there were no tears left and his body just shuddered. The army moved, but Jor'aiden was carried on a litter, staring up at the sky. And when the army stopped for the night, he didn't rise, just lay there, staring. He refused to eat, refused to drink, refused to speak. So Xadrian told them to leave him there, to let him be, to let him have whatever peace he could find in the recesses of his empty soul.

The Magister shook his head. Time had ceased to have meaning and the days and nights bled together. From the corner of his eye he noticed someone standing there, waiting for him to acknowledge them. He looked to see it was one of the members of Vivien's vanguard. He could tell by the white cloth they wore around their upper arms, each with a black wolf's head, hand drawn from the ashes from the fire. The man swayed from foot to foot, and he swallowed nervously.

Jor'aiden beckoned the man over, but to his surprise, it wasn't just this one man who had been waiting, but fifty. The men, and two women, surrounded him. The entire area suddenly quieted when, as one, the group went down to one knee.

One man spoke. "Grand Magister, we feel your loss. While we realize it is nowhere close to yours, we still feel it. We are honored to have fought for the Wolf. He was a great leader. But Vivien, she was too. It was she who brought us together, she who gave us the strength we needed to persevere over our enemies. Grand Magister, we fought for the Wolf, but we died for your daughter. You are, and always will be, and honored man in our hearts. Thank you for being the man she deserved. Thank you for letting us know her, if even for such a short time."

The group bowed their heads then, every last one, and when they rose, one of the men, one of the mages, approached. His red-rimmed eyes were bloodshot and his complexion was pale. "My Lord, please hold out your arm."

Without thinking, Jor'aiden did as the man asked. The mage tied a white cloth around his upper arm, and when he was finished, he bowed and walked away. At his cue, the rest of the group followed suit.

The Grand Magister just stood there, looking at the scarf around his arm. It looked just like the ones the rest of the vanguard wore, with only one difference. The wolf on his scarf had green eyes.

ELVISH JEWEL

The scorched landscape stretched before them as far as their eyes could see. Blackened husks rose as silent sentinels from the ground, the remnants of great trees that had been burned in a raging wildfire that lasted until torrential rains snuffed it out, rains so heavy that rivers were engorged and depleted lakes restored. Their travel-weary boots were coated with drying mud and the sun beat down mercilessly upon bare shoulders usually covered with protective clothing. They followed the river towards the swamp Vivien hated so much, the one the vanguard had traversed not so long ago. Not far lay the travel packs they had left behind, filled with the extra clothing they needed, and well as other supplies that would make their journey back to Rithalion more bearable.

Vivien groaned inwardly, her aching feet sweating inside her boots. Her body was tired, more tired than she'd ever experienced, and she ached in places she'd never ached before. She put a hand against her lower back, just held it there and applied as much pressure as she could. It offset the ache for the briefest moment, giving her some small relief.

"Vivien, do you need to rest?"

She looked up to see that she'd fallen behind the Wolf. He'd stopped to wait for her, creases of concern between his thick brows. She shook her head. "No, I don't want to stop. I want to reach our packs by nightfall."

He grinned. "No worries about that. The bog lies just over the next rise. We are getting close."

She gazed ahead of them and frowned. "I see nothing. How do you know?"

He winked. "I caught a whiff of it on the breeze a time or two."

She curled her upper lip, remembering the sickness she'd suffered whilst they traveled through that terrible misbegotten place. And now that she thought of it, she'd noted a mild stench in the air a time or two herself.

True to his word, they reached the swamp outskirts over the next rise. The fire hadn't been as devastating here, as the vegetation was more damp, constantly in proximity with a water source. Even the air was damp, and coupled with the heat of approaching summer, it weighed on her like a sodden winter cloak.

They walked across the edge of the bog, and once reaching the place where Ravn recalled the vanguard walking out, they began following the path they had taken towards what would become the battlefield. The longer they walked, the more memories flooded Vivien's mind, memories of the vanguard— the men talking around their fires at night, the stories they told, the camaraderie they'd shared. Those people had let her in, let her be a part of the family they had become, a part of something bigger than she'd ever had before. Those people— she'd known all their names, heard about their families, their lives, their loves, their fears. Everything.

And now they were gone.

Vivien suddenly stopped, tears rolling down her face. She put a hand to her belly, feeling a tickling there, like the fluttering of butterfly wings from within. It was a curious sensation, one she'd begun to feel more and more often as of late. It wasn't a bad one, but it worried her, for she'd never felt anything quite like it.

Thick arms wrapped around her and she leaned against Ravn's solid chest. He just held her there, saying nothing. He caressed her hair and her back, offering her all the comfort he could, and she took the liberty of crying for a few moments. Didn't her people deserve it? Really, they deserved much more than the tears of the general who led them into battle.

General. She'd never thought of herself in that way before, but truthfully, that's what she was. She was a general who had led her people into a battle they could never win. She had killed them and managed to save herself by running away.

Her voice was tremulous. "I am a coward. I left them behind. I should have stayed with them."

His hands took her shoulders and pulled her away from him. His face was determined as he looked at her from stormy gray eyes. "No! You forget how it happened. The fire was between us and the rest of the army. We had no way of getting to them."

She just shook her head, her body shaking with the force of her sobbing. "No, I left them! I left them behind!"

The Wolf shouted. He shouted louder than she had ever heard him shout before. "No! You never left them. We fought the giants to allow them to escape and got separated. We had nowhere else to go, Vivien!"

Her breath hitched in her throat. His hands were tight on her shoulders and they were beginning to hurt. His face was gaunt, thinner than she'd ever seen it, and without the full beard she was used to, pale. He was a little bit scary, his eyes bright with conviction, tendrils of curly hair springing loose from the braids she'd plaited along the sides of his head.

Ravn saw her fear and instantly retreated. He released her shoulders and took a step back. She did the same, her body shaking. "Jash'ari..." He lowered his head and shook it, "...Jashi, I am sorry. Please forgive me."

She heard the anguish in his voice and instantly went to him. She wrapped her arms around him as best she could and lay her head on his chest.

Ravn was still for a moment before he spoke again, his voice broken, "I never want you to fear me, ever. You are everything to me. Everything. I would never harm you." His arms shook as he gently placed them around her. They stood there for several moments before he spoke again. "Please, tell me you forgive me."

She looked up at him. "There is nothing to forgive."

He closed his eyes and whispered, "I made you afraid of me. That is enough. Please tell me you have forgiven me. I need to hear the words."

"I forgive you RavnWolf."

His body instantly relaxed. "Thank you." Then he paused. "What? RavnWolf?"

She gave a small smile, momentary fear melting away inside of her. "Yes, I see you both. I see the man I knew a long time ago, and the man I have known more recently. You are both here, with me now."

He nodded and put a renegade tendril of hair behind one pointed ear. "All right. I can accept that. You may call me whatever you wish." He took her hand. "Come, let's get our packs and decide how we will proceed."

Vivien grabbed his tattered tunic where it lay across his chest and gripped it in her fist. Her eyes were intense as she looked into his. "Whatever happens, always remember I love you. I love both parts of you that make the man I have before me now. Promise me you won't forget."

He frowned as he stared back at her, his eyes searching hers for an answer he couldn't find. "I will remember. I promise."

She released the tunic and stepped back. "I...I am ready for what lies before us."

He nodded and they continued. It wasn't long before they reached the scrub-laden hill where the vanguard had left their packs. Only...the packs were gone.

"Wolf, is this the right hill? It looks like it, but..."

He shook his head. "This has to be it. This is the one I remember."

Vivien continued searching, looking behind one bush, then another, and another. Several feet away, Ravn did the same. Then she found it. The sight made her heart skip a beat and her breath stopped.

"Ravn..."

Hearing the odd tone to her voice, he rushed over. There, on the ground before them, were two travel packs. Vivien could tell they belonged to her and the Wolf by the color of the thread used for stitching and the ornamental buckles. Surrounding them were a stack of rocks, and within the circle with the packs were what appeared to be personal items, precious things left by the people who had left the memorial. There were engraved mugs made of platinum, jewel inlaid scabbards, and finely made daggers. There were jeweled rings, bracers, and earrings. There was even a rope of long braided hair that shone golden in the sunlight.

Knowing what the memorial meant, Vivien's heart soared. She turned to Ravn and they held one another in a fierce embrace. This time they both cried, not tears of sorrow, but happiness. For members of the vanguard still lived, and by the number of precious gifts given to her and the Wolf to serve them in the afterlife, more than half. There, in a sheath, lay the broken blade of Arisil as well.

Ravn took her arms in his hands. "You know what this means!"

It was a statement, not a question. But Vivien cocked her head to the side in reply, wondering.

"It means that our army is probably still out there! I didn't notice it before, but look at all the trampled shrubbery, look at the ground! It looks like dozens and dozens of people have walked here!"

She looked where he pointed and she dared to believe. "That means, if so many people cared to come back here..."

The Wolf nodded. "We won, Vivien! We won the battle!"

Her voice was an incredulous whisper. "I'm so afraid to believe you!"

"Then we travel. Lets follow where these footsteps lead!"

They took their packs from the shrine that had been erected around them, opened them to extract dried food and the extra sets of clothing still resting within. It felt strange to have cloth around her now, after so many days with nothing but fabric around her breasts and hips. They then carefully loaded their packs with the treasures their brothers and sisters had left behind, and they did just Ravn said they should do. They followed the beaten path, a path that led towards Rithalion, towards HOME.

They entered the forest and it was good to see land untouched by fire. For two more days Vivien and the Wolf followed the path made by a large group of people, and on the third day, it joined a path that grew exponentially wider. Along that path they could tell where the army had settled for the night, as seen by places where large numbers of tents had been pitched and fires made. Their excitement grew, and on the fourth day after finding the memorial made in their honor, they entered a clearing in the wood and that was at least a few miles long and wide. It was then they saw a smudge in the distance ahead...the trailing end of the Elvish army.

Vivien and Ravn turned to one another and laughed. She dropped her pack and rushed into his arms. He picked her up and swung her around. "Woohoo! We did it, Jashi! We made it, just like I knew we would!"

Her heart was almost filled to bursting by the time he put her back down. Happy beyond belief, she surged forward and put her lips to his. It was impromptu, supposed to be a quick kiss, but he put a hand behind her head and deepened it. She was flooded her with love, and she could feel his devotion in every movement of his mouth over hers.

Elvish Jewel

They parted, breathless, and Ravn put his forehead against hers, eyes closed. "You are in my heart always."

She smiled. "You are in mine."

He shifted, threading his fingers through hers. "In my dreams I..."

She silenced him with fingers on his lips, "Shhh, let's talk about them later. I want to meet our people, free them from their grief, free me from mine."

Ravn nodded and she grabbed her pack. They started to walk, faster and faster until they were at a slow jog. Slowly they bridged the gap and Vivien prayed her father was there, alive and well, and Mikarvan, and the Lady. Her fatigue had somehow bled away, replaced by excitement and fierce determination. She looked at the Wolf. He grinned, and then, just like he had the day they left Rithalion in the company of ninety-eight soldiers and mages, he lifted his head and howled.

His fervor was contagious and Vivien followed suit.

They increased their pace and jogged faster, the grasses swishing against their legs. Ravn howled again and Vivien joined her voice with his, the tones embracing one another in the air. And then, when the air was quiet for a moment, they heard it... an answering howl in the distance ahead. Then there was another, and another and another. Before long, the air was filled with distant howls, all of them coming from the army ahead.

Vivien turned to the Wolf. She saw the look in his eyes, nodded her assent, and began to run with him. Faster and faster they ran, the grasses whipping past, their packs bumping against their backs. The howling continued, getting louder and louder.

And then they weren't running alone anymore.

In the distance ahead there were others, their voices lifted in wolfsong. Closer and closer they approached. The howls got louder. Vivien felt her legs begin to tire, but she wouldn't stop, couldn't stop. The men ahead began to spread out, and when they were finally in proximity, they didn't stop, but ran past her and Ravn, circled around behind them, and fell into place. First there was Gregor, followed by Tyrell, Seamus, Cedric, Donal, and Enya. Before long, what remained of the pack was running in formation behind them, and ahead...

...the army had stopped.

A path had begun to form, a path lined by the Elvish army. The wolf pack got closer, closer, closer. And then Vivien heard their voices, voices raised in joy. The army was cheering! No, not just cheering. Their voices were raised in a litany, *"La'athai! An'drath! Elthari Jashi! La'aithai, An'drath, Elthari Jashi!"*

Tears streamed down Vivien's face, tears that cooled her heated cheeks. These people were cheering for the vanguard! They were cheering for the Wolf! And, much to her surprise, they were cheering for her!

They ran down the path the army created for them, the people hooting, hollering, and cheering. Even the injured joined in, propped up by their able-bodied brothers. Vivien's heart soared on wings of rapture. No one had ever cheered for her before. Ever. Ahead there were more and more people, but then someone was blocking the path. It was a man.

Vivien began to jog and the Wolf slowed with her. Behind them the rest of the pack followed suit. The litany came to a stop, as did the cheering and hollering. Within moments the area grew silent. The man wasn't just any man.

The Wolf and the rest of the pack stopped and Vivien continued alone. She began to run again, and her heart thundered in her chest. She stripped the pack off her shoulders and let it fall as she continued forward, forward to the man at the end of the path. No, not at the end anymore. He was running too, his burgundy robes waving like a banner behind him.

The look on his face was one she would never forget as long as she lived.

And then she was there. Strong arms wrapped around her, the same ones she always remembered from when she was a girl. She hit the solid wall of his chest and wrapped her own arms around his neck, her body shaking with the power of her emotion.

"Jash'ari! My Little Jewel! You have come back to me!"

She heard the tears in his voice, the anguish he had endured thinking she was gone from him forever. She put her lips to his ear, "Father, I am so glad to see you, so glad to be home. I love you so much. Keep holding me; hold me tight and don't let me go!"

And he didn't.

Chapter Fifty-Five
The Story

Gregor's voice filled the bivouac. "You saw them! Those giants were bigger than any human man, any elvin man! And they were killers, you could see it in their eyes when their collars were released. This one roared, so loud the trees shook, and An'drath roared back!"

The audience was captivated. Ravn looked beside him to see Vivien sitting there, her attention on the storyteller on the other side of the fire. Ravn had to accede that Gregor was good, quite good.

"Elthari Jashi commanded us to go, but she didn't know we all stood there for a few more moments, watching the battle unfold. An'drath told her to run, but she refused, saying she would stay by him and fight!"

The audience clapped and Gregor paused with a big smile. A few people turned to look at Ravn and Vivien, their eyes alight with the joy of seeing them there, sitting among them. It filled Ravn's heart with a wonder he'd felt a very long time ago when he was laird of his own people.

"The giant smashed its mighty club to the ground and it shook with the impact. Elthari Jashi called her magic as An'drath roared again and charged!"

Ravn recalled the words he had spoken to Vivien before that moment, words the storyteller hadn't been able to hear. But Ravn heard them– in his mind, in his heart. He continued to look at Vivien until she turned. She smiled, her eyes dancing with happiness. "You hearing this? I can't believe he tells it so well!"

"The fae came to her call, leaf-like fae that swirled around her like a fierce storm before flying at the hideous giant with single-minded abandon. She summoned more, and more, while the giant swung at An'drath, the end of the club crashing to the ground and splintering with the impact. Elthari Jashi still called more and more fae, and before long they were a peppered layer upon it's flesh. But it didn't stop the giant from attacking again. An'drath barely leapt out of the way of another vicious swing of the club!"

More clapping ensued, and people whispered among themselves with the building excitement.

"Then the giant decided he would crush our fearless leader! This time An'drath could not escape. The huge hand came down, but An'drath caught it! With his mighty strength he kept the hand from squashing him into the earth for as long as he could. Elthari Jashi continued to cast, to no avail. The weight of the giant was simply too much and the monstrous hand crashed down onto An'drath's breast plate. Blood spewed from the wound in his side, and pooled on the ground beside him!"

Ravn once more looked at Vivien. Her face had gone pale, and her lips trembled. It was then he realized that this was a nightmare for her, and she was reliving it with the tale Gregor told. It was a tale meant to honor them, but the pain it inflicted was acute. He was about to say something, when Gregor then stood from his place and shook his head.

"Alas, that is the end of my story. The fire swept between us and our leaders and we were forced down the hill where our Mistress had commanded we go. We waited for them to emerge, but they never did."

The audience groaned, disappointment showing on every face. More glances were cast at them, glances that had become more hopeful instead of just happy. It took a moment longer for Ravn to realize what they were hoping for. The people wanted him or Vivien to tell the rest of the story.

Oh Gods, I don't know if I can do this. Every eye will be one me. I will be scrutinized...

Then he paused and took a deep breath. *Does it matter? Does it matter if I'm scrutinized? I should tell the story. Gregor's tale spoke of two heroes, one sounding much better than the other. That rendition was wrong, but only I know the truth.*

Vivien stared at him as he rose from his place beside her. "We never emerged because we still fought the giant."

The audience clapped, whistled, and raised their fists in the air. Gregor's smile reached from ear to ear as he sat down to hear the next part of the story. The encampment then fell into silence, every person wanting to catch every word.

"I was being crushed by the weight of the giant. It was heavier than anything I'd ever felt in my entire life. I couldn't breathe and I thought I was going to die. It pushed, and pushed and...suddenly it stopped."

Ravn looked down at Vivien. She looked up at him, pain flashing through her eyes. He knew what she was thinking; that she hadn't done enough to help him in the fight.

"The giant lurched off of me and lifted its massive arm. There, at the pit, was a TREE. From something as hideous as this giant, a tree had come to life and grown. The thorns were like swords and they sundered flesh from bone. Blood poured down its side, down its leg and onto the ground. It was going to come for me again, but another tree grew from its knee. The monster roared and fell before another tree spouted, and another. I hefted my hammer, and with all the strength left in me, I brought it down..."

Silence reigned. Ravn looked over the crowd that had gathered. The Grand Magister stood there, his eyes wide, and the Lord of Swords and Truth stood at his side. People looked at Vivien, who just stared up at him in wonderment.

His voice rose so that everyone could hear. "The flames closed in on all sides, and men of the Iron Coast overtook us in waves. Together, we ran. We ran from the fire, ran for our lives. We ran towards Dreaming Lake. The enemy had broken, but the fire chased us as a hungry beast. It enveloped the trees near the edge, and consumed them like massive, smoke filled teeth. We had come to the lake, and our only option was to climb down. So climb we did. I was so tired and bleeding. Only Jashi's presence there with me kept me going. Once at the bottom we fell. Fed by winter runoff from the mountains, it was bitterly cold, and it sought to pull us into the dark depths forever. We were swept along towards the falls. There was nothing we could do but hold on to one another for dear life."

He could hear people's hushed breathing, feel the tense expectancy in the air.

"And then we fell again. I blacked out. I don't know how long I was gone, but I knew I was dying." Ravn looked down at Vivien, saw the tears in her eyes that she blinked away so that no one could see. "When I awoke, I was in a sphere of silver beneath the water of the lake, and she was kissing me!"

There were chuckles all around the camp and some of the men jabbed one another in the side. Vivien's cheeks flushed with embarrassment and she lowered her head.

His voice was stronger as it rose over the murmuring. "But it wasn't just any kiss! She was breathing into me, and somehow, with the magic she called, with strength she no longer possessed, she saved me."

Once again there was silence. The Magister's eyes sparkled with pride and...something more he couldn't determine. The Laird looked to his partner and the story stuttered in his mind. He remembered the caves, his dreams. Ravn shook them off and raised his arms from his sides and turned around for all to see him. "We were deposited in underground caves and had to find our way out. And so you all see me standing here before you now."

The bivouac erupted into cheering and clapping. *"Elthari Jashi! Elthari Jashi!"*

Ravn turned to Vivien and bowed before her. He put out his hand, palm up. "My Lady, I am forever in your debt."

Vivien hesitantly placed her hand in his. He brought it close and swept his lips over the top. "I am in your service; please use me well."

Vivien bowed her head, shaking it back and forth, as the cheering continued. Ravn knelt at her side and whispered in her ear. "Everyone wants to see you Vivien, just like the La'athai did at the end of every day. Do you remember?"

She sniffed and looked up at him, her eyes shimmering with tears. She nodded. "I remember."

Vivien rose to stand beside him and the encampment erupted. *"Elthari Jashi! Elthari Jashi! Elthari Jashi!"* The men surrounded them. They all wanted to take her hand or to talk to her. And if they couldn't do that, they were well enough just to touch her shoulder or her arm, offer her a smile or a salute. Tyrell went so far as to rush forward and embrace her. Ravn took her hand and slowly led her over to where her father stood beside the Lord of Swords and Truth. Once there, he went down on one knee.

Again the encampment quieted. Both older men looked on in confusion as Ravn unhooked the sword sheath from his belt and handed it to Xadrian. Even though there was no hilt, it was easy to tell that there was something inside the sheath. When the Lord turned it upside down, a blade fell out and onto the palm of his outstretched hand.

Xadrian's lips curved into a slow smile and his fingertips caressed the rune inscribed metal. He looked up at Ravn, an expression of gratitude on his face, and then at those who were still gathered. In spite of the chance of cutting his hand, he held the blade aloft. "Arisil Doomslayer has come home to my family!"

The people cheered again and Ravn heard his Elvish name raised in litany, *"An'drath! An'drath! An'drath!"*

The Lord of Swords and Truth put a hand on his shoulder. "You have become like a son to me, Wolf. I am blessed to have found you."

Ravn winced and placed a hand over Xadrian's. "My profound thanks to you, Lord. You honor me."

The people finally began to disperse and the camp prepared for the night. Ravn led Vivien to the tent she shared with the Magister, and when they approached, Master Healer, Mikarvan rose from the fire he had prepared in front of it. Ravn kept back while she rushed over to her friend and he couldn't help noticing the fervor with which she joined in his embrace. It was plain to see that she loved him, and even more, that he loved her as well.

A pain swept through Ravn, swift and hot, searing him to the core. *Oh gods, what am I doing here? There is no hope for me with her; I know this, have always known this.*

He had the sudden impulse to run, run far from here and never come back. He loved Vivien with everything he was, and she said she loved

ELVISI) JEWEL

him. He also knew that elves had many loves during their long lives. Her problems with her lord were the talk of everyone in Rithalion, and he had dared to hope inside his deepest heart that she might come to him once her freedom was restored. He respected her as much as he loved her, and he never wanted to own her, to cage her, but to be considered and loved openly. He had followed her, had supported her, but to be passed over for anyone was too much. He could barely stomach the thought of it. He knew she was married, understood that Torialvah awaited her somewhere between here and Rithalion and if he was wise he would realize his folly and welcome her into his arms. But somehow, that wouldn't hurt like this. Even if she could choose, she would ever choose a wild thing, without a drop of Elvish blood. He let the knowledge creep over him like a cold cloak of thorns.

Ravn unobtrusively watched, saw how Mikarvan's hands lingered over the small of her back, her hips, her sides. And when he put his hands alongside her face to say whatever endearment Ravn chose not to hear, Vivien reached up to place her hands over his.

Ravn turned and began to walk away. He didn't belong here. He needed to leave. He would take what few things he had and abscond in the night. Vivien wouldn't know until morning. She might miss him for a while, but as the years passed, she would learn to forget him.

Even though he would never, could never, forget about her.

"Wolf! Wolf wait!"

He turned at the sound of her voice, his heart thundering in his ears. Oh gods, how he would miss the sound of it. She jogged up to him and stopped when she saw the look on his face.

"Ravn, what is wrong?"

He shook off the melancholy that threatened to envelop his entire being– heart, body and soul. He forced himself to relax and gave her a small smile. "Nothing is wrong. I'm fine. I was just going to find my tent and get some sleep."

Her brows furrowed and she searched his face for the truth hidden there. However, she continued on as though she'd never found it. "I know it is getting dark, but..." She hesitated and an expression of sadness passed over her face. She shook her head. "I'm sorry, you must be tired. Good night."

He took a step towards her. "We both know how the rest of our lives can be snatched away at any moment. Say what is in your heart." His hands shook a bit. He realized how important her words were at this moment and he swallowed past the painful lump in the back of his throat.

"I...it's just that...I was hoping you could stay? I'm so used to having you with me, that I have this feeling that I might not..."

Within the space of a single breath, Ravn had closed the gap between them. The words he spoke were soft, but they were dictated by the beating of his heart instead of his fear. "Of course I will stay. I'll stay as long as you need me."

She gave him a tremulous smile. "Thank you."

They walked over to the fire and sat down. A pot hung over it, and there were mugs sitting off to the side. Vivien poured the contents of the pot into two mugs and handed one to him. "Mika says this tea will help restore us." She grimaced. "He says we look too thin."

Ravn chuckled at the expression on her face and took the mug. He took a sip and was surprised to find that it tasted good. His thoughts calmed, and he realized he had been thinking too rashly. Vivien had said she loved him, and she'd proved it to him time and time again during their travels. She would be hurt if he simply left without any type of farewell. It had been wrong of him to even consider it.

They just sat there for a few moments, staring into the flames. "Are you going to tell your father who I am?" The question had been on his mind, and he felt there would really be no better time to ask it.

She nodded. "I was thinking about doing so in a few days, after the fervor of our return has died down. I want to choose a good time; it will come as a bit of a shock."

He nodded. "I agree."

A slight tension arose and her own question hung between them. Ravn sucked at his upper lip. Damn, he should have been more thoughtful of the questions he asked. And now that the topic had been breached...

"Ravn," her voice was hesitant, "how have you not aged all these years? How have you not... passed away yet?"

Her gaze locked with his and they remained that way for several moments. The sounds of the bivouac had receded as people settled around their fires for an evening meal, and talk was quiet. The feel of her beside him was comforting, and that fact figured into his reply. "That is a long story, a difficult story. It will be hard for me to tell it, but I will do it for you."

Vivien continued to look at him, her eyes sweeping over his face. Her expression was one of utmost solemnity as she put a hand on his cheek. His beard was growing back, and she smoothed the short hairs with her thumb. Her voice was almost a whisper. "Sometimes I still can't believe you are here with me, that I might still awake one morning and you will have been naught but a dream."

He said nothing, mesmerized by the way she looked at him. She leaned in, slowly moved closer and closer until her lips almost touched his. In his language, she whispered, "I love you Ravn of Blacach."

He didn't move. He didn't breathe. He was tempted to close the gap, but he waited. He waited to see...

Her lips pressed to his. They were soft and warm, caressing him with tender sweetness. He trembled as he finally breathed, taking in the wonderful scent of her. He raised his hand to rub his fingertips over her face the way she always liked to do with him.

She pulled away and he felt bereft. The kiss was much too short when he wished it could last forever. He thought about the dream in the cave, of loving her with all he was and everything he could be. She ran her thumb over his lips and whispered it again, "I love you Ravn. I love you."

He kissed her thumb and brushed errant strands of her hair behind one ear. Happiness surged through him, and for the first time in longer than he could remember, he felt a sense of peace. Finally, after a journey that had taken him more than a century to complete, he had finally found what he was looking for.

Epilogue

No man or beast had dared approach Pergatium after the flood. Even now, many, many years later, after some of the waters had receded, the same could still be held true. The stench alone could bring a man to his knees, but the death...the death was what really kept them away. The death of so many elves in one place had been, until that fateful night, unknown, and it left a pall that was difficult to contemplate...until you were there.

Esgrynn flew over the city that had become a stinking cesspit of swamp. Nearer the outskirts, the tops of some of the taller buildings that hadn't been taken down by the initial wave stuck out above the water like sentinels over the dead. Nearer the center, where the land began to rise, more and more of the buildings could be seen, until finally, the streets of the central plaza came into view. And it was there, at the apex, where the academy stood.

The Academy of Learning and Excellence was where all formal education had taken place in the city of Pergatium. It was a sprawling series of buildings, but the most important one was at the center. It was the one that housed the library, one of the greatest in Elvish history, containing myriad books and scrolls, some of which were so old they dated back from before time was recorded in writing.

Esgrynn urged his mount into a downward spiral. The wyvern had proven to be a good neighbor over the years, and the two had formed a warm camaraderie. Whenever he needed something done, or he needed a ride, all he had to do was call and his wyvern friend would be there. Every time, the wyvern was given the reciprocity he deserved, whether it be food, companionship, or anything else he might desire within Esgrynn's ability to give it.

They descended into the central plaza, the wyvern's wings creating a small whirlwind of dust and dead leaves as they settled. The beast then lowered himself to the cobbles to allow Esgrynn to dismount, then rose to his full height, a staggering twenty feet tall from foot to head, large for a male wyvern.

Pekoh'nah, Old Friend, was very old.

Esgrynn walked slowly towards the domed epicenter. Statues of gods lined the walkway, starting with the Mother of Light, Deep Green, Maiden of the Hunt, Lord of the Sun, God of Journeymen, Goddesses of Birth and Rebirth, Destiny and Time. Following them was a slew of demigods including Courage, Mercy, Honor, Strife, Greed, and Suffering. The staircase leading up into the building crumbled where he walked, and he had to be careful of his steps. The doors rumbled on their rusted hinges, much more difficult to open then he remembered. The effort made him sweat as he pushed and labored.

Finally he stepped through and looked around the darkened chamber. The first thing he saw was a statue, the largest one by far. It was man, clad in flowing sorcerers robes. In one hand there was a book, and in the other, a staff topped by the head of a dragon. He recalled it being built, remembered the sorcerer for whom its likeness was taken. Kalshamar had been an arrogant man, full of himself and the dreams he had for the future of the elves who followed him. All that it had gotten them was decades of misery.

Esgrynn stepped around the statue to the other side. There he saw two long dead elves forever locked in mortal combat. The woman wore plate mail that had been so severely burned, it looked like it was melting off of her. She sat astride her opponent, her longsword piercing his chest through to his heart. His hand clutched at the blade, his face a rictus of pain, and both were scorched, not with a normal fire that would eventually disintegrate them, but something more– Dragonfire. The only thing that remained unaffected was the sword. The blade was covered in Elvish script and the hilt filigreed with gold and silver inlayed with amethysts.

It was imbued with magic, family magic.

Before the flood, the people of Pergatium had fought a bitter civil war, the elves divided into two factions: those who believed only in the use of faery magic and those who preferred dragon magic. Brothers and sisters fought, summoning the greatest fae and dragon allies they could muster to fight alongside them.

Esgrynn shook his head as he stepped past the combatants. *Such a waste, really. Families destroyed forever.*

He walked further into the chamber. It was dark, darker than it should have been for the greenish-brown muck that coated the windows in spite of the spell placed upon the place. He supposed it had only worked for so long without someone to maintain and strengthen the wards. He walked up the stairs to the second level, knowing where he wanted to go in search of the texts he desired. They were arcane texts, ones that would have survived the flooding, ones that could help him unlock greater levels of the knowledge he sought.

Knowledge of dragon magic.

Glowing chandeliers gave light in the pervading gloom, showing him glimpses of the majesty that had once been. Staircase after staircase lead up to different levels or onto balconies, all of them holding shelves of books and desks for study. Many remained intact despite the surrounding carnage and these he moved around with the ease of someone who knew the place like the back of his hand. He walked with swift efficiency, up one staircase and across to another, between the fallen bookcases, searching amid the moldy tomes. One by one he found them, lying here and there like small beacons of light. He continued purposefully around the periphery of the dome, placing them in his shoulder pack, each one on top of the other. And when he was finished, he made his way back down the stairs.

It was then he thought he felt something.

Esgrynn walked slowly towards the entry. It still lay half open, letting the sunlight stream through into the darkness that prevailed within. He wracked his mind, trying to think what it was that had him so on edge.

He walked through the narrow aperture and into the light of day. He breathed a deep sigh of relief, glad to be out of the musty old library, away from the ghosts that pervaded the place. He settled his pack more firmly on his shoulder and then felt it again.

It was the sensation that something was wrong, and that is was coming...

Without thinking, Esgryn drew his sword and held it before him. He looked out among the statues of the gods and goddesses, straining to see...

And it was then he noticed movement.

His breath hitched in his throat as they emerged from hiding, stuff from out of the nightmares that had plagued him for the past hundred years.

It was the fae.

They came rushing from out of the shadows. They weren't the tiny fairy fae that everyone called on a whimsy, they were the larger, more powerful, more dreadful kind. They weren't just of the seleighe variety. The unseleighe were also there, and that meant that the all-wonderful fae elves weren't so magnificent after all.

These fae were elf sized or taller. They looked like bundles of sticks or rocks in man form, fantastical animal and insect hybrids, humanoids with armor of leaves or bark, all with deep glowing eyes that gleamed eerily in the early evening shadows. They slunk toward him from behind broken walls and the skeletons of drowned homes where they had made their hiding places, and his heart went cold in his chest.

Oh gods...

Esgrynn shouted a warning to *Pekoh'nah*. The wyvern started and took flight even as a few fae broke free and darted towards him. Esgrynn watched him leap to safety as the wizard ducked back into the library. He thought to close the door behind him but quickly thought better of it. It was far too difficult to move, and they would just end up battering through it.

Esgrynn was no fool. They had come to kill him, just as they had killed any dragon elf they could find all those decades ago during the war. What was startling was that they were still there, imprisoned in this place, bound to it for all eternity.

If he'd been in any other situation, he may have felt pity for them, may have tried finding a way to free them. But as it was, he was soon to be in a fight for his very survival.

He proceeded to the rear of the room, tripping on the thick vines that had grown through one of the shattered windows and wound along the floor and up the adjacent walls. He crouched among them and waited, peered from behind the shelves that still managed to stand despite the ravages of time and the elements.

A thorny missile flew past his head, followed by several others, making *thunk thunk thunk* sounds against the thick wood of the shelves. They fell to the floor and he jumped back when they began to sizzle. Faery poison. It would have eaten the flesh from his bones and left him to suffer for days. That is, if the other fae didn't get to him first.

Esgrynn battled the wild beating of his heart. All of what he'd learned the past several decades fled his mind before he finally found a moment of calm. He cast his spell and he felt it rush over him. It didn't cause the pain it used to, a pain so acute it would make him cry out, his voice echoing through the lonely chambers of his cavern home.

Esgrynn flexed arms and legs, rolled his head until he felt his neck pop. The thickened skin over his body would protect him from many missile attacks. He glanced beyond the shelves again, saw a gnarled fae and barely ducked out of the way before a whip-like vine whizzed over his left shoulder, barely missing his neck. He made no retaliatory move as the barbed rope retreated along the floor. He cast his next spell, then took a deep breath, raised his palm to his lips, and looked again.

The fae was directly in front of him, its face a mass of ropey sinew that looked like something from out of a nightmare. But before it could act, Esgrynn was blowing into the palm of his hand...

A stream of fire erupted.

The fae emitted a frightening sound, a blood-curdling shriek that shook him to the bone. Esgrynn darted from behind the shelves, leaping over vines and dodging around desks, glancing back only to see how dire were his circumstances.

And very dire they were. The fae were closing on him, and there was no escape.

Esgrynn ran as fast as he could along the periphery of the chamber. Missiles embedded into his tunic and trousers, hanging there when they caught in the fabric after failing to pierce the summoned *Dragonhide* underneath. A trembling shook the floor and before him it suddenly opened up to reveal a yawning pit. He managed to jump to the side just as he was about to fall in, steadying himself at the edge by holding on to a thick vine.

Damn, if only I can get up to the next level! But then what? I'm still trapped. Oh gods, what if...

He opened his pack and fumbled around inside, and when he found what he was looking for, he brought it out. It was the smallest of the books he'd found, a book of many names. He started to cast another spell, the only one he could think of that would stop so many fae, and he flipped through the pages and found the first name he could read. He lifted his voice and it echoed throughout the chamber.

It was the strongest summoning spell in his repertoire, one he'd never dared cast. And with the name...

"Zah-rahm!"

Winds of power swept through the place, and everything stopped to see what was about to happen.

It didn't fly to him the way the wyvern did, or the little fire-lizards he conjured every so often. Out of a vortex of wind, fire and lightening the dragon arrived, creating a splash of heat that reached every inch of the chamber. It was huge, easily four or five men long. And then there was the tail, at least another four. It's scales were the color of living flame, shining in hues of crimson, orange, and gold, and the eyes– the eyes were blood red.

The dragon named Vengeful Flame gave a mighty roar, one so loud Esgrynn slapped his hands over his ears. When it was over, all he could do was stand there in stupefaction, his ears ringing. This wasn't just any dragon! *Oh gods, what have I done?*

Seeing him standing there, the dragon swung his massive head down, stared at him from one eye hauntingly devoid of soul. Esgrynn shook uncontrollably, so much that his bladder threatened to release as twin tendrils of smoke rose from nostrils that flared with every breath the massive beast took.

"So, you are the puny being who dared summon me here?"

Esgrynn startled when he heard the words in his mind. He'd always known dragons were intelligent beings, but not that they could speak. The eye narrowed beneath a thick, bony ridge, making the dragon look more sinister than he did already, and the tendrils of smoke thickened.

"I cannot speak the way you do, but you can understand what I am saying because of the connection we now share."

Esgrynn felt his eyes widen. *By the gods, the creature could understand his thoughts! No one had told me about this!*

The dragon's head rose, and the beast stood there before him at full height. *"You are a fool. You are naught but a novice, a stripling boy who happened upon a piece of knowledge best kept hidden from eyes such as yours. Of course I can understand your thoughts. You would have known that had you studied the spell you cast to bring me here!"*

Esgrynn's bladder released and warmth saturated his trousers. He could hear the anger that suffused the dragon's words, and he knew an attack was eminent if he did not regain some semblance of control. "My apologies, noble one. My brethren have dissipated since the battle that took place here over a century ago. But I needed help this day, and I knew not where else to obtain it."

The dragon hissed. *"Help? You needed help so you summoned ME to help you deal with some paltry malcontented faery folk?"*

Esgrynn swallowed heavily and began to scramble away from the pit, searching for cover from both deadly foes and fatal new friend. He glanced about the chamber. Even the fae stood still, as though hoping to avoid the gaze of the greater dragon that stood in their midst. It somehow made him feel a bit better, knowing that everything else was just as afraid of this being as he was. "Yes, noble one."

"And what would you give me in return?"

Esgrynn faltered. Oh yes, in his rush for aid, he'd forgotten that he needed to have some kind of recompense, some bit of payment for the service he requested to be rendered.

The dragon noted his silence and a tension filled the air. *"You called me here with a request for aid, but you have nothing to reward me?"*

Esgrynn bowed, but kept his eyes on the dragon. "My apologies. You are right. I am young and inexperienced. I was wrong to call one such as you here. And my mind slipped. I forgot..."

The dragon's voice rang through his mind. *"You FORGOT that you would need to pay me? You called me all the way here, and you have no payment?"*

"I... I am sorry, great one. I will endeavor to be better the next time."

The dragon hissed again. Esgrynn began moving before a roar shook the chamber. *"There will be no next time!"*

Esgrynn rolled out of the way as a bolt of hot flame swept past. Out of the corner of his eye, he saw the fae moving as well, everyone getting out of the way of something that could char them in an instant. It was more than just hot... it was searing, burning the tips of his ears and the end of his haphazardly braided hair.

He darted across the chamber back towards the entry, past the two elves locked in immortal combat and godlike statue of the dragon-magic sorcerer. Behind him Zah-rahm gave chase, his hot breath at his back.

And it was then he realized... there was no escape. Not for him. The dragon would simply follow him out of the academy and snatch him up. Gods only knew what he would do...

True to his nature, Esgrynn began the casting of another spell. It was the one he'd been teaching himself before he decided to make a madcap journey into a doomed city filled with death. Chanting to himself, he erupted out the front door and to the outside. Fae stood there, waiting for him. In any other circumstance, he may have skid to a halt and assessed his situation. This time, he barreled right on through.

And behind him was the dragon.

With a deafening roar, Zah-rahm burst through the partially open doors. Splinters flew, and Esgrynn fell as he was struck across the back by the debris. He heard a thunderous crash from behind the dragon and he knew the giant statue of Kalshamar had finally fallen from its lofty post. In spite of the distraction, he continued with the spell, heard the screaming of the fae when a massive gout of fire cut a swath through the air over him.

From the ground he felt the heat like a hammer. A sleeve caught fire even with a near miss, and the wizard tore it free and let it flutter away. If not for the _Dragonhide_, Esgrynn certainly would have perished. As it was, the defense would only hold so much longer.

He scrambled to his feet, ignored the pain that blossomed in his side with the movement. He ran, dodging around the statues of the gods he'd passed on the way in– those and the new ones of the fae the dragon had just created with his wicked flame. In a way, the blackened forms were more grotesque than they were in life, their terrified faces immortalized forever, just like the two combatants inside the academy.

Then the spell was complete. At the end of the plaza, as the ground began to slope downwards, Esgrynn turned around to face the dragon. The beast was larger than life, his scales shimmering in the late-day sun. His eyes blazed as though with a demon light and razor-sharp teeth ringed his open maw. Esgrynn could feel a shift in the air, telling him another burst of flame was eminent. With one last wyrd, he threw the spell, and the dragon, recognizing it, lurched forward, hoping to escape...

But it was too late.

By some unseen force, the dragon was jerked back. And for the briefest of moments, Esgrynn could see it, the _Bind_ that kept the dragon there. It was a thin, gossamer rope that wrapped around his neck, sparkling like a thin chain of diamonds before it was invisible again.

"Damn you! You can't leave me here! Set me free!"

Esgrynn just stood there, his heart thundering in his chest. He clenched a hand over the wound in his side, blood seeping between his fingers and coating the side of his tunic where a thrown shard had struck. He moved backward and stumbled over the steps, falling to his knees.

Damn you! Daaamn you! I know your name and I'll be coming for you! Just you wait. I'll be free of this place one day!"

Esgrynn stumbled down another few stairs.

The dragon roared, speaking in a tongue he couldn't understand. Winds of power swept though the place; a spell had been cast, or an oath made. He doubled over himself, and only then did he realize that something was wrong, something inside of him was broken.

A trumpeting sounded overhead. Esgrynn looked up and blinked in surprise to see his wyvern friend hovering there, bluish scales glinting in the last rays of sunlight. His mind reeled with the sight, for he never imagined his neighbor would have awaited him in the face of so much adversity. There was no way he would be able to repay him. The wyvern knew that, but had stayed anyway...

The wyvern alighted upon the stairs, but only long enough for Esgrynn to grab hold. He swung himself up and over the reptilian back, anchoring himself in place with his legs. He then lay over the wyvern's shoulders and they lifted, higher and higher.

With a sigh of relief, Esgrynn looked down. He saw the plaza, the academy with the domed roof, the surrounding learning center. He saw the cobbled pathway, the statues of the gods and goddesses, the carbonized remains of the fae. And among it all, like a fiery sun, was the dragon looking up at him as he flew away.

Tracy Renee Ross (aka. Chowdhury) was born in the small town of Tunkhannock Pennsylvania in 1975 and moved to Cincinnati Ohio when she was twelve years old. Growing up, she was an avid reader, especially of fantasy and science fiction, and she loved to write. She attended college at Miami University in Oxford, Ohio and studied her other passion, Biology. She graduated in 2002 and worked in cancer research for several years. During that time she picked up her love for writing again, and in 2005, her first book, *Shadow Over Shandahar- Child of Prophecy*, was put into print. With the help of her co-author, Ted Crim, the sequel, *Warrior of Destiny*, was published two years later.

Tracy currently lives in Montgomery, Ohio. She is married with eight children, a big dog, four cats and three ferrets. She does various home renovation work, and in her 'spare' time she continues to write and promote her books. In 2011 the Shandahar novels were picked up by a small press, Loconeal Publishing, and the original duology was re-mastered and separated into smaller volumes to make a series. More books have followed, as well as several short stories, and she is currently working on the final installments of the series. More information about the books can be found on her website at www.worldofshandahar.com, and she can be found on Facebook and Twitter.

James Daniel Ross first discovered a love of writing during his high school education at The School for the Creative and Performing Arts in Cincinnati, Ohio. In those early days, in addition to this passion, he was an actor, computer tech support operator, infotainment tour guide, armed self defense retailer, automotive petrol attendant, youth entertainment stock replacement specialist, mass market Italian chef, low priority courier, monthly printed media retailer, automotive industry miscellaneous task facilitator, and ditch digger!

James began his writing career in simple, web based vanity press projects, but his affinity for the written word soon landed him a job writing for Misguided Games. After a slow-down in the gaming industry made jobs scarce, he began work on his first novel, *The Radiation Angels: The Chimerium Gambit*. Soon after came the sequel, *The Key to Damocles*, followed by other novels in the sci-fi/fantasy genre: *Snow and Steel, The Last Dragoon, The Whispering of Dragons, The Echoes of Those Before*, and many novellas and short stories. He shares a Dream Realm Award with the other authors in the anthology, *Breach the Hull*, and two EPPIE awards with those appearing in *Bad-Ass Faeries 2* and *3*.

ROSS €ROSS

James' books can be found on Amazon.com and at many retailers across the country. James himself can be found on facebook. Most people are begging him to go back to ditch digging.

There are good guys and there are bad guys...and guys who turn into wolves...

But life is never just black and white.

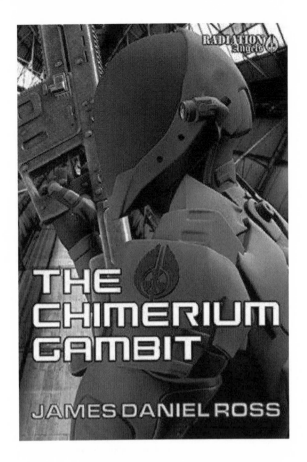

They Say You need three things: Honor, Integrity, and Courage.

What you really need is the nerve to fly half a billion light years, touch down on alien soil, and fight in a major land war… every other week.

When the enemy sets foot on your soil, when civil unrest or revolution raise their bloody hands to the stars, when governmental factions leave words behind and reach for guns and knives and bombs, there is little that the aerospace navies can do. This is when planets contact mercenaries, the last scions of professional ground troops.

Led by their Captain, Todd Rook, *The Radiation Angels* must wager their fortunes, their friends, their very lives on a plan that will make them rich beyond kings, or ensure their painful demise: **The Chimerium Gambit.**

Shandahar is a cursed world. People will live and die. Wars will be fought, kingdoms built, discoveries made. For centuries, history will proceed apace... and then everything will come to a grinding halt and start all over again.

Shandahar is a world brimming with darkness, filled with no promise of a future but one. A prophecy. Spoken by the renowned seer, Johannan Chardelis, there is a divination that tells the coming of someone who can stop the curse. The snag? They have failed four times already.

Enter a world swirling with mystical realms and bloody battles, with enchanted forests and crowded cities where things are not always as they seem. Enter the World of Shandahar.

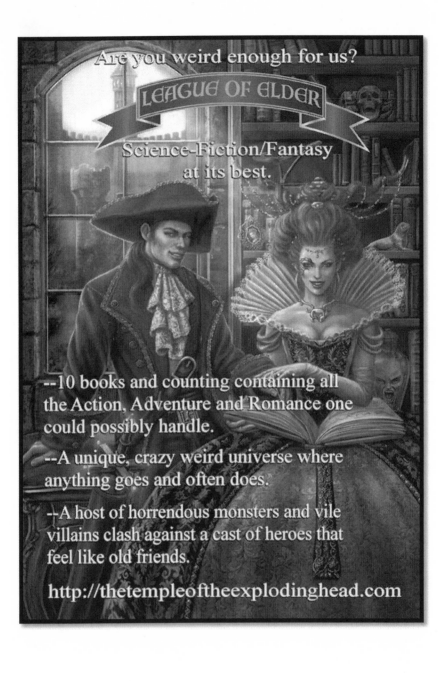

Are you weird enough for us?

LEAGUE OF ELDER

Science-Fiction/Fantasy
at its best.

--10 books and counting containing all
the Action, Adventure and Romance one
could possibly handle.

--A unique, crazy weird universe where
anything goes and often does.

--A host of horrendous monsters and vile
villains clash against a cast of heroes that
feel like old friends.

http://thetempleoftheexplodinghead.com

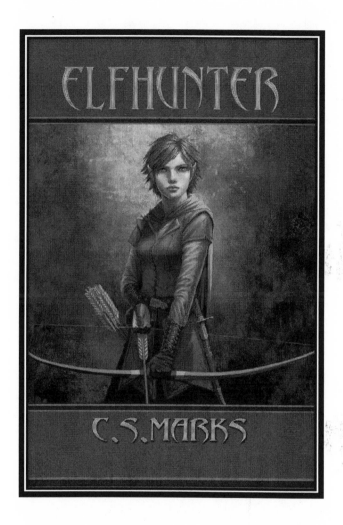

This is the tale of Gorgon Elfhunter, a monstrous, mysterious creature who has sworn to destroy all the Elves of Alterra–until none remain. It is the story of Wood-elven heroine Gaelen Taldin, who has sworn to rid her world of the Elfhunter even as she is hunted by him. The conflict between them creates a tangled web that blurs the line between Light and Darkness, love and obsession, free will and fate.